HALFKINDS VOLUME 1: CONTACT

By Andrew Vu

Recoil Books
ISBN-13: 978-0988520608
ISBN-10: 0988520605

1
CONTACT

Table of Contents

Chapter 1 – The Detective

Contact

November 15, 3040 5:31 AM

I got the tip to investigate a homicide in a small town called Primm, about forty miles outside of Las Vegas. I normally don't take calls so far away, but seeing that it was 5:00 in the morning and there weren't any responders, I figured why not.

I had just started my day and woke up at around half past three to take my shower. The water was cold that morning; damn heater must have been broken again. I guess I get what I pay for in this apartment.

I popped some toast and eggs in an insta-cooker, and a second later it was all done. I couldn't cook that well and, with no lady around, that box was my only personal chef. All I had to do was pop in a little pea size pod, and a few seconds later, I had a full meal. Sure it didn't have the human touch I enjoyed, but it still tasted pretty good. Amazing what technology can do these days.

I got my badge and gear, and hopped into my hovercar towards the police station in Sloan. The morning air was crisp and fresh. It looked like it was going to be a relatively hot day in November. I turned on my car's AI and asked what the weather was going to be.

"Eighty five degrees. There will be light showers at 4:42 PM, but skies will clear up by 8:15 PM. Is that all you require, detective?"

"One more thing, when will the sun rise?"

"From your position, it will rise at 5:45 AM. It will be to your left. Is that all?"

"Yes, computer, thank you."

"You're welcome, have a nice day."

A fifteen minute, quiet hovercar ride had passed and I was at the station. As I exited my vehicle, the dispatcher buzzed in about the tip, just before five. The tipper said he heard gunshots around 4:00 in the morning and a woman's scream, so I quickly chimed in to the dispatcher and said I was available to investigate.

"It looks like today is going to have some action after all, what a time to be alive in the thirty first century," I said to myself, and I was on my way. It is where I am now, in my car, en route to the crime scene.

A quiet fear overtakes me. It's the same fear I always feel before an investigation like this. Robberies, vandals, I can deal with, but homicides are different. The sight of a dead body always irks me, the possibility that the killer hasn't left is even more troublesome.

It'll take about twenty minutes to get to Primm, and my thoughts are the only things that keep me company. Sometimes I wish I had a partner, but with the budget so small and the robots taking care of parking and speeding tickets, I guess I should be happy that I have a job in the first place. Not many can say they've had a long career in law enforcement, but being a detective sure helps. There's only so much that artificial intelligence can cover without a human mind.

It also doesn't hurt that I'm a cop in one of the most crime ridden areas in the United States. They say you can get anything in Las Vegas. Want to blow your life savings on a game of craps? Go ahead. Need a fix? Just go to any shady corner and you got it. And you can be sure there's something that will satisfy you no matter what you're into.

It's not the gambling, drugs, and sex that cause the chaos, it's the crowds. Things get rowdy fast. That's what happens when you have all these species mixing in with each other. We already live in a world where the wolves hate the dogs, the gorillas are at war with the lions and everyone pretty much hates humans. God, I wonder what it was like to live back in the old days, when people were the only ones who could think for themselves.

These animals got too smart too fast, and all of a sudden they're all fighting for their share on this planet. Worst part is that we humans allowed it to happen.

I think about this kind of stuff when I'm on my way to these cases. I think about how crazy a world I live in. I guess we humans got carried away with our dreams and ambitions.

But I am getting distracted. I can't be thinking about this right now, not before walking into a crime scene. I have to remain focused.

Primm is usually known for being a hooker town. Since Las Vegas is strictly a no prostitution zone, all the neighboring towns have cashed in. Boulder City, Goodsprings, Mead, Moapa, all those places are a haven for selling sex. Thank God Sloan hasn't turned out that way, because I have seen some weird shit over the years.

Species stick to their own species. Human hookers have human clients, dog hookers have dog clients, that's the way it is because it's against the law to have interspecies relations. The worldwide government banned it a long time ago, right when the other animals started to become equals with humans. We don't want it, and neither do they. But here in the Vegas area, laws are always broken and once in a while I'm forced to put some sick dog or human or whatever to justice.

It's hard because a lot of the pimps are in control in these areas, but even interspecies clients are something that most pimps want nothing to do with. It's the taboo of all taboos, and when they are found they get cracked down on hard.

Sometimes I think it's strange how all of this came about when other species started to get smarter. You would think that intelligence would bring a level of sensibility and morality within creatures, help them see what is right and what is wrong. But quite the opposite happens. Smart or not, every being has its own desires. Intelligence allows those desires to be realized.

Primm is particularly notorious for this kind of stuff, maybe because it's so far south, away from the grasp of civilization. A lot of murders and busts happen down in Primm and, with their lack of law enforcement, guys like me usually get called there to check things out. They don't have enough resources to handle this dangerous place. That's why I have that feeling of fear every time I have to check out a homicide, especially in Primm.

"Computer, what's the ETA of my destination?"

"Ten minutes. You will travel on Troup Road for approximately three minutes and then make a right on Chakming Drive. Continue on for seven more minutes and you will arrive at 1523 Chakming Drive. Do you need anything else?"

"No, that is all. Thank you."

I look out my window and see the poverty filled streets of Primm. There's litter everywhere, and several homeless species. Dogs, humans, even a bear, all with "help me" signs and tattered clothing. The bear looked particularly out of place; they normally don't like the heat of Vegas. But I guess when you're homeless, you're homeless.

I make a right on Chakming Drive, and I notice the street is completely empty. There are no businesses, no stores, just a few vacant homes spaced out by unkempt lawns and broken down hovercars. This homicide victim must be the last resident here. It seems like the rest of this area has been abandoned for years.

I arrive at the address, 1523 Chakming Drive. I must have driven down the road for about a mile before reaching this empty house at the end of the street. It was the only house left at that point, and when I arrive I can see why. It's old, run down, and shabby looking to say the least. It stands at one story high with no fence. Weeds are growing onto the street. There are rusted hovercars in the driveway. Whoever lived here didn't travel much judging by the condition of the vehicles.

I park my car and take my gun out of the holster. I charged it overnight, so it is at one hundred percent energy. I open the side door and get out, slowly looking around to make sure there is no one else in the area. The killer could very well have returned to the scene of the crime, so my gun is switched to fire mode.

I make my way through the yard, and right away I notice the front door is open. The dispatcher was right about the freshness of the crime because the killer made no attempt to cover it up. He must have been in a hurry.

I make my way up the porch, and squeaking noises radiate out of it with every step I take. I'm now in the house, gun held with both arms as I use my head to peer through the hallways, and it's pretty empty. I see only a few signs of life scattered about: a dining table in one of the rooms I had walked past, faint shoeprints on the hardwood floor that I was walking on. There are some lamps dispersed here and there, and several closed doors.

I also smell a foul stench. It smells like rotten fish mixed with eggs. It's horrible, and it only gets stronger as I approach the kitchen. The floor continues to creak with every step I take. And then I arrive at the kitchen and see the source of the odor.

On the ground, there is a body, a woman whose skin is pale and limbs are stiff. She has an almond face, though it is a bit bloated, and long brown hair that reaches down to her back. She is curvy, big bosoms and thighs, but also short. She seems to be just over five feet. She was probably quite the looker when she was alive.

I cover my nose as the stench is at its strongest. This woman must have been dead for at least a week, judging by the stink she is emitting. There was no way the crime could've happened this morning.

I step closer to examine her body and I see no gunshot wounds, no seared flesh from energy pistols, not even any blunt trauma. It appears that the woman had died from natural causes. She looks too young for that, though. Judging from her appearance, she was probably only seventy or eighty years old. Natural death usually occurs when someone is over one hundred fifty.

All this speculation is useless though, the only way I can get the real story is if I do a scan, so I take out my bio scanner from my pocket and stand above her. I turn the handheld device on and two laser emitters shine onto her body and travel up and down several hundred times in a matter of seconds. The first examination is complete, so I do the next one. I cover my mouth and take a latex glove from my pocket. I then open her right eye a bit and place the scanner on top of it. I flash the lasers over her retina. The second phase is complete, so it is now on to the third.

I place the scanner above her left wrist. Two small needles protrude from it and prick her forearm. The blood sample is taken. The scan is complete.

"Analyzing," the computer says, "estimated completion time five minutes."

I really need to upgrade my software, because five minutes is a goddamn eternity compared to some of the newer models out there. With five minutes to kill, I continue my investigation of the house.

It is odd, I see signs of life around the house, but what I don't see are signs of a full life. There are no books, no TV, not even a music player. The house just has things that were necessary for living. Clothes, some unclean dishes in the sink, a few credits lying about. That was it, nothing else. This woman seemed to live far away from the modern world, like a hermit.

I walk out into the living room and notice a door on the wall. It must be a closet, so I approach it and nothing happens. Its motion sensor must be broken, I'm going to have to do this the old-fashioned way. I reach into its indented groove, get a firm grip, and pull hard. Really hard. After a few seconds of struggle, I'm able to pry it open. It is a closet, filled with dusty boxes. Whatever is in them hasn't been touched for a long time.

I open one of them to see its contents - a bunch of photo frames, lots of them. I grab the nearest one and take a look at the picture. It's her, the woman, kneeling on a porch next to what appears to be a group of children. At least, they look like her children, though there sure are a lot of them. The photo is dusty so I use my shirt to wipe it clean. I take a closer look at her. She is smiling and looks healthy.

I then look at the children. They look 'different' to put it nicely. I don't notice at first, but as I stare closer at each one, they don't appear to be human. Some have long hairs coming out of their faces, others have no hair and their skin looks scaly. One in particular looks like he has some stripes on his face. I have never seen a picture of children like that before. They almost look like animals.

Was this taken during Halloween? These costumes look pretty real. What kind of freak show was this?

"Analysis complete."

I nearly drop the scanner as the sound of the AI breaks my thoughts.

"Name, Maya Lawton, age of death, eighty two. There is a thirty percent chance victim died of natural causes. The rest is inconclusive."

"Natural causes at this age? I find that hard to believe. Computer, any unusual traits found on the body?"

"Inconclusive."

I have never heard the computer say that.

"Computer," I say, "please be more specific with your response."

"Subject appears to have some damage in the uterus area, but I cannot find a match to a historical case similar to what was scanned."

"That's strange. Computer, cross reference your search on uterus damage with multiple births. Victim appears to have a group of several children. Could the toll of multiple births combined with your findings of uterus damage have been a cause of death?"

"Computing...... It is possible, but inconclusive."

It looks like I am going nowhere with the cause of death.

"Computer," I say, "please state medical history."

"No recent records found. Last known medical appointment occurred on February 13th, 2990."

"Damn, that was over fifty years ago. Computer, state criminal record."

"Maya Lawton alias Maya Howl. Five counts of illegal prostitution. Last known incarceration was in 3014, sentenced to ten years for unlawful interspecies intercourse. Was released with good behavior in 3016."

I look at the pictures. "3016, that was twenty four years ago. That means this picture was taken after that. Interspecies intercourse? It can't be…. Computer, summarize most recent research on interspecies breeding."

"With other species gaining intelligence spanning hundreds of years, research on interspecies breeding suggests it is still only in theory. Scientists are unsure of the probability that one day interspecies breeding is possible. Case in point, there is no conclusive evidence proving or disproving the possibility of mixed species existing. However, public opinion has remained that this subject is taboo."

The computer tells me what I already know, but my eyes do not. I see a picture of half- man, half-animal children and I learn of their mother's shady history as a prostitute. I put the clues together and hypothesize that this woman gave birth to abominations, monsters or something.

But where are they? I see no signs of life at all. Not even a sound. It's as if the only person who lived in this house was her.

Creaaak!

I hear the footsteps of someone else. I am not alone in this house and quickly run to a wall, gun pressed against my chest. The steps come slowly, thump, by thump, by thump. The sound emits from the front of the house. I am in the living room, right beside it. The only thing that separates us is a thin, decrepit wall.

I don't think the intruder heard me shuffle to my cover, because its footsteps sound calm. There's no rushing or sudden movements. I slowly edge myself closer, and continue to hear the lingering thuds of each step. He's now walking away from my position, towards the kitchen, towards the woman's body.

Does he know her?

This is it, no fear. I slowly peer my head over to see who it is, but his back faces me. He wears a large sweatshirt, head covered with a hood. He has thick, brown boots on, which explains all the heavy thuds I heard when he entered the premises.

From my position, I can see him kneeling down over the woman's body. His back is still turned. He's vulnerable, it is time to make my move. With a rush of adrenaline, I run to him and point my gun.

"Freeze! Hands up!" I yell. He's caught off guard and stands up immediately. His hands remain at his side.

"I said hands up!" He does nothing. "Hands up!"

I sense his fear, his head is shivering.

"It's okay, I just need to ask you some questions, now hands up!"

Still nothing.

"Now!" I yell.

In a blink of an eye, he runs towards the kitchen counter. I'm shocked that he doesn't obey my orders. I still have my gun pointed at him, and his sudden movements make my trigger finger itch. But I remain calm, even as he makes his mad dash to the counter.

I must remain calm. I must. Until…

… I see him reaching for a butcher knife in the sink.

When you only have a few seconds to react, time stays still. I see him reaching for the knife and my instinct is to move, but my body can't compute this. I want to move my arms, my legs, to charge after him, but I can't. That moment is frozen in time, and I feel paralyzed.

The only thing I can move is my finger. I fire a shot directly into his chest. I fire another one to make sure.

His arms fly violently above his head, and he stumbles backwards. His legs flail up into the air and his head jerks back. The knife that was in his hand falls down as he does. I see all of this millisecond by millisecond. That's how it's always like when I have to kill someone.

Time speeds up back to its normal pace. The attacker isn't moving. There are now two dead bodies on the ground and I have a good look at his face. I walk over to examine it and I am floored.

His skin is shiny, and the greenest of greens I had ever seen. His eyes are on the side of his head. He has no nose, it's more like a pointy snout, and his mouth is as wide as his head. His legs are strong and muscular. He looks like a frog, but there is something strangely human about him.

It is like he was made of puzzle pieces that aren't supposed to fit. The overall picture is completely unnatural and extremely frightening.

What have I stumbled into?

Chapter 2 – Leonard Lawton

Homecoming

November 15, 3040 5:01 AM

I didn't want to leave my brothers and sisters, but I couldn't abandon her. My mother had died, and we left her for the flies. It was wrong; it's not the way mothers should be treated.

Tiago strongly objected when I told him that we should go back, that we should have given our mom a proper send-off. After all, she raised us through blood, sweat and tears, kept us away from the humans, dogs, wolves, and other animals who won't understand what we are. Tiago never liked her, though. He said she was a whore behind her back and that the only reason we existed was because of her whorish ways.

I may be the youngest of all my brothers and sisters, and Tiago may be the oldest, but what he said was incredibly immature. How could you say that about your own mother?

I would hear her talk about the outside world. She would say society would deem us freaks, that they would never understand us. She made sure that we never left the house, that no one could ever see who we are, and I could see her point. I read the news, watched the TV shows and movies she let us see. All of those animals I saw on those programs, none of them looked like us. I saw dogs and cats, humans and frogs, bears and lions, they all looked like what they were supposed to. We, on the other hand, didn't completely look like other humans, we didn't completely look like other animals, and I didn't look like the normal frogs I've seen. No, we looked different; we were special.

My mother was a human. I can see her human traits in myself. When I was young and I asked her who my father was, who was this mysterious frog that was part of me. She would always avoid the question.

"It's not important," she would say. Eventually, she said it enough times that I believed it wasn't important. I had my mother, and that's all that I needed.

It wasn't until I was a little older that Tiago told me the truth about her, that she was a prostitute who serviced not only her kind but other species as well. Gross. My mom said that all eleven of us were unique, that we were the first of our kind. She was right. When I looked things up on the infospace, the results stated that scientific findings proved interspecies breeding is impossible.

Maybe mom was different. Maybe there was something about her body that allowed it to be possible. She never went to the doctor. Last time she had an appointment was forty years ago, or so she said. She insisted there was nothing to figure out and pretty much balked at the idea of finding the answer. Even if she knew the answer, she wasn't telling us. All of that was a part of a past she wanted left behind.

But there are some things you can't run from.

All those times Tiago called her a whore, he was right. She bore eleven children in the span of six years. I guess since we were a mix of different species, some of us were faster to pop out than others. Or maybe mom's unique physiology sped up her maternity. I never really understood the science of it, but all of us are here, and it happened.

I also learned about the baggage we carried. I had seen a lot on the news, and I researched what I could on the infospace. Interspecies prostitution is universally frowned upon in practically all corners of the world. She was a whore in the most vile sense.

When I first found out, I was disgusted with her. I didn't talk to her for days. She didn't ask why I was angry, but I think she figured it out. During a dinner, when it was just me and her, she asked me what was wrong.

"Nothing," I said.

"What did your older brother say to you?" she asked.

"Nothing."

We didn't say anything for the rest of dinner, but later that night I heard her quarrelling with Tiago in one of the rooms. It was hard to make out, but I could hear what they were arguing about.

"What did you want me to tell him?" I heard Tiago yell.

"Anything but that I was a prostitute!" she said. "That was almost fifteen years ago. It's something I want to leave behind!"

"Well, it's hard to leave behind considering the eleven freaks you raised as your own."

"Don't call yourself that, you're not freaks!"

"If we aren't, then why do you keep us locked in this house? Why can't we go outside and explore the world?"

"You know why. They'll hunt you. They'll take you away from me. Even worse, they'll make you experiments. You do understand why I have to protect you from the world, don't you?"

"Yeah, I do, it's because you're a paranoid psycho."

Tiago then stormed out of the room and went to the backyard to let off some steam. I didn't understand him.

For a guy who claimed he wanted to see the world, he could have left anytime he wanted to, but he didn't. I guess he was as afraid of what was out there as the rest of us. We all were scared, my mother made it very clear that we would not be welcomed into society. She got to him, too.

It didn't matter to me, though. I had no desire to leave. My mother loved all of us, cared for all of us, and that's all that mattered. When we needed food, she provided it. When we needed clothes, she gave them to us. And for the most part, our family got along. Even Tiago, the sibling I feared the most, was someone I could call my brother. We looked out for each other because we were family. It was the only thing I needed. Let the world figure out its own problems, because I didn't want to be a part of it.

The house was a great place to live. It was a little rundown, and it was only one story, but what you couldn't see on the surface was that there were a whole slew of rooms underground. That's where my siblings and I lived for most of our lives. We congregated and spent time as a family upstairs, but we had our own space below. My mom lived upstairs. As she put it, it would give off the right appearance in case someone came knocking, though we hadn't encountered anyone in ages. Our street was practically a ghost town. I suppose it was another way my mom kept us under wraps. For the sixteen years I've been alive, the only people I knew of were my family and what I saw on TV and the infospace. I had never seen the outside world other than through what I saw on a screen.

And I had no desire to see anything else. The world doesn't seem that great of a place. I heard about wars between species going on in some areas of the world. I read online that things weren't always this way, that hundreds of years ago, humans were the only animals on the planet that ruled. But then something happened and other animals became smarter. Not all kinds, but many did. And when you have that many species aware of how smart they are, conflict is bound to arise. I liked my bubble, it kept me away from them.

But my dream scenario eventually crumbled. Without warning, something happened. We were all eating dinner, like we always did in the evenings, the eleven of us gathered around the supper table enjoying a meal prepared by mother. As we talked about the day's events, mom started coughing really hard. She had always had an issue with her throat, but it was usually very mild. This time she was coughing up a storm. We were all concerned, but after a small fit, she assured us she was okay, so we went back to our meal.

But then, five minutes later, it happened again. She coughed and coughed and coughed and then collapsed to the ground.

Immediately, we rushed to her side. My sister Iris quickly raised her head and Isaac, her twin brother, got a glass of water and tried to make mom drink it. She wasn't having it, though, and furiously puked it out. I looked at what she spewed and I saw pieces of blood in it. She turned over to her side and continued to cough and vomit violently.

"We need to get a doctor!" I yelled. The others looked at me, with uneasy expressions. They wanted to do it but couldn't because of the repercussions.

"You know we can't," Tiago said. I nodded sadly. We could only sit there and watch.

The convulsions came. She started to shake violently, flopping around like a fish out of water. One of her arms flailed around so forcefully that the ground cracked.

I turned around to a corner and shielded my eyes away from the sight. But soon there was nothing to see. Her convulsions stopped and all I heard was silence. I looked over to see my brothers and sisters gathered around her with their heads down. She was dead.

And so it came to be that my mother, the only person who took care of us all these years, had died in front of my eyes.

That night, we gathered in the living room to figure out what we were to do next. There was already talk amongst my older brothers and sisters that the only plan we could pursue was to leave, but we needed to figure out a strategy.

"We can't leave her!" I proclaimed.

"Well we can't stay," Tiago said. "Eventually, someone is going to come. Bill collector, mortgage officer, someone is going to wonder why things haven't been paid. You know mom was a on a daily collection plan because of her bad credit. If she was a day late, she might have gotten a visit from the local collector. None of us have access to her information, either. She kept that all to herself. And if we stay here, we're going to be found out. It might take a day, it might take a month, but it's for certain. And you know what's going to happen. We're practically dead if they catch us."

"And what makes you so certain they're going to harm us?" I asked.

"Are you a fool?" Tiago yelled. "You spend your time on the infospace, don't you? Have you seen what they do to anyone who is different? Did you read about what humans did to their own kind thousands of years ago? What they do out of fear and ignorance? Mobs of people are going to hunt us down and hang us. At one time, they were considered the most intelligent animals on the planet, and look at how they behaved when faced with something unknown. Things haven't changed. Any animal that can think for themselves will act the same way. They'll murder us."

"Perhaps Leonard is right," my brother Oscar said. "Perhaps you're only thinking of the worst scenario."

"The worst scenario is the only scenario," Tiago said sharply.

"Look," Isaac said, "regardless of how the outside world is going to treat us, we should discuss whether staying here is the best option."

"I think we should consider exploring the outside world. We can't stay here forever on what food and supplies we have alone," my sister Maddie told the group. "We'll eventually have to go out, as we only have a few weeks of rations. There's no way we can order anything, since mom's insta-item is linked to her accounts. We don't have access to them. Perhaps we should take this time to leave and go to a place where no one will be looking for the bills that aren't going to be paid. There's nothing for us here anymore."

"And where do you suggest we go?" my brother Alex asked.

"There are plenty of abandoned buildings around here," Maddie continued. "We can stay in one of those, at least until we figure out what to do next. No one will be looking for us there."

"How do you know they're abandoned?" my brother Lombardi asked.

"I know. You're not the only one who goes sneaking away at night," Maddie said. Lombardi looked embarrassed, as did all my brothers and sisters.

"Looks like Maddie is right," Oscar said. "What do you guys think?"

I looked around, and I saw everyone nodding their heads in agreement.

"It seems wise to find a better hiding area," Tiago said. "Then we can plan what to do from there. We'll need to gather as many things as possible and move during the night so we are unseen by any nosey bystanders. Everyone, start packing your things. We're moving out when the sun sets, in less than two hours."

"But what about mom?" I asked Tiago. "We can't leave her."

"We don't have time," Tiago said. "We have to move as soon as possible."

"No!" I yelled. "That's not right. She raised us and we can't even give her a proper burial?"

My ten brothers and sisters looked away from me, avoiding eye contact. I saw the shame in their eyes. I knew they were thinking with their brains, that survival was their priority, but I wish they thought with their hearts.

Tiago approached me, "I know this is hard for you to hear, but it's the only thing we can do right now. You're scared. You were the closest to mom and heeded all her advice. But let me assure you, the last thing she ever wanted was for us to be in danger. She didn't want to see us hunted down by an angry mob, but that's what's going to happen if they find us here. C'mon, Leonard, we have to move."

His words made sense, yet I was still unsure. But with all of my sisters and brothers leaving, I didn't want to be left behind.

"I suppose, I suppose you're right," I said hesitantly.

"Good, now get your stuff, it's time we leave this place," Tiago said.

I took an hour to get my things and met everyone out front. Maddie told us the abandoned building was a warehouse two miles away. We started to walk away, and I looked back to say goodbye.

Thirty minutes later we finished our trek and arrived at our destination. It's a large building, and it was very empty. We easily broke down the door and entered. All eleven of us made camp and lived off the food and water that we were able to bring with us. Tired from the journey, we settled in and dozed off.

I had dreams that night of my mother. Well, not so much dreams, but nightmares as I replayed her death over and over and over in my mind. I still couldn't believe she was gone.

A day passed and I missed her.

Two days passed and I missed her more.

Three, four, five days, and all I could think about was her corpse rotting without a proper burial.

By the sixth day, I had had enough. I needed to go back home to get some closure, to say goodbye, to give her a proper burial.

It is 5 AM, and my brothers and sisters are sleeping. A week has almost passed since that fateful day. I look for something that will hide my face, and I find a hooded sweatshirt, boots, and some sweatpants. This will do. I make sure no one sees me and I slink into the morning light to make my way back home.

Things need to be ended.

I arrive in the front of the house. It's a strange feeling coming back. This is the place that I grew up in, the only home I knew all my life. And now I am coming back to it, like a stranger. Only a week has passed and already I feel like I am not welcome home anymore. It makes me sad.

I walk through the front door and slowly approach the kitchen. I smell the stench of death, and it is foul. A part of me is scared of what time has done to her body. If the odor is any indicator, it has not treated it well.

I reach the kitchen and see that her once beautiful face is now bloated. Her peach-colored skin is now grossly discolored, a mix of yellow and light purple from her dead veins. She is still trapped in her shocked state, it looks anything but peaceful.

I shed a tear. This is not the way she should've gone. She deserved better. A part of me is angry at my brothers and sisters. How could they have abandoned her in this state? All that time she spent raising them and this is the thanks she gets? It is pathetic. How is it that I am the youngest of them all, but I am the only one who understands the meaning of respect?

I kneel down over her body. I am sorry mother, I should have never left you.

"Freeze! Hands up!" I hear. I am not alone. My thoughts are interrupted, the shock of this discovery rocks me to the core.

The man repeats his call again. I am too dumbfounded to comply. How could this have happened? How is it that a man, a cop no less, already knew to come looking for us?

The man is armed with a gun. He is not here to collect bills, he is here to capture something.

He repeats his order one more time. I slowly stand up and think about how to handle the situation. If he takes me into custody, I will surely be a lab rat or killed, like my mother warned me. If I run, it will give him another excuse to shoot. Either way, this will end in disaster. I wouldn't be surprised if there is a mob already waiting to take me out.

I don't know who this man is, but I am not going to be taken. I look down at my mother and remember the lifetime of warnings she gave us. All these years we had doubted her claims about how the world would view us. It looks like she was right.

I am not going to be killed. I can only do one thing - fight. I know she's looking down on me. It's what she would have wanted me to do. Time to make her proud.

I see in the corner of my eye a kitchen knife in the sink. It is the only weapon available, so I make a quick lunge for it. I'm counting on being faster than this man's trigger finger.

But I am wrong. After I grab the weapon, I turn around and feel two hot burning sensations hit my chest. It is painful, but I can't tell because things are starting to black out. My chest feels like there's nothing there. It's hollow and I can sense movement going through it, like wind flowing through a tunnel.

It's the last thing I feel.

I'm sorry mother, I failed you.

Chapter 3 – Simon Trevor

Debrief

<u>November 16, 3040 6:05 PM</u>

I got the call from headquarters earlier in the morning about a special assignment. It had been about four months since my last case. I am a commander for the Human Council, their star detective. When they call me up, it's usually to investigate a crime and lead a team to complete it. If there's a suspected terrorist in a town, I'd be the guy who would find him. Got tech that's been stolen? I'll help you search, track, and recover it.

So when they told me that they had something extremely high security, something that they knew only I could handle, I took it. It's from an order from the United Species Alliance, high priority stuff. The Council doesn't hand out these assignments freely and being on their good side will certainly help in the long run.

My superior called me at 4:00 in the afternoon and told me that if I was willing, the case would start in Las Vegas. I usually have time to prepare first, to get my things, but my superior told me that he needed me in as soon as possible. I never heard him sound so hasty, so I knew it was something big. I packed my bags, put on a shirt and pants, took the first teleporter into Las Vegas, and headed to the local United Species Alliance headquarters for my debriefing.

When I get out of the teleporter station receiver, a hovercar is there to pick me up and take me to HQ. Sometimes I laugh at the idea that through all this technological progression, or maybe lack thereof, we still have hovercars, especially when we can teleport across entire countries. I guess it's necessary. If we were teleporting around left and right with no order, you'd have people bumping into each other. It'd be chaotic, and in times like these, even the slightest order is good order.

Besides, we can't invent things like we used to. Those days are long gone thanks to all this change in society. Maybe one day when things settle down, we'll be back on track.

About fifteen minutes later, I arrive at HQ and meet up with my superior, Agent Leons. He's a large, portly man, standing well over six feet. He has a mustache and bald spot over his oval shaped head. His double chin hangs over the collar of his shirt, and his blazer is slightly wrinkled.

He's the man who usually notifies me about these assignments and always gives me the run through on what I am up against. I've probably worked with him for twenty years or so. He's straight forward, seems relaxed and carefree, but under that exterior lies a competent manipulator. He talks a lot, and sometimes tells me more than I need to hear. To put it bluntly, I don't fully trust the man.

We walk past the lobby and head towards the elevator. I had been to the Las Vegas branch before, but I still have a hard time navigating myself around. It's a grand office building, and when I enter, I see steel colored walls reaching to the roof. Giant screens adorn them with the day's news. The lobby is quite a sight, and there are several agents walking about. I politely make my way through the crowd as I follow Agent Leons to the elevator. He presses up, and we wait for it, standing next to each other in an awkward silence.

The elevator opens, and we walk in. He finally speaks.

"So you ready for some strange shit?" he asks me.

"I've seen a lot, don't know if what you plan to throw my way is really going to surprise me," I respond.

"That's what I thought too, but once I got the details, I was pretty shocked."

"You could've given me a small briefing on the phone."

"If I did, you might have had second thoughts."

"Have you ever known me to not accept a mission?"

"No, but I can't be certain I know anyone that well."

"What's with the rush anyway, Don? "

"It's time sensitive. You'll probably only have until the end of the night to prepare."

"It's already 6:00 PM."

"Yup."

"That high priority, eh?"

"Yup."

The elevator opens and he makes a right, in the direction of one of the debriefing rooms. They all look the same, so I follow him to prevent myself from getting lost. He opens the door and I enter a large conference room with a beautiful polished desk in the center and a humongous screen on the wall. It looks like a standard debriefing room, but much nicer than what I am used to.

"Have a seat," he says.

As I sit down and make myself comfortable, he tosses me a thin tablet device. I turn it on and see an image of a brunette woman. Judging by her appearance she looks to be in her fifties or so.

"That is a picture of Maya Lawton," Agent Leons says. "She's currently fifty five in that picture, but it was taken about twenty five years ago. Quite the looker, eh?

She probably ran the racket on clients, don't know why she got into the shit she got into with that face."

"What did she get into?" I ask.

"You'll see."

He turns on the screen and immediately a hologram of a corpse flashes from it.

"This is a more recent image of her," he says smugly.

"You want me to investigate the death of this woman?" I ask Agent Leons.

"Hold off on the questions until after the briefing," he says.

"Okay."

"Maya Lawton was also known as Maya Howl, a prostitute who was a member of this man's stable of hookers."

The screen shows up a hologram of a fat man, well past his hundreds. He is bald and disheveled looking. He's wearing a loose shirt and his neck is adorned with various pieces of jewelry.

"This is Eddie David, grade A asshole, low level pimp. He had a small operation down in Primm. Eddie was incarcerated for running an illegal prostitution ring there. The judge sentenced him to life without parole in 3014."

"Life without parole? That seems pretty harsh for just running a prostitution ring."

"The ring specialized in interspecies prostitution."

"Ahh, I see. So he's currently sleeping in a prison pod right now?"

"No, he's dead. Before he could carry out his sentence, someone murdered him during his transport to Mojave Penitentiary. Files say it was a former rival that arranged his hit. Man, sometimes things are easier when you let these scumbags take each other out. Makes it less messy for us members of the law."

Agent Leons is never one to shy away from his opinions.

"I see," I say dismissively. "What happened to Ms. Lawton?"

"She was sentenced to ten years in a correctional facility. They didn't put her to sleep. She only served two until she got released for good behavior. However, with Eddie gone, her source of income was limited. She stayed off the radar and eventually vanished, or so it seemed. The only thing registered to her was a broken down house and some energy and wireless bills. In actuality, she was still servicing other species."

"So no one ever found out?"

"No, she was actually pretty good at lying low, other than the whole whoring herself out to animals part."

"How long did she do this for?"

"We don't have conclusive evidence, but we're guessing she stopped doing it by 3024. Thank God. This brings us to today."

Another hologram emanates from the screen. This time it is a man with scruffy hair, aged probably into his eighties as well.

"This is detective Scott Marsden. Last morning, he received an anonymous tip about the residence of 1523 Chakming Drive. It was where Maya lived. When he entered, he found her body in the kitchen, as I had showed you in the previous slide. He also encountered this."

The screen renders a hologram of something I've never seen before.

"What the fuck is that?!" I yell.

It's an image of a human, except he doesn't look completely like a man. He has green skin, big bulging black eyes on the sides of his head and a large, wide mouth. His face looks like a frog. The rest of his skin is green as well. But as I examine the photo more closely, I see that he has thumbs, hands like a human. He is wearing human clothing. He's much too large to be a normal frog, yet he definitely doesn't look like anything I've ever seen.

"That, my friend is what the folks around here are calling 'halfkinds', that is what this is all about," Agent Leons says.

"Halfkinds?" I ask Agent Leons.

"Well that's what these beings are, half mankind, half animal-kind. From the bio scanners and medical analysis, we've determined that thing has both human and frog DNA. And guess what, the human DNA was a match to Ms. Lawton."

"But that's impossible. There have been no successful cases of animal human splicing so far."

"That's true, but we also had the medical team look at Ms. Lawton, and from their analysis it seems to suggest this wasn't the work of a rogue faction of splicers, this was something else. We're guessing this thing was her son."

"You're saying she gave birth to it?"

"Indeed I am. The medical team did an autopsy on her and they found tons of illegal tech in her body. Biotics, biological robotics, stuff that works inside you. It looks like she wasn't only whoring herself out to other species. She was whoring her body out to some black market implanters. Mix both of them together, and I guess this is the end result. People will do anything for cash."

"What did they put in her?"

"We can't determine yet. It's kind of a jumbled mess of bionic and robotic implants in her uterus. It's hard to determine what kind of tech we're dealing with since all of it seems off the market."

"Do you know the purpose of the implants?"

"Not exactly, but early word from the science lab is that all the implants are related to birth enhancements. Makes sense. Genetically engineering a half man half animal creature would no doubt be on the radar of the United Species Alliance. This group needed something less detectable, so why not have a bunch of paid whores do it the old fashioned way? It's kind of just a hypothesis, though. We won't know until they have more time to research. It's only been a day after all."

"Well your team does work fast."

"They do think that it attributed to her early demise. All of that biotech had traces of synconium in it."

"Isn't that stuff poisonous?"

"Sure is. I'm surprised she lived so long considering what was in her. But since synconium poisoning happens in a flash, she probably had no idea she was going to die so soon."

"I can't believe she agreed to put that stuff in her body."

"She was desperate, and I'm pretty sure the last thing that tech went through was any kind of safety test. She probably didn't even know what was in her. With all the shit she willingly did in her life, I would guess she wasn't the brightest bulb in the bunch."

Agent Leons walks to the other end where a water dispenser lies. He takes a swig of the liquid and goes back to the screen.

"We don't know who did it either," he continues.

"Maybe a group of fanatics? Perhaps, they're trying to manipulate the evolutionary process, kind of like what happened about a few hundred years ago?"

"That's what we think. This is definitely some underground work. Our information is sparse and it's pretty shitty. We don't even know if Maya was the only person involved with these implants. I suspect she wasn't, but that information is up the chain. I can't get access to it."

"So to wrap up what I've learned so far, we suspect that there's a rogue group of biologists out there that are working with women like Maya to breed half human half something else species?"

"That seems to be the case."

"Is there any evidence to suggest that Maya is still involved with this group?"

"That's the thing, we don't have any messages or records that suggest it. They, or she, probably cut ties with each other after this one was born."

"That's why I'm here then, huh? You want me to find this renegade group, find out who's performing these operations?"

"No. Right now that trail is cold. All of this is theory. We haven't had enough time to sift through the evidence that we found at her house to determine what the story is exactly. When we do get something concrete, we'll go after the group responsible for this. For now, what we need you to do is find the others."

"Others?"

"This guy right here, this frog thing, his name was Leonard. I find it kind of funny she gave them such normal names. I would have given these freaks freak names to match their appearance. When our team completed searching the Lawton residence, we discovered that he has brothers and sisters. "

"What?"

"After Detective Marsden subdued Leonard, he investigated the house and stumbled upon the basement, a very large basement, with several rooms built underground."

He goes to the next render and it shows a hall with ten or fifteen corridors.

"All this was constructed below the surface," Agent Leons says. "This was where his brothers and sisters lived."

The structure impresses me. The hallway is quite spacy and, from what I can tell, the rooms look rather roomy. I can't believe all of it was built underground.

"How many are there total?" I ask Agent Leons.

"A lot," he responds. "Including Leonard, eleven."

"Are they all half human, half frogs like Leonard?"

"Not quite. It's kind of a potpourri of species mixing."

He goes to the next hologram. It is of a creature, a large one. He has the face of a human, but it's covered with fur, striped orange and black. His eyes are round and yellow, like a cat's. He has long, bushy white hair flowing from his head. His body is bulky, but muscular. The same striped fur adorns his arms and legs. His hands are like a human's, but the fingers a round and stocky. They look like paws.

"We were able to gather quite a bit of evidence from the rooms in the basement. That's how we created these renders. There were documents, pictures, personal effects, all of them helped piece together the information you are about to receive now. This one's name is Tiago,"

Agent Leons says. "We're guessing his father is a Bengali Tiger."

"Good guess."

"He appears to be the oldest of the group. From what we can tell, he's roughly twenty two years old. I'm going to show you the profiles in order of age, if you don't mind."

"No problem. Anything else you can tell from him?"

"Not really, but since he's the oldest and one of the biggest of the group, we're guessing he's a natural fit for leader. You'll have time to go over our findings later on. All the documents should be in that tablet I handed to you."

"Okay."

Leons pulls up the next image. It's another massive creature, much larger than Tiago, teetering on the obese side. His body is covered with a light brown fur. His fingers are long and at the end of them are claws. His face is round and a large snout protrudes from the center. On the top of his head are two fuzzy ears.

"Father was a bear?" I ask him.

"From the looks of it. Grizzly, you think?" he asks me.

"I guess, I can't really tell. Not exactly an expert on this stuff."

"His name is Oscar. We figured his age is twenty two as well."

"How'd she give birth to him so quickly when she just had Tiago?"

"The frog, Leonard, he was sixteen, and he was the youngest. We're guessing she kept pumping them out. The implants in her body also might have expedited her pregnancies to a few months each."

"I see. What do you think this one's role in the family is?"

"We're not sure exactly. We think he's big enough to be the muscle of the group, but from his personal writings and journal entries that we found, we get the sense that he's somewhat of a pacifist."

"What did you find from Tiago's writings and personal effects?"

"He's more hostile."

"Did all of them have private journals?"

"Almost all of them. The ones we confiscated are the only way we could figure out their personality profiles."

The next hologram morphs on the screen. It's of a hulking creature. He is big, like Oscar, but muscular, rough looking. His skin is grey, eyes small and beady. He is bald and has the ears of a human. Oh, and there is a giant horn sticking out of his face where his nose is supposed to be. He is in full scowl mode in the image I see.

"This is Alex," Agent Leons says. "Age is about twenty one. He's one of the two who didn't have a journal. The horn is a dead giveaway that he must be part rhino. Judging from this mug, if Oscar isn't the muscle, he definitely is. Good luck trying to take this bastard down. Let's go on to the next one."

This creature is the strangest looking so far. He has feathers, for starters, shiny brown ones, along with a beak and wings as limbs. I do see human fingers extending to the tips of them. His eyes are globular and very noticeable. He's wearing a jacket and pants, yet coming out from the bottom aren't feet, but talons.

"The biologists can't really figure out what kind of bird he got his traits from, but most likely it's a Golden Eagle, the only true intelligent bird out there," Agent

Leons says. "It's pretty indistinguishable, especially with the human traits mixed in there. What we do know is that he's the same age as Alex, just a few months younger. He's also another one without a journal, so it's hard to put a finger on what he's like."

"What's his name?"

"Lombardi. I call him the ugly one. On to the next."

This one is the most human looking. Its posture is hunched over a bit, and it's a lot hairier than a human. Its nose is flattened and there is a long gaping mouth under it. It has long, styled hair, and it's wearing short shorts and a pink tee shirt.

"At first we thought this one was human, but later we figured she was part chimp. And yes, you heard right, that's a girl. I guess you could tell from her attire. She had a journal and from what we read, she's a pure technical ace."

"How do you know?"

"We found a lot of device manuals, blueprints, and hacking files in her living quarters. Schematics and some unassembled machines. It seems whatever she got her hands on, she took time to understand how it worked. She's probably the group's mechanic and genius. Her name is Candy and her age is twenty."

"Candy? Seems kind of an odd choice for a name."

"Haven't you heard? Her mom was a hooker."

Agent Leons presses the button to move onto the next image. This being is quite different from the other one. This one is hideous. His skin is a dark green, almost mud colored, and scaly. His eyes are serpent like, bugging out of his head. Sharp teeth burst past his upper lip, overlapping his bottom one. His hands are large and scabby like the rest of his body and each finger has large claws on them. He is the third biggest after Oscar and Alex.

"This is Curtis. He's obviously reptile, so we're thinking he's bred from a crocodile. We're guessing he's about twenty. Unfortunately, he didn't have a journal, so we're not sure how he fits in with the family. I theorize that if he does have a role, it's not good."

I fixate on his sharp teeth and leathery skin. It sends chills down my spine. Next to the rhino halfkind, he'll be the hardest to take down.

The next hologram image has two halfkinds in it. The first one looks very similar to Tiago, but leaner, skinnier, and with spots. His fur is yellow instead of orange. He also has a large yellow tail, also spotted. The other one has smoother looking skin, though I could see some short hairs on it. It's black and white, and has a large pink snout for a nose. It's also bigger, kind of obese like the half bear that Agent Leons showed me earlier.

"Meet Ace, the half cheetah, and Maddie, the half cow. Each one of them idolizes a different older brother. Ace wants to be like Tiago, Maddie wants to be like Oscar. Oh, and if you couldn't tell by her name, Maddie is female. And now we come to the last two. Both of them are in their late teens."

Agent Leons moves to the next hologram and I see two catlike beings. The first one is has orange fur, its body type is lean and well defined. He has whiskers and hypnotizing cat eyes. His fur covers his whole body and his ears point up. He's bipedal like all the others.

His counterpart is similar to him, except everything is more delicate, feminine. She is the only one who I could tell was a girl off the bat. Her eyes standout since they are so enormous, and her face is thin and soft looking. She has a long tail that sticks out of her clothing. Her fur isn't as long as her brothers, and while she did have the cat ears, she also has long, silky human hair on her head. In a strange way, she is very beautiful, alluring almost.

"These are the twins, Iris and Isaac," Agent Leons said. "They're part cat, and probably about seventeen. And that's all we know about them really. They didn't have a journal or many personal effects."

Agent Leons eyes Iris perversely.

"But, man, too bad that one is a cat abomination," he says. "In a weird way, she looks pretty good."

I imaginarily roll my eyes at his comments. "What can you tell me about the one who died, Leonard?"

"Not a lot, only that he loved his mother very much."

"And the detective just shot at him?"

"No, Leonard attacked first with a kitchen knife."

"He was hostile?"

"It seems so."

"What is my mission exactly?"

"You are to assist in the hunting and termination of these eleven halfkinds."

"Why?"

"It's an order from the Council via the United Species Alliance."

"Seems like a pretty shady order. I'm not a hired assassin."

"Well, you're not. You're a soldier. And soldiers do what they're told."

"They think for themselves, too."

Agent Leons looks to the ground and shakes his head.

"Look, Simon," he says. "I don't decide the orders, but this is one from the top. You already know how much a taboo interspecies relations are. If word got out that these things exist, it'll be chaos. It'll be opening a can of worms that will lead to God knows what. People, animals will take this as another accident, like what happened a few hundred years ago. Suspicion and fear will ravage the streets. These things are atrocities and their very existence shouldn't even be put into light. If this interspecies breeding begins, within a few generations people will wonder exactly what it means to be human. And it's not the way Mother Nature intended it to be."

He takes another sip from his cup.

"Messing with genetics," he continues, "playing God, it's not our role. If our ancestors had only known the repercussions of all this experimenting, then we'd still be on the top, instead of sharing it with all these others animals. But here we are again, put face to face with an evolutionary crisis. It's not only the Human Council that wants this done, it's been decided among all the species councils that these things need to be put out because of the threat they bring to all life, for future generations. This time, we have to put a stop to this before it can even begin."

He puts his cup down.

"Goddamn, think of all the shit us humans could've done if we hadn't messed around, if these animals never got smart. We could've been walking around this planet like gods, dominating the world with all the advances we would've made the past few hundreds of years. I can't even imagine all the cool shit that'd we'd be playing with right now. But that stuff never happened. We had the plans, but once the animals were as smart as us, the plans were put on hold. Now we're stuck in a loop of politics and ever increasing shit."

He looks me in the eye and moves in closer. His face changes from business to a more relaxed expression. A slick smile flashes, like one a used hovercar salesmen would have. The pressure I feel from him makes me uncomfortable.

"This is from the top," he says. "If you do this, the Council, hell the United Species Alliance, won't forget it."

He's right. I don't want to let down either group and the credits they would pay me would be pretty nice. With a direct order like this, I might be the one giving out briefings in the future.

"All right, I'll do it then."

"Good. Follow me and I'll introduce you to your team."

"Team? I normally work with people I know."

"Well this isn't a normal case."

Chapter 4 – Iris Lawton

Outcasts

November 15, 3040 11:21 AM

When we woke up this morning, we discovered that Leonard had gone missing. I remember earlier seeing him asleep next to us on the dingy ground of this abandoned building, and then mysteriously, he was gone.

We're not sure where he snuck off to, but Tiago has a good idea. He knew how much Leonard loved mother, we all did. We remembered how outraged Leonard was when we left so hastily, that we didn't even give her a proper burial. Tiago thinks that Leonard went back home to let her rest peacefully.

I personally didn't want to leave mother rotting away in that house either, but things happened so fast, and we were afraid because mother had told us so much about how the outside world would persecute us. When the others said that someone could stop by the house within a day or two, I was petrified. If we are discovered, they'll kill or capture us for their experiments, like mother warned us. I don't want to die. That's why I agreed with the others to leave so quickly.

But Leonard, I could tell that he didn't want to. He said nothing, but his face gave it away. When Leonard was sad, his upper lip would tremble a little, and his large, black eyes would blink rapidly. I saw both of those things happen the moment we left home.

It was hard for him. It was hard for all of us. I didn't sneak out like Maddie or Lombardi did, so that house was the only place I knew for seventeen years. Mother kept us in a very sheltered existence. She let us go on the infospace to learn about the civilization around us, but it wasn't tangible. We couldn't interact with it physically.

From what she told us, I figured the world wasn't a nice place to live in. But the idea she reinforced most often was how all of them, humans, dogs, gorillas, pigs, all of the animals, would be against us. We were different, too different for a world like this.

I didn't want to believe her, but who else was there to believe?

"He should be returning at any moment," Tiago says. He had sent Ace to go back to the house, to see if Leonard was there. Ace was eager to help out and he is the best equipped to scout the area, even in broad daylight. He's part cheetah, meaning he runs the fastest of all of us, and the paws he has help him tread lightly. He boasts about his prowess, how he's so good he could run circles in broad daylight. It's not something I would do, but his cheetah ancestry also means he's not that smart.

"Do you think Leonard really went back home?" I ask Isaac, my twin brother.

Isaac twitches his nose and his whiskers shake. "I don't know Iris, but it seems pretty likely. He was the closest to mom. Remember how much she used to baby him? He always was her favorite."

Isaac speaks in the past tense and it irks me a little. Mother is dead, and we now have to talk about her as a memory, not someone in the present. It makes me sad. I wasn't as close to her as Leonard, but she was still my mother. She took care of me and my brothers and sisters, and it's something I couldn't shake in just a week.

I twitch my nose and sniffle a bit. I try to prevent the tears from coming out of my eyes, but in doing so I let out a faint sigh. Isaac senses my sadness.

"Are you okay?" he asks me. Isaac is the one I am closest to, he is my twin after all. He is usually my confidant and can sense my emotions better than any of my other siblings. He's earnest and on good terms with the rest of the family, but they usually refer to us as one entity. They say it must be a cat thing, that we stick to our own kind. I think it's because Isaac understands me, and I understand him.

"Yeah, I'm okay," I say.

"You're sad about mom, aren't you?" he asks.

"Yeah. I mean, who isn't."

"Tiago for one."

Since mother had died, Tiago quickly took his place as the leader. Throughout the week, he was the one who had been giving orders and telling us how to ration our supplies. He was also the one who commanded Ace to search for Leonard.

I can't imagine how it must be to have the weight of ten other siblings on your shoulders. Isaac thinks that in the last few days, Tiago has come off way too cold, especially the way he handled us leaving in the first place. I could tell Isaac disagreed with how we left mother and the house so suddenly. It seemed wrong to leave her corpse to rot. He wanted to punch Tiago in the face.

But I know what we did was for the greater good. Tiago was thinking rationally. It was too dangerous to stay in one place, and Tiago had to do what he could to protect us. Sometimes the best decision isn't always the most popular one.

Tiago has also been discussing with our second oldest brother, Oscar, on what our next move should be. It's odd that they are working together, they've never really seen eye to eye on anything. One is a softy, one is as hard as a rock. I guess to formulate a plan, you need to hear both sides.

We can't hide in this warehouse forever and our supplies are slowly dwindling. The younger ones, like me and Isaac, have to rely on their leadership in order to get through this.

I myself am scared of what the future holds, but I've always been afraid. What kind of future could I ever possibly have? We have no home anymore and we can't bounce from place to place forever. Even worse, if something did happen to Leonard, if he got found out, our existence would be known. We'd be mobbed down and murdered.

Thinking about my future makes me shudder.

Suddenly, we hear knocking from the back entrance of the warehouse. I grab a lead pipe I had been sleeping next to. We had locked the doors tightly, but we are still on edge over possible intruders. First we hear three fast knocks, followed by a pause, and then two more fast knocks. I ease up a little. It's the secret knock we had made before. Ace has returned.

"Ace, is that you?" I ask.

Isaac shushes me. "Let Tiago handle this."

"Ace, what is the code?" Tiago asks.

"Aww, c'mon, just let me in," Ace says impatiently.

"The code," Tiago says again sternly.

"Eight," he says.

Tiago had made a coding system for us during the week. If there was someone with us or someone had taken us hostage, we'd respond four. If we were injured, we'd respond fifteen. Eight means everything is clear.

Tiago instructs Alex to open the locks. This place isn't automated, it's old. We were able to find some industrial padlocks in the warehouse, but only Alex has the strength to unlock and lock them thanks to his rhino DNA. Alex usually does a lot of the physical work in our family, like lifting heavy things and helps with the tough manual labor. His personality is rough, like his grey skin, and brutish, like his large physique. He usually hangs with Tiago. I feel Tiago keeps him around for protection, like a bodyguard. Personally, Alex kind of frightens me.

Ace bursts through the door, breathing deeply. He is wearing a coat that is hooded and wide lens black sunglasses. We concealed his identity as much as we could, especially since he's moving in daylight.

He rests his body on his knees to recuperate.

"Give me a minute," he says, panting.

We back up and wait, all of us are on pins and needles to know what he discovered. Isaac and I exchange glances. I have a worried look on my face, but he shakes his head reassuringly. Ace finally gets settled in.

"What did you see?" Tiago asks.

"I was able to make it about a hundred feet away from the house. When I got there, there was already a group of people snooping around. They were taking our things and putting them into a large storage hovercar," Ace says.

"Were they bill collectors?" Maddie, my half cow, half human sister asks. Some of my brothers look at her dumbfounded. Her question doesn't surprise me though, she's not very bright.

"I don't think so," Ace responds. "They look like they're members of law enforcement or something. I saw the letters USASD on their vehicle."

"United Species Alliance Science Division," Candy responds. She's probably the smartest in our family, and is usually on top of the world's current events and scientific breakthroughs.

"The United Species Alliance?" Oscar asks. "What do they want with our things?"

"I don't know," Ace says.

"You heard him," Tiago interrupts, "It's the science division. They come to experiment on us."

"You don't know that," Oscar says defensively.

"What other reason could it be? It's their science division," Tiago emphasizes the science. Oscar is silent. I look around and see the grim expression on everyone's face, even Isaac's. The hard truth is becoming apparent, mother was right about the outside world.

"What about Leonard?" I ask Ace. "Did you see him?"

Ace is quiet and looks at the floor. His nose begins to twitch and I hear a small sniffle. His whiskers droop down and his pointed ears fold to the side of his head.

"Yeah, I saw him," Ace says. "The science team packed him away in a body bag."

I don't understand what Ace means at first. Body bag? Why would they need that? But then Ace makes it all too clear.

"Leonard is dead," he said.

The room is silent. I think back to when Leonard was a child and mother held him in her arms so proudly. I remember how much he adored her, how he never questioned her, and always went by her word. He was endearing not only to her, but to all of us. A baby brother to everyone. He was the only one who cared about mother enough that he went back to see her off. And now, he was dead for it.

"How did it happen?" I asked.

"I don't know. I just saw him being carried away into the truck."

None of us want to speak. Leonard was so young and caring. He didn't know the world like we did, because it wasn't his nature to acknowledge the brutality around us.

But that's what caused him to die. He deserved better.

"He was murdered," Tiago says angrily.

All of us acknowledge the truth that Tiago speaks, but none of us step up to respond to him.

"That science team probably ran into him and killed him," Tiago says. "Mom was right, they want to experiment on us like we're a bunch of freaks."

"Now let's not jump to conclusions," Oscar says. He stands up from his sitting position and looks Tiago straight in the eyes.

"It's the only conclusion!" Tiago yells. "What else could have happened?"

Oscar is silent. He knows Tiago is right, but doesn't want to admit it. Admitting it would show the truth that we were not welcome in this world, that we would be killed without hesitation.

"What do you think we should do now?" I say, interrupting the conversation in order to ease the tension.

"Well first thing's first, we're running out of supplies." Tiago replies. "We'll need to go into the city and get some food. But we can't do it now, not in broad daylight. We'll have to wait until the sun goes down. We'll only be safe moving in the shadows, to avoid running into anyone. We'll need enough supplies to last us until we decide to move on."

"Move on to where?" I ask.

"Away from here. We need to leave Primm," Tiago says.

"Oh, really?" Oscar says skeptically. "And where do you suppose we run to."

"The Moon," Tiago says.

All of us are shocked by the bomb that Tiago has laid. Leaving our home was hard enough. Leaving Primm would be even harder, but leaving Earth, that was just insane.

"The Moon?!" Oscar yells. "You've lost it."

"You know as much as I do that the Moon is probably our only bet for living a safe life," Tiago says. "Leonard was killed by a government agency. Do you think they're going to leave us alone now? Do you think even if he hadn't died, that we could hide around Primm forever? We've been hiding all our lives, I'm done hiding. I want to live in freedom."

"But why the Moon?" I ask him.

"The Moon may have been finished terraforming fifty years ago, but it's far from being as organized as Earth," Tiago says. "There are still areas of the Moon that are uninhabited and developing. Areas away from governments or scientific agencies, away from the kinds of people who are and will be looking for us. These kinds of places are the only ones left for us. If we stay here on Earth, we'll be found and killed. At least on the Moon, it will be a lot harder for anyone to track us down. It's our only option if we want to live a full life, and not one in hiding."

"But how do we get there?" Candy asks. After learning Tiago's plan, Candy suspects there will be tech involved. My guess is she knows the answer to her question, and her expertise will come in handy. She is not asking 'how do we get there', but rather 'how can I help us get there'.

"There are teleport stations in Primm," Tiago says. "They can instantly transport us from one station to a larger hub that will teleport us to the Moon. I did research a while back, before all this happened, and if we can connect to the San Francisco teleport hub from Primm, then we can get to the Moon via the station there. "

"But we can't waltz into a station without causing a commotion," my brother, Isaac, says. "We won't be able to hitch a ride in broad daylight, we don't have credits, so how are we going to get access to a live one?"

"We'll have to break into one of the stations at night," Tiago says. "Once we're in, Candy, we'll be counting on you. We'll need you to figure out how to operate a teleporter and send us out of here and to San Francisco. Then when we make it to a station there, you'll need to send us to the Moon. Are you up to the task?"

Candy looks hesitant yet eager at the same time. She moves her hairy arms and puts her long fingers on her chin. She walks forward and then backward, dragging her other knuckle on the ground, much like a chimp would. She wants to take on the challenge of learning new tech, but is unsure about her abilities. But then she looks at the rest of us, knowing that our escape hinges on her skills. She can't let us down and she knows it.

"Yes," Candy says. "I can do it."

"Good," Tiago says. He then turns to Ace, who has now fully recovered from all the running he did earlier. "You did good, Ace. Without you we wouldn't have been able to get the information we needed. We would've never known how much danger we're in without your help."

"Really?" Ace's eyes are beaming. I know Ace has an admiration for Tiago. His approval means the world to him.

"Yes. Do you think you're up for another task?" Tiago asks.

"Of course. Anything to help out the family," Ace says.

"Good. This is going to be a riskier job, but I need you to go and get supplies for us. Food, water, clothes. We'll give you a list of things we'll need. Don't worry, we'll wait until night so it's safer for you."

"Where do I go to get these things?"

"There's a supply depot about a mile away from here. It should have all the things we'll need. You can use our packs to carry everything."

"A supply depot? I don't think I know where that is."

"We can draw you a map."

"Um…" Ace looks confused, unsure of the task given to him. This mission requires intelligence that he doesn't have. A map in his hands would surely lead to disaster.

"Let me go. I can get the supplies," a shaky voice from behind me says. It's Lombardi, my older brother. He's usually pretty quiet, not one to talk. He lacks confidence because of his appearance. While we look different compared to a normal human, Lombardi would be considered uglier than all of us. He's the only one with a beak. It's large and sticks out of his face. It's kind of an eyesore. He also is the only one with feathers, and they're usually oily. The rest of us either have a light layer of fur or hair, or none at all, but his feathers make him look dirty. His arms are wing shaped, but he cannot fly, and he has small, grotesque hands sticking out of them.

Lombardi is also somewhat socially awkward, most likely from a lack of confidence generated by his appearance. He wasn't big and strong like Alex, nor was he tough, like Curtis, whose rough, scaly skin matched his disheartened interior. He couldn't run fast, cheetah like speeds like Ace, nor was he smart like Candy. And he definitely wasn't a natural leader like Oscar or Tiago. Lombardi was kind of useless. It was sad to say, but he was an outcast among outcasts.

And because of that, he always wanted to prove himself. This time was no exception.

Tiago looks skeptical, almost annoyed, that Lombardi has volunteered to help.

"This is not a task for you," he says.

"Aww, c'mon big brother," Lombardi says. "You know I was able to sneak out when we lived in the house. And I can read maps like a charm. In fact, I know these neighborhoods pretty well thanks to all the creeping around I've done."

Lombardi did have that going for him. He is the most knowledgeable about the surrounding area.

"No," Tiago says firmly.

"He has a point, though," Oscar says. "I don't think any of us has had as much exposure to this area as Lombardi."

Tiago looks at the rest of us and then looks at Lombardi. Lombard is frozen, his eyes wide open, hanging on Tiago's response.

"All right," Tiago says hesitantly. "We may act tomorrow night. Don't fuck this up."

"I won't!" Lombardi responds eagerly.

They and Oscar walk to another side of the room to go over the details of the supply raid. I walk over to

Isaac. Everyone else also separates, doing their own thing until the night comes.

"What do you think of the plan?" I ask him.

"Which one? The supply raid or Tiago's master plan?" he asks.

"Tiago's plan."

"I don't know, sis, I'm kind of skeptical."

"Me too."

Isaac looks at me curious. "Any visions or senses?"

"No," I say dodging his question. "You didn't finish your answer. What do you think?"

"On one hand he has a point. The Moon is the ideal place to live. It's just like Earth climate wise, and since things haven't completely settled down there, he is right. We could live there unnoticed. We could find a place, and get food and supplies teleported to us online. We could live anonymously. Hell, mom was able to do it so well that no one even knew we existed."

"What about the other hand?"

"It seems kind of rushed. I don't know if Tiago has fully thought this plan out yet."

"Oscar doesn't seem too confident about it."

"Do you blame him? Tiago is shooting for the stars on this one, figuratively and literally. A week ago, none of us would've even considered being away from home and now, all of a sudden, we're being asked to leave Earth? It's too much to ask in such little time."

"We're running on a short timeline. It looks like people are going to be searching for us sooner than we thought, with Leonard being taken away and all…"

We both stop talking to let the words of my statement sink in. Neither of us can believe that our little brother is dead.

"He didn't deserve it," I say.

"I know, sis."

"What if… what if we're next?"

"Hey, don't say that kind of stuff," he says reassuringly.

"I mean it. If they were able to take out Leonard so easily, so quickly, what chances do we have? None of us know how to fight and we don't have any weapons or anything."

"Hey, we have each other."

"I'm being serious."

"So am I! Look at me," I tilt my head up and look at his eyes. His arms are at his side, paws clenched together. His tail lies perfectly still.

"Nothing is going to happen to you or me," he says. "I promise."

"Thanks, brother."

His words comfort me, but that comfort fades away the more I think about the next day. The future scares me.

Chapter 5 – Fenrir Snow

Allies

November 16, 3040 7:00 PM

I got the call last night from the Brotherhood of Wolves about a special assignment they wanted me to undertake. They said that a mission had come up in Las Vegas and a tracker was needed. Wolves are natural trailers, and amongst them, I am the best. The Brotherhood can vouch for that.

Naturally, I accepted their mission, no questions asked. I come from a long line of loyal soldiers. The Snows have militaristic prestige written all over their names. I would do anything my fellow wolves ask me, especially the high council in the Brotherhood. I'm battle tested due to my service. Unlike humans or pigs or any other animal, I am not greedy. I do it simply because my kind asks me to.

This mission is organized by the humans, which initially caused some hesitation. I'm not fond of their kind, but the Brotherhood needed someone who can speak human. I don't need to rely on those stupid translation boxes. A computer doesn't do my speaking for me, I do.

They allowed me to rest for the night before I journeyed off, but I couldn't get any sleep. I hate Las Vegas, it is human territory. Most of North America is, only the coldest of North America is our territory, the Wolf's Den as the humans call it. They gave us that wasteland when the negotiations happened hundreds of years ago.

Just the mere thought of being around so many of them makes me nervous. I have never trusted them and I know of their history with wolves. Before the Event, wolves were their sport. We, the natural hunters of the wilderness, were reduced to dodging their weapons. Many of us were pushed out of our homes, brought to near extinction. And for what? To make them pretty coats? To be targets in their games? I would hardly consider the slaughter of my brothers a game. They could do what they wanted because they had weapons we couldn't compete with. First, it was bow and arrow and then it was guns. We never stood a chance against them.

I still don't understand why after the Event, when the playing field became even, we remain underneath them. We had formed our society, formed our civilization, all within a few hundred years. Their technological development hit a brick wall. Despite all these handicaps, humans still dominate society, even today. We have our own guns now, but we still do not dare to strike back at the real alpha in this world. It's a numbers game. There are far too many humans for us to fight. Even if all the intelligent animals banded together, we still wouldn't be able to take them on.

They spent century after century killing and reducing the numbers while multiplying. And then, by their own foolishness, they gave us the gift of intelligence. But even then, our numbers had dwindled so much that we still cannot fight back. There are only millions of us, while there are billions of them. I guess that was their back up plan. As long as they didn't kill each other off, they would still rule the land.

It's not right. We are superior to them in so many ways. We're faster than them, stronger than them, more durable than them. They cannot fly on their own, they can't swim without their precious machines. They can barely out run the slowest of winds. The only thing they had to their advantage was their brain, but even that isn't much of an edge anymore. No, it's because of their numbers. It's the only advantage they have.

We should be the rulers of this world, not them.

But I didn't come to Las Vegas to spew my anti-human ideology. I came here for a mission and I intend to serve as best as I can.

I'm currently sitting in a large conference room in the local United Species Alliance headquarters in Las Vegas. The escort picked me up from the teleportation station and brought me straight here. He is a rookie human agent for the United Species Alliance, probably some gopher that gets stuck with all the remedial tasks. He tried to make small chatter with me, but I pretended that I didn't speak human, so he quickly shut up.

I learned how to speak human during basic training in the Brotherhood's Academy. It's a tricky language for wolves to pick up, as our physiology prevents us from making certain sounds, but I try to cover my wolf accent as best as I can. The Brotherhood tells me that it is barely noticeable, yet sometimes I tend to stumble on 'b' sounds here and there. Other animals say I sound like I'm growling, but that is not my intention.

I'm glad that humans only speak one language. I heard long before the Event, humans used to have hundreds of languages among them. Then, they started to unify it into one universal language to make communication easier. Thank goodness.

I was briefed earlier about the mission from my own wolf superior, so I didn't have to be briefed by the human superior agent. It's a case of some renegade human group deciding to play around with genetics, again. But now I and a group of other animals are stuck cleaning up their mess. Typical. Just like a careless human, they never learn their lesson the first time. Though I should be grateful to the first time, I wouldn't be standing where I am today if they hadn't.

These things are half human, half something else. I will probably be the primary tracker on this team, meaning I will be the one responsible for catching their scent and hunting them down. There is a dog on this team as well, but their skills are weak compared to us wolves. They have to rely on their toys. They're only here because they're good at sucking up to humans. Dogs have spent their existence being pets. The funny thing is even after the Event, when they were free to do as they pleased, they still play second fiddle to humans in their society. They support the humans any way they can. They are their waiters, their cleaners, their butlers, their servants. They do have their own government, the High Dog Council, but they always vote with the Human Council in the United Species Alliance. It's pathetic. They may not be on a leash physically anymore, but humans hold a metaphorical one over them.

The room is filled with my other team members. First is the aforementioned dog. I do not know my dog breeds that well, but judging from his large size and golden yellow coat, he is a Labrador. Like many other Labs I've seen, he looks big, friendly, and dumb. He sits on the floor with a pleasant demeanor. He has a black Dog Alliance uniform on, which is the High Dog Council's police force. It covers his body and legs, but leaves his paws exposed. It's made out of a strilium high fiber polyester synthetic. I've been told that it is light and can nullify most small energy projectiles. It's human technology, so I know it's top notch stuff. Humans were always good with their tech, and they share it with their closest animal allies.

I, on the other hand, am wearing my standard issue reflector uniform, black in color. It's not as high quality stuff as the strilium, and it doesn't nullify energy projectiles, it just deflects them. But it's wolf technology and I'm fine with that. There isn't much human tech outfitted for wolves anyways. The humans don't think there's a market for their goods in the Wolf's Den. I'd say that's a true statement, we don't want their overpriced wares.

The uniform is also extremely light. My fur had already been reinforced with wolfspray, a high aerosol alloy that strengthens my fur's durability. It's standard for any member of the wolf military to go through this procedure. We already have a natural coat, so why not reinforce it with something resilient?

Sitting across from me is a gorilla. His kind I can respect. They share roots with the humans, but unlike the dog, they have carved out their own niche instead of being servants and second tier citizens. Together, them and animals like them such as chimps, along with the lions, were able to claim the southern parts of Africa as their own. The humans gave them some land down there as part of the negotiation, but it wasn't enough. Thus, the rebellion against the humans in Africa started, and the gorillas were highly adaptable. They already had the physiology similar to humans, so retrofitting human weapons and equipment for their own needs was a piece of cake. Within twenty years, their alliance with the lions helped them push most humans out of South Africa. Naturally, once the struggle was over, their agreement was broken and the great war between the gorillas and lions still rages on today.

I'm guessing eradicating these halfkinds was so important that the Gorilla Government decided to send one of their own to help out.

Most of the intelligent species have already claimed certain areas of the world to call their home. We wolves occupy Northern Canada, dogs are spread out across the world, sharing whatever territory they live in with humans, the pigs have Australia, and countless other animals claim other parts of planet Earth. It's all chump change compared to how much the humans still have.

The weird thing I find in all of this is that despite all these new territories, we still call them by their human names. Our territory is called the Wolf's Den, but it's an unofficial name. The official name is still Northern Canada. The pig's territory doesn't even have an unofficial name, it's still referred to the human name Australia. The city names haven't even changed. I hear stories that long ago, when humans ruled the world, when settlers came to the United States, they used names given by the natives there. I suppose the same thing has happened, but out of convenience. We already know Canada as Canada, so why change it?

I see it as a subtle reminder that humans are still the principal species, that we have to speak their language, use the names given by them. Even though they don't own the lands as they used to, they still have that level of control.

The battles on Earth may have died down, but the real battle has only begun with the terraformed Moon still in its current state. Politically, it's a mess. There have already been some colonies set up by different animals, but colonies aren't a big deal. Territories will cause conflict, large designations of land assigned to different species. We've only started to flesh out what that might look like. When animals start stepping over their boundaries there, claim this territory over that one, a new war is going to be at hand.

I continue to observe my peers. There's an elephant standing in the corner of the room. I'm actually surprised he is here. I've never met an elephant before, as their territory is mostly in parts of Asia. From what I hear, elephants are quite peaceful. But I also hear in battle, they are durable, that their tech makes use of their large size and powerful frame. The elephant I see is quite gargantuan and he already has some armor on, a standard heavy padded plasma absorber that all members of the Elephant Force get issued. It's made to take heavy fire, especially heat. I suppose he'll be useful in his physical durability alone. Still, given their soft reputation, the United Species Alliance could have sent a better tank, such as a rhino. But perhaps I'm stereotyping.

Last but not least, I see the pig. If there's any other species I distrust more than humans, the pig would be it. Even before the Event, their reputation among humans was that of greed and it is still well deserved today. Their kind has been known to be hard negotiators and gluttons for resources. They take whatever they can from whomever they can and refuse to broker alliances for what they collect. The whole government they have set up in Australia is based on the principal of greed, an every pig for themselves mentality. It is the opposite of what I was raised to believe. I was taught to stick to the pack, to fight not only for yourself, but for each other.

I am jumping to conclusions. I haven't talked to this pig yet. Perhaps my prejudice is getting the better of me.

Through their trading with the humans, pigs have gotten decent at gaining and developing new tech. It shows through this one's uniform. He's wearing a suit made of the same strilium the dog is wearing.

This is the team that I've been assigned to work with, handpicked by the United Species Alliance, a group consisting of the leaders of all intelligent species. They could've sent others, a different combination of species and personalities, but they picked us. And now we wait for our human commander. He's the leader not because of his leadership skills, but because this is a mission spearheaded by the Human Council. I will never consider a human my leader.

Suddenly, two humans walk in. One is a tall, portly man with a mustache, Agent Leons. I had heard about him for the first time when I was briefed earlier and I already don't like him. He seems like a jerk. The other is a leaner, more well-toned man that I have never met nor seen. He has a shaved head and strong profile. His jaw is square but his head is appropriate for his average height. He looks young. Judging by his appearance, he is probably in his fifties.

"This is the team," Agent Leons says to the younger man. "All six of you were picked by your respective councils and governments to undergo this mission, approved by the United Species Alliance. Consider yourself lucky, for you are the elite not only of your kind, but of most animals out there today. You've all probably seen me in your briefings, but you haven't met this man. His name is Simon Trevor, he'll be heading this mission. He's a specialist in obtaining illegal contraband and weapons. Simon, meet your team."

"Hi, I'm looking forward to working with all of you," he then turns to the dog. "Good to see you Apollo. When was the last time we caught up?"

"A month ago?" the dog replies.

"That long? Well, drinks will be on me after we're done with this."

"Oh, so you two know each other?" Agent Leons asks.

"Yes, Simon and I worked together hunting down some illegal drug runners a few years ago. We've been keeping in contact since," the dog replies.

"I would consider Apollo one of my combat buddies."

"That's good!" Agent Leons says enthusiastically, but I can sense his bullshit a mile away. "Always nice to have friends on the same team. Makes cooperation a lot easier."

The dog is sucking up to the human. Typical.

"Well," Agent Leons says, "since you spoke first, how about you introduce yourself first. We'll all go around in a circle and give our helloes."

"No problem," the dog says. "I'm Apollo Bradley. Like Simon, I'm a specialist in tracking and finding illegal contraband. I'm thirty four years old and I've been with the Dog Alliance for about seven years."

"Apollo here is shy," Simon says, "he's a rising star over there."

I'm surprised at how young the dog is. For a task like this, I would imagine that his superiors would have sent someone much older, maybe in their fifties. Most every intelligent species' lifespans have been greatly bolstered since we became aware.

The gorilla speaks next. "Colbo Zuma. I'm a heavy arms specialist and I've served a few tours in the Gorilla Lion Conflict. I've also done some secret operative work for the Gorilla Government. Classified, naturally."

"Of course," Agent Leons says.

"Erawan Bornoa, member of the Royal Elephant Service."

That is why the United Species Alliance chose this elephant. The Royal Elephant Service is the elephant's secret service group, protecting the leaders of their government. He's probably the highest decorated member of this team.

That is all Erawan decides to say, and that is all he needs to say.

"I'm Borton Freely," the pig says. "I'm also a tracker, like Apollo, but I specialize in the tracking of currency. I usually handle covert operations involving money laundering."

Borton seems like a questionable choice on this team. He can find things, like me, Apollo, and Simon, but his specialization is currency? C'mon. He probably got assigned to this mission because of politics.

It is my turn to speak. "I'm Fenrir Snow, member of the Wolf's Den Task Force. Like some of the others, I'm a tracker, but I specifically hunt wanted criminals. As you know, the Task Force has a reputation for finding the toughest escapees and threats to our society of wolves. I can't go into the details of my missions, though, they're classified."

I shoot Colbo a wink. He responds with a smug smile. Asshole.

"Great, now that we got all our introductions out of the way, we can start with the mission," Agent Leons says. "You've been briefed. We suspect that the halfkinds are already on the move, but still in Primm, so we'll have to come up with our own strategy to hunt and find them. Your orders are to kill. We'll gather in the war room so you can get your gear and work on your plan of attack. Follow me."

I am uncomfortable with being a hitman for these humans, but if the Brotherhood deems this mission is worthy, then I will do it for them. When the hour comes and I stand face to face with a halfkind, I will be ready to pull the trigger. The only thing I will think is that I served my wolves well and nothing more.

Chapter 6 – Tiago Lawton

Weakling

<u>November 16, 3040 4:35 PM</u>
"Do you understand the plan?" I ask Lombardi.

"Yes," he responds with a lack of confidence.

It's right before sundown, and all of us are gathered around to make sure he knows what to do and where to go. We had gone over it for the last hour, testing him on every detail of his mission. We only have one shot to get the things that we need.

Luckily for us, Primm is a rundown city and its supply depots don't exactly have the most state of the art security. Candy was able to use her compcube, a small device that opens up a holographic interface, to do some research on the kind of defense mechanisms Lombardi might expect during his task. She was surprised, as were the rest of us, to learn that the Primm-Phillips supply depot only had a full building sensor installed and nothing else. No security drones, no indoor alarm trips, nothing. They didn't have the funds to invest in all the bells and whistles.

Not like they had to. Judging from the Primm-Phillips catalog, the only things that were stored there were food, clothing, and some other essential survival items. It wasn't where they stored all the good, pricy objects. Most importantly, though, there was an insta-item there.

Still, if Lombardi messes up and sets off something, you can be sure the next day the drones will be warding the depot floors in droves. He needs to be quick, and silent, as if nothing was there in the first place.

I don't have much confidence in Lombardi. I would have preferred Ace to handle this task, as I know he is quick and his skills in stealth greatly outmatch Lombardi's. However, Ace does not know the outside world too well and he isn't the smartest sibling. Lombardi tells me he knows this area better than anyone else due to all the sneaking around he's done. The family seems to trust his claim on this, so I have no choice but to trust it.

To say the least, I am skeptical of Lombardi. Having grown up with him I know his abilities and personality, like I know the abilities of all my brothers and sisters. Each one of my siblings has something to offer. Alex and Curtis are both huge, providing the strength that my smaller brothers and sisters don't have. Oscar is a leader, I guess. Ace is quick and light footed, that's why we always send him on scouting missions. Candy is book smart, able to pick up things fast and is a technical genius.

The twins are pragmatic, especially Iris. She can see things in others that most of us can't. She knows how to look into future events and has a sense for what's coming up. Both of them are also the glue to this family. Their intuition to others' thoughts and emotions help calm my siblings down in times of stress. They also can talk sense into the most irrational of family members. They are well liked by Oscar and I. Oscar respects their thoughtfulness and compassion, I respect them for the ways they can handle my brothers and sisters. Those kinds of things are invaluable.

Each of us have certain talents, well at least most of us. I wouldn't say Maddie is the most useful sister I have. She's part cow, and like all cows, she's only good at eating and following. No wonder humans used to devour them by the millions. Fortunately for Maddie, Oscar constantly defends her. Leaders always have a devout follower. Maddie would be his.

Supposedly, Oscar is a strong leader, but he has too much compassion. He feels sorry for our weaker brothers and sisters, which explains why he takes Maddie under his wing. I am the opposite. While Oscar dreams of a world where everyone gets along, I see the world for what it is, a place for survival. And for creatures like us, we have to fight for it. I am more realistic than he is. He values weakness, I value those who can help contribute to our chances. That's why I'm better at what I do.

That has always been the key difference between us. For years, I led the rallying charge against mother and her plans to keep us in Primm. The others looked at me to tell her that we didn't want to be cooped up forever, that we were not prisoners in her house. I spoke for them because they could not speak for themselves. Oscar, on the other hand, would always try to negotiate and make peace between mother and me. He wanted all of us to be together because we were family. I love my family as much as he does, but I love them enough to fight for them.

As Oscar has his follower Maddie, I have mine, the ones that I know I can depend on. Ace's loyalty has never been questioned. I know, and the others know, that he looks up to me, that he idolizes me. And Alex has always been my bodyguard. His size is intimidating; his demeanor is frightening to the others. He's a bit of a punk, but in a good way.

I am unsure about where the others lie in their allegiance, but considering our situation, they need a leader who can lead them into battle, not one who is looking for peace. Oscar cannot provide this to them, only I can.

We live in a world where we are the ones who will be hunted, Leonard's death proved that. The only chance we have is if we use the abilities given to us to take our lives back. If you have nothing to offer, then you are nothing to me. Stragglers don't have much use, family or not.

From what I observe, Lombardi has nothing to offer. He is part bird and the one thing he should be able to do, he can't. I look at him and I see wings, or at least arms that look like wings. But they're not hollow and their span is not great enough. Lombardi can't fly. What use is a bird when its wings have been clipped at birth?

He has too much human in him and those traits stand out to me. He isn't graceful like a cat or strong like a rhino. He is uncoordinated and weak like a human. He's slow like a human, he's fragile like a human.

He's not even as bright as a human. Lombardi claims to be smart. I do not consider being familiar with an area a form of intelligence. He simply knows a few things that we might not because we haven't been sneaking around like him. The others consider him to be smarter than Ace, but that's not something to brag about.

The only thing Lombardi has going for him is that he's eager. He wants to prove himself worthy to me and the family wants me to give Lombardi his chance. He knows I'm not fond of him because of his inherent uselessness, but the family believes in him. If I didn't have the family swaying me, Lombardi wouldn't even be an option. Now is not the time for charity. I'd rather have the people who I know can do their part do their part.

But I must go with the voices of my siblings. I can't risk alienating myself too much.

"So let's review what your plan is," I say to Lombardi as the others watch me question him. "After you leave this building, where do you go?"

"Let's see, um, the depot is only a mile away from here," he says. "If I run, I should get there in six to eight minutes. I exit through the west of this building and travel south on Junket Street for half a mile, until I get to Tangerine Road. I am not to take any streets other than Junket. It's the least traveled, making it the safest for me to go on."

"Good so far. Once you get to Tangerine Road, where do you go?"

"Straight. It leads to the Primm-Phillips supply depot, which should be empty. Business hours have ended more than three hours ago. Security should be scarce, too. No drones, no guards, nothing. It should be easy for me to walk around unnoticed as long as I disable their surveillance sensors."

"And what are surveillance sensors?" It's an easy question to answer, but I want to make sure he knows everything.

"They are laser scanners attached to the walls. They emit tracking beams that scan the area and create holographic recordings of the depot overnight. In short, if they're on, they'll be able to make a hologram of any intruders that walk the premises unauthorized."

"Good," I am actually surprised at how thorough his answer is. "How do you intend to disable their security?"

"Underground. According to the information Candy was able to obtain on the infospace, there's a sensor along the perimeter. However, their master command box is hidden deep underground and I can access it there.

Before the supply depot, there should be a grating hidden on the floor. The Primm-Phillips supply depot was constructed on top of older land, so there's a series of tunnels underground that was built there long before. They were called sewers. I can go into them and reach the master command box. Once I'm in, all I have to do is program the surveillance routines off."

"And how will you do that?" I ask.

"With this," Lombardi says. He takes out a piece of paper and shows it to the group. "This is a list of detailed instructions on how to disable their routines. Candy has made it easy to follow and I've gone over with her what to do. Thanks, Candy."

"No problem," she says. "Sorry it's on paper and not on a data cube or tablet, I didn't have the resources. Remember that there is a time limit. If you don't do it fast enough, you'll get shut out and the alarms will sound. But don't worry, my instructions will work, I've spent all day researching and hacking. It actually wasn't that hard to learn how to deprogram a Tang Corporation Phalanx Security System Model 3, the thing is practically a piece of junk. Better secured places are on Model 9."

"Don't worry, Candy," I say. "None of us doubt your skills."

She looks at me and smiles at the compliment given to her. Sometimes it amazes me how smart she is.

"After I get the security system off line," Lombardi says, "I can go in. Then it should be easy sailing. I'll get this list of items and be out in a flash."

"Remember," I say, "we don't know where the items are held, so you'll have to do a little bit of exploring in order to locate them. They definitely should be in the warehouses though."

"Got it," Lombardi says. "I'll have my pack emptied so I can try to grab as much as I can, but I'm not sure how much I can carry."

"It's okay," Oscar says. "Grab what fits in your pack, but make sure you get enough credits and, most importantly, get us an insta-item. Without that, we are screwed."

"Understood," Lombardi says. "Other than that, so far what I have is clothes, food, and some compcubes."

"Yes, you have the list," I say. "Just remember the insta-item."

I take out a small metal container. It is a cylinder, no heavier than ten ounces. It has a clicking device rigged to the top of it.

"Here," I say as I hand it to Lombardi. "This is for you. Candy made it earlier."

"What is it?" he asks, taking it with his hand. He examines it, but he is still confused in its purpose.

"It's a small explosive. Candy rigged it together with some of the things she found around here. It's pretty crude, but it'll get the job done. You trigger it by pressing the clicker on top. You'll only have a few seconds after you start it before it blows. According to Candy, it's pretty powerful, so be careful."

Most of my brothers and sisters look stunned by what I had handed to Lombardi. He looks relatively shocked as well. The one who looks the most surprised is Oscar.

"Candy, why did you make this?" Oscar says, as if he's been betrayed.

"Tiago asked me to," Candy says sheepishly. "I just want to help out."

"You have a problem with this?" I interrupt. "What's the issue?"

"This is not necessary," Oscar says. "If he uses this thing, the alarms will sound and he'll have more to deal with. What you're giving Lombardi is a death sentence."

"He gets caught and doesn't defend himself, it's already a death sentence," I say defiantly. "Have you already forgotten what happened to Leonard? It was last morning. They, the outside world, the government, whomever, killed him in cold blood. Someone is after us, and they're out to destroy. I'm giving Lombardi something he can defend himself with."

"Is that so? This will help him defend himself? Or are you giving him something that will send a message to our so-called hunters."

"Sometimes, brother, you need to do both. It isn't always so black and white."

"I don't approve of this."

"Of course you wouldn't. You're not thinking of the big picture. You want to live in your peaceful dream land. A place where the world will leave us alone and let us be, where we are free to do whatever we want without persecution. Unlike you, I live in the real world, and in the real world, people will never accept us. We are too different, we shouldn't even exist. They'll make sure that is so. Just remember what happened to Leonard, never forget."

Oscar looks at me, eyes beaming. This is another example of his leadership weakening over the past week. He's losing his grip on our siblings and he knows it.

"The bomb is a precaution," I tell Oscar. "Hopefully, Lombardi won't have to use it."

"I hope so, too," Lombardi says.

"Once we get our supplies, we can focus on getting to the Moon," I tell everyone.

"Lombardi, you don't have to bring the bomb," Oscar says.

"Oscar…" I say in an irritated tone. "Don't start."

Lombardi senses the tension and looks at Oscar. "No it's okay, really. I probably won't even use it. It's insurance, that's all."

Oscar backs away. Good boy, Lombardi.

In a few days, we will make our break for the Moon. I've already discussed it with the family. There are two teleportation stations in Primm that can send us to any other station out there, including San Francisco. It shouldn't be too hard to get it running, especially for Candy. Even I understand the basic concept of how a teleporter works.

Like any other mode of transportation, in order to get from point A to point B, you basically need to know where you're going and how to get there. Our destination is the Bay Area, the transporters is how we'll get there. All those things need is for the power to be on. There are delivery and receiving teleporters, one to send and one to arrive in. Once we fire it up, we locate a receiving teleporter to travel to. Receiving teleporters are duty free, so we can arrive anytime without being noticed. After we walk through the teleportation gate, and when we get to the other side, we're in the Golden State. Then we use the more powerful San Francisco delivery teleporter station to go to the Moon.

The great thing about teleporters is that when you choose your destination, it automatically turns on the receiving one. It's not possible to walk through a gate if the receiver is off, because if you did, you wouldn't exactly end up anywhere. Automatically turning on the other side is a failsafe created to prevent that from happening. And if, for some reason, the other side isn't working because the power is out or it's broken, the delivery teleporter will fail to open the gate to the other side. It's incredible that these provisions have been built into the machines.

We'll be breaking in during off hours, so we'll have to trust in Candy's abilities. She'll need to figure out how to disable any security systems, activate the power in the teleportation station, and enter the destination. I'm confident she'll be able to do all three. She's been researching vigorously on the technical aspects of our plan. She's already demonstrated a knack for disabling security systems, as she was able to figure out how to aid Lombardi on his task. She still has a few days to figure out how to start the power and run the machine, and a few days is plenty of time for someone of her scientific caliber. I have complete faith in her, she hasn't let us down yet.

We should reach the Moon instantly after teleporting there. Then, we'll sneak into the undeveloped areas to carve out our new home. There's still a lot left to be discovered on the Moon. The Moon may be terraformed, but it's a long way from being a new Earth. There's a lot of unsettled land and politically it's a nightmare as every species is still trying to claim a piece.

Our family can survive as long as we have the insta-item. With the credits that Lombardi will swipe for us, we'll be able to order food and other items that will keep us afloat online. The supplies will be teleported directly to our insta-item machine, no questions asked. That way, we can get what we want anonymously. Long ago, humans used something called mail to do this. I can't imagine a world where I would have to wait in order to get something I ordered.

We have the maps of the Moon, we know what's populated and what's not. Unlike here, there's plenty of land up there. Living undetected and in peace should be much easier. We just have to worry about getting there. It's still a long road away, but if things go right for us, we can make it.

There is a big problem though, the others. Someone is after us. Mother had spent all of her life terrifying us about the outside world. I didn't believe her. I always thought she was crazy, that the years of prostitution had taken a toll on her mental health. She would rant and scare us about the horrors that existed out there. When I was younger, I was afraid, but as I got older, I saw what she really was, a liar.

Or so I thought. It appears I am wrong and she was right.

When Ace came back and told us about Leonard's demise, I was shocked, a little from the news of his death, but more so because of who was responsible for it. A government science crew was on hand so quickly after he died. They were eager to learn from his corpse. When Ace delivered the news to all of us, I realized that mother was right.

We went into hiding right away as a safeguard. Even I didn't know what we would face, and I needed time to figure out what our plan was and what threats would come our way. We lived off the supplies that we had gathered, but within a few days, I saw that our stash was dwindling. We would have enough food to last another week, but hiding out in an abandoned building is no place to live a life. We'd spend the rest of our existences like cockroaches.

Yet, I didn't know what to do, the world was still a mysterious place to me. I had no idea the kind of reception me and my siblings would receive if we stepped out into the public.

I wanted to think that the world wasn't that bad of a place. I, after all, was always arguing with mother, doubting the merits of her warnings. But to say that mother's words didn't have an effect on me while growing up is untrue. Mother may have been crazy, but that didn't mean she couldn't have been right. I needed to test out exactly how dangerous it was for creatures like us.

And then, in the wee hours of last morning, I saw Leonard sneak out. He didn't see me, though, if he did, he surely wouldn't have left. At first, I wondered where he was going, but after a few minutes of thought, I knew exactly where. It didn't take a genius to know that he was heading home, back to where mother's body was, back to say goodbye.

In terms of his usefulness, Leonard was right there on the bottom next to Lombardi. He was young, naïve, and too emotional to be counted on. He didn't have anything that he could offer to our family. Even Lombardi had a certain level of enthusiasm and courage, Leonard did not. He was a coward, and I knew that in the future he would be a liability. That's what I thought of when I saw him sneak out.

He was my brother and I loved him, but in the fight for our survival, he would only hurt our chances. I couldn't babysit him forever, and when he snuck out that morning, it proved to me that my judgments were correct. He wasn't thinking about his family. His foolishness could have jeopardized the safety of all our brothers and sisters. So I did what I had to do, I called the police and let them know that there was a homicide at 1523 Chakming Drive, Primm, Nevada.

When I sent the tip I was unsure about what waited for us outside. Was it harm? Was it help? What kind of welcome would we get? There was too much I didn't know. Leonard would help me find out.

And when he didn't come back that morning, when Ace arrived with the news of his of death, I got my answer. We were on our own, and there would always be someone ready to hunt us.

In his death, Leonard ended up as the most useful member of our family. He gave my brothers and sisters the motivation to get a move on. We had all been unsure about where to go, if we should stay in Primm, if we would be safe here. Leonard's death made it all too clear that we were not. He gave us the sign that we needed to think of an escape plan.

Most importantly, he let me know that mother was right and that I was wrong. The world is the dangerous place she talked about, but I would have never figured this out on my own.

I am sorry baby brother, but I hope you can find it in your heart to understand. At least you're with her now.

Lombardi is about to leave and begins to say his goodbyes. The others gather around him, but while no one is looking, I tap Ace's shoulder.

"He's leaving soon," I whisper to him.

Ace nods quietly, so none of the others can see.

"You know what to do?" I whisper again.

He nods silently once more, and I nod back. I know I can count on Ace, he's hasn't let me down yet.

Chapter 7 – Simon Trevor

Sundown

November 16, 3040 7:15 PM

Our debriefing has finished, so Agent Leons shows us the way out of the conference room.

"We need to figure out our strategy first," I tell him as we walk through the hallways with the team behind us.

"Hold on, son," he tells me. "First we'll have to stop by the armory, reception said the team's special packages have arrived."

"These things are going to be on the move, especially after one of their own has been killed. The more we wait, the farther they may have gotten."

"It's night time, no one is going anywhere this fast. All the ways out are closed. You need to slow down there, pal. You can't fight a battle if you don't have anything to back it up."

We're all different species, so the headquarters here doesn't exactly have everything each of us need. For example, for handguns, I require a standard issue Tang 534A Pistol. It fires pulsed energy shots at a target, hot enough to char through the skin of a crocodile and leave him dead.

However, other members of my team may not have fingers to operate my firearm. Most quadrupeds have to rely on side harnesses to hold their weapons, and their mouths or tails to pull the trigger. This is the first time I have met my team, so I'm not sure what kind of arms they plan to use. All of their gear had to be ported in earlier this morning, according to Agent Leons.

We get to the armory and I see six bags on the floor. They're all the same color, granite black, but each is tagged and one says "Trevor." Another says "Snow," and another says "Bradley." "Freely," "Bornoa," and "Zuma." Looks like they packed their gear, too.

"I see that some of you have your equipment on. Nice armor big guy," Agent Leons says looking at Erawan. He does not appear amused. "All except Commander Trevor. I'll provide you with some standard issue protective gear after your strategy session. I believe the rest of you brought your own weaponry, since we're running low on animal arms around here. Don't know why you brought your own stuff, Simon, you know we have plenty of toys for you to play with."

"I like to work with my own tools."

"Work with your own tools, eh? What movie did you get that line from?"

I look into my bag and pick up my Tang 534A. The pistol is one of my favorite weapons. It has a long battery life and is speedy and accurate. It's also equipped with a silence mode that suppresses noise at the cost of lower firepower. I glance at it to make sure it hadn't been damaged during the delivery and set it aside.

I then take out a longer, heavier gun. It's a Tang 700 series energy rifle, also known as a Spitfire. Its nickname derives from its plasma shots, hot enough to burn through several metals, but its energy cost is higher. I probably can only get one hundred rounds or so until I need to recharge. I saw the images of the rhino and croc halfkind, Alex and Curtis. I have a feeling my Tang 534A won't cut it, so I may have to rely on the Spitfire instead

Those are the only two weapons I need, though I'll be sure to pick up some pulse, mini, and sound grenades from Agent Leons before we leave.

I observe the others' gear. I'm familiar with dog and wolf weaponry, since I worked with Apollo on a several missions, but I'm not aware of what Borton, Erawan, and Colbo might have in their arsenal.

Colbo pulls out a large gun from his bag. It looks like my Spitfire, but twice the size. Gorilla weapons are similar to human weapons in that they are carried by arms and require opposable thumbs to operate, but they are usually bigger than what humans use. I doubt that a gorilla would want to be seen with a ridiculously small gun on them and a trigger that their fingers can barely squeeze.

The leading gorilla weapons manufacturer is Silverback Industries, and their arms are known to have quite the punch. Gorilla's themselves tend to favor heavy weaponry as opposed to pistols. They have a reputation for hitting hard and hitting fast. I can't even recall the last time I've seen a gorilla with a pistol or light firearm.

"I trust that you guys have grenades and pulse bombs," Colbo says to Agent Leons.

"Sure do, but they are Tang models. Hope you don't mind using human weapons," he says.

"That's fine, a bomb is a bomb. I should be able to use it like you humans."

Erawan uses his trunk to pull out a large, metal stick. At first I'm not sure what it is, but after looking at it, I know. Designed by Shivato Tech, the elephants call it a firing stick. Basically, it's a large stick where one end fires an energy shot, while the other end is held by the elephant's trunk. A trigger is in the form of a panel on the stick and when an elephant wraps his trunk and applies pressure, the shot is fired. It can also be used as a melee weapon.

Borton rummages through his bag and pulls out a harness looking apparatus. It looks like it is supposed to fit on his back. From it protrudes two energy pistols. Pigs don't have an independent weapons manufacturer. They rather negotiate and haggle for weapons instead of using their resources to make their own, so they have their weapon designs contracted out by other species. This looks to be the work of a human developer, since it's a bunch of human weapons stitched together for a pig to use. Attached to the triggers of the energy pistols are wires that lead to a helmet looking contraption.

My curiosity gets the better of me. "So how does it work?"

"What, my weapon?" Borton say. "Well, basically I put this harness on my back and this helmet on top of my head. The strings that connect the harness and helmet go near my mouth, and when I'm ready to shoot, I bite down on the string which is attached to this small controller. The buttons on the controller retract the cords, which pull the triggers on the pistols you see on the harness and, boom, weapon is fired. I know it seems primitive by human standards, but it's effective."

I then look at what Apollo and Fenrir have. Canine weapons, regardless of wolf or dog, are produced by the Beo Group. The only thing they need is a helmet, which is for both protection, storage of devices, and weapons. Their trigger is voice activated. Once the command is spoken, shots of various type, electric, plasma, ballistic, come out of their helmet. For stealth shots that don't require a vocal command, a sensor is aimed at their tails. If they move it in a certain manner, left, right, whatever depending on how it's programmed, directives are interpreted.

I've seen Apollo use it before, and the firepower that comes out of those helmet cannons is pretty impressive.

Fenrir has something else, though. It's a small box that looks like it should be attached to his front leg. I've never seen it before.

"Is that some kind of communication device?" I ask him.

"No, it's a marble shooter," he says. "Marble shooters fire out small balls of energy in a forward direction. It rolls across the floor, like its namesake, and after a ten second window, it explodes. The blast radius is the same as a small grenade. However, they are required to roll on a flat surface. Any uneven ground makes it unpredictable and inaccurate. I have it just in case. They're best used as an element of surprise."

"All right everyone, you have everything you need?" Agent Leons asks.

"It looks like that's the case," I say.

"Good, then let's go to the war room. You'll need to figure out your plans."

We put our gear back into our bags and follow Agent Leons into another large conference room. It's called the war room, but it looks exactly like all the other rooms we've been in. Colbo and I take a seat, but the rest stand since there appears to be no chairs that would fit their body type.

"Commander Trevor will take the lead from here," he says.

The team's attention turns to me and I walk to the front of the room to address them.

"After our debriefing, we know there are ten halfkinds remaining. You've gone through their profiles,

I assume?" I ask the team. They all nod. "Good. We know that Maya Lawton's corpse had been there for about a week, thus, I think they vacated 1523 Chakming Drive immediately after she had died. It seems they didn't even take time to bury her properly, which meant they were in quite a rush to leave their home."

"Judging from the evidence that we've obtained, they had lived there their whole life. Why would they be so quick to leave?" Apollo asks.

"Perhaps they knew someone would be coming," Borton interjects. "Maya was on a daily plan for her energy bill since her credit was so bad. That means she had to pay every day or else a collector would be coming. The Las Vegas County Energy Department has always been very punctual about bill collections, and for someone who already had late incidents before, they wouldn't hesitate to have someone stop by."

"It seems that they want to keep a low profile. But why?" Apollo persists.

"Because they think we are hostile," Colbo interrupts. "Think about it, when that frog half-man, Leonard Lawton, saw Detective Marsden, what was his first instinct? To attack him. He didn't ask any questions, didn't give any terms of peace, he went straight for a weapon. Judging from what I've read on Maya's profile along with the actions of Leonard, these things fear us."

"Do you blame them?" Fenrir asks. "You all realize that our mission is to track down and kill these creatures, right? Maya Lawton raised her children with the right mindset, that they will be feared and attacked. Her upbringing made them understand their place in the world."

There is an awkward silence in the room after Fenrir's comments. The reality of our mission sinks in. We are given our orders, but we are not the good guys. We are the predators, hunting a prey that didn't ask to be hunted.

"As long as I get paid, that's all I care about," Borton says.

"Of course," Fenrir responds. "That's all you pigs care about."

"Excuse me?" Borton says defensively.

"Calm down both of you," I say sternly. "We're here to discuss our plan, not argue with each other."

Borton and Fenrir stop their squabbling, but give each other dirty looks. Apollo interjects to ease the tension. "My original question wasn't answered, though. Why do you think they left so abruptly?"

"I thought my statements answered that question, but I guess I have to spell it out for the less intellectually inclined," Fenrir says. "They're afraid of making contact with the world. They're motivated by fear, avoiding any creature that comes their way, especially ones that ask questions. They'll do anything to keep their secrecy, even if it means leaving their dead mother to rot in the house they grew up in."

"Sounds cold," Apollo says.

"Survival is their only mission. Sympathies are trivial," Fenrir says casually.

"Okay, so we know they're on the run," I say. "They've been out there for a week. How do you think they are on supplies?"

"From the reports at Maya's crime scene, it seems that they took things with them. Not personal items, but the house was scarce of any items that are necessary for their survival," Agent Leons says.

"Food, water, clothing?" I ask. He nods. "How much do you think they took?"

"A lot," he responds. "It's hard to determine, but there was barely anything in the house, in terms of that stuff."

"What about their insta-item?" Apollo asks.

"Negative, that was still there," Agent Leons responds. "Maya had one linked to her accounts and it was a special security model. It had a bio scanner on it, so it would only work if she activated it. The thing is useless without her. They wouldn't be able to order any supplies with it, nor receive any goods unless she was physically alive to get it for them. Seems that she wanted to be the sole provider."

"That's good news for us," Colbo says. "That means they'll be running out of supplies eventually."

"You're correct," I say to Colbo. "You all know how the insta-item process works right? The items that you can order through the intsa-item are stored in supply depots. Various delivery companies have many scattered about small towns, like Primm. That's where all your food and goods are held. When you make an order through the insta-item, it's automatically processed in a supply depot. So, say you want to order a bag of rice. The supply depot gets the order and sends it through their teleporters to the coordinates sent via the insta-order. Once it's sent from their side, it only takes a couple of moments until it pops in your insta-item. Ingredients for your day's dinner are ready."

"So," Borton asks. "You think that once their stash runs out, they'll head to a supply depot to get what they need?"

"Yes," I respond. "I assume they don't have an insta-item with them, so they'll need to go directly to the source to get their goods. I think our first task should be to stakeout all the depots in Primm. They'll be bound to try and get supplies sooner or later, and we should be there to intercept them when they do. Apollo, do you have your compcube with you?"

"Yes," he says.

"Do a quick search on all the supply depots in Primm."

He takes out his cube. The user interface appears in front of him, a floating hologram. He uses his paws to navigate the menus and search my query. Within a few seconds he has an answer.

"Looks like there are six different ones in Primm," he says.

Great. There are six of us, and I can't risk sending one animal to each supply depot. We have the weapons to take them on, but if we spread the team thin and it becomes a "one on ten" situation, whoever that one is will be screwed. Yet, I need to make sure all of the supply depots are monitored.

"Leons," I say. "Is it possible to bring in reinforcements?"

"Yes, but it'll take at least a few days tops to get all the necessary permissions. It was already hard enough for the Human Council to maneuver through the bureaucracy to get this team assembled."

"Damnit. We can't risk sending one team member to each depot, but we need to have them all covered. How about drones?"

"Again, more paperwork."

"Shit!" I say to myself in a frustrated tone.

"They don't have an insta-item right? That's probably the only thing they need, that and credits," Fenrir says to the group. "We should cross reference Apollo's results with depots that carry insta-items."

Once again Fenrir impresses me. His logic makes sense. "Apollo, do it."

Apollo quickly enters the query into the compcube. "Looks like there are three depots that carry insta-items. Primm-Phillips, Primm-Austen, and Primm-Burke."

"That's where we should start looking then," I say. "We can split into teams of two and each pairing can do recon there. We'll want to stay low and only spring into action when we encounter the targets. Does anyone object to this plan?"

No one raises a hand. However, Fenrir speaks. "Remember, when we're on stakeout, we want to stay inconspicuous. The halfkinds won't be expecting us to act so soon, so the element of surprise is key here. It could take a day, or five, to stakeout the area, but they'll come eventually. They'll have to."

"I want to focus on these three depots only," I say. "I can work on the paperwork to get the drones out, but the earliest we can get them here will be in a week. We can't wait that long, so for now we'll have to make do with what we have."

"When do you want to start?" Borton asks.

"Tonight," I say authoritatively. "We don't have a moment to waste. Apollo, has there been any reported break-ins to any of the depots?

"Give me a second, I can check." Apollo scans the information presented to him on his compcube. "Nothing in the past few days. No stolen items, no missing inventory. If anything came up, it would have been reported and I can't find anything."

"Good, that means they haven't made their move yet," I say. "But they'll make it soon, I can feel it. I hope you all got enough sleep, because most of our operations will happen at night."

"If you don't mind me asking," Borton says, "why is that?"

"You heard what Fenrir said," I respond, "they're scared of what's out there. And right now they're hiding. Why would they want to go out in broad daylight and risk being seen?"

The answer is obvious and Borton knows it. His face shows frustration, as if he angry at himself for asking such a stupid question.

"How do you want to assign the teams?" Apollo asks me.

"We will take Primm-Austen. Fenrir and Colbo, you'll secure Primm-Phillips. Borton and Erawan, take Primm-Burke. Are you all okay with these assignments?"

They all nod their heads.

"We have to act fast, team, so let's go back to the armory and suit up."

We head back to where our gear is stored, but I wait for everyone to pass until Erawan walks by. I want to have a word with him. I am curious that he remained silent during the entire strategy session.

"Something on your mind, Erawan?" I ask him.

"No sir," he says.

"You didn't say one word during our meeting, something must be on your mind."

"No sir, just the mission."

I know his background. He is a member of the elephants' elite guard, probably the most decorated animal on our team.

"I would have expected more talk coming from someone so experienced," I say to him.

"Experience is the reason I stayed quiet. I've been on more of these kinds of missions than anyone on this team.

I've seen it all, been on covert assignments on the Moon, fought secret wars in Africa, things I can never tell anyone. That is the key to my point, a true soldier has nothing to say unless he needs to say it. And right now, there is nothing I need to say. I will fulfill my mission. Everything else is optional."

He walks away without a hint of emotion. I was wrong to question his lack of participation and now I realize that. This is my team and I will respect how they operate.

Time to get started.

Chapter 8 – Fenrir Snow

Hunters

<u>November 16, 3040 9:50 PM</u>
The night sky is shaded with a hue of pink and orange. The lights from Las Vegas make stars non-existent in this part of North America, especially in Primm which is thirty miles away from it.

Colbo and I have arrived at the Primm-Phillips supply depot. We stand outside its gates and I see no sign of a break in. The local law enforcement has been surprisingly cooperative with giving us full access to most of the public buildings in Primm. We didn't really give them any specifics about our mission, just that we were hunting fugitives and that they were most likely hiding within the confines of one of these depots. When law enforcement gets the order directly from the highest members of the United Species Alliance, they tend to cooperate hastily, even if it means answering to a lowly wolf or gorilla. In human territory it's still a human mentality.

The police have provided us with general access keys, allowing us to get past any security the depot may have. When I first heard about what systems they have, or lack thereof, I thought it was a joke. I almost let out a laugh, but then I realized this is all they really have. I guess I wasn't expecting a human city to be in such shambles.

When you're in a close proximity to a place as morally questionable as Las Vegas, these kinds of things aren't surprising. Corruption tends to leak from the source. Just look at all the cities surrounding it. They are hotspots for prostitution, gambling, and illegal drugs. Interspecies hooking, an act that is strictly punished and looked down upon by most societies, human or otherwise, could only happen in a place as poor as Primm.

We walk through the front gate toward the main entrance. It's automatic and slides open the instant we are in range. The area inside the gate looks decrepit. Dead plant life litters the premise.

With the access keys, Colbo and I plan to enter through the front door. The supply depot itself isn't difficult to navigate through. Trevor handed us the floor plan, and I examined every detail on it.

There's a front lobby that is no larger than an average living room. Two doors are at opposite sides, leading to two different areas of the depot. The left one, marked 'holdings,' goes to a hallway that leads to an enormous warehouse where all the supplies are kept and processed. It holds several items, but what the halfkinds are looking for will most likely be food and the insta-items. The warehouse is a large maze of stacked boxes and automated conveyor belts that lead to different teleport stations. Someone far away orders their item, it gets processed through the belts. At the end of all the twists and turns, it is sent out for consumption to whomever ordered it. There are cranes and mechanical arms that help in the shipping process, picking certain items and dropping them in the teleporters for jobs that the belts can't handle. I've never seen these things in action before, but I heard when it's working, the only thing you hear are hundreds of gears and robotics moving simultaneously at one time. So many parts are in motion, too many for the naked eye to keep track of.

The other door in the lobby leads to the clerical rooms. That is where workers do their inventory checks, making sure that all the orders are processed correctly. Machines do most of the work flawlessly, but bugs still occur in the programming and it's up to these workers to maintain things. They set up these offices in case any manual labor needs to happen.

Colbo and I are here mainly to patrol and investigate the warehouse. That's where the goods are, that's where the target will be snooping around. I doubt we'll even step foot into the office side of the depot.

"So Colbo, what do you make of all this?" I ask him as we head to the entrance door.

"Make of what? Our mission?" he asks me quickly as he looks around for anything suspicious.

"No, of this whole situation. These halfkinds and their existence."

"My opinion doesn't matter. I'm here for the same reason you are, because my kind asked me to."

"You obey your orders blindly? Don't you ever stop and think about if they're right or not?"

"Judging by your question, it seems you are the one who has trouble with what we've been assigned to do."

I look at him sharply.

"Not even," I say. "I am loyal to the Brotherhood of Wolves and would never suspect any of my orders. I'm curious, that's all."

"It is not my place to question the motives of my leaders," he says.

"Ah yes, of course not. But I assume you do know the Gorilla Government is in cahoots with the humans. I imagine the Human Council will now be funding a chunk of your war against the lions in South Africa thanks to this mission."

I get under Colbo's skin and he looks mildly angry by my comments.

"Since we have just met, I'll be polite and refrain from knocking the fangs out of your mouth," he says. "And you should be one to talk. Rumor has it that the wolves need some upgrades in their tech. I'm sure human engineers are jumping at the opportunity to help your kind out…"

I flash a small smile.

"Whatever you say," I say. "Guess both of our governments are free dealing then. Politics aside, why do you think they, the Human Council and the other species, want these things dead?"

"I think they feel that these halfkinds are a threat to the balance our world has maintained."

"Balance?" I scoff. "Last time I checked, our world is anything but balanced. The humans are still in control. They have the leg up on all of us, always will. They got better tech, higher numbers, and more resources. We're second class citizens compared to them."

"Better than no class," Colbo says matter-of-factly. "There was a time when we didn't stand a chance. Much has changed and now we are equals in our intelligence. We aren't on the verge of extinction like in the old days."

"Yes, and now we are on a mission spearheaded by their council. And to do what? To make a new species extinct. Seems that things haven't changed at all."

"Don't be so cynical. They are abominations and shouldn't even exist. Their conception only happened through the most perverse actions that the sickest minds could think of. I do not see eye to eye with the Human Council all the time, but I can see why they pushed for this operation. These things are a disgrace to the laws of nature, created by bio techno monsters, a rogue group that is playing God. We need to send a message to those who think they can wield such power."

"If I recall correctly, the last time humans played God, our intelligence was created. Perhaps it's something we should encourage more often," I say wistfully.

"But if I recall correctly, they lost their path to a perfect world. They had everything before we came around. Teleporters had broken through. There were plans for advanced biotics, technology that could be integrated into your mind. Imagine watching a TV without having one, it appears in your eyes. Amazing. So much could've been created. But all of that became lost after the Event, after we showed up. Their development stood still. It's a miracle that they were able to finish completion of the terraformed moon."

I sneer.

"Who cares about the humans, it worked out for us," I say.

"Not this time," Colbo says. "It could open a plethora of issues. People trying to breed halfkind children, genetic mixing that shouldn't exist, and none of us, wolves, gorillas, humans, would be able to control the chaos that might ensue from it."

"Seems like we're picking and choosing."

But in a way, Colbo is right. The existence of halfkinds would bring upon issues that could put society in a panic. Things have barely smoothed out after the Event, the world was not ready for another one.

"I see your point, Colbo," I say. "But what we're doing isn't a mission, it's an assassination."

"What must be done must be done," he says. "It's the cold reality of what we signed up for. Besides, you don't seem like the type to care."

"I don't."

We have reached the front entrance. Colbo takes his access card and puts it in front of the scanner. It takes a few seconds to complete, but when it is finished the device says "Security systems already disabled."

"Our access cards didn't do anything," Colbo says. "It looks like the security system is already off."

"What do you make of this?" I ask him.

"Either the security system malfunctioned or someone turned it off already."

"If it malfunctioned, repair drones should have been sent already. This was a manual shutdown. Someone is here."

We both look around.

"Did the police say if there was any maintenance scheduled for today?" Colbo asks.

"No," I respond.

"We should contact Commander Trevor to report our status."

"No, I think we should investigate first. I don't want the human to get involved yet."

"It's protocol Fenrir, just do it."

"Fine."

Begrudgingly, I activate the communicator that Trevor has given to us. It provides direct communication via headset to all our squad mates, and has video holographic capabilities.

"Trevor, do you read me?" I ask.

Trevor's face pops up on a video hologram in front of me.

"I read you, Fenrir. What is your status?" he says.

"Colbo and I have entered the Primm-Phillips supply depot," I say. "The security system was already disabled before our arrival. We both agree that an intruder has turned it off. Do we proceed?"

"Yes, but be careful. Over."

We both walk through the front door and, as the schematics tell us, there are two doors, one that leads to the warehouse, the other to the offices. Without hesitation, we head to the warehouse and slowly saunter through the hallway, trying to be as discreet as possible.

The warehouse machines are off, so the whole building is silent. If there is an intruder in the premise, they must be very good at keeping low because I can't hear anything.

We make our way through the warehouse doors and hit an outsized cage that separates the entrance of the warehouse from the rest of it. There's a small doorway that has a manual handle, as opposed to all the automatic doors we had walked through. Since I do not have hands to operate the human handle, I motion to Colbo to open it. He proceeds to gently pull it down, creating a large enough crack for me to pass through. I motion for him to wait until I scout the area, since I am shorter and possess the stealth that his hefty frame doesn't.

All I see are stacks of boxes everywhere. They are labeled with the product names. One box says Alphabrans, a popular cereal among the human population. Another is labeled peaches. It seems this place stores fruits and vegetables. They must be pumped with fresheners. I don't see how a peach could last long in a dank warehouse like this.

All the boxes looked untouched, as they are still piled up neatly. If there was a halfkind looking for supplies, it hasn't happen yet. Things would have been strewn about messily from the rummaging that would have taken place. Either that, or our would-be intruder took every precaution to mask whatever evidence they would have left. I doubt they are that good.

I pace around to see what else is in the warehouse, but I become disoriented by the clutter and shipments. I look back and can't even see where Colbo stands. The fact that my vertical height reaches just over three feet prevents me from seeing over the stacks.

None of the machines have been operating. There's a compcube nearby, so I walk to it and turn it on. It has an encryption device, but my access card allows full rights to go through it. I quickly navigate the menus to check the operating logs of the building.

The first thing I go over is when the last shut down was. The menus are voice operated, but that shouldn't be an issue. There's no one in the warehouse to alarm.

"Computer, state the last time of operation," I say.

"Last time of operation was at 7:00 PM," the computer says.

"That was three hours ago," I say to myself. "Computer, when was the security protocol activated?"

"Security protocol activated at 7:01 PM."

"When we entered, it was off. Computer, when was the security protocol last disengaged."

"Security protocol was disabled at 9:55 PM."

I look at a clock on the warehouse wall. The time reads 9:58.

"Hmm, three minutes ago. Computer, was the security protocol shutdown as a scheduled routine?" I ask.

"Negative, shutdown was disabled manually."

I didn't see any manual override rooms when I was looking at the floor plan. Wherever it was, it wasn't in the warehouse.

"Computer," I say, "where is the manual override located?"

"Manual override controls are located approximately thirty feet below this current room. Its entrance is via manhole in the northwest area of this building."

"If the security protocol was disabled three minutes ago, and it was done manually, that means whoever did it is probably still there. We have to get to that manhole."

I motion to Colbo to let him know the coast is clear. He does not see me, though, so I navigate myself through the labyrinth of boxes and supplies, back to the front where he is waiting.

"What did you find?" he asks me.

"The security protocol was disabled manually, according to their system logs. It's about 10 PM, the system was shut off at 9:55. And the manual shut off is underground, right beneath this very room."

"That means whoever turned it off is still here!"

Suddenly, Colbo and I hear an earsplitting clang hit the floor. It comes from the northwest area of the warehouse, which is the opposite side where both of us stand.

"Manhole cover," I whisper to Colbo, "that's how you get down there. I'm certain that's the noise."

"Let's go investigate," he whispers back, "but we must stay silent."

We walk toward the direction of the clink quietly, traversing through the stacks while remaining on our toes. I hear slight grumblings and heavy panting as we inch closer to where it is.

We are now just around the corner from where an intruder stands. The murmuring is even louder. I can almost make out what he is saying to himself. Colbo wants to proceed, but I tell him to stay behind me. I want to get a glimpse of what we're dealing with before we charge in.

From around the corner, I peer in and see a man. But this man has feathers. And he has a beak. And he isn't wearing any shoes because he has talons instead. It is the bird man from the briefings, it is Lombardi Lawton.

I retreat back to where Colbo is hiding and look at him. I nod my head and give the motion. Before we do anything, I turn on my communicator to reach out to Commander Trevor.

"Commander, we have an ID on a hostile," I say to him. "It's one of the halfkinds, the bird one."

"Is he alone?" he asks.

"Positive, it's just him."

"Good. You have your orders. Engage the target."

"Understood."

I turn off my communicator and give Colbo the signal.

Chapter 9 – Lombardi Lawton

Prey

<u>November 16, 3040 9:31 PM</u>
When I left our hideout, I was a little teary eyed. I had never been prouder. The fate of my brothers and sisters rested on me. Not once had I ever been entrusted with such responsibility, and now, it was finally time to prove my worth. I would not let them down. I'd rather die than have failure be an option.

I have always been seen as one of the weak links in our family. I am an outsider among my brothers and sisters. The facts are hard to ignore. While some of them were given gifts of strength and beauty, I never had anything to offer. I was considered ugly and useless. Some of my siblings tried hard to conceal the truth. Iris and Isaac, for example, included me in their conversations and treated me with respect. Candy sometimes tried to explain all the things she was working on. Even though I didn't understand it most of the time, I still appreciated the gesture. But some of my other brothers weren't like that, they weren't kind at all.

Tiago always has had it out for me. When we were young, he used to beat me up. He teamed up with my more brutish brothers, Alex and Ace, and ganged up on me. I couldn't compete with Alex's raw power, nor outrun the cheetah speed of Ace. They used to bully me to no end. Growing up was hard. I might as well have been their whipping boy.

Everyone had someone in our family. Tiago had his little gang, Iris and Isaac had their twin connection, even the other weak links had someone they could confide in. Maddie hung out with Oscar, and Leonard was the mama's boy. I had no one.

It wasn't like I didn't try to fit in. Actually, I tried really hard. Even when they pushed away, excluded me from all their little games, I persisted to get in. I think the more they refused, the more I wanted to belong. Even if they rejected me, it was still a sliver of interaction. As pathetic as it was, even that small amount was enough for me to keep trying. I wanted to be in Tiago's circle. It never happened, though, I was still on my own most of the time.

Maybe that's why I ended up sneaking out at night so many times. I wanted to get away from home, to get away from my loneliness. After everyone was in bed, I would climb out of my room and slip through the back door. Our house was far away from the civilization Primm offered, so the back door led to this open field that connected to the outskirts of town. Sometimes, I would walk outside and look at the night sky for hours, thinking about the future and where we would end up.

Other days, I explored. I snuck in the shadows of Primm's dim city lights. The town was relatively quiet at night and deserted for the most part, so getting around wasn't too difficult. I made sure I had a hoodie on to conceal my face. I didn't do it too often, maybe once or twice every other month. Mother was good at keeping us sheltered in the house, and I didn't want to run the risk of getting caught, so I only left when I had strong urges.

That's how I got to know the area around us. I knew the streets well enough. Ace couldn't even locate the Primm-Phillips supply depot. When he got confused, I knew it was the opportunity I was waiting for. It was finally a chance for me to prove myself. A chance to shine, a chance to be someone the family could count on. No more being picked on, no more being seen as the weakling, no more feeling that I didn't belong.

That was then, this is now. We're all grown up and we're all fighting for our survival. And who does Tiago entrust the most critical task to? Not Ace, not Alex, but me. That says a lot. I guess all those years, all that hardship I went through, Tiago was testing me, to see if I have what it takes when the time called for it. I'm not going to let him down.

I ran as fast as I could toward the Primm-Phillips supply depot, tote bag on my back, instructions in hand. The night has already blanketed the city and I was able to hide within the darkness as I made my way to my destination.

A block or two after I had left, I referred to the map that Candy had drawn. It was a simple straight path to the Primm-Phillips depot, and I avoided any major streets where I could be easily spotted. I had to make my way down Junket Street, where most of the businesses were either out or not around anymore. It was a street littered with emptied out lots and rusted storage bins, with tall buildings and little lighting. It was easy to go unnoticed.

I didn't really need the map, I already was familiar enough with the area to know where to go. It was just a mile away. If I hurried, I could get there in about eight minutes, but I didn't want to rush. I was fearful of bumping into someone. Quietly, I ran from building corner to building corner, hiding behind emptied bins, old vehicles, basically anything I could. And every time I took cover, I peered out to see if the coast was clear and continued the same thing over again.

This got old fast, though. About half a mile in, I hadn't encountered anything. No people, no dogs, no cats, not even a rat. This street was as dead as the night.

I decided to change up my strategy. I was only less than half a mile away, so at that point, a non-stop sprint would get me there in a few minutes. I was already hooded. Face, arms, everything was obscured by my clothes and nightfall. Even if I did bump into someone, I would be running by them so quickly that they wouldn't even have time to realize what had crossed them.

I positioned myself in a runners start and lost myself. I can't ever remember running that fast before, but the adrenaline from the danger coupled with my motivation attributed to my speed. I think I would have even impressed Ace with my swiftness. If only my brothers and sisters could see me.

And now I am here, standing in front of the Primm-Phillips supply depot with the weight of my brothers and sisters on my shoulders and a few breaths to catch. I look at my watch and see that it is already 9:30.

I start to search the grounds for this grating Candy had described. It's supposed to lead to an underground tunnel system where the main security controls are. According to her instructions, the grating is somewhere towards the back end of the building, opposite side of the entrance.

I walk to the rear and look at the ground, but I still see nothing. Candy has provided me with a flashlight wristband, so I turn it on and point to the ground. All I see are weeds and blades of grass. The plant life has grown wild and thick. Candy assured me the grating is here somewhere, so I get on my knees and tear away at the weeds. I have to move quickly.

The security system is only activated when an intruder enters the building unauthorized, so the outside grounds between the outer fence and the depot is safe. I am paranoid, though. I'm afraid that there might be some surveillance equipment or sensor that Candy failed to catch. Her research and hacking skills are amazing, but mistakes happen.

I continue to pull the weeds furiously, until my hand hits something hard on the ground. I stop in my tracks, turn my hands into a fist, and knock on it. It's dense. Carefully, I feel the surface. It's cold, smooth, and rusted. This must be the grating.

I remove any roughage I might have missed until I uncover the whole thing. It's a small, metal circle no larger than two or three feet in diameter, severely rusted from the ravages of time. Since it's so old, I don't have to worry about locks or anything like that, Candy's instructions state I can remove it manually. It's heavy, but with all my strength, I lift it briefly and slide it to the side. The hole reveals a ladder, which I climb down.

I make my descent into the ground below. It smells horrible, like aged feces. Humans used to dispose their waste down here, long before modernized toilets had the capability to disintegrate droppings on the spot. The smell must be from the remnants of the shit and urine, left to rot for decades, even centuries maybe. I can barely stand it, but I continue on with my mission, walking down the north end of the tunnel as my directions tell me to do.

The floor is a little moist. It's dark down here, but there are a few lights adorned on the ceiling that help me see. The air is colder than on the surface and occasionally I feel a few drafts of wind. It is larger than I thought it would be, and longer, too.

At the end, I reach a large metal door. It looks new, probably something that had been built over the remains of the sewer. It has a numeric pad digitized on it, meaning a code is needed to open it. Behind it lies the main console that will allow me to disable the security system. According to the specs given to me, there should also be a metal grating on the ceiling of the room, which I can use to gain direct access to the warehouse floor.

But first things first, I must get past the secured door. Luckily for me, Candy was able to hack into the Primm-Phillips secured servers and obtain the access code for this door. She says it was pretty easy to do so, something about their server walls being breakable and a weak infrastructure on their encryption. It was a lot of technical jargon that I didn't understand.

I enter the ten digit combination: 4815162342. And as usual, she doesn't fail. Her access code works like a charm. I hear a click and clank within the metal door and it slides open. When she first gave me the code, I was wondering why I couldn't use an access code on the top entrance. She told me the locks used to fortify the security system were older than the rest of the security in the building. They built that first and later upgraded the security upstairs. Then they simply never upgraded back the stuff underground. Really shows you how well maintained this place is if everything is so out of sync.

I walk in to see a room very different from the dank tunnels. It's clean and smells much better. The walls are white and on the opposite end of the door is a giant computer. It's equipped with hologram technology, meaning there's no screen and, when powered on, a graphical interface appears in thin air. The room wasn't exactly state of the art, but compared to where I was earlier, it is a welcome change.

After I enter, the door shuts behind me. I turn back to Candy's instructions to see what I need to do. According to her, it's a standard Tang Phalanx Third Generation, meaning it's one of the earlier models. These ones have a manual override, which is configured by remapping certain wires on the circuit board. The newer models, which Candy said were in the ninth generation at this point, removed this feature, but I guess they didn't bother upgrading this console.

I open a small panel at the bottom of the box and I see nothing but a sea of wires attached to the circuit board. Candy's instructions make it very clear where I should place what. Switch circuit A from port A1 to A2, wire R from port B2 to B5 and so on. The goal of all this switching is to cause a system failure without making it obvious to the system. If I go about randomly pulling wires, the system's AI will be aware of tampering and automatically cause the alarms to go off. The wires I'm programming are masked switches that the artificial intelligence purposely ignores. Then after I'm done, the system failure goes off before the AI can react. It's a manual override designed to trick the AI from doing anything about it. It was installed in case the AI goes haywire and prevents a manual override. Once a system failure is detected, and after the AI realizes it can't do anything about it, thanks to the override, it automatically shuts down the security programs and my task is done.

After I make my modifications, I put the panel back in place and fire up the console. The graphical interface appears to me and it boots up. The artificial intelligence then speaks.

"System failure, going into automatic shutdown mode," it says. "Security programs will deactivate in five minutes."

It works! A timer then appears on the screen. I guess they give a five minute buffer in case someone wants to manually turn the security programs back on. So now I wait until I can enter the grounds.

During the five minutes, the console has computing capabilities, meaning I can use it to enter the infospace. With some time to kill, I decide why not. I open a new window and use the graphical interface to move some windows around. With my hands, I guide the display in front of me and open a browser.

Although I am not as technically gifted as some of my brothers and sisters, I am good enough to browse the space. It's easy enough. Once a window is popped open, simply enter your query and all this information pops up. The infospace has been around as long as intelligent animals have, probably longer. In its infancy, it was called the internet, but now the moniker has evolved to the infospace. I guess it's to emphasize the size of it. I heard back then you actually had to wait to open up browser pages and that it would take multiple queries, or searches as they called it, to find what you really wanted. They even had to remember web addresses. I can't imagine living in a time like that. Now, all you have to do is ask a question and ninety nine percent of the time, the results you're looking for get to you in a flash. Thank God for modern tech.

There's still about two minutes left and what I want to investigate is our next move. Tiago mentioned using the teleporters to connect to the Moon via a stop at San Francisco, but he might want to know some information about the teleporter stations around here. I use a quick query to get the locations of all the local teleporters near our hideout. The infospace returns information on two stations, the Li and Gonzalez stations. I wonder which one Tiago plans to lead us to? The Gonzalez one is closer to our hide out, it's probably that one.

Tiago and the others would no doubt need to know this, so I decide to retrieve the information. A few seconds later, a data cube pops out from the console.

"Security programs shut down," the computer says, breaking my thoughts.

It's time to go, but before I do I take some time to scan the warehouse, to get the locations of the items I plan to grab. I use the console to do an inventory search and I take note of where the food, insta-items, clothes, and other things are. I take the floor plans that Candy has handed to me and mark the locations on my map. The list has been double checked and I take one last look at it to make sure I have the rundown. I then climb up the ladder and open the grating that leads to the warehouse floor. It's lighter than the grating outside, making it much easier for me to remove.

I get above surface, put the grating back on the hole, and take a look around. There are boxes piled sky high.

"Crap, how am I going to sort through all this stuff?" I ask myself. "I didn't expect this place to be so crowded. I thought it was a small supply depot."

Digging through them might be more difficult than I thought. But it shouldn't be that much of a problem. After all I had done thus far, I feel a new sense of confidence that I have never felt before. I knew I could achieve, I just needed the opportunity to do it.

But then, my eyes go back to floor level and I see two figures in the shadows. The light from the Moon shines through a window on the wall, and from the darkness they step through it. A wolf and a gorilla appear before me, wearing militaristic uniforms. The wolf doesn't look too armed, he has some odd looking helmet headset combo on him and some kind of box on his front leg, but the gorilla looks menacing. The main thing I notice is his very big gun.

These must have been the animals that killed Leonard, these must be the animals that are after us.

"Stop right there," the gorilla says. I'm surprised because his human speech is very good for a different species. I understand him clearly.

I tense up and put my hand on my tote. I remember the explosives that Tiago had given to me and wonder if I should use them. It's too early, and I am seriously outgunned, so I wait for them to speak again.

"Drop the bag," the gorilla instructs me. I do not.

"Who are you?" I ask. "Are you here to kill me?"

The wolf then speaks. "Yes. On orders of the United Species Alliance, straight from the leaders."

A part of me is shocked. This was a direct order from the top of the top of the United Species Alliance. I knew they were involved in some scope, but I didn't think the big bosses were involved. This is larger than I imagined. The world really is after us.

Suddenly, without warning, the gorilla props his gun up from his arms and aims it at me. I only have a few fractions of a second to react, so I dash to the side, reaching for cover behind a stack of boxes.

I hear a deafening blast echo behind me, causing items to fly everywhere. The force from it sends me flying headfirst and I use my arms to break my fall forward. Dust and debris rise and it becomes hard to see. I am little discombobulated, but uninjured.

The boxes don't provide much to hide behind, but since there are so many of them, they keep me hidden. I quickly get to my feet and hide behind another one as I try to figure out where my pursuers went after the first shot.

"Damnit, I missed!" I hear the gorilla shout. I realize that they're not far and that my only option is to bolt out of here. The supplies would have to wait if I want to live.

I start running towards where I think the entrance is, knocking down piles of boxes that stand in my way. Unfortunately, my sprint is a dead giveaway and another shot from the gorilla's massive gun comes hurdling my way. It once again misses about three feet from me, but it's still enough to knock me off my toes and cause another rain of supplies.

Once again, I am disoriented, but I hear the footsteps of the two coming my way. I look around to see if there's anything I can use as a weapon. I still have my bomb, but now is not the best time to use it unless I wanted to blow myself up in the process.

Luckily, though, fate intervenes. I see a button on a nearby pole that says conveyor switch. I'm not one hundred percent sure, but I believe it turns on the machinery in this room and might provide a good enough distraction for me. I dash to it and press the button.

The machinery starts to run. Boxes move and the warehouse becomes noisy from the echoes of gears and devices.

"He's turned it on!" I hear faintly hear the gorilla say. "I can't hear shit."

Not wasting an instant of time, I make my way to the exit, bulldozing anything in my way. I don't care about the noise I make, I just need to get out.

I see it, the chain link fence with the word 'exit' marked on top. Never in my life do I feel so relieved to see a sign. I might not have what I came for, but at least I'm going to make it out alive.

Or so I thought. Something jolts me from the side. Feathers poof into the atmosphere. I fall to my right and tumble on the ground face first. Instinctively, I try to get back up, using my arms for balance. But as I lift myself up, my arm suddenly has a strong stinging sensation, like someone has pinched me. I collapse and once again my body hits the floor. I roll over, face up, and I reach my right arm over to my left, where the pain comes from.

To my surprise, a dark, thick liquid covers my hands. It is my own blood. I look to the left, the direction the blow came from. It is the wolf. His helmet protrudes a barrel that is smoking.

The gorilla rushes over.

"Nice shot!" he says to the wolf. "It's a good thing we decided to split up. Now let's end this."

I look directly into the eyes of the wolf. They are cold and empty. I sense that he has no satisfaction in what he is doing, but from his lack of emotion, I know he is going to kill me.

But I will not go down like that. I reach in my bag for the bomb and press on the trigger. I hear a high screeching noise, take it out, and throw it in their direction. I then jump as far away as I can.

Time freezes. I hear the explosive hitting the ground, the bellow of the gorilla yelling to move. And as quickly as I threw it, I hear an ear shattering boom behind me.

This is the third time I have been knocked down this evening. The gorilla's shots barely moved me, but this bomb flings me clear across the room. The force throws me directly into a wall, back first. It feels like someone has slammed me with a sledgehammer.

I lay on the ground, bones probably broken from my encounter with the wall. Everything on my body is sore, my legs, back, arms and head. I look at my arms and legs and see that they are bleeding, but at this point, I can't even locate where my wounds are. I see that they are painted with a thick coat of dark red. I touch my head and I feel the same thing.

I guess it's the adrenaline, because under normal circumstances, I would have been out cold. But things are visible, I can still see, and what I see is a large cloud of smoke in the air. Everything in my field of vision is dusty. I don't see the gorilla or the wolf either, nor do I hear them.

"Did I kill them?" I say to myself. But before I could even continue speaking, something trickles from the smoke. They're bright and blue, like a neon light. They're also small, and bounce on the ground toward my direction. They look like little spheres of lights.

"What is that?" I ask.

And then suddenly, I am flung from the ground again. The little blue spheres burst in front of me with violent aggression. Each explosion is like a tiny bomb and the collective of them sends me into the air and tears up my body. I feel things that I have never felt before, cuts so deep that it feels like something is eating at my flesh. Things I had control over suddenly do nothing. I try to move my fingers as I hit the ground, but I have none.

My body falls to the floor, and I know that pieces of me are gone. I cough as smoke and fumes enter my lungs. My vision is fuzzy, my ears are ringing, and I look down to my waist and see that my right leg is gone. My left hand has disappeared too, replaced by a stump that oozes out red liquid. My feathers, once glistening and healthy are now charred and burnt. My body is in agony, but the shock and adrenaline make it hard to focus on any one part. I am literally smoking.

There's nothing left to feel. I have failed. I came this close to being good enough, to being the guy who my family could depend on, but success evades me even until death.

I see the wolf emerging from the cloud of smoke, the barrel from his helmet still out and pointed at me. I hear him say something, and I'm not clear what it is. It sounds like fire, but it doesn't matter anymore. It's the last thing I hear. Seconds after the wolf speaks, I feel a jolt hit my head. An incredible pain occurs, like my skull is collapsing on itself. Everything turns black.

Looks like I didn't have what it takes.

Chapter 10 – Oscar Lawton

Leaders

<u>November 16, 3040 10:45 PM</u>

It's been a little over an hour since Lombardi left on his quest for supplies. He should've been back by now.

I am worried about my brother. He isn't strong like the rest of us. He's slower than the runners in our family, and can barely lift half the weight that I've seen Alex or Curtis press. He's no genius like Candy, either. But I can see why he volunteered. He wants to prove himself and who am I to brush off his request? He probably isn't the best among us, but I believe in him. He is my brother and I know he won't let us down.

Some of the others aren't like me. They don't have faith and this attitude is broadcasted by the likes of Tiago. We've never really seen eye to eye, Tiago and I. While he wants to dictate his commands to the group with an iron fist, I see the value of compassion. You can't scare people into doing things for you, especially your own family members. We both hold the heavy burden of being the leaders among my brothers and sisters, but the way we handle things are worlds apart.

Being the two oldest siblings is always a big responsibility, but being the two oldest in a family on the run is even harder. My little brothers and sisters look up to Tiago and me for direction and, so far, the struggle for leadership has been difficult with someone like him to bang heads against.

When we first decided to leave home, I agreed with him, but unwillingly. It was a decision that I didn't want to make, but I felt the pressure from my siblings and I agreed to make the call. But I knew Leonard wouldn't follow us quietly. Mother and he were inseparable. It was like we were practically asking, no, demanding, him to amputate one of his limbs. Even though he agreed on the surface, I knew he had doubts, but I didn't know that he would act on them.

When Ace came back with the news, I was devastated. I played a part that lead to his death and that will stay with me for the rest of my life. We should have been more sensitive, I should have spoken for him, but I didn't. He is dead because I failed to lead.

The more and more Tiago shouts his orders, the less control I feel I have. I wasn't even aware of his grand scheme to go to the Moon when I should have been. I knew we'd eventually have to make a run somewhere else. We couldn't live in this building forever, but things happened so fast that I didn't have the time to formulate our next move.

When he told us his plans, I was caught off guard. I thought we would coordinate everything together, that no decisions would be made without each other's blessing. And then he goes and announces to everyone that the Moon would be our final destination. He didn't even hint his idea to me. I was as surprised as everyone else.

I didn't and still don't, like his proposal. It's far too risky. He thinks we can waltz into a teleporter, hitch a ride to San Francisco, and make it to the Moon? What about security, what about actually using a teleporter?

I normally don't doubt that he hasn't considered these issues, but the way he's been acting the last few days gives me major concerns. Tiago has never struck me as a compassionate person, but he's been too cold, even for him. When mother died, he didn't flinch an inch. No remorse, no pain, no emotion. And when news of Leonard's death reached us, he was already making preparations. Most of my brothers and sisters were struck with grief, not him.

Most of them at least. Tiago has his entourage and they look up to him for guidance and direction. They emulate what he does and obey his every command. And in that sense, they dominate my other brothers and sisters.

You have Alex, Tiago's bodyguard, brutish, with the durability of a tank. He is Tiago's muscle. Then you have Ace, Mr. Covert Operations. He can be in your proximity, and you'd never know it thanks to his speed and grace. He is not mentally gifted, but his ability to walk unnoticed sure makes up for it.

Finally, there's Curtis. I've known him all my life and I still don't know much about him. He hangs in Tiago's circle, but he rarely says a word. On the outside, he looks like a monster. Long, sharp teeth, tough as nails scales, and the bug eyes of a reptile. He has a prehensile tail that sticks out of his back and razor sharp claws. Yet, when I dig past his physical appearance, he does not strike me as a killer. He looks sad most of the time, like living in this world brings him great agony, and this was before we were on the run. He could probably match up with Alex in a fight on any given day, yet he mopes around behind him. And he's an amazingly oversensitive individual. Sometimes, the slightest insult is enough to pierce his psyche. I don't understand how someone so strong can be so weak.

Yet, despite his mental frailty, Tiago shelters him. Perhaps Tiago still sees a use for his physical gifts, despite what he lacks in his confidence. Having two bodyguards is better than one.

I always feel that when it comes to leaders, I have to speak for the rest of us who won't stand up to Tiago and his gang. We are brothers and sisters, but that does not mean we are shielded from the politics that every group must face. Those who aren't in Tiago's entourage don't fall in line with his militant command of style. Candy has always been more interested in learning than in following. I can't say she's a devotee of Tiago exactly, but I do know that he respects her intelligence. We all do.

The twins are also a neutral party. The only ones they really stick with are each other. But for the most part, they get along with everyone. Just as Tiago respects Candy's intelligence, he sees value in the twins' intuition and empathy. They seem to know things we don't.

The rest of the family members are the ones I have to lead. They are the weaker ones: Maddie, Lombardi, and Leonard. Tiago and his cronies would be so cruel to them when we grew up. He used to bully them, tease them, steal their things, and whenever they tried to fight back, it wasn't him they had to face, but the clique. I always stuck up for them whenever it happened. I wasn't afraid of Tiago. I was bigger than him, bigger than most of them. I would go toe to toe with Alex if needed. Bears are juggernauts in their kingdom. Behemoth in size and swift in speed. And when we were growing up, I grew and grew and grew. None of them can take me.

I feel it is my responsibility to help those weaker than me. Maddie, Lombardi, and Leonard didn't have a choice in what God gave them. Maddie's cow DNA means she is clumsy, slow and lethargic. But she is also sweet and kind. I admire her for that. While the others live in a world that is harsh and cruel, Maddie lives in one that I wish I could be in, a place that doesn't know the brutal realities I see. I will always protect her from it, no matter what happens.

But it's funny how some people react when they need saving. Leonard sought mother's protection, Maddie looked to me, and Lombardi, he kept coming back to Tiago for more. I guess sometimes you don't want to be saved by someone else, it's a rather shaming thing. But I didn't care, I just wanted to help.

And now, as we're grown up, on the run from who knows what, I feel this is the time that my younger siblings need me the most. Some things don't change. Tiago doesn't physically bully my younger brothers and sisters anymore, but he isn't going to take care of them either. It's always been an every man for yourself mentality with that guy, family is no exception.

When mother died, I was scared like all the others. I was too afraid to think on my own and Tiago was brave enough to react for all of us. But now, after Leonard's death, and as I fear the worst for Lombardi, I'm not so sure if his leadership will lead us to the right path. He is far too selfish to care for us all. I've known this all my life. I need to speak up.

One of them is dead, possibly two. Tiago's orders are leading my brothers and sisters to their demise, and he goes about his business like we're some kind of army. My brothers and sisters are not collateral damage, they are family, and family should take care of each other. Tiago is no general, so why is he acting like one?

Tiago has already made another order without consulting me. When it reached 10:30, and we started to think something might have gone wrong, he told Ace to investigate the supply depot, check to see Lombardi's status. Naturally, Ace went without hesitation, and while I don't doubt that it's a good idea to send our scout to actually scout something, they way he did it came off cold. He didn't tell Ace to see if Lombardi was okay, he told Ace to see what was taking so long.

I knew, the minute Lombardi volunteered, that Tiago was irritated. Just like when we were kids, Tiago still sees Lombardi as a weak link, someone not to be trusted with such a valuable task. But I had faith in Lombardi. It's not right to keep everyone in the dark, and if he said he can do it, then damnit, he can.

Tiago unwillingly sent Lombardi. He's waiting to see when he will screw up so one of his guys can make the save.

Worst of all, when he sent Lombardi on his task, he gave him a bomb. Is this what things have come to? Shoot first, ask later. Does he want our brother to be killed, to have a big target on his back? I tried to tell Lombardi not to take it, but he assured me that it wouldn't be used. Then why have it at all?

I believe when Tiago gave that bomb to Lombardi, he was setting him up for a fall.

Suddenly, the front door of our hideout opens. Lombardi? No, it's Ace, and he's breathing heavily.

"You're back!" I say to Ace warmly. Even though he runs with Tiago, I'm still glad my brother is safe.

"Did you find him?" Tiago asks Ace.

"Yes," Ace says.

"And?"

"He's dead."

I feel like someone has punched me in the gut. It's the same thing I felt when Ace told us Leonard had died. Another one of my family members is gone. The times when we were young, under mother's roof, flashes before my eyes. It seems like only yesterday, we were carefree children. I've failed to protect another one.

"What happened?" Tiago asks.

"I don't know. I got there and saw a group of animals snooping, United Species Alliance vehicles parked all around the depot. The building looked like it had gone through some damage. There was a cloud of smoke and dust hovering above it. I carefully snuck into the building and I hid in the vents and observed. Those animals were putting something in a body bag, and it had a hand sticking out from it which had feathers..."

All of us are silent, but I can't stay silent anymore.

"This is your fault," I say to Tiago.

"What?" he says immediately, voice raised with a hint of anger.

"This is your fault. Didn't you hear what Ace said? The building had a cloud of smoke over it. Your bomb probably went off. You sent him to his death when you made him take it."

Alex inches closer to me as I make my accusation, but Tiago puts his hand in front of him, holding him back.

"Don't throw out accusations at me, brother. Lombardi knew the risks when he volunteered to go. We all knew the dangers. I gave him that bomb in case there was someone in his way and it looks like there was. It probably would've happened with or without the explosive."

His callousness surprises even me. "Are you listening to yourself? How could you brush off our brother's death like that? You act as if it's expected. Do you even care about any of us?"

He grimaces his face toward me. "How dare you say that! Don't even question my love for my family. Everything I've done, every instruction, every plan, every move that I've made was for this family!"

"Then why are you so hardened? Does Lombardi's death mean nothing to you? Why are you so unrelenting in your pursuit?"

"Because we don't have the time to relent. Two of us are dead and it's because of them, these agents of the United Species Alliance! They're after us, they're moving in for the quick kill. If we don't act fast, there's going to be more of us to mourn over."

"Two of us are dead because of your plans. Leonard would have never left us if we had given him the time he needed. Lombardi would still be alive if you hadn't given him that bomb."

"Oh really? Correct me if I'm wrong, but wasn't it you who vouched for him? You're the one who sent him on the suicide mission when I wanted someone capable like Ace."

"I sent him to get us supplies, not bomb it."

"Stop it both of you!" Iris tells us. "This is getting us nowhere. You can fight later, but for now we need to consider what's going on. Leonard and Lombardi are gone, and we don't have anything to sustain us."

"Uh, actually..." Ace says meekly. He takes his backpack off his shoulders and reaches in. He pulls an insta-item out and some packs of food.

"Unbelievable," I say to myself. "You sent Ace to get supplies, didn't you?"

"No," Ace says hastily, "I got these myself after the Alliance was gone. Tiago didn't tell me to get anything."

"Liar!" I yell. "Stop covering for your hero."

"Shut up, Oscar," Tiago says. "I didn't tell Ace anything, but at least we have what we need to make it to Moon."

"The Moon, that's the only thing you care about. You want to be as far away from home as possible and it doesn't matter who goes down in the process. You're not a brother, you're a dictator. And I'm done taking orders from you."

"What are you saying, brother?" Tiago says.

"What I'm saying is I'm not going to follow you into the slaughter. Your quest to get out of here is going to leave a lot of bodies and I won't be one of them."

He shrugs off my threat. "Fine, but you'll be on your own."

"No, he won't," a voice says behind me. It's Maddie. "I'll follow you wherever you go and I'll be able to find us shelter until you figure out what we should do next. I'm sorry Tiago, but I'm not ready to leave so quickly, not after all that's happened."

I look at her with a nod. "Thank you."

"Fine, take her. Anyone else? Anyone?" Tiago asks skeptically. No one responds. "Just as I..."

"We're leaving, too," a voice says. It's Isaac who speaks and Iris follows behind him. I'm actually shocked that it's them and Tiago looks just as stunned.

"Brother, sister, why? You know you two will always have a place with us," he says.

Isaac takes a moment to speak. He looks at me and Maddie, and then he looks at Tiago and the others. "I'm sorry, brother, but if we go with you, we're going to die. I feel it. I can't follow you on your path to destruction."

The words break Tiago's emotional wall like a battering ram through a castle gate. He has always liked both the twins. He believes there's something extraordinary about them, and their rejection hits him hard.

"And you, too, Iris?" Tiago asks her.

"Yes. You know I go where my brother goes," she says.

His face changes from a stupefied stare to a dark glare. "If that's what you two want, then so be it. We don't need you anyway."

He raises his arm and points to the exit.

"All of you, get out of here, you're not welcome anymore," he says.

"But where will they go?" Candy asks in a concerned tone.

"There's another abandoned building near here," Maddie says. "It used to be a casino, the Spades and Diamonds Casino, but I don't think it's been in business for quite some time, at least a year. I used to sneak out there, they have a lot of neat things, even if it is dusty and abandoned, I think we can hide there until you figure out what we should do next, Oscar."

I look at Maddie, and nod supportively. "Sounds good, Maddie. I guess that's where we'll be heading."

The four of us make our rounds and offer our goodbyes to the rest of the family. Some of them, like Candy and Ace greet our farewells warmly. Alex doesn't shake my hand when I offer it to him. Curtis gives a curt nod to me and I nod back.

I then walk up to Tiago and look at him eye to eye. He doesn't move a muscle and glowers straight back at me.

"I guess this is good bye then," I say. I offer my hand out as we continue our stare down. He holds his stance and doesn't move an inch.

"I guess so," he says. "Good luck to you."

"You too, brother."

We gather our things and walk to the exit. I take one quick glance behind me and look at the brothers and sister I leave behind. No one sees it, but a small tear rolls down my eye.

If only we could have stayed a family.

Chapter 11 – Iris Lawton

Origin

<u>November 16, 3040 10:55 PM</u>
We walk in the darkness and remain quiet as we follow Maddie's lead. I think about why we're on the run in the first place.

Our mother didn't teach us much when we were younger, but she made sure we learned two things: history and why we were different. I'm not sure if the others paid attention, or if they had any fascination about animal history, but I sure did.

We are half human, half something else. In the eyes of the leaders of the world, we shouldn't exist. They can't decide what we are - abominations, the next step of evolution, or a new species.

All of the animals have something to fear about us, but as I think about it, I suppose the humans have the most to lose. They have co-existed with intelligent species for some time, dividing land and power among themselves. And I think we represent the threat of a new power, one that would ruin what little balance exists. I suppose that's why whoever is in charge needs to kill us. They fear that we would join the fight for power and there's no more room for sharing.

There was a time when nothing was shared, when the one and only ruler of the Earth were the humans.

In the early twenty third century, humans had reached the pinnacle of their development. They had doubled their lifespan. The technological advances of teleportation and terraforming were going into full swing.

Artificial resources were being perfected, lowering starvation, crime, and poverty on a global scale. Cities were becoming larger and more decadent. They flourished in ways they only dreamed of a few hundred years before that.

More importantly, they had achieved something that had eluded them for a long time - a lasting peace. Humans had united on a worldwide front. Political arguing and threats of war were non-existent. Countries worked together more than ever before, seeing each other not as people of different colors and customs, but as one in the same: a member of the human race. A universal language had formed and it broke down any barriers that existed. They were no longer a species divided among nations, but a species unified under one front.

And thus, many of the arms were disassembled. All their weapons of mass destruction were put out of commission. They used to have fears that a nuclear war would end the world, but there was no need to worry about that anymore. The minutes to midnight were gone.

Yet, they still had problems. Earth was becoming more and more toxic by the pollution that ravaged it. Thus they made powerful initiatives to clean up their planet, spending all their assets on this goal.

With a flurry of resources and manpower, humans were able to restore much of the environment that they had destroyed within a few decades. Technological advances reduced the waste that previous generations built up. Non-pollutant energy sources were the only forms of power. Lost habitats were regrown thanks to advanced aging techniques. The ozone layer was strengthened thanks to chemical experiments that fortified it. Since they didn't have their conflicts to distract them, humans could focus on cleaning up the mess they made.

By the mid twenty third century, the planet had blossomed back to its environmental prime, owing its bloom to the ingenuity of human beings. It was these methods that allowed the humans to terraform the Moon much quicker than they had estimated, and it was these methods that restored the Earth to its peak condition. Mother Nature was easy to fix because it lacked its own will. The creatures they shared the Earth with were a different story.

More animals were on the endangered list than ever before. Whole groups of species, not just specific breeds or subsets, were on the verge of disappearing from the Earth. Gorillas, rhinos, crocodiles, and lions were a few on the short list that faced extinction if the humans did not act fast.

This was unacceptable to them. They had conquered their environmental issue, it was now time for them to take on the task of getting these animals off the endangered list.

There was a problem, though - the creatures weren't breeding. Gorillas, rhinos, crocodiles, lions, and a bevy of other endangered animals didn't know how few of them were left. How could they? Thus, they had no reason to procreate at a rapid pace.

Scientists, biologists, and zoologists tried everything to get these animals to breed. They tried artificial pheromones that supposedly increased their reproductive drive, but it was unsuccessful. They tried studying mating patterns and applied all their understanding of different animal customs in hopes that they would repopulate their kind, but that also failed. They even tried cloning techniques, but experts recognized it was a behavioral issue and that cloning would only be a crutch if the drive wasn't there to procreate.

There were many theories as to why these endangered species were breeding less and less. Some say that years and years of being exposed to the pollutants in the air caused shifts in hormonal development, thus reducing their drive to copulate. Others say that since the world around them changed so much, from the advances of humans, they were overwhelmed and didn't reproduce. Some think they just gave up their fight to exist.

Whatever the case, both the humans and the animals were on the edge. Then a breakthrough initiative was made by the powers that be. In most circles, it was believed that the problem was a behavioral issue, so what if you change the way animals behave with a boost of intelligence? When a creature is aware of the danger they are in, they react. The problem was that these endangered species didn't know they were in danger, but if you made them understand their situation, they would proactively do something. A bit of intelligence would give the animals this drive. Let the animals know they needed to make offspring or it could be the end of their kind.

Naturally, this caused a load of controversy among humans. People were worried it would lead to the downfall of their kind. Humans got to where they were because of their intelligence, if you give it to other animals what would stop them from becoming the rulers of the world? From the way things are today, their fears were justified.

Others didn't know if such an outrageous plan was necessary. If these animals couldn't do it on their own, maybe it was nature's way of letting them go. Was destroying the balance worth it if extinction was part of the plan anyway?

Yet, a typical human trait was confidence and, at the time, they had an over-abundance of it. They had cured most diseases, brought peace among themselves, and restored the environment to its former glory. They believed what they were doing was good and their accomplishments backed up their claim. Leading animals to extinction was not something they were going to allow.

They also thought they had things under control. Their intention was not to make animals super intelligent, but intelligent enough for their cause. They would still be primitive in nature, still rely on their survival instincts, and would lack any true knowledge, or so they hypothesized.

The leaders assured the world there would be no threat to humanity. Never in a million years did the humans see an Earth where animals would be speaking their language, engaging in their government, and be seen as their equals.

Riding on their earlier success, they overlooked any possible risks and went forward with the plan. It took some time to unlock the properties of intelligence boosting, but after twenty years or so of research, they were ready to begin testing. By the year 2285, The Ark Project began its mission to slightly raise the intelligence of endangered species and have them repopulate the Earth.

The first Ark Project was dedicated for testing only, picking animals that were in no real threat of dying. They chose five groups of species, four of them, dogs, cats, pigs, and cows, were domesticated animals. These animals were chosen because they already had above average intelligence and were easy to obtain. The other species they tested was a chimp. Though not as tamed as the others, their mental acumen was something that was sought after.

The first Ark Project was intensive with many tests and developments. And throughout all the trials they conducted, the people on the Ark Project noticed that progress was being made. Animals were being brought in by the thousands. The dogs and cats responded and learned commands much faster than their untested counterparts. The same went for the other animals as well.

The animals showed no sign of super intelligence at first. They adapted and figured things out impressively, but they weren't even close to being as smart as the dumbest humans on Earth. The results were still remarkable, though. Scientists studied these animals and put their brains to the test. Eventually, they were able to train animals to do advanced things, including breeding.

The project was considered a success and plans were being made to conduct phase two, which would be exposure to endangered species. This time, they would select nine groups of animals deemed to be at risk for extinction. Different breeds of wolves, gorillas, lions, eagles, rhinos, crocodiles, bears, elephants, and tigers were brought in for intelligence boosting.

Meanwhile, the animals of phase one were done with their clinicals and would be released back to their natural environments. This was the beginning of the downfall for the humans. They were so busy with phase two that they failed to thoroughly monitor the phase one tests subjects. If they did, they would have seen that these animals were still growing smarter and smarter as time passed. In a matter of years, they became as smart as humans, right under their noses.

But for their part, the phase one animals were quite tight-lipped about their newfound mental capabilities. They had become aware enough to know the destructive nature of mankind and kept their abilities under wraps. They knew they would be killed if they showed a slight hint of their super intelligence. Thus, they formed a secret society of phase one animals and gave the outward appearance of ignorance to hide what they really were. The intelligent groups also reproduced, increasing their numbers and spreading their intelligence to the next generations.

Fifteen years later, towards the beginning of the twenty fourth century, phase two had completed. The nine endangered species were much smarter than they originally were. They were still held under captivity, so scientists could monitor the rate of their repopulation, but things were improving. The procreation rate within the small subgroup of animals they held was slowly increasing.

Just like the phase one animals, the phase two animals also grew smarter than the humans had anticipated. Just like the phase one animals, they kept this all cloak-and-dagger for the same reasons. And like the phase one animals, the formed their own secret society.

One hundred years later, by 2400, the animals of phase two had swelled to a numerous mass. The Ark Project was considered a success and it was ready to move into phase three, reintroducing these animals to their natural habitats so that they could thrive and return things to the way they were. By 2420, phase two animals were living on their own in special, adapted habitats

The secret society of phase one animals covertly communicated with the secret society of phase two animals for the next twenty years, sharing information between the species. It was primitive by all means, with eagles relaying information between groups. But by

2440, there were super intelligent animals pretending to be savage, living among humans.

For the dogs, cats, and chimps, maintaining this secrecy was easy. They were treated by their human counterparts well and had no reason to shed light on their gifts. For the cows and pigs, it was harder. They were still a source of food for the humans, and there were many times when they wanted to rebel. But they stayed tough. When the cattle watched them go into the slaughterhouses, they kept their act for the sake of keeping appearances. They waited for the day of rebellion, and with plans being formulated between the phase one and two animals, that day would come soon.

Over another hundred years, by 2540, the repopulation effort was finally deemed a success. The phase two animals were taken off the endangered species list, the goal of rapid repopulation came to fruition. The humans believed their work had saved these animals, but they were right in ways far beyond their scope.

During those hundred or so years, the animals created an underground army. The phase one and two generations had development teams that were veiled and secretly researched human technology. They learned how to modify human weapons for their own use. Hiding was easy enough, especially thanks to the air support the eagles offered. There are some places humans can't get to because they are human. And thus, the stockpiling happened. Weapons were being created in unknown locations, preparation for an all-out assault to gain freedom.

The plan was simple - create enough damage and fear that it would force the humans to negotiate with the phase one and two animals, now known among themselves as the Ark Rebels. The terms were reasonable, each group of animals wanted their own land so that they could cultivate societies, no longer in secret.

A hundred years is a long time to plot and plan for an attack and there was one more thing the Ark Rebels had on their side - the element of surprise. Humans were still prospering in their peace and spent few resources on arms divisions. They only had their local law enforcement to rely on. They would be unprepared. Humans still had the numbers, but the lack of anticipation would help even the odds.

So, on January 1st, 2541, when the humans were celebrating and at their most vulnerable, the Ark Rebels and their army of super intelligent animals struck. They planned spread assaults across major cities around the world. Gorillas, lions, and chimps ransacked Southern Africa as humans scrambled in the confusion. The same went for the wolves and bears of North America, Australia, and Europe. In Asia, the rampage was spearheaded by the tigers, with crocodiles and elephants providing ground support. Eagles still provided communications, and the animals also created low grade messenger devices. Since the dogs, cats, cows, and pigs had agents everywhere, they aided their brothers in all parts of the world.

These rebels fought valiantly, plundering smaller cities and keeping their stance in the bigger ones. They were ruthless and killed humans left and right. It was the only way they could make a statement.

Thirty days of fighting raged on and the humans were still dumbfounded at what had happened. Overnight, the world they knew changed and a threat they didn't see coming invaded their homes. It took them a week to realize how things came to be, that the Ark Project was responsible for all the carnage. But within two weeks, they rallied their troops to bring things to a stalemate. By the fourth week, both sides realized the struggle was at a draw, so the humans wanted to talk to the rebellion's leaders to map out a negotiation.

When the leaders stated their terms, humans balked at the idea. Despite all their changes and all the good they had done, they still retained their one trait that made them human: greed. Humans are never good at sharing, and giving up their land and power was ridiculous to them. Throughout their entire existence, they had been the ones who ruled Earth and, in one short month, their reign was being threatened. They refused to give in to such threats.

They were still dominant. The Ark Rebels had caught the humans in a weak moment, at a time they least expected. They weren't fully armed or prepared for the battle, but the rebels knew it would only be a matter of weeks before the humans would be ready to fight. It only took a month to bring things to a tie. Even with all the repopulation and preparation, the rebels could not engage in a full war with humans because they would lose the numbers battle. There were too many of them to fend off and in a few months, the rebels' efforts would be lost.

But the Ark Rebels had an ace up their sleeve: weapons of mass destruction. Humans had deconstructed their WMD cache centuries ago, but the rebels had learned the technology and developed it over the past hundred years. They researched human documents and schematics. It wasn't a nuclear or atomic bomb, but it was enough to get the job done.

With their efforts dying and negotiations crumbling, it was time for the rebellion to act. They gave one last plea to the humans, warning them of the consequences if they did not agree to their terms. The humans arrogantly brushed off their threats. They were now winning the war and thought the rebellion could do nothing but watch their effort die. WMD's hadn't even come into the humans' minds. They greatly underestimated their foe.

On March 2nd, 2541, the rebellion launched a bomb at the coast of western China. Over a million humans lost their lives that day. This day was forever known as the Event.

After that, the humans had the choice of walking down one of two paths. The first was to reinstate the nuclear program and continue an all-out war that would lead to the destruction of the planet. The second was to negotiate terms with the animals. They chose the latter.

The rebellion got what they wanted, their own place to live. It took a few years to figure and settle the territories, but in the end each group of animals got what they wanted. The pigs got parts of Australia, the wolves got parts of Northern Canada, the lions and gorillas got parts of South Africa, and so on. Most of these places were areas already uninhabited by humans, except for a few.

Territories had and still have names, like the Wolf's Den for example, but the geographical designation that humans gave the land still applies. Thus, the Wolf's Den is still known as Northern Canada to most people, though sometimes the terms get mixed around. It depends on who is talking. A human is more likely to call it Northern Canada while a wolf would call it the Wolf's Den. The city names are the same, which leads to more confusion on what we call certain cities or territories. But most animals usually know what you're talking about regardless of which nomenclature you use.

Also as part of the terms, the rebellion was forced to disarm any remaining WMD's they might have had. There are rumors that there's a secret stash somewhere on both sides, in case it needed to be done again. But that's only a rumor.

Initially, the animals lived in relative seclusion from humans, so the United Species Alliance was formed to keep diplomacy between all species. After the Event, bad blood brewed for decades between the humans and their non-human counterparts. Luckily, no major wars raged on, only minor skirmishes would appear at the borders of the territories. Humans still owned most of the land on Earth. Yet, people resented their new neighbors. Many of the humans who were forced to move out of their homes remained bitter and angry.

However, as a few centuries passed by, things started to die down, and human-animal relations started to improve. Cats and dogs have integrated within human society, with some cities being designated as cat towns or dog cities. The other animals have frostier relations with humans, but for the most part they are civil with each other.

Separatist groups within certain species tried to replicate the Ark Project's research. In 2803, lions tried to recreate the process on some of their feline brothers, like cheetahs, when conflicts rose between them and the gorillas. They needed more allies, so they tried to create their own. And pigs tried to do the same on frogs. But the Ark Project could not be replicated successfully, thus the result of the lions and pigs trials led to intelligent cheetahs and frogs, but not super intelligent ones. They're smarter than the average wild animal, but slower than a human.

When the other members of the United Species Alliance discovered this, they quickly sent a strike team to put an end to these operations. Since then, any attempts at boosting intelligence leads to the harshest of punishments. In fact, any genetic engineering is forbidden.

The world has been this way for more than four hundred years and sometimes I find it hard to imagine what life must have been like for humans. They used to eat cows and pigs, which is ludicrous nowadays and would lead to jail time. Chicken and fish are the most acceptable meats to eat.

I sometimes think about how strange a balance it was back then versus now. For example, cats used to be the humans' pets, loyal companions that were cherished by them. And when the rebellion happened, mother said cats and dogs were the most resistant to engage in the carnage that the gorillas, pigs, cows and wolves were pushing for. Unlike them, they had no real reason to hate humans. They weren't their sport, nor were they mass produced solely to be eaten. They simply went along with the plan because they didn't want to be their pets forever, but that didn't mean they hated humans. Even today, cats, dogs, and humans have probably the strongest relationship among species. They were given their own territory in Europe, yet as time passed, cats and dogs slowly integrated back into human land. I guess the bond between humans and their domesticated pets doesn't change, even in the most dire circumstances.

The relationships humans have with other species aren't as pleasant. Most of the other animals hate humans, due to the thousands of years of abuse. I'd hate them, too, if I were them.

Humans don't have to worry, though. From what I read on the infospace and according to Mother, humans still are in control in the world. They outnumber all the intelligent animals combined.

But it must irk them knowing they have competition when hundreds of centuries ago they had none. It probably burns them more because it's their fault it happened. Maybe that's why the world is after us. All animals, humans, cats, dogs, all of them, probably would do anything to prevent another uprising like that and I guess they think we have the ability to do so.

The true irony of it all is that in their quest for altruism, Pandora's Box was opened. Ever since the rebellion and the Event, humans have never been able to attain the level of peace they once did. They didn't have to worry about each other, but they had new enemies. The arms companies quickly went back into business when the paranoia first spread and now it's regressed back to pre-peace times. Poverty is back, as is the political game between species. During the time of peace, humans never had to negotiate with each other, politics was handled on a philanthropic level. But that can never exist now with so much animosity and fear in the world.

Humans could have achieved so much if they didn't have the animal uprising as a distraction. They were at the pinnacle of their technological developments, but after the Event, things slowed down. There were too many threats, too many things that veered them off the accomplishments they were so close to having. Before the Event, there was a boom in breakthroughs, but now, it's hard to come by anything amazing. There isn't time for it. With so much conflict and tension on the Earth, the only thing there's time for is violence and fear. Those things never lead to anything great.

These are lessons that mother left us with her death, the explanation of why we are hunted. Back then, the animals who rebelled were the freaks that were pushed against the wall. It seems like the world thinks we're the next ones to start the fire and they want to put it out before it spreads.

No matter what you think, destruction has always been the easiest answer, and now my siblings and I have to hide in a musty casino because of it. Mother was right, it's a cruel world indeed.

Chapter 12 – Apollo Bradley

Partners

November 16, 3040 9:36 PM

Our mission has been relatively quiet. When we got past the entrance of the Primm-Austen supply depot, everything looked normal. The equipment was off and the place was empty. There was nothing to raise suspicion. Commander Trevor is looking through the warehouse floors to find anything that might be a clue. Hair, feathers, blood, but his examination is empty.

I use my nose to sniff out a trail, but nothing puts me on notice. It's the usual aroma of rats and dust. I've gained a database of thousands of scents over my short career. I've even got some aromatic biotics, implanted memories of smells, which aid my tracking skills. It's a pretty standard procedure for a canine tracker like myself. I know each and every one of them, so I know what is standard and what might be out of the ordinary.

Still, you can't be too careful.

"Scent amplifier," I say. Out from my helmed weapon slides a scoped device that places itself in front of my nose. Commander Trevor looks at me with a funny expression on his face.

"What does that thing do?" he asks.

"It's a Cerberus Scent Amplifier, newest model, top of the line," I respond. "It basically makes it easier for me to pick up scents that are otherwise impossible for my nose to detect. With this, I could probably tell what has been lurking as far back as a month ago."

"Impressive, but isn't that going to cause like an overload of smells? I can't imagine it's pleasant to be bombarded with the stench of things that are months old."

"There are filters that help control that. I won't smell a fart that some maintenance worker ripped five days ago."

"You dogs and your tech," he says in a joking manner. "I'm surprised there's stuff that dogs can't smell."

"Even with aromatic biotics, there's only so much the body can do on its own."

"True. I never see wolves with something like that, though."

"Eh, they're too proud and feel that technology weakens their hunter's spirit, whatever that means. They tend to act more... stubborn than us dogs. I mean, have you met Fenrir?"

Commander Trevor lets out a light laugh.

"Well I'm glad your candidness is still around after all these years," he says.

I first met Simon a few years back. We were tracking drugs that were being created in Seadog, Florida, a booming dog city on the southern tip of the panhandle. It has wonderful beaches and top notch law enforcement thanks to the resources given by humans.

Even though Seadog is considered a dog city, it owes its development to humans. Humans provided financial funding, and even to this day, human law enforcement helps patrol the streets when dogs need assistance. As a return, they get a small portion of the local tax charged to Seadog residents.

Drugs were a new thing in Seadog. This place was still relatively young and, while prosperous, over time, poverty crept its way in. There was a rumor that an illegal stimulant was being produced in a sleeper operation. The drug was some sort of hyper steroid, allowing the user to enhance their physical abilities greatly for a short amount of time. On the street, though, they were known as "wall smashers" mainly because of the rage a user would feel while under the influence.

Since humans had a strong connection to Seadog, the raid was a joint effort by the Human Council and High Dog Council. They sent a team that included Commander Trevor and me to get these drugs out of Seadog and persecute those making them.

I was fairly young at the time, but our enforcement branch, the Dog Alliance, saw me as an agent with unlimited potential. I was smarter than my peers, faster, and had a better nose. A drug operation like this was ideal for a dog with my skills.

Dogs and humans have a natural bond with each other, even after we were no longer their pets. We never harbored the hatred that so many of our animal brothers had, especially the wolves. And, in turn, humans never really held a grudge for us from the Event. They saw we were held at the mercy of our animal allies. These reasons are why dogs and humans are capable of coexisting in the same land. We have no need for separate territories like the other animals have, we are perfectly fine living in an integrated society with our human friends.

This has always been a subject of controversy, though. Our canine brothers, the wolves, see us as weaklings. We got our own territories like the others, but they've scoffed at our openness to live among people. They think that we are still their pets, second class citizens in a human dominated society. I've never seen it that way, I've always seen humans as compassionate neighbors. There used to be a saying, that dog was man's best friend, but I think it's a two way street.

I remember the first time I met Commander Trevor.

"You must be Apollo," he said to me. "I've heard a lot about you. My intel from the Dog Alliance tells me that you are one of their most valued members. I'm glad to have you on this mission."

He was all business, but had this friendly way about him. On that mission in Seadog, Commander Trevor and I worked as a team, much like we are working now in Primm. We went looking for traces of wall smashers, but on our first few locations, we found nothing. When I sniffed the area, I smelled no clues.

It was frustrating. A lot was hinging on my tracking ability, but every time we went to our targets I couldn't find anything. Up to that point, I hadn't been used to failure and my senses never faltered.

I was young and I started to feel the pressure of the team on my shoulders. Like a rookie, my confidence started to crumble with each empty search. I could sense the disappointment coming from my teammates. But Commander Trevor had faith in me. When the other humans and dogs went grumbling about how I was doing nothing for them, Commander Trevor told them to shut up, that the mission shouldn't fall on one dog or human, that it was a team effort. These admonishments helped lift the burden from my mind.

On our fifth search, I once again fell short and things had reached a boiling point. One of the other dogs wanted to take the lead in tracking and said the only reason I got to be the head tracker was because I was sucking up to the Dog Alliance. He didn't see any of the so-called potential I possessed.

That's when Simon took me aside. "Don't listen to him. He's trying to talk you down. He knows you're young and that a promotion is in line for the lead tracker. He's trying to snipe for that promotion and he's not above belittling team members. Remember, I'm the commander on this mission and I'll decide who does what. And until I see any other reason, you're still going to lead the hunt."

That was the jolt I needed. I did one more search of the place and I smelled something funny. It smelled like human blood, yet scrubbed away with so many chemicals that even the greatest sniffer could barely smell it. But I did. I alerted Simon and he told me to hold on to that scent. I kept sniffing, and sniffing, until I smelled traces of what we were looking for - wall smashers.

The scent trail had been discovered and with my new-found confidence, I did some of the best tracking of my life. Two days later, we found the source, the drugs were destroyed, and wall smashers would never be distributed again in Seadog. My work lead to a promotion that helped me get placement on some elite teams. I owe all this to Commander Trevor.

Since then, Commander Trevor and I talk to each other on a regular basis. We hadn't worked together again until today; nevertheless, we're always willing to get a drink whenever we're in each other's town. I've made my residence in Seadog and Simon is always fond of the beaches there. He's one of the few animals, man or dog, that I can call a good friend.

I am done searching the area and found nothing suspicious. Even with the scent amplifier everything seems to be the way it should.

"Looks like I have zilch," I say to Commander Trevor.

"Me either," he says to me. "My scanner picks up nothing. I've been looking all over the place and there's not a single hair or scale that would help me."

"Should we report to the others?"

"I guess so."

I'm about to activate my headset to let our team members know our status when, suddenly, I hear a buzzing noise. It's an incoming message from one of our squad mates in the other depots.

"Identify yourself," I say.

"This is Fenrir Snow with a status report. We got one of them."

"This is Commander Trevor," he chimes in. "You got the target? Are you still at your location, the Primm-Phillips depot?"

"Affirmative," Fenrir responds.

"Is the halfkind dead? How many hostiles did you encounter?"

"Only one. And yes, we have a fatality."

"Which halfkind is it?"

"The eagle one, Lombardi Lawton."

"Borton, Erawan, do you read me?"

"Borton here," he says, "Read you loud and clear."

"How is your investigation going?"

"We have nothing to report. Seems quiet here."

"Abort your location and head to the Primm-Phillips supply depot. We'll rendezvous with you there. Do you confirm?"

"Confirmed."

We turn off our headsets and look at each other.

"Looks like they sent a scout," I say.

"Yeah, that's pretty smart of them not to put all their eggs in one basket," he says. "Let's head over there to investigate, pronto."

"Got it."

We quickly get in our vehicle and make our way to the Primm-Phillips supply depot. It looks like a warzone when we arrive. There are demolished boxes, food, and supplies scattered about everywhere. The dust has just cleared, even though the battle had finished ten minutes ago.

"Didn't really go for stealth did you?" I say to Fenrir.

"Stealth is hard when your target throws a homemade grenade at you," he snaps back.

"Where is the halfkind?" Commander Trevor asks.

"Over there in that corner. I've covered him with a blanket. You're more than welcome to investigate."

"You haven't searched his body?"

"I figured I should wait for you. You are the Commander," he says with a hint of sarcasm. The wolf in our team is acting like an asshole. What a surprise.

Commander Trevor and I walk over to the body while the others trade information in the center of the warehouse. He lifts the blanket from the ground and it is a mess.

"Unbelievable," I say to myself.

Blown apart limbs, charred feathers, and a gaping, bloody hole in his temple are some of the few things that I notice. Fenrir and Colbo really did a number on this poor guy. If I hadn't seen a hologram of him earlier, I would have barely recognized what I am looking at.

As I get past the cuts and dismembered body parts, I'm able to get a better view of his feathers. He has the beak of a bird protruding from the center of his face, although it is now painted with dried blood. His eyes are small and black. His head is rather large in proportion to his body, but his general anatomy is human. He has the feet of a bird, talons and all, but he is bipedal. His arms are a mixture of limb and wings. He's wearing clothes, pants and a shirt with a jacket, and most of it has been ripped to shreds at this point.

He also has a pack wrapped around his arms.

"Any of you guys look inside the back pack?" I yell at the others.

"Like I said," Fenrir says, "we were waiting for you."

I open it and stick my head in. It's rather spacious and partly burnt, but for the most part empty. The only things I smell are scrap metal and some electronic devices. However, just as my head is about to exit, I smell the faint trace of something familiar. I grab it with my teeth and spit it on the floor.

It's a partly charred data cube, and it looks like it's still in working condition. I nudge the button on it and a holographic image floats in the air. Something looks familiar.

"What did you find?" Commander Trevor says to me when I make my discovery.

I turn to him and say, "I think I know where they're going."

<u>Chapter 13 – Tiago Lawton</u>

<u>Sacrifice</u>

<u>November 16, 3040 11:08 PM</u>

"What do you mean they know?" I yell at Ace in frustration. We're having a private conversation in a corner of the building, a status report on how his scouting mission went and what he observed while at the Primm-Phillips supply depot.

"When I was hiding in the vents," Ace says. "I saw one of their team members, the dog, pull out a cube from Lombardi's bag, and an image popped up. I couldn't make out what it was, but when the dog talked to the human, I heard them say our next move was to leave Primm. It appears the cube had information on the teleporter stations around here and that tipped them off."

"He must have gotten a data cube with a teleporter schedule or map or something. So they know for sure that we're heading to either one of the two teleporter stations here?"

"It think so."

Damnit Lombardi, how could you have been so stupid? How could you have left such vital evidence behind? We didn't even need it, Candy could have easily looked it up for us. What were you thinking?

Then again, it's my fault. I shouldn't have let you go in the first place. Such a vital task and I gave it to such a liability. I should've listened to my instincts instead of appeasing my brothers and sisters. I'll have to think of a way to cover Lombardi's mess.

"How did the rest of your mission go?" I ask Ace.

"Just as you planned. I left here at 9:50, Lombardi had already disabled the security system. His confrontation with the law was the perfect distraction while I got supplies. The action was happening on the other side of the warehouse and the wolf and gorilla were too busy with Lombardi to even notice I was there. After I got the goods, I slipped into the vents and made my escape."

"Did you have a tough time getting there?"

"Yes, but my speed was able to make up for my lack of direction. Besides, Lombardi left a bit of a trail, feathers were dropped here and there. I was able to follow that."

"I'm surprised. That's rather clever. Good job, Ace."

"Too bad our family didn't pick me in the first place."

"I agree. I didn't have time to argue for you. I should have."

He looks at me curiously.

"How did you know there was going to be someone there waiting for Lombardi, though?" Ace asks.

"I didn't. I figured if there was no one there, you could have helped Lombardi get the stuff. But in case there was, he would be the perfect decoy, especially with that bomb packed with him," I say.

"I'm sorry it had to be him."

I stay silent and think of my brother. He wanted to please me so badly and I never understood why. Maybe it was because he wanted to belong, but I wished he hadn't tried so hard. I wished he would have come of age on his own. That was the real way to win my approval, not by sucking up, but by proving. But I knew he'd never do it, so I had no choice but to use him like a pawn. I had to ensure one of my knights made it out alive.

"Yeah, I'm sorry, too," I say to Ace.

"The rest of the family, they just think that I went to look for Lombardi?" Ace asks. "They must never know of our plan."

"Don't worry, they won't. Even if they did, I doubt it would make a difference. Oscar and the others are gone. I will sacrifice all that I can to ensure the rest of us make it through this alive. This is my true family, you are all that matter."

"Thanks Tiago. Are you okay, though, with Oscar leaving and all?"

I knew that along the way sacrifices would be needed, but I didn't think we'd be fractured. Oscar thinks my leadership is too brutal, but it's a necessary evil. I will question my decisions one day, but not tonight. Oscar's soft heart doesn't have the strength to make those calls, mine does. It's the mentality you need if you want to live.

My actions are justified. Leonard would have slowed us down. He could have led our pursuers to us. Lombardi would fail getting the stuff we needed, so I had to send Ace. He wouldn't have had a chance without Lombardi's sacrifice. My brothers didn't die in vain, they died for the greater good, for the siblings that matter.

I wish Oscar could see that, but we are a family divided. Maybe we were always this way. Ace and Alex have constantly been loyal to me and I've never been that close with the likes of Leonard, Lombardi, or Maddie. I can't let down those who look up to me, not when the stakes are so high.

"Hey, Tiago, you there?" I have blanked out and Ace still wants an answer to his question. "Are you okay with Oscar leaving?"

I pause before I say anything. "Yeah, I'm fine. By the way, were you able to find the special items I requested?"

"Yes, I'll show you."

Ace reaches in his bag and rummages through it. I hear some clanking noises, like plastic banging into each other. He pulls out a small, stringy device.

"This is the transmitter you asked for," Ace says. "I only found wrist mounted ones. You can send a signal out and it'll beep when it is sent and received, but nothing else. You can't hear or talk through it."

I take it from him and observe. It's larger than I expect, but I wrap it around my arm and it fits, barely.

"It's kind of loose," I say to Ace. "How many did you get?"

"Four."

"Good. Did you get the other items?"

"Yes, I have a whole bunch of them, let me fish one out," he says. His whole arm is now in the sack. "Here you go."

I look at it. "Thanks, Ace, you did well."

He is holding a small Tang 320A light energy pistol. I did some research on the Primm-Phillips supply depot and looked specifically for small guns that we could arm ourselves with. It's a featherweight, handheld firearm, mainly used for household protection. It won't blast through walls, but if we need to take on our followers, this will get the job done.

Ace says it's the United Species Alliance that is after us. These are the big leagues, professionally trained soldiers. In a head on fight, we might as well be dead. The guns will offer some small form of safety, but I pray that we won't end up in a firefight for our lives.

"I got at least ten of them, along with the insta-item, food, and credits," Ace says.

"And the other item?"

"I have that too."

He pulls out a few disc-like objects and puts it in my hand.

"I'm surprised they had them," he says. "Seems too heavy duty to be in the inventory of such a shitty supply depot."

"Yeah, but I did my research. I saw it was there. Don't worry about the discs, they are for Curtis."

"What are they exactly?"

"Nothing important," I say as I look at all the supplies. "Hopefully, this will last us our trip to the Moon. Once we get there, we can set up our insta-item and live in solitude for a while."

"That's the plan?" Ace asks.

"That's the plan, at least for now."

"But how will we sustain ourselves in the long run?"

I don't have a good answer for him. Eventually our credits will run out and we'll be forced to find some way to pay for the things we need. But there isn't any time to think too far into the future, I have to focus on now.

"One thing at a time, brother," I tell Ace.

"What do we do now?" he asks me. "We have our supplies, should we start heading to the teleporters? Which one should we use, the Gonzalez station or the Li station?"

"I've asked Candy to do some research, let me consult her before I decide our next move. Wait here."

I walk over to where Candy is sitting. She's furiously working away on her compcube. After I told the others we were going to the Moon, I had asked her to start investigating how to get the teleporters working. With

Candy at full focus, there's no doubt in my mind that she'll get it done.

"Hi Candy," I say to her. "How's the search going? Did you figure out how we can use the teleporter?"

"Hold on one second," she says to me. I hear several beeping noises and after a few moments she looks up. "Okay, sorry about that. To answer your question, I think I got it. Not that hard, actually. Both stations around here, Li and Gonzalez, have routes to San Francisco. All we have to do is power up one of the teleporters and program its destination to the Bay Area. Then when we get to San Francisco, we'll do the same thing for the Moon."

"And I assume you know how to do all of this," I ask her. "Powering up the stations and programming our destination won't be a problem?"

"I've been at this for a while, what do you think?"

I give a light laugh. "Sorry, I shouldn't second guess you. What about the security there? How will we get in?"

"Security systems are actually maintained through a central server," she says. "I can hack into it and disable them via the infospace. I've already found weaknesses that I can exploit, so give me the go and I'll be able to shut them down."

"Can you shut down one at a time or will you be able to shut them simultaneously with your commands?"

"I can do both."

"Impressive."

"But why do you need both?" Candy asks suspiciously.

"As a contingency plan, just in case. We'll be heading to the Li station, but you never know what trouble we'll run into. Better to have two ready than one."

"Good point."

"I don't mean to rush you, but you might have to shut them down sooner than expected."

"Why? When are we leaving?"

"Tonight."

"So soon?"

"Is that a problem?"

"The process of getting things powered up isn't difficult, but it isn't fast either. I'll need some time to set up and get things started."

"How much time?"

"At least three hours."

I start to think about the scheduling of my plans. I'm unsure how much time we have, but then an idea pops in my head.

"I don't think that should be an issue, I just need to make some last minute decisions with Ace. Good work so far, Candy," I say.

"Thanks," she responds.

I walk back to Ace.

"Candy says she's ready, but once we get to the teleporter, she'll need time to get things ready, at least three hours," I say. "The United Species Alliance knows we're going to a teleporter. I need you to throw them off in order to buy that window for her."

"How do I do that?" Ace asks with concern.

Before I tell him what I'm thinking, I hesitate. Do I really want to do this? Will I be so ruthless in order achieve my goals, in order to save the siblings who are with me? Leonard was one thing, Lombardi was one thing, but what I'm thinking is a sin on an entirely different plane.

But if Candy can't work uninterrupted, then there won't be a life left to live. This is vital. I need to create a diversion that will throw off our chasers. I have to do whatever it takes.

We're the alphas, they're the betas. They branded themselves the moment they left. Oscar and Maddie were never strong and it showed in their actions. Yet something perplexes me. I don't understand why the twins went with them. They're like us, on the top. They should be hanging with the best instead of the worst. Why did they keep such low quality company?

"What's the plan?" Ace asks me, breaking my thoughts.

As much as I revere the twins, I must do what I must do to save my true family.

"In a few minutes, I'm going to write a message and I want you to sneak back to the Primm-Phillips supply depot. Is the United Species Alliance still there?"

"When I left, it didn't seem like they were going anywhere," Ace says.

"Good. Take that message and leave it where they can see it. On their vehicles, near the front door, wherever, as long as they get it."

"And what's in the message?"

"The location where Oscar and the others are hiding."

Ace looks at me stunned. "What?"

"Candy told me that she needed time to prepare the teleporters. If the United Species Alliance agents are busy checking out Oscar's hideout while Candy is working, it'll guarantee she'll have a long window to get it done."

"But... but...our own brothers and sisters. This isn't right."

Ace is hesitant, and rightfully so. I already have enough difficulty with giving the order, I can only imagine what it must be like to carry it. But this must be done if we are to survive. I must be strong for the others, I must make the choices they won't.

"It wasn't right that they left," I say coldly and sternly. I must be callous. If I show any sign of weakness, Ace won't do it. "This team knows we're heading to the teleporters thanks to Lombardi's tip. They'll be hot on our trail. We need to do this to divert their attention and stall them while Candy works."

"But…"

"No buts, Ace. If we don't leave today, we'll be dead. Do you want that?"

He shakes his head no.

"Then, can you go through with it?" I ask.

He nods his head quietly. "Yes, but don't tell the others. I don't think they'll forgive us."

"It's our secret. When you get back, we'll be ready to head to the Li station."

"The Li station? Why not the Gonzalez one? It's much closer to us and the Primm-Phillips supply depot."

"Exactly. The agents of the United Species Alliance are probably thinking the same thing. They know we plan to use a teleporter to get out of Primm. Now that they took down one of our own, they know we're nearby. If I were them, I'd be banking that we'd be heading there. We can't be that predictable."

"What if they split their team?" Ace asks in an anxious tone. "There are two teleport stations and six of them, they can send two teams to the two stations."

"That's true," I answer, "but if you fulfill your task, they'll have to split their team in three. With your tip, they'll want to check out the casino. They can't spread their squad too thin and I doubt they'll take that risk."

"But…"

"Don't worry so much, just trust me."

"So, you sure you want me to do this?"

We need to act fast and can't afford to encounter any hazards at the Li station. Oscar knew the risks. When I and the rest of my siblings are on the Moon living in peace, away from this mess of a home, I'll be looking back at these moments and I will understand why I did it.

"Yes, that's all we need to talk about for now. Get ready to leave soon. Also, see that bag about five feet away from us? Retrieve it for me. And bring Curtis over here," I tell Ace.

Ace runs to the bag and slides it next to me. He then walks over to the other side of the building where Curtis is laying down.

"Hey, Curt, Tiago wants to talk to you," Ace says.

Curtis gets up, without saying a single word and walks in my direction listlessly. His scaly, prehensile tail sways like dead weight. His yellow eyes look sullen. There isn't a smile or a frown on his face, just a blank slate. When he gets to me, he doesn't say a word. No hello or greeting or anything, only a simple nod to acknowledge his arrival. He frightens my other brothers and sisters and even I admit he scares me sometimes.

"Do you still remember the plan we talked about?" I ask.

He nods.

"Okay, it looks like we're going to go forward with it. You'll be headed to the Gonzalez station," I say. "I'll tell Candy to disable the security systems, so all you have to do is enter, no sneaking around. But before you leave, are you sure you want to do this?"

He nods.

"You don't have to," I say. "I've done a lot today, but this is your call. No pressure from me, no schemes, nothing. Even if it gets down to the last second and you feel like you want to abort, you're free to do so and I'll totally understand. One more time, are you sure about this?"

He nods again.

"Okay," I say. I grab the bag that Ace had delivered and the disc objects he had swiped, and hand them to Curtis. He opens the bag and checks its contents. Everything looks satisfactory to him and he slings the bag around his right arm. He looks me dead in the eyes. He doesn't nod this time, but they tell me that he's ready to start.

"You better go now," I say. "I'll tell the others you left. As you requested, I won't tell Candy what you plan to do, just Alex and Ace."

He looks at me skeptically.

"Don't worry," I say. "She didn't ask why she needed to make it. It won't raise any suspicion."

Curtis nods and walks toward the door.

Before he goes, there is one more thing I want to say. "Remember, if you feel like coming back, we'll be here with open arms. You're not bound by your mission, you can stop any time you want."

He looks back at me and says, "Don't worry, that won't be the case."

The large door opens and he is gone. I look at Ace as he prepares to deliver the message that I will write. I think about the twins and a sudden sadness overcomes me. I don't understand their betrayal. It's a mixed feeling of frustration and gloom.

And then I think of Oscar and the others. Questions fill my head. Will they forgive me? Do they understand?

Asking is useless, I already know the answers, and I don't care.

Chapter 14 – Curtis Lawton

Monsters

November 16, 3040 11:25 PM

I'm on my way to the Gonzalez station, ready to help my family one last time. It's only been minutes since I left, but so much is on my mind.

When we were growing up, I would go on the infospace and see what other animals looked like. Humans, crocodiles, dogs, cats, tigers, all of them are so beautiful. They look the way that God intended. But when I look in the mirror, I don't see any of that. I see this grotesque mess of human features with scales, teeth, and monstrous eyes. I see something that is a mistake, something ugly, something terrifying. I become frightful, yet entranced. And then, I realize that I'm looking at myself.

And I become disgusted.

I hate myself. When I was a child, I learned what I truly was, what my place was in this society. Since then, not a moment goes by where I wish I wasn't dead. I don't belong here, I don't belong anywhere. Not among my family, not among the rest of the world. I am a monster.

What Tiago fails to see, what the others fail to see, is that the world is right. He thinks that we are one of a kind, that we deserve to live, but I disagree. We are abominations. I wonder sometimes why we are here, what purpose do monstrosities like us serve? But I can't find any answers.

My mother told me I'm part man, part crocodile. I don't see it. The only way I could be of those two species is if someone put a human and a croc right next to each other, got two mallets and started smashing away until the two separate entities became a single being. A mixture of teeth and bones, skin and leather, hands and claws. Then you would have me.

Out of self-pity, I would ask why am I like this? I don't know who I was asking. It certainly wasn't God. I don't think he would've made me the way I am and if he did, he doesn't seem like a God to me.

Growing up was hard. My brothers and sisters didn't say anything, but I could see it in their eyes, they were afraid of me. Some, the more cowardly ones like Leonard, Lombardi, and Maddie, showed their fear with utmost clarity. Their voices would shake when they talked to me, their hands trembled when they approached me. I've known them all my life and it has always been the same. I didn't have the most approachable demeanor, but when your brothers and sisters can't even look at you face to face, you realize that perhaps you are the monster they fear so much.

The other siblings also dreaded interacting with me, but the terror they displayed was much more subtle. Instead of it showing on their faces or voices, they did it with their actions. I was always the elephant in the room, their interactions with me were awkward and hesitant. I couldn't bond with any of them like true family. It's hard to have deep conversations when a pair of knife-sharp jaws are glaring from your mouth. It's hard to horseplay and have fun when a wrong tug means a dislocated shoulder. Even our supposed tough guy, Alex, didn't want anything to do with me, probably because he knew I could snap his arm off if I wanted to.

I wouldn't dare, though, because I love my family. Even through all this hell, they mean the world to me.

There is one brother who doesn't fear me - Tiago. He doesn't act the same way as my other siblings do. I don't see him avoiding eye contact when we talk and I don't see his body posture shrivel up. He stands chest out, head high, eyes focused. He walks confidently when he approaches me and speaks to me like a normal being. In fact, sometimes I sense a bit of arrogance, as if he's demonstrating his authority. He wants me to know that he's not scared. I'm not sure if I'm the one who should be petrified.

That is the way my oldest brother is. He wants people to know that he is the alpha male, that he is the boss and he doesn't have to say a word. He just has to stand there and act like himself.

Still, it was nice to have someone to talk to. Tiago and I wouldn't have serious chats about the meaning of life, we just spoke of things any youth would speak about. Dreams of leaving Primm, of finding a place away from mother's control, a place where we could be accepted. I hold these talks close to my heart.

He knew, and still knows, that behind this rough, horrifying exterior lies someone who is dying inside. At first, he didn't understand why I loathe myself so much. He tried to convince me I had power. I was, and still am, bigger than the others. I'm supplied with natural gifts and could easily outmuscle my brothers and sisters. Tiago couldn't fathom why someone with such natural ability didn't try to take advantage of it.

I would tell him it wasn't for me. I am not one to seize power for my own. I am one who merely wishes to exist, who wishes to be happy. My appearance makes me elude this goal. It causes me great pain to know that some beings can't find joy in the world.

But despite my self-hate, I will not act in fits of rage or take what is not mine. I won't release my pain on others, just on myself.

Tiago is like that, searching for power, for survival. It is his way, not mine. Many times he has tried to convince me otherwise and many times I tell him I'm not interested. Sometimes his persistence bothers me, he doesn't like to hear the word no. Most times, I wonder why he is so tenacious in the first place.

I see what he has done with Alex. My rhino-like brother is much like me, behemoth in size and strong with tough skin and natural weapons like horns and a thick skull. When we were young, he was feared by my brothers and sisters, much like me, that is, until Tiago took him under his wing. He offered Alex that powerful hand of friendship and now Alex is Tiago's personal muscle. If there is ever a struggle for Tiago's life, rest assured Alex will be the one fighting for him.

Some of the others think the same of me, that I am Tiago's lackey, simply because he treats me differently than they do. They mistake his gestures of civility with those of manipulation. When he talks to me confidently, they see a puppet master pulling the string. And when I respond politely, it only supports their argument further.

I wish they could see it's not exclusive, that I want to act the same to them. My brothers and sisters are the only creatures that I've known my entire life. Twenty plus years under one house, one roof, without contact to the outside world. Blood is thick. I have an obligation to them and I know that they have an obligation to me. They are afraid of me, I understand, but despite their anxiety, I know I can still trust them. I would never do harm to them, I would do anything for them. I wish they could understand that.

The idea of family is a strange thing. We don't talk much, we don't connect much, but I am compelled to protect. I can't explain it. If they were anyone else, I could care less what happens. But because of that last name, we are bound to each other. They aren't strangers, they are my kin and I treat them that way.

Sometimes a few of them actually attempt to reach out to me, like my brother Oscar. I get the feeling that he wants to connect, but he can't find the courage to do so. He's made past attempts. As children, though apprehensive about it, he would try to play with me. It was kid's stuff back then, hide and go seek and playing with these toys mother had bought us, but it was something. Yet, even as children, his trepidation showed and eventually we disconnected.

As we grew older, it was the same. We didn't talk much and when we did it was always short. My relationship with Tiago was getting stronger. They didn't get along and my connection with Oscar deteriorated because of it. We never became as close as we were when we were young.

I don't hate him for it. Actually, I admire him more for it. An effort is better than nothing. Sometimes I feel gratitude. I have this underlying suspicion about Tiago's actions, that there's a hidden agenda. I don't have that concern with Oscar. I don't question his sincerity.

This was all I had to look forward to when it concerned my family, bits and pieces of interaction. It left me with an incredibly lonely existence. We were already outcasts in this world and I was the ultimate cast off. It wasn't like some of the others, such as Lombardi. He was ousted because of his awkwardness and social ineptitude, but at least he was given a chance to belong. I never got it.

How does one cope with being viewed as a terror among the people he loves? To be willing to give anything to those who are ready to run away at your very sight? The only thing I can say is that it's soul crushing.

As the years went by, I spiraled deeper and deeper into depression. I had so much love to give, but no one wanted it because they were too horrified to take it. Life in that house was so lonely, and I was confined to it every day. I was a prisoner trapped in despair and the only thing I could do was wallow in it. A mind alone is a dangerous thing. You wonder about things that don't seem possible. With no one to talk to, it would only be me and my thoughts.

Going to sleep was the worst. The darkness blanketed me, covering my eyes so I couldn't see myself. I felt things, but I didn't know if they were really there. I heard things, but I didn't see the source of the sounds. The only thing that was real to me were my thoughts and they weren't tangible.

I questioned my existence. It was surreal that I was what I was. There was nothing on this Earth like us, so what if we weren't real? What if the life I was living was some kind of fabricated lifetime? How would I wake myself up?

I knew the answer to that was obvious. It's something I think about all the time.

I wonder if any of the others thought about suicide, or if the long run had ever entered their minds. Mother had told us the horrors of the world. That's why she kept us on lockdown. It would make me question what kind of future I would have. A lifetime of living in that house would drive me insane, a lifetime of living outside of it wouldn't last very long. I look like a mutant, I would be killed like one. The only solution I had to accept was that there was no future for me.

I wanted to kill myself so many times. I wanted to get one of those kitchen knives and jam it into my neck. I just never had the guts to do it. Death is final, uncertain, I wasn't ready to face it so abruptly. So instead, I continued to suffer without a friend to talk to.

And then, mother died. I had spent my years worried about being trapped in our home forever. It was now time to face the other fear, living out in the ruthless world she described.

When we left our house, I started thinking. Our plan was to be on the run, to hide until we could find a place to be free. But I realized that it's as bad living underground as it is living in captivity. We'll never get to live full lives, despite what Tiago or Oscar might think. The only life we could have is that of a rat, a vermin living off the scraps of others, doing whatever decrepit thing it takes to survive.

I was a bigger target than ever. No doubt when someone sees me, they'll start shooting. The others looked unique, almost beautiful, I do not. No life to live indeed.

My worries came collapsing down and I had nowhere left to go. We were backed in a corner, I was backed in a corner. It was time to react or suffer forever.

Two nights ago, I decided to react. I mustered the courage, I wasn't going to be afraid anymore. When the others were sleeping, I grabbed something I had been working on all week. To the average eye, it was a long, hallow pipe. But at a closer glance, one would realize its tip was sharpened. I spent the days in our hiding place fashioning a spear, so I could jam it right into my heart. Like I said, I wasn't going to be afraid anymore.

I carefully walked away from our hiding place into the night sky. The Moon was out that night and it was mesmerizing. I could see the specs of green and blue reflecting its way back to Earth, illuminating the sky stunningly. There was a small patch of grass behind the warehouse and I stood there to look around. It was oddly out of place, a tiny field of green that shimmered brightly, stuck in the middle of the dank Primm backdrop.

For a quick moment, I reconsidered what I was about to do. The majesty of the night and peculiar peace I experienced was enough for me to have my doubts. Such magnificence was found in the middle of this ugly place, I felt right at home. Perhaps there was a place for me after all if I could enjoy a moment out of such simplicity.

But then I realized moments are fleeting. They don't exist forever. What exists forever is the hardship and cruelty of this world, one that allows this monstrosity known as myself to exist. What a horrible place indeed.

I grabbed the pipe with both hands, extended it forward, and pointed it down at my body. I closed my eyes and thought about my family.

"Such a shame," I said despondently.

"Indeed it is," someone said behind me. I recognized the voice. Tiago.

"Come to talk me out of this?" I said with the metal still grasped tightly in my hands.

"No, I've come to understand why this happening in the first place."

"You know me, brother. We don't have a chance out there, especially me. Who would accept us?"

Tiago let out a short breath. "Our goal shouldn't be to gain acceptance, it should be to survive."

"So run like fugitives then? Always fearing what lies behind the corner?"

"Run yes, but not like fugitives. Run to freedom, Curtis."

"And where does freedom exist?"

Tiago looked up at the night sky, his eyes fixating on the blue and green orb above us.

"The Moon," he said. "It exists there."

A part of me was shocked by his announcement. Tiago had infinite amounts of ambition if that's where his endgame would be. I knew he already had a plot formulated in his mind.

But the other part of me did not care. The Moon, Earth, Mars, another galaxy, it did not matter where we hid, there was still no future for us and I had my own plans to execute.

"I don't know what crazy scheme you have," I said, "but I don't want to be a part of them. My path is set."

I looked at Tiago and saw an expression I rarely see - sadness.

"But what about us?" he asked me. "I thought we were family."

I choke up a little bit.

"We are family," I said teary eyed, "but I can't live this life anymore."

His body drooped down and his breathing became heavy. "I... I... understand, brother, but this can't be the way. We can't lose another."

My eyes narrowed and I remained stoic. "It's the only way."

He paused for a bit before he responded to me and looked right at my eyes to see if I was bluffing. I wasn't, and he knew it.

"All right, brother, I'll respect your decision," he says. "But before you do whatever it is you plan to do, perhaps there's one final way you can help out the brothers and sisters you claim to love. You say you would do anything for family, correct?"

"Correct," I say softly.

"Then I have a plan for you."

Two nights later, as I head to the Gonzalez station, I feel ambivalent. What he wants me to do will help aid my family's escape. It's pivotal that I get this done. At the rate the United Species Alliance is going, it won't take long before we're all dead. My role in all this can put an end to them.

But I am also angry. I wanted to go out on my own terms, not as a person being used in a scheme, but as an individual who is putting an end to all his suffering. To take that away and put the guilt of the family on my head makes me question Tiago's concern. I've become a pawn in one of his schemes after all.

His leadership has been questionable these past few days. He let Oscar and the others slip from his fingers so offhandedly, without even a word of persuasion. It's like he didn't care about them at all. I care about them and I didn't want them to leave. I would have gone with them, too, but at that point, I had already committed to Tiago's plan. I didn't want to jeopardize the safety of those that remain, the objective still needed to go through.

Now I hold a slight grudge. When they left I didn't say how angry I was at Tiago, but he knew. He tried to convince me the importance of family, the importance that we do what it takes to make sure the family lives. I believed him, that's why I agreed to his proposal that night.

Then he turns his back on one of our brothers. Sometimes I wonder when Tiago talks about all that family duty crap, if he just means the family members that matter to him. His actions against some of the others have been less than loving. On the other hand, he protects those he personally cares about. I'm not sure if he thinks so black and white, but that seems to be the case.

And I'm not sure if I'm one of those he will toss in the wind. But then I remember all those times that we were kids and how he was the only one who could look me in the eye like a brother and not a beast. I suppose my paranoia is getting the best of me.

When I departed our hideout for the Gonzalez station, he knew I was mad. He asked if I wanted to back out, but I brushed him off aloofly. I wanted nothing to do with him. At the time, I thought he was a scumbag.

But as I think about it, I realize that I told him not to tell the others what I was going to do. He had told Ace and Alex from the get go, because he tells them everything, but he made sure not to tell anyone else. Not Oscar, not the twins, not Candy, who was the only one left after Oscar's camp departed. I asked him this because I didn't want them to be worried. Tiago fulfilled his part. None of them know. Things like that show me I can trust Tiago, that there's nothing to be paranoid about. It's a true demonstration of familial bond.

Even in this final hour, family comes first. That is why I'm doing what I'm doing. This is for them, my last act to give.

Chapter 15 – Simon Trevor

Risks

November 16, 3040 11:32 PM

The remnants of storage boxes, bits of food and clothes, and destroyed electronics surround us. I doubt that Primm's law enforcement will be happy with what we've done, but there's not much they can do about it. The United Species Alliance gave us full jurisdiction, so we're able to do whatever the hell it takes to get the job done as long as no one dies. Still, as I look around, I can't help but think that Fenrir and Colbo's actions were a bit excessive.

"Didn't really go for the quiet approach, did you?" I say to Fenrir, who is a few feet away from me.

"You didn't tell us we had to," he says sarcastically.

"Guess I didn't."

Another halfkind is dead and there's nine left. This one had a weapon with him, which tells me he was expecting us. I wonder how prepared the rest of them are, that when the time comes, if they'll fight back like he did. These things are scared, desperate, and fighting for their lives, which makes them very dangerous. I guess Fenrir and Colbo did what they had to do in order to get the job done.

"All right, let's gather up and go over what we know so far," I say. The team has been spending the past hour looking for clues, documenting evidence, and doing forensic tests to find anything that could help in our investigation. Fenrir has been on scent duty. I told Colbo and Borton to seal the area and find out what the halfkind was trying to get. Erawan is on guard duty.

Apollo had already finished his investigation. He discovered some very vital evidence - a data cube Lombardi Lawton had in his pack. I think we've gotten what we needed and it's time to figure out the next plan.

"Everyone gather around," I say. "Apollo, share with the group what you found in his bag."

"Information on nearby teleporters," he tells the squad.

"We also checked the security console from where he entered," Fenrir says, "The history log suggests he was on the infospace looking for the same thing. Let me take a look at your data."

Apollo shows Fenrir the display and he examines it.

"Yup, the information from the log matches with what you discovered," Fenrir says. "It appears they're trying to leave Primm as soon as possible."

"It makes sense. I'm not surprised that's their next move," I say. "Two of their family members are dead. If I were them, I would leave here in a hurry, and if they make it to and are able to use a teleporter, tracking them down will be very, very difficult."

"Where do you think they're going?" Borton asks.

"We don't know, but does it really matter?" I respond. "They could travel to anywhere in the world in the blink of an eye."

"How many teleporters are there in Primm?" Colbo asks.

"There are two, the Gonzalez and Li stations. The birdman's data was for the Gonzalez station, probably because it's closer to here, so I'm guessing that's probably where they'll be heading," I say. "This also gives us a clue as to where they're hiding out. With no vehicle support, it means they're on foot. They have to be at least within a one to three mile radius from here and the Gonzalez station is in this area. They can't risk being in the open for too long, even if it is at night."

"Perhaps we should be finding out where their hideout is," Colbo says.

"No," I interrupt. "We know where they're going. If we go looking for their hideout, it could lead to a wild goose chase. Why not meet them at their target and stakeout the area? It'll be the perfect trap."

"But what if we're the ones who are being trapped," Fenrir says, breaking into our conversation.

"What do you mean?"

"Think about it, this is too obvious. This halfkind creature got blown to bits by Colbo and I. We tore him apart, just look at his corpse, and he conveniently leaves us a nice, fat clue to cash in? Doesn't it seem a little odd that someone we destroyed is leading us somewhere so obvious?"

"Perhaps," Colbo says, "but it's not like he knew that we were coming after him."

"Didn't he?" Fenrir says. "He had a bomb with him, after all. Maybe he was sent on a suicide mission, maybe he died because he wanted to leave a message."

I interject. "That's a lot of maybes and if that's the case, you think these halfkinds would sacrifice their own like that? Send some kind of kamikaze soldier to set up this trap?"

"It's not out of the question."

"But he's their brother," Apollo says, "it seems pretty extreme to make your own family do that."

Fenrir pauses to think about Apollo's observation. "When survival is on the line, extreme decisions are always made."

"Maybe," Apollo says hesitantly. "But the only other teleporter here is the Li station and that's nearly four miles away from this supply depot. If they are heading to that one, they'll have to risk being seen and there are nine of them around. Seems like an unnecessary gamble to be walking out in the open, in such a large group, to a station that's farther away."

"So, should we check out the Gonzalez teleport as the Commander suggests?" Colbo asks.

"It's up to him," Fenrir says bluntly. "But I'm still skeptical. Make your call, Trevor."

I go over the situation in my mind before I confirm. The Gonzalez station would be the most likely place they would show up next. Lombardi's evidence practically spells it out.

Fenrir does also make some excellent points. Things seem too good to be true. I'm not fully convinced, though. I just don't think a family would sacrifice their own like that. I've seen a lot of things in my career, but that seems too merciless to me.

"I think we should stakeout the Gonzalez station," I say. "It's the next logical move for the halfkinds. But I want to make sure we're all in agreement before we execute it. Who's in and who's out?"

"I'm in," Apollo says. "There's no reason to suspect otherwise. Just because the pieces fit doesn't mean we should disregard the facts."

"Yes, the obvious answers are obvious for a reason," Borton says.

"And you Erawan?" I ask him. He nods in agreement. "Colbo?"

"The halfkinds are scared, they know we're after them," Colbo says. "I don't think they care for strategy now, I think they want the fastest way out."

I then look at Fenrir. Judging by his body language he's still suspicious.

"I'm guessing you're the only one who thinks this isn't a good idea," I ask.

"I'm unsure," he says. "Things never come this easy and we are underestimating these halfkinds too much."

"Well there's not much we can give them credit for," Borton says. "Two of them are dead and their attempt to retrieve supplies has been a spectacular failure. I don't think they have a master plan or grand scheme. I think they're running around with their heads cut off."

"Still," Fenrir continues, "the second we let our guard down is the second they'll strike."

"What do you think we should do?" I ask Fenrir.

"We should split up," Fenrir says. "There are two stations here in Primm, one team of three can check out the Li and the other team can check out the Gonzalez station."

"I don't know," I say. "I think if our team is taking on nine possible hostiles, we should be at full strength. They may not be armed like we are, but a three on nine situation is never safe. I don't want to take the risk on a hunch."

"But if they're as clueless as we think they are, three on nine is plenty," Fenrir says.

Taking on so many of them with a handful of squad members could be suicide. But if I cash in all my chips on the Gonzalez station, and the halfkinds go to the Li station, my mission will be over.

"Okay, Fenrir, we'll do it your way. I'll send half of us to the Li station and half of us to the Gonzalez station. Borton, Apollo…"

Suddenly we hear a knock echo from the front door.

"Did you hear that?" I ask the others. They nod. We're not alone. "Fenrir, Apollo, exit through the front door and see what that was. I'll follow behind you for back up. The rest of you, stay here for now."

"Why can't we go?" Colbo asks.

"You're all too big," I say as I walk away. "You might scare it away."

Apollo and Fenrir head toward the knocking. I trail behind them, gun in my hands pointing downward. We exit the warehouse and slink through the hallway leading toward the front. It's quiet, like the warehouse, but different at the same time. The warehouse has an openness about the silence. I could hear wind blowing against the outside walls and small pieces of metal getting thrown around softly. The hallway has deft stillness, the kind of sound that surrounds you as the adrenaline pumps in your body and you brace for a clash.

The front door opens and the two canines step outside while I observe from my view inside. Fenrir looks to the left, Apollo looks to the right. They see nothing and trot around the front area. I step outside as well.

We survey the landscape and see squat, just an empty lot.

"Apollo, use your scent device," I say. "Fenrir, see if you can pick up anything too."

Apollo equips his scent device and sniffs the ground diligently. Fenrir does the same, without the gadgets.

"Got anything?" I ask.

"No, it's hard to pick up a scent if I don't know what I'm sniffing for," Fenrir says.

"I smell something faintly, but nothing solid. The earlier battle has spread all this debris, there's too much bombarding my nose," Apollo says.

"Don't blame this on me, dog," Fenrir snaps back.

"I'm just saying."

"Enough fighting you two, we need to…"

Suddenly something catches my eye. On my vehicle lies a note stuck tightly on the side. It flutters violently as the wind blows against it.

I walk towards my hovercar and snatch it off.

TWO OF US ARE DEAD. IT'S TIME WE TALK. MEET US AT THE SPADES AND DIAMONDS CASINO IN ONE HOUR. DON'T BE LATE.

"What is it?" Apollo asks.

I don't answer him. My brain needs some time to process the message. I hastily make my way back in. "Let's get inside, we need to talk to the rest of the group."

I rush into the warehouse and address the others.

"So what was outside?" Colbo asks.

I hand him the note and he passes it around to the others. After they read it, Fenrir speaks. "This is a trap."

"Another trap?" Colbo says. "Is your mouth on repeat?"

"Well what could they want to talk about, the weather?" Fenrir says.

"If this is a trap, then what about your theory on the Gonzalez station?" Borton asks. "That also another scheme they have?"

Fenrir is at a loss for words. "I suppose I was wrong in my earlier assumption. Maybe they're trying to draw us into one place while they make their escape at the teleporter."

"That does seem like a wise strategy," Apollo says. "Perhaps in this case, it is a good idea to split up."

"I agree," I say. "This is most likely a ruse they're setting up. I don't think they want to talk. But even if they are setting some kind of con, I still think that the Spades and Diamonds Casino is worth investigating. If we split up the squad, one group should take the Spades and Diamonds and another should check out the Gonzalez station."

"And the Li station?" Fenrir asks in a concerned tone.

"Sorry, but I don't want to divide us any further. If we don't find anything at either location, then the Li station will be our first priority. But for now, we should focus on these two. Is that a deal?"

I look at the others. They all are in agreement, except Fenrir. But as my eyes continue to pierce at him, he finally relents.

"Fine," he says begrudgingly, "we'll do it your way."

"Good," I say. "The assignments will be Apollo, Borton, and I to the Spades and Diamonds Casino, Erawan, Colbo, and Fenrir to the Gonzalez station. I'm splitting up the trackers so that there's one on each team. In case this is a diversion, I'll concentrate the heavy firepower at the Gonzalez station. I'm looking at you Colbo and Erawan."

"Don't worry, we got it covered," Colbo says.

"We'll be Team A, and you are Team B," I say.

"Try to be a little more discrete this time," Apollo says. "It's one thing to blow up a cruddy supply depot, it's another to destroy a teleporter station. The Alliance won't be too happy if the bill for this mission runs high."

"We'll do what we need to," Fenrir says. "Besides, it's not our fault that birdboy threw a bomb at us."

"Noted," Apollo says dryly.

"We're leaving now, Commander?" Colbo asks.

"Yes, but Team B will set up a perimeter on the Gonzalez station. Your assignment will be to wait on my command before you engage. I want to check out the casino before giving the go on an assault. The more information we have, the better, and if the casino is empty, I don't want Team B to be stuck in the middle of an ambush. I have a suspicion that if this meeting is a trap, they'll be waiting in full numbers at the Gonzalez station. If you wait, I can relay our status via our communicators and give you the signal to lead your strike. Is that understood? Don't engage until I tell you to, I repeat, do not engage unless I tell you."

"Yeah, yeah, we got it Commander," Colbo says nonchalantly.

"Good. We'll be departing for our respective locations in ten minutes. Finish up whatever you have left to do and get ready to move," I say.

The others disperse and start to pack their gear. Once again, I notice Erawan has stayed mute throughout the strategy session. He doesn't have much to pack and silently stands still while the others rustle through their items.

"Nothing to say again?" I ask him.

"Not much, Commander," he says.

"What do you think of the plan?" I ask.

"It's solid. I see your reasons for spreading the group and I understand why the teleporter stations are high priority."

"But it seems that something is bothering you. You haven't said anything since we got here."

"It's because there's nothing to say. There's one thing I do disagree with, though."

"And what's that?"

"Your assertion that these halfkinds aren't desperate enough to sacrifice their own. They may be intelligent like you and I, but that doesn't mean they have lost their survival instinct. In the end, all we want to do is survive, primitive or intelligent. And with a group as dangerous as ourselves hunting them down, and their desperation increasing every second, I wouldn't be surprised if sacrifices needed to be made."

"But they're family."

"Does that ever matter?" he says bluntly. "Excuses like that are conveniences we can afford because we're smarter than the primitive animals out there. But in the end, our core is made of those primitive instincts."

"You sure are battle hardened, Erawan. I wish you would speak more, you're experience could help guide the others."

"Talk is useless, experience can only be gained through actions. Whatever I say would be lost on them."

"I see. So do you think Fenrir is right, then? Do you think they sent their brother to deliver this message?"

"Perhaps, but it's a guess. My knowledge can only go so far. We creatures are too unpredictable."

"Well for the sake of the mission, let's hope our gut feelings are right."

"Yes, for the sake of the mission," he says as he walks away. I sense a subtle sarcasm in his words, as if the assignment means nothing to him. But I can understand, after years of these kinds of tasks, importance and meaning get lost in the sea of memories you obtain. You do what you're told and don't think a second about it. Even the best of us get worn down eventually.

Chapter 16 – Oscar Lawton

Runners

November 17, 3040 12:05 AM

After two miles of walking, we've arrived at The Spades and Diamonds Casino. It has been about one hour since we left the hideout.

The road wasn't easy. I was worried about the risk involved, as the casino had only been closed for about a year. Something shutdown so recently might have drones sweeping and cleaning, gutting the place up so that it's ready for the next owner to move in. Inside, there might be squatters like us or maintenance workers doing jobs the machines can't.

Maddie, however, had told me she had been there a few times before and it is indeed empty. The Spades and Diamonds Casino used to be a relatively successful gambling hall, but hard times reduced it to an eyesore in Primm. Given the city's already poverty filled state, that was hard to do. Its owners went out of business, abandoning mostly everything. There were rumors that the local mob drove them out of town. They left in such a hurry that they had no time to flush the building out.

There have been talks of investors coming in to refurbish the place, but there's been no resolution. Poor conditioned slot machines, tables, and decaying furniture is all that you'll find inside. It's like a ghost town in there, which makes it the perfect temporary hiding place while we decide what to do next.

Maddie says she doesn't think anyone has set foot in it for months, that the only inhabitants you'll find are bugs and rats. I believe her. Unlike others, I trust and respect the opinions of all my family members. That has never been the case with Tiago, he only cares about the people who are deemed worthy. He treats our family like a food chain, and if you're not at the top, you don't matter. A family shouldn't be that way, structured like some kind of power ladder. All of us should matter, not just the ones that are the highest.

I'm done living under that kind of rule. I still care for my brother, but there's no place in my heart for his brand of leadership.

And I can't follow him on his suicide mission to the Moon. He thinks it's an end-all solution, but what he fails to realize is how crazy it is. I think about all that could go wrong and I'm glad we decided to leave. I've already seen him brush aside two brothers so carelessly, I wonder how many more must die until his goals are complete.

There are so many faults with his plan. What if Candy can't figure out how to work the teleporter? What if the United Species Alliance finds them? It's quite obvious that escape will be a priority for us and a plan like Tiago's will attract a lot of attention. I think it's better to lay low until things die down, but Tiago wants to leave as soon as possible. He doesn't think of the repercussions. I had to do what was best for the others, offer them an alternative to his madness.

I wish it didn't have to end up this way. I wish we could have been a family as one. I wish mother hadn't died. I wish none of this had happened. But wishes do nothing. This is reality, this is the situation, and I can't hopelessly think about what could have been if I am to lead Maddie and the twins away from death. I must be a strong leader for their sake.

We stand at the front entrance. The windows have already been broken, providing an easy way to slip in. Maddie takes the lead, guiding us through the trail of broken glass. The building isn't very large, no bigger than the warehouse we were at, but it seems roomier thanks to all the gambling machines lying about. None are working, and I doubt there are any credits around. Looters raided the place right after it had closed down, taking anything of value with them. There's also no electricity or water, as the utility companies cut it off immediately after it closed.

There are some chairs and sofas strewn about. There are green, matted tables, all of them dusty, some overturned. The floor has dark red and black checkered carpeting with diamond and spade designs imprinted on them. The walls are a mahogany color, but the paint is already peeling off. Still, it's a lot better than our old hideout.

Traces of life still remain, though their state has been worn down considerably. There are some broken, grimy glasses and empty bottles sprinkled about a dingy bar that hugs a wall nearby. Playing cards messily cover the ground. There are stairs leading to a balcony that surrounds the main playing floor.

It's dim, but the bright street light crawls its way through the windows and crevices to provide enough illumination to see through the darkness.

I see a plush, red couch, drop my belongings, and plop myself right on it. The walk here was long and tiring, especially for someone with my weight. Maddie does the same, but I see the twins rustling through their things.

"What are you doing?" I ask them.

"I was able to swipe some stuff from Tiago's stash before we left, I want to make sure it's accounted for," Iris says. "Don't worry, it's not anything they'll miss. They still have quite a lot of stuff."

"What'd you take?"

"Food, water, and some clothes. Also, some portable lanterns from our previous hideout."

"And the insta-item?"

She shakes her head no. "I didn't see it in his stash. I think Ace only got one and Tiago must have it on lockdown."

I figure that would be the case. The insta-item was the most important thing he wanted Lombardi and Ace to retrieve. It's a key element in his plan, so I figure his muscle, Alex, is guarding it.

"How long do you think we'll last with the supplies you got?" I ask Iris.

"If we ration it, probably about two weeks," she says.

"We'll have to make another run to the supply depot?"

She pauses. "Regretfully so."

I hate to admit it, but Tiago at least had that right. The insta-item is the way to go because I don't know how many times we can sneak around. And now that the United Species Alliance is after us, it'll be harder to go in and get what we need. If only I had thought of that earlier.

Iris takes some of the portable lanterns and places them around our squatted campsite in the casino. They're nice, but there's still plenty of light coming from the Moon. I trace the beams of lights shining from the few windows, I stare at it, and my mind wanders into space. It's actually quite beautiful and with the light reflecting off of the blue and green from its terraformed surface, it looks like a grand jewel in the night sky. I can see the land formations and I imagine life fluttering there. Many parts of the moon are uninhabited. It's only starting to take shape, but I find it amazing what intelligence can accomplish.

Iris notices and says, "You think Tiago is really going to make it?"

I wake out of my trance. "He might."

"Are you being honest? If you really thought that, we would have never left him in the first place."

"I didn't want to leave because of my doubts. I didn't like how he was running things, we seem expendable. I would want to follow a leader who actually cares about the people he's leading."

"But you really think that? You think he would throw us under the bus if he needed to?"

I think about Tiago, about the hard times he gave some of my brothers and sisters while growing up. And I think of Leonard and Lombardi.

"There are some things I want to believe," I tell Iris, "And then there are some things I just know."

"I see," she says.

"Why did you and Isaac join me? It always seems like Tiago respects you two, I don't think you're on his 'weakling' list."

"I don't know, I guess I have a feeling that he's going to lead us to our end. I can't really pin it on anything. I mean, I have no real concrete evidence to do so. It's just, I have this sense, this intuition that something is going to happen, something bad, and no matter what I say to stop him, he's already set on his way. In order to save myself, in order to save Isaac, in order to save the rest of us, we need to stay away from him and his schemes."

"One of your visions?"

She looks embarrassed, dismissive.

"Uh, I guess so," she says.

Suddenly, Isaac barges into the conversation.

"What's the plan, Oscar?" he asks me.

I pause to think. If there's a time for a group meeting, it's now. I motion for Maddie to come over. All four of us are huddled with a blanket of lantern light covering us.

"I think we should lay low," I tell the group. "Tiago is charging into the situation with full force, he's bound to run into our pursuers eventually. He's not going to be quiet about things, either. I think while the United Species Alliance is distracted, we can obtain an insta-item from one of the supply depots. We have to finish Lombardi's job. But we can't go right away, we'll have to wait until the dust clears because they're on high alert after the first raid on the depot. We can live on our supplies for now, but eventually we'll have to make our move."

"What about Tiago? What if he and the others get into trouble?" Iris asks.

I hesitate saying what I want to say. I would help Tiago if needed. I know his hasty decisions will lead to carnage left and right and he could use assistance. But I can't. I have to do what's good for the rest of my family.

"Tiago's a fierce fighter," I say. "And the rest of the family has what it takes to endure. I know him and the others can take care of themselves, trust me."

"But we're abandoning him," Iris tells me softly.

"No, we're not," I say sternly, "we just have to take care of ourselves first."

"You know who you sound like? You sound like Tiago," Isaac says bluntly.

"I am not like him," I snap back. "If you died, he wouldn't even flinch at it. He would probably push you into the law so he could get away."

"You don't know that. I don't think that would happen to Iris and I. You're assuming," Isaac says. "Your judgment is clouded by your bad blood."

"That's not true. You saw how quick he passed over Lombardi's death and went straight to business afterwards. He didn't mourn over his brother, Lombardi meant nothing to him."

Isaac stands silent.

"Oscar's right!" Maddie says. "You don't know him like we do. Tiago is a terror. He's always had respect for you and Iris, but it's different for the rest of us."

"He's not that bad," Isaac says. He continues to defend Tiago. I suppose if I were him, I'd do the same. Isaac has never really had a reason to distrust Tiago, but I've seen Tiago's treatment of Maddie, Leonard, and Lombardi. I know how much of a bully he can be.

"Yes he is! Why did you even come with us?" Maddie shouts as her eyes get watery. Isaac remains tight lipped, but Maddie persists. "Why?"

"Because I made him," Iris interrupts. "I told you about my premonition, that something bad is going to happen if we stayed with Tiago. No one else would have believed me except Isaac. He's here because of me."

"Is this true?" I ask him. He nods silently. I pause for a few seconds then address him. "Isaac, I'm not mad at you. I understand that you might be questioning things, that you might be scared you made the wrong choice, but trust me, I'm here for you, I'm here for all of you. You aren't soldiers in my army, you are my family, and I won't let anything happen to my family."

Isaac's face softens a bit. He no longer has the frown that covered his face earlier. My speech has affected him.

"Okay, Oscar, I trust you," he says.

"Thanks," I say. "It's been a long day and it's already midnight. We should probably get some rest soon."

They all agree and slowly get settled in for the evening.

After our talk, I am optimistic. We may not have our whole plan figured out, but we have each other's support, the kind that was missing when we lived under Tiago's regime.

I think we're going to make it after all.

Chapter 17 – Simon Trevor

Assault

<u>November 17, 3040 12:50 AM</u>

Borton, Apollo, and I are on our way to the Spades and Diamonds Casino. We're in our transport, possibly heading toward a trap, but we're fully armed and prepared for what may come. I have my energy shotgun and pistol, Apollo and Borton have their gear. We also have a cache of smoke and pulse grenades.

The Spades and Diamonds Casino is about four miles away from the Primm-Phillips supply depot, but we only take the hovercar three miles. We proceed on foot for the other one. This is what I decided. If we take our vehicles to the front, we might alert them, and the only way we can control the situation is to utilize the element of surprise.

We're here. The shabby casino sign I see used to shine brightly in the Primm landscape. The once glorious marquee has a gaudy diamond and spade on it, but it's been reduced to chipped plastic and cracked glass. We get out of the hovercar cautiously. I motion for Apollo to survey the area and sniff out any traps. He sprints and investigates a half mile ahead of us and comes back. He shakes his head, everything seems okay.

I kneel down.

"Okay, so let's go over the battle plan one more time," I say. "There are two entrances to the Diamond and Spades Casino. I will take the front entrance, Apollo and Borton will take the back one. It's a pretty small building. The Spades and Diamonds Casino is a single floor, one room gaming complex."

"So the back entrance and the front entrance are in relative proximity from each other?" Borton asks.

"Yes. I will have my weapons stowed within my armor and will appear non-hostile," I say. "I don't want to trigger any unwanted aggression since they're the ones who invited us to talk. I'll distract them while you two sneak in the back. My communicator will be on sound mode, no graphical interface. I want you two to tell me your observations while staying hidden. It is vital that you let me know how many there are and what, if any, kind of weapons they have. I'll need to know what I'm dealing with."

"Understood," Apollo says. "We'll get a head and item count for you."

"I'll try to negotiate with them to stall," I say. "And then, when I give the signal, you two will attack from the rear and all three of us will work to disarm and capture the halfkinds."

"Only capture?" Borton inquires.

"Yes, only capture. Remember," I say, "when we are in pursuit, you're to obey my commands at all times. I don't want either of you charging into the situation head first."

Apollo I trust, but I've never worked with Borton before so I'm not sure what to expect from him.

"What if we take down one of the hostiles before you?" Apollo asks.

"Engage, but only subdue. I repeat, only subdue. I don't want any fatalities yet, understood?" I say to both of them.

"Excuse me, Commander," Borton asks, "but isn't the purpose of this mission to terminate them? Why are we only going to subdue?"

"Because they might have some useful intel. Besides, we're not executioners Borton, let the Alliance deal with them."

"But it's the Alliance who made the orders. They told us very clearly to kill them."

"Look, if they are hostile, then by all means do what it takes to keep yourself safe, but if there is no resistance, then your orders are to simply capture. I'm not going to be responsible for the murders of defenseless creatures."

"Um, defenseless? You saw what that one did to the supply depot, right?"

"He was provoked. This is different."

"But as I said before, I have strict orders from both my pig superiors and the United Species Alliance to terminate at all costs."

"These are my orders," I say sternly. "And you will fall in line."

"If you say so," Borton says begrudgingly. "Just know that if I get any flack from the uppers, I'm going to direct them to you."

"By all means go ahead, I can handle them. So we know what to do?" Apollo nods his head. Borton does too, but unwillingly. I tap on my communicator and Fenrir pops up on my graphical interface. "Team B, how are things going?"

"We've just arrived and set up a stakeout area on the Gonzalez teleporter," he says, "There doesn't seem to be anyone inside, at least not from our vantage point."

"Okay. Hold your position. Do not engage until I tell you to."

"Understood."

The holographic screen shuts off and I shift my attention back to the team. "Let's go."

I walk to the front of the building and motion for Borton and Apollo to go around the back. I tap my ear to my teammates, which reminds them to keep their communicators on sound mode only. I don't want any holographic interfaces to go off and blow our cover.

Borton and Apollo turn the corner and disappear from my line of sight. I hug my back against the wall and sneak to the front door. There's tons of broken glass on the ground, but it's hard to say if this is the work of a halfkind or looter. The sound of crushing glass will surely tip them off, so I take a peek inside before enter. I don't see much because of the dim lighting, only some haggard looking furniture and broken down gambling machines. It looked like the casino was empty and I start to worry that we have fallen into a trap.

I tiptoe my way in and try to make as little noise as possible. A few scratches and crunches are made, but there's no reaction from inside. I open the partially broken door.

Creak!

Shit, that was loud! Immediately, I hear rustling and swift movements. They must have been resting, the door no doubt startled them.

A small light turns on, but a slot machine blocks my view on its source.

"Apollo, Borton," I whisper, "Are you there? Have you entered the building?"

"Yes, we're here," Apollo says. "We're hiding behind a door that leads to the back. We're unnoticed."

"A light has turned on in the main casino, but my view is blocked. What do you see?"

"Four halfkinds. The twins, the cow, and the bear. They're on high alert, something must've startled them."

"That was me," I say embarrassed. "What are they doing now?"

"They just woke up, but they're surveying the area suspiciously. Oh, wait, one of them, the bear halfkind, he picked up a lantern."

"There are only four of them? Where are the other five?"

"I don't know."

"Something is wrong."

"Hello?" the bear halfkind shouts. I hear him talk to the air. His voice is quivering and I can sense his fear. "Who's there?"

"He's starting to walk around," Apollo says to me on my communicator. "He's, oh shit, he's headed our direction."

"We need to engage," Borton interrupts.

"Negative!" I say, "That's not part of the plan. You need to wait for my signal."

"Hello?!" I hear the bear halfkind shout louder. "Who's there?"

"He's walking right toward us!" Apollo says. "He's going to find us."

"We need to engage," Borton repeats.

"No. You two stay there. I will intercept."

I walk towards the light and make myself visible to the halfkinds. I see the four of them, huddled near the lantern, eyes wide open in my direction. This is the first time I've come in contact with them. They have a blank look on their faces, mouths quaking, bodies shaking, paralyzed in fear. They're terrified at the mere sight of me. The only one who reacts is the bear man. I look at him as he holds his lantern up high. I don't know what to say, so I blurt out the first thing that comes to my mind.

"You speak human," I say.

"Who are you?" he asks me, voice shaking. "Are you the ones who are trying to kill us?"

"No," I say calmly. "I'm just here to talk. We got your message."

"Message? What are you talking about?" the bear halfkind asks. He looks genuinely confused. This is the first time he's heard about the note.

"Your message, the note you left on my hovercar," I clarify. "You said you wanted to talk, well here I am, so let's talk."

"Talk? Note? I don't know what you're saying. Is this a trick?"

I observe his expressions. Something is going through his mind. It causes him to be in a state of both surprise and shock. He's realized things have gone terribly wrong and his bewilderment shows all over his face.

"You don't know what I'm talking about?" I ask him.

"I... I..." he doesn't respond coherently. I look at the other three, still frozen with fear. I don't see threatening items near them. No guns, no weapons, just some open food containers and back packs filled with items. These ones are different from the ones we encountered so far. The first two were prepared to fight. One attacked that detective with a knife, the other carried a bomb. But I see nothing to suggest that these halfkinds are battle ready.

"Listen," I say. "Even if you weren't the one who sent out the invitation, I'm just here to talk. I'm not here to hurt you. Why don't we sit down and we can discuss what…"

Suddenly, I hear a shouting from my communicator followed by a charging sound.

"One of them has a gun!" It's Borton.

"What?" I say perplexed. "No, stand down, Borton, I don't see any…"

But it's too late. Seconds haven't even passed and a shot has been fired. It's aimed at the halfkinds but misses. It hits one of the lanterns and the impact creates a large flash that blinds me. My eyes feel like they're engulfed in flames and my eyelids tense up as I close them. I hear a screaming and the sound of footsteps running away from me.

"Borton, back off! Stand down," I yell sightlessly.

"No, they're armed. They were about to fire at you!" he yells back. My vision slowly recovers, but I'm still dazed from the flash of the lantern.

"Damnit, Borton!" I yell. "I told you not to shoot."

"And I'm telling you they're armed. They scampered off to the right, while you were down, and are holed up behind those blackjack tables and slot machines," he says. "I'm going to take them out."

"No Borton, stay here!"

It's too late. I can see him chase after them in the haze of my eyes. In a few seconds things went from peaceful to chaotic and I'm stuck on one knee wondering how this mission has failed so horribly.

Chapter 18 – Oscar Lawton

Ambush

<u>November 17, 3040 1:00 AM</u>
"Hello?!" I shout at the darkness. "Who's there?"

A few minutes ago, we were dozing off and now I stand here fearing for my life. Someone has entered through the front door. I heard the creaking noise moments ago, but it's too dark to see anything. I have a lantern in my hand. However, the surrounding slot machines and tables block any visibility.

I hear some whispering, but it's too soft to be audible. It sounds like the intruder is having a full conversation with someone. Is there more than one trespasser? Who is he talking too?

I don't have much time to ponder, though. Someone steps out of the shadows and into my light. It's a human, tall, medium build, but toned. He's wearing tactical gear. This is one of the men who have been on our trail. I'm sure this group is responsible for killing Leonard and Lombardi. A sudden weakness overcomes my body. The fear has set in and I begin to wonder if this is the end for me and my siblings.

The human himself looks a bit flabbergasted. This is the first time any of us have come face to face with our pursuers. I'm sure he already had an idea of what I looked like, but seeing it in the flesh probably blows his mind. After all, we aren't the norm. We're the freaks. Judging by the way he looks, he's thinking the same thing.

We both stand in awkward silence, unsure of what to do. Finally, he says something to break the tension. "You speak human."

His manner surprises me. I didn't expect him to ask so calmly. I, on the other hand, don't have time for idle chit chat and cut straight to the chase.

"Who are you?" I ask, voice shaking. "Are you the ones who are trying to kill us?"

"No," he says again in that relaxed tone. "I'm here to talk. We got your message."

"Message? What are you talking about?" I don't understand. I never sent a message, and neither did the twins or Maddie. They had been with me the whole time and we hadn't encountered anyone on our way here.

"Your message, the note you left on my hovercar," he says. "You said you wanted to talk, well, here I am, so let's talk."

Hovercar? Note? What the hell is this gibberish? Perhaps it's some kind of trick, because I certainly didn't want to meet with him, I just wanted to stay hidden. There's no way anyone should know where we are. I was very careful on our way here, making sure not a piece of evidence was left behind. In fact, the only people who knew where we were was…

….no, it can't be… it can't… can it? He wouldn't have. He couldn't. But then I think about it, our history and arguments. Clashes flash before my eyes and I realize… he did.

"You don't know what I'm talking about?" the human asks me, breaking my thoughts.

"I… I…" I'm at a loss for words. The revelation that my own brother probably sold me and my siblings out causes my brain to overload. I can't fathom the reasoning for it. Why did he betray us? What purpose does this action serve? Is he so callous that he would sacrifice us, like pawns in his master plan? Does he feel nothing for his family?

"Listen," the human continues say. "Even if you weren't the one who sent out the invitation, I'm just here to talk. I'm not here to hurt you. Why don't we sit down and we can discuss what…"

Suddenly, I hear something scurrying in our direction behind me.

"One of them has a gun!" a voice yells. He lies. We have no weapons.

"What?" I hear the human say. He continues speaking but his words are unclear. The noise from behind masks his voice.

I hear a sharp whizzing noise and a bright flash hits my eyes. Something has exploded and I hear Maddie let out a shrill wail. Whoever is behind us has fired a shot and it nearly hit her. Luckily, it missed and she is uninjured. The only thing that is damaged is one of our lanterns, which has been blasted to smithereens.

The chaos is actually a blessing in disguise, it's the perfect distraction. I look at the human and he's blinded by the flash, so I quickly signal to the others and we bolt to the other side of the casino. We sprint rapidly and find shelter behind a long stretch of broken down slot machines.

I peer through the cracks and see what we're up against. Other than the human, who still appears to be disoriented, there's also a dog and a pig. The dog has run to the human's aid, but the pig continues to rush our way. If I don't act fast, he'll be here in a few seconds. I see a rusted steel chair nearby and throw it in his direction. It flies up in the air and arcs its way down, right onto his head. He tumbles over his own footing and comes crashing into a table, causing it to flip to its side.

"Damnit!" I hear the pig say as he writhes in pain. "Assholes hit me right on the head! I'm taking cover."

He slowly stumbles behind the table that had overturned and sits. The human seems to be okay now, and he and the dog rush to the pig's location. He gets a nearby blackjack table and pushes it to its side, hiding behind it.

I hear some mumbling and arguments from behind their table, but I can't understand what they're saying.

"Why are they attacking us, we didn't even do anything!" Maddie asks in a frightened tone.

"One of them thinks we have a gun," Isaac says.

"Did that pig say we shot at him? I couldn't hear anything," Iris responds.

"I don't know what they're talking about, I was totally still while that guy was talking to you, Oscar," Maddie says.

"Shh, quiet!" I whisper.

We don't have time to sort things out. I hear the sound of metal clinking in succession and then it stops. From behind the slot machines, I see a small silver orb a few feet from us. It beeps and I am generally perplexed.

In the blink of an eye, smoke sprays out of it. We all start to cough violently, and scatter away to get ourselves to clean air. Maddie and the twins scramble to the right, I run doggedly to the left.

As soon as I am clear from the haze, I feel something blow by my head, like a swift wind. I then feel another, as I continue to run forward. I look behind me and see things getting knocked down. Cups and chairs are shattered right before my eyes. Small holes explode from the wall in eruptions of cheap wood and dry paint. From the corner of my vision, I see a large column, big enough to cover me. I make a straight line for it while things continue to fly left and right. Through perseverance and fear, I make it to my destination.

The opposite side of the column starts to blast away, debris flies all over the place.

"Borton, that's enough!" I hear the human say, and the shooting stops. "They're not firing back. I don't think they have any weapons. Go check on the others, Apollo, and I will get the big one."

I take a quick look at my siblings. They're holed up at the bar. I can see them from my angle, hiding behind the counter as the pig approaches him. He has guns on both sides of his body. My brother and sisters hear him, step by step by step. They are petrified. If I don't do something quick, they'll be killed.

I look at Maddie. She's shivering, crying hysterically with the panic and dread. She looks the same way she did when we were kids, when Tiago and his crew bullied her. I was the one who got her in this mess, it's time for me to get her out of it.

I step out from behind the column and have my arms spread open.

"Don't shoot!" I say. "I don't have anything on me."

The pig looks over, but his body and guns are still pointed at my brother and sisters. The human points his weapon straight at me and takes a long glance.

"He's telling the truth. I don't see anything on him. Where were these guns you were talking about Borton?" he says angrily. "They're obviously unarmed, not a single shot has been fired from their side."

The pig remains silent, but doesn't show any remorse for his lie. The human puts his gun down and stows it in a holster on the side of his pants. I continue to walk forward slowly with my arms in the air.

"I give up," I say. "Take me in."

He approaches, takes out a metal stick, and presses a button on it. An orange glow shines and from the ends, two short beams uncoil like a snake. I've seen them before, they're energy cuffs, concentrated light that is flexible, strong, and near impossible to break.

I put my arms together and present them to the human. He grabs one, but before he can get the cuffs on, I knock his hand away. The force of my swing causes the device to fly to the other side of the room. He looks a bit surprised, but the minute I stick my hand toward his waist, he knows what I'm trying to do.

His gun is so close to my reach, I can practically feel my fingers touch it, but before I can make contact, I feel something, like a mallet, hit my face. It's the human's fist.

"He's going after my gun!" he yells at his teammates.

"Just shoot him already!" the pig yells.

"No, I want him alive!" he fires back. He quickly unholsters his gun and tosses it to the dog. "Keep this away from him. I can take him down myself."

I'm still a little staggered from his first blow, but I recover to my feet. I have claws and a huge size advantage, but my fighting skills are less than impressive. I throw a wild swing at his head, but he reflexively ducks under it and strikes a blow to my stomach. I crouch over in pain, but before I can even clutch it, his knee hits the front of my face. It feels like a brick and I am certain my nose is broken.

I wobble backwards and land on my ass. I put my hands over my nose to try and contain the bleeding. My stomach is in agony, my face is soft and tender, probably bruised beyond belief. But even as I'm wrought with pain, I look at my family, who have now emerged from their hiding place to watch my moment of heroism. I can't let them down.

A second wind comes over me and I lunge at the human. He thought I was down for the count and I catch him by surprise. I collapse over him. My whole body covers his head, and I can feel him struggle to breathe below me. I use my weight to my advantage and attempt to smother him. He violently moves his arms and legs to try to get me off, but it is useless. I actually might win this fight!

"Ouch, goddamnit!" I yell. Right there and then, I feel a sharp pain pierce through my leg like a dagger. Pieces of flesh and delicate tendons are being torn into and it is excruciating. "What the hell?!"

I look behind me and see that the dog has a firm grip on my heel with his jaws. He crunches down on them hard and I start to experience the muscle getting ripped from my bones.

It is too much for me to take, so I turn around and try to kick him away. But in my attempt to shoo the dog, I lose my position and the human speedily recovers. My back is turned to him and he instantly wraps his arms around my neck.

The dog lets go of his grasp and says, "Stun mode."

A baton protrudes from his helmet and I see an electric spark shoot out. I feel a sting on my chest and things quickly turn black. I'm out cold.

Minutes later, my consciousness sluggishly blurs back into place. Feeling to my legs and arms returns. I'm sitting down in a squatted position, but I can't move. Something is holding them down. I struggle to try and get free, but no matter how hard I try, my attempts end in failure.

I see the human in front of me. My brothers and sisters are now exposed from their cover and they're on their knees. The pig still has his guns pointed at them.

"What happened?" I ask the human.

"Apollo stunned you," he says. "It was the only way we could bring you down. You almost had me when you tried to go for my gun. Good thing he was there to save me."

Beaten and bloody, restraints tying my hands behind my back and my legs to the ground, I am exhausted and defeated. We have lost.

"What's your name?" I ask the human.

He looks at me curiously. "Simon."

"I'm Oscar, but you probably know that already," I say lethargically.

"I'm afraid I do. I have information on all of you."

"So that was you the other morning snooping around our home? We saw your science division investigating."

"Well, not me exactly, but yes, it was an order by the United Species Alliance to investigate your house."

"They still there?"

"Not anymore," he says as he shakes his head, "they're done with their job, we already have all the information we need."

"How'd you find it in the first place?" The pace of my voice is slow as I continue to catch my breath.

"A local detective ran into one of your guys. Your frog-like brother."

"Leonard..." I look around and the realization of how screwed we are hits me hard. "Why don't you just kill us already?"

"I told you, we aren't here to kill you," he tells me.

"But you killed my brothers. Leonard, Lombardi, they were both murdered by you."

"Leonard was killed by the detective I mentioned. It was out of self-defense, your brother attacked him first. Lombardi threw an explosive at two of my team members. They thought he was dangerous."

I knew that bomb was nothing but trouble. I start to breathe hard, as the adrenaline wears off and the pain starts to make its presence known.

"Still," I say. "They're both dead."

"It wasn't by me," the human says.

"Well, that is the plan. Are you going to kill us all eventually?" I ask.

"Those are the orders I've been given, but it's not my plan," he says dryly. "I need some information from you."

"Information?" I pause to think about how I'm going to respond. "Can you do me a favor? Can we speak quietly? I don't want my siblings to hear."

"Sure," he says in a softer tone.

"What kind of information?" I whisper.

"There are only four of you here. We were expecting nine. I have another team looking for the rest of your family. Anything that could be useful for my squad would only make things easier for you."

"Easier for me? Like how?"

"For starters, I'll make sure that none of you will die."

His offer is tempting, but after what I've been through I'm not sure if I can trust him.

"Even if you're not lying, why would I help you?" I ask. "Why would I betray my family?"

"Because from the expression on your face earlier, it looks like they already did it to you," he says bluntly. "I saw how you reacted when I told you about the supposed meeting. The shock on your face meant only one thing, you didn't set it up. And no one else on this planet knows of your existence, let alone where you're hiding. No one else except your own kind."

I look down at the ground in shame. He's right, my own brother sold us out.

"Don't you want to get back at him? Don't you want to help us?" he asks me.

I glance at the twins and Maddie. They're still being held up by the pig. They look tired and drained. This is his fault. We wouldn't be in this mess if it wasn't for him. He ruined everything for us and if anyone deserves to get what's coming, it's him. He's my brother, but I want him dead for this.

Yet, I think about what has gone through my head. Am I thinking clearly? Have I changed as well? Before all of this, I would never even see myself capable of having these thoughts. If I help our enemies, rat him out, I would be just like him.

"I'm sorry, sir, but I'm not like my brother," I say. "I will not help you."

He looks disappointed to say the least, but he's not angry. "I understand."

"What happens to us now?"

"You're going to be put under custody while we figure out what to do. I'll need to consult my team and construct our plan."

And just like that, grand visions of us living freely have been dissolved in front of my very eyes. The end came so swiftly. I am the fool who couldn't see the obvious, even when it was right in front of me.

Some leader I turned out to be.

Chapter 19 – Curtis Lawton

Deserter

<u>November 16, 3040 11:45 PM</u>

I'm almost at the Gonzalez station, I'll probably be there in fifteen minutes at the latest. My walk here has been uneventful. Primm isn't Las Vegas, it's a dead city. You would think that around midnight there'd be people walking the streets, partying their lives away, but not here. It's not exactly safe after the sunset and the only creatures that would be up would be the shady ones. You know, the types that would be into interspecies intercourse.

I guess I should be grateful. If it wasn't for those losers, I wouldn't be here. Or maybe I shouldn't. They've cursed me to this existence. If I found out who my father is, these claws and teeth would see some action. I'd follow Tiago's advice and use the gifts given to me.

My mother's a different story. I would never lay a finger on her. Just like I would do anything to protect my family, my mother is the same. It's too bad she died. There's been a lot of controversy over what happened to Leonard. Though my brothers and sisters are sad that he died, the overall feeling I get is that they don't understand why he did it. Why go back home and risk everything for someone who's already dead?

I get it, though. She was the one who raised us, our blood. She sacrificed so much to help us get a taste of a normal life when we should never have been afforded such luxury. We did nothing to repay her, to show our respects. It's too bad.

The others can't read me well, they're too scared to look me in the eyes. But if they did, they would have seen that I was ashamed to call myself her son. I already was ashamed of my own existence, but at least I knew someone loved me. My brothers and sisters may have been afraid of me, even Tiago to a degree, but my mother was not. She saw me as her boy. I wasn't coddled by her like Leonard was, I didn't need it. But I did love her just as much.

I'm so misunderstood by my family. Because I run with Tiago, they think I have the same opinions as he does about mother. They think that I hate her like Tiago does. I do not. I would've gladly done what Leonard did when he decided to leave. I'd be killing two birds with one stone, giving mother the proper send-off she deserved and getting the send-off I wanted. If only I had thought of it first. Poor Leonard.

Candy has given me a route that I can safely take. It's simple enough and runs through an undeveloped part of town. It seems there are a lot of those in Primm. If I stay on her track, I should encounter nothing. There are some street lights here and there, but I make sure to avoid them.

My path isn't a street, but rather a dirt track that used to be a train line when those things existed. The tracks are buried deep beneath the ground. It's impossible to grow anything on this soil, so the walk is quiet and abandoned. It makes me feel alone. My mind drifts to the dark side. I think of the suicide that should've happened, the years of feeling like an outcast. I was going to be rid of my pain forever, but my brother intervened. I wonder why I took this job for Tiago when

I wanted to end things on my terms. How did I get sucked into one of his schemes?

I guess it's because I feel I owe it to my family. What I'm doing will help protect them from these bastards who are chasing us. It could help get them off our tail completely. Just the thought that they'll be left alone gives me a shred of happiness in an otherwise chronically depressed mind.

But then I think about whom exactly I am protecting. Tiago is the one who hatched this plan. Is it just for him? Oscar isn't with him, only Tiago's cronies are. I'm not even sure if Tiago cares about Oscar. But when I think about the plan that Tiago has outlined for me, I can't see how it wouldn't help everyone. Even if Tiago is only looking out for himself, what I am going to do isn't just for him. Getting rid of these agents will surely benefit us all.

I was going to end it all a few nights ago, but it seems my contract with our maker has been extended. If living on this God forsaken planet for a few more days will help my family, sign me up. I'm in.

There aren't many things to look at on this deserted road, but there's a nice view of the Vegas lights. It's so bright. They're twenty miles away, but the neon signs illuminate the sky giving it a rainbow of hues. Beams shoot into the air, the result of the spectacles the different hotels offer. Some of the lodgings tower so high above the skyline that even from my position, I have to tilt my head up to see where it ends. It seems to stretch more than a mile into the atmosphere. Hovercars zoom around the landscape like bees in a hive. I wonder what it's like to live that kind of life. Must be great.

The view itself impresses me. It's nice. I don't think I've ever had the chance to see it. Our house was facing the opposite direction, so live images like these were a rarity. The only way I could see something like this was if I snuck around and I didn't do that often. I'm not exactly the stealthy type.

Looking at this beauty depresses me further. I know this is the closest I'll ever be to experiencing that kind of life. Imagine me walking around Vegas. The gamblers and hedonists would no doubt run in terror. I'd be spending the whole time dodging gunfire. It'll be like what we're doing now, on the run, except in tenfold.

"Spare some creds?" a gravelly voice says behind me. I look to where it came from and I see a homeless lion sleeping on a cardboard bed. His mane is grimy and dirty, his fur stringy and greasy. He looks malnourished or hung over, maybe both. He's wearing tattered clothing and has a chewed out hat to his side. It appears to be a military cap.

"Um, sorry," I say discreetly. "I don't have any."

"It's okay, brother. Didn't expect anyone to be walking around here anyway. Sorry if I caught you by surprise."

"Uh, no problem."

I realize this is the first time I've talked to someone from the outside world. I'm nervous, I don't really know what to say. I've never talked to any creature other than my own family members and I could barely keep a conversation with them. Now I am talking to someone who is part of that world I learned to fear. I'm terrified, yet curious at the same time.

I'm actually surprised he hasn't run for the hills yet. But I look at him, eyes half open, laying in the light. On the other hand, I am concealed by a veil of shadows. I'm also covered from head to toe in clothing. Hood, thick sweater, pants, I'm wearing anything to hide my identity.

It must be hard for him to see what I am. I feel a little relieved.

"What are you doing out here, anyway?" he inquires. "Seems kind of late for someone to be around this part of the neighborhood."

"I was just, um, going for a late night walk," I say. He talks slow and slurs a bit. He sounds like he's under the influence of something, but I'm not familiar with what substances are out there. I'm hopeful that my answers won't trigger any suspicions, but in his state, it would be hard to recognize if anything is off. His awareness has gone out the window.

This is a rare opportunity. I can actually interact with another being consequence free and my curiosity gets the best of me. I wonder what this lion has to say.

"What are you doing out so late?" I ask him.

He gives a yawn and licks his snout area. He uses his paws to scratch the top of his head.

"I'm running," he says. "I've been on the run for a while."

"Running?" I say. "From what?"

He looks at me oddly and peers straight at me. I get a little nervous, unsure if what I said has tipped him off. I don't think he can see anything, though, it's too dark and I'm too covered. After a few moments of piercing glances, he lowers his head down and looks at his hat.

"You speak human," I say.

"Of course," he says. "All military members, human, wolves, lions, learn all the languages. In a human city like this, it comes in handy."

He bites his hat and flings it my way.

"You see this hat?" he says. "I was a soldier in the conflict."

"Conflict?" I say.

"Geez man, where have you been? The conflict!"

He raises his voice as if something I said angers him. I step back cautiously and he notices.

"Sorry, pal," he says. "I didn't mean to get testy. I just haven't had a good drink for a while. Anyways, the conflict, you know, the Lion-Gorilla War?"

I'm vaguely familiar with what he's talking about. I wish I had paid more attention to current events.

"So, you're fighting in that war?" I ask him.

"Was fighting. I left about a year ago, went AWOL," he says. "Somehow I ended up in Vegas and blew my creds away. Now I'm stuck in this goddamn city trying to get whatever I can."

"AWOL? You mean you left the war without permission?"

"No shit."

"Why'd you leave?"

"I got scared, pal."

He shakes his head and pauses. He looks at the ground and moves his head up and down in a dazed fashion.

"Yeah, I got scared," he said. "Got drafted into it when the gorillas started their attacks. They came to my house, threw me a uniform, and shipped me off. I didn't even have time to say goodbye to my family. You know what that's like?"

"I think I do," I say.

"Basic training wasn't so bad. Got some good food there, learned some cool shit, and made some good friends. In fact, I trained with my company from the start. Those guys are like my brothers. We even made a pact to make it out alive, through thick and thin."

"Brothers? So you were part of a team?"

"I was part of a team, but I ain't anymore."

For a brief moment, he snaps out of his dazed behavior and has a moment of clarity. Talking about his team triggers something in him.

"So, what happened to your team?" I ask.

"I... I left them," he said.

"You left them? How?"

"I snuck away. I didn't even go and fight. I got scared. During training, they showed us movies to prep us up. I saw videos of the war, lions getting their heads blown off from all sorts of weapons I didn't even know existed. I wasn't ready for it, I would never be. I'm no fighter, I wouldn't survive one day out there. I left the training grounds and took the first teleporter I could away before they could shipped me off to battle. Never fought a gorilla in my life."

"What happened to your friends?"

"What about them?"

"You said they were your brothers, your family, you left them?"

"Of course I did. I wasn't going to die because of some silly pact."

"Wow, you really have no honor then. I guess the outside world really is a shitty place."

"What the hell are you talking about?" he says as his voice rises.

"You ran off. You're afraid of death," I say.

"Yeah, whatever, like you aren't."

"I'm not afraid of death, I welcome it. I welcome it so much that I invite it in so that it can take my place instead of the people I love. How could you leave the lions you call your brothers to die alone?"

The lion stands up. He shakes his head and inches closer to me. My face is still obscured, but if he keeps at it he'll know what I am.

"Don't talk to me, you shit," he says. "Try and judge me about how I shouldn't leave. What the fuck do you know about family and courage?!"

"I know more than you'll ever know!" I yell. It catches him off guard and scares him. He steps back but maintains his ground.

"You don't know jack shit about me," he says defiantly.

"I don't need to," I say. "I know that you left your family behind right before they needed you most. You made a pact with each other and you broke it. They could be dead and your promise meant nothing. You aren't their family, you're a nobody."

"Shut up! I'd do anything for those guys. I mean it when I call them my brothers. I got scared. I was thinking and thinking and thinking, and my nerves got the best of me okay?"

"Yeah, sure. You did a lot of thinking, but it was only about yourself. You are a coward."

"Hey, fuck you!"

His curse echoes faintly through the sky.

"So what if I left them?" he says. "We're all in in it for ourselves, pal. You think they give two shits about me? Show me one creature who wouldn't do the same thing I did!"

I step from the shadows and take off my hood. My face and body are now clearly visible to him. I tower over him like an ant, my hands protrude from my sleeves and my claws stick out. I give him a demented smile to make sure he sees my razor sharp teeth.

He looks at me with utter terror in his eyes. His face shakes and he steps back slowly, but with each step he walks faster, and faster, and faster, until he's far enough to sprint away. I stare at him until he is out of my view completely.

"Just as I thought," I say to myself. I put my hood back on and continue on my path. It should only take me a few more minutes until I'm there.

Chapter 20 – Apollo Bradley

Spared

November 17, 3040 1:16 AM

The bear halfkind, Oscar, looks like he has thrown in the towel. I can tell from his body language he knows his fight is over. Commander Trevor has made it clear that he, his brothers, and sisters are to remain alive. Simon has always followed an admirable code of conduct and this order doesn't surprise me. After all, how right would it be to murder a defenseless group of creatures, especially after they had already surrendered?

"Hey, can I ask you a question?" A disheveled Oscar asks Commander Trevor.

"Sure, what is it?" he responds.

"How come…" But he never finishes the question. I hear a shrill pop and I instantaneously see his body jerk back fiercely. Small flecks of red fly from his skull. And then, his head slumps down and his body slouches.

"What the hell happened?!" Commander Trevor yells. "Apollo, get over there and check his vitals!!"

"Got it!"

I dash to him and call for my bioscanner. A sensor emits from my helmet and scans his body. When it's done, a holographic screen pops open with the results and I hurriedly review them. I am hopeful for the best, but the output doesn't lie.

"He's dead," I tell Commander Trevor.

A loud bawling erupts from the mouth of the cow halfkind, Maddie Lawton, and echoes throughout the casino. She falls to her knees and uncontrollably weeps in despair.

The two cat halfkinds, Iris and Isaac Lawton, don't whisper a peep. They look too shaken by the events to even emit a reaction.

"What happened, what happened?!" Commander Trevor yells demandingly.

"The scanner says it's a fatality via gunshot wound to the head," I say.

"Borton…" the Commander says grudgingly. We both look at the suspected murderer. "It was you!"

His gun is smoking from the plasma it has fired. He stands defiantly tall, in a firm position. He doesn't even bat a lash at Maddie Lawton who continues to sob wildly. His eyes narrow and his face sneers with disgust.

"I did what you couldn't, Commander."

"What I couldn't?" Commander Trevor asks angrily. "You disobeyed an order! I specifically said no one was to die!"

"I disobeyed your order," Borton says. "But I followed the orders given to me. Hunt and kill, remember?"

"Those weren't my instructions!"

"I don't care about your instructions. I only care about my superiors and that's not you. You're just my teammate."

"He's our commander," I snap back. "You have to report to him. What you did could get you discharged from the mission."

Borton looks at me smugly. "Fine, go ahead, tell on me, you suck up. But what are you going to do, really? Try to get me in trouble for subordination? I was doing what the United Species Alliance asked me to do. You really think they're going to side against me in this argument? I did them a favor."

Commander Trevor kicks a chair in frustration. It falls and slides across the floor. "What you did was cold blooded murder!"

"What I did was my job," Borton responds.

"But, he was about to say something," I interject. "He could have given us valuable information."

"He wasn't going to give us jack shit," Borton says bluntly. "Even if we tortured the poor bastard, I doubt he would've talked."

"It wasn't your call!" Simon yells. He walks away in disgust, hands on his head and paces around to cool his temper. Borton looks at him apathetically, while I observe the situation. I'm still appalled by what has gone down.

I can't believe Borton disobeyed the Commander. I'm even more surprised that he killed Oscar so callously. I know we were given orders by the Alliance, but I agree with Commander Trevor. They were restrained, we had the situation under control. It was wrong to fire on Oscar. I don't believe Borton's whole 'I'm carrying out my duty' shtick. He executed someone.

"Why are you so determined to kill them?" I ask Borton. "It seems that's more important to you than following orders."

He looks at me suspiciously. "None of your business, dog."

"There is something else then? I believe you have a hidden agenda."

Borton looks even angrier than before. "You can believe what you want to believe, but I'm not talking."

"Or… firing mode," I say. A gun barrel protrudes from my helmet. "You can tell me why you want them dead."

Borton suddenly looks afraid and yells, "Commander, are you seeing this? Tell him to put his weapon away!"

Simon looks at me and shrugs. "Proceed, Apollo. I'd be worried about him. Unlike you, Borton, he's good at following orders."

I shoot him a smile and then shift my focus back to Borton. "So, tell us!"

I see sweat trickle down his brow.

"All right, all right! I did it because I don't get my fee unless the mission is fulfilled!" he blurts out. "If there are any left alive, then this mission isn't fulfilled, is it?!"

"That's what this is about, getting paid?" I ask irately. I put my weapon from firing mode back to safe mode.

"That's what it's always about," Borton says. "Don't tell me you don't get any compensation for these jobs."

I stare at him blankly.

"Wow, you dogs really do get taken for a ride. Guess the whole 'man's best dope' stereotype is true," he says.

"And I guess you pigs get the reputation you deserve," I reply. "Greedy bastard."

"Watch it, dog," he warns me.

"So that's all you are, Borton?" Commander Trevor says, "Just a hired gun?"

"Don't do that," Borton retorts back. "You both act like you're better than me, because you hide behind that veil of your honorable service. But when it comes down to it, you're no different. I'm just smart enough to make some credits off of it."

"Whatever, you're a low life mercenary," I say.

"I don't care what you think, brownnoser," he shoots back.

"Enough!" Commander Trevor says with a raised voice. He pauses to collect his thoughts. "I'm not going to judge your motivations, Borton, but your actions defied my direct commands and I won't stand for that. From now on, you will listen to me at all times. If you're worried about the Alliance, don't be. You should be worrying about me first. And, you will treat your squad mates with respect. If you continue to have this attitude, if you fail to follow one more order given by me, I'll have you off this team in a heartbeat. You can practically kiss that paycheck good bye."

Borton looks at him cautiously. He's trying to determine if he should call Simon's bluff.

"All right, Commander," he says. "You win. No more renegade actions."

"Good. You can make up for what you did by cuffing the others. If I see you harm a single hair on them, you're done."

"Yeah, yeah," he says dismissively.

As Borton approaches the rest of the family, I notice something odd about Maddie Lawton. She's no longer weeping, but what's strange is that it happened so suddenly. A few minutes ago, she was crying her brains out and now she's as quiet as can be. She might have calmed down when the three of us were arguing, but I'm not sure.

Her facial expression is even more peculiar. Her eyes are bugged out and her head is shaking. She's on one knee and her hands, which are very human like, are placed firmly on the ground, like tree trunks. Her posture is intense.

That's when I notice an item in her hand. It's rusted, long and narrow, like a stick. I take a closer glance and realize it's a piece of debris that resulted from our assault. She grips it tightly, but I'm unsure why she has it.

If I had more time to analyze the situation, I would've realized what she was about to do. But because we spent so many minutes arguing, I didn't keep track of her movements. It is now that I realize what she is planning and I only have a few seconds to react. But I am too slow.

Borton is only a few feet away from her. In a savage moment, she jumps towards him, rod clutched tightly with both hands, and jams it straight into an exposed area on his neck. He is caught off guard and probably doesn't even know what hit him until after the metal stick is already lodged in his head. He squeals out and falls to the ground, rolling in agonizing pain. Blood spews out of his neck like a water fountain on a hot summer day.

Maddie still has her hands grasped on the rod and her attention turns to the Commander. She starts to lunge at him the same way she did at Borton, but before she makes it to another victim, I say "Fire!"

A shot from my helmet goes careening out of the barrel and makes its way directly to her head. It knocks her off her feet and blood flies across the room on impact. Her body lands hard on the ground and ends up in a contorted position. Now two halfkinds are dead.

"Are you okay Commander?" I ask him.

He ignores everything and rushes to Borton. He's still squirming on the floor, flopping around like a fish out of water. I hurry over to see if I can help.

Commander Trevor uses his hand to cover the wound and tries to contain Borton, but it's difficult because he's moving around too much. Simon's palms are painted a crimson red and more blood flows everywhere. The red liquid seeps through his fingers and a pool starts to form under Borton.

"Apollo, I'll take care of Borton, go restrain the others," Simon says.

But when I look to where they are, something horrifies me - they're not there.

"Commander, the twins are gone!" I yell.

"Shit!" Simon screams. "What else can go wrong? Apollo, there's no way they could've gone far. You need to find and capture them at all costs. Use whatever tools you have at your disposal, just get it done. I'll stay here and try to treat Borton's wounds."

I look at Borton. His screaming is fading by the seconds, his skin has turned pale. He's already lost a lot of blood and I literally see life draining from his dead eyes.

"Um, Commander," I say trying to make him see the obvious.

"Just go!" he yells.

That's my cue. I equip my scent booster and sniff the area. Within a few seconds, I have a lock on their trail and follow it. It leads me out the back door and into the alley from which Borton and I had entered. I look around and see no signs of them.

The night sky colors the streets with a shade of orange and the only noise I hear is that of the wind blowing on an empty street.

I continue to sniff their trail methodically, making sure not one footstep goes unnoticed. It goes for ten feet, then another ten, and then another. With each stride I feel like I'm getting closer and closer.

But suddenly something unexpected happens - the scent turns cold. I can't smell them anymore. It appears they have disappeared into thin air. I'm confused at first, I don't understand how this could've happened. Then I realize the feeling of the ground has changed from the gripped surface of pavement to the smooth, slipperiness of metal. I'm standing on top of a manhole cover, a remnant of the once glorious sewer system humans were so dependent on. I'm sure this is where the twins escaped to.

There's only one problem, I can't open it. My paws can't lift the metal enclosure. Not to worry, my suit has grappling hooks in case of situations where opposable thumbs are needed. I fire them and they latch on to the small holes of the lid. I then retract the wire and the manhole cover slides open.

It's dark down there, so I say, "flashlight." A white stream of light comes from my helmet and I look down. I'm worried the drop will be huge, but, after I shine the light, I see it's only about ten feet deep.

I gracefully hop down and smell a foul odor. The sewers haven't been used in some time, but their stench still remains. It's too much for my nose to handle, so I unequip the booster and try to sniff out the twins' trail. It's faint, covered by the musk and lasting filth of the sewer, but it's still traceable.

The sewers are even more silent than the ground above. I hear a few droplets of water here and there, its impact on the floor timed out like a metronome. It's nearly pitch black down here, the only source of light is some dimly lighted bulbs, but my eyes are able to adjust.

I follow my nose for another hundred feet, when suddenly, the trail makes a sharp U-turn back the other way.

"That's odd," I say to myself, "Why is it going the other…"

I don't finish my thought. A flat, dizzying, throbbing sensation hits the back of my head like a wrecking ball. I hear a thunderous clang noise behind me. My vision takes a straight nose dive to the ground. The cloudiness of my consciousness makes it hard for me to piece together what has happened, but it comes to me - I've been struck a heavy blow to the back of my head.

I am paralyzed. I try to move my legs, but the slam has tired me and my perception is less than coherent. The only thing I can feel is a deep ache at my neck. All I see is a hazy picture from my eyes. Two blotches emerge into the fold. I hear discombobulated, but recognizable, speech coming from them.

"What... should we... do now... Isaac?" I hear one of them say in a distorted tone, slow in pace.

"We... should... kill him for... what they've... done," he says.

"But... he's... defenseless... right now...."

"So... was... Oscar..."

I'm breathing more heavily than before. I feel my awareness slipping from me into a cloud of grey. But I stay steady to hold on, even if it's just for a few more minutes, a few more seconds.

"No.... Isaac..." the voice responds. "It's...not... right...It wasn't.... his...fault... it was...the...pigs'."

"Sister... if we don't... kill him... now...he and... his team... will kill us... later..."

"Isaac, please.... don't...do it... please..."

I am a victim at his mercy and can only pray his sister's intervention is a success. A few moments later, I hear a clashing noise and see a metal pole drop to the ground.

"Fine... sister...we'll... do it... your way..."

After those words, the two shapes walk away. Their size gets smaller and smaller until they fade into small specks that I can't see anymore.

I take a few deep breaths, until my mind gives up and things fade into darkness.

Chapter 21 – Iris Lawton

Refuge

November 17, 3040 1:28 AM

"Now's our chance," Isaac says to me. We're still on our knees, but the dog and human are too busy tending to their injured comrade to even think about us.

"But what about the others?" I ask him. Maddie had attacked the pig and now she's dead. Oscar was shot without warning. My brother and sister were killed in front of my eyes and I was helpless to prevent their deaths. I look at their bodies, splashed with blood, twisted and deformed as they lie lifeless. I've lost so much these past days.

Isaac's voice interrupts my thinking. "If we don't move now, we'll be like them."

"But the human promised that we wouldn't be killed," I say.

"That promise might be broken if their teammate doesn't make it."

I look at the pig, screeching and thrashing in misery. Red liquid stains the floor and gushes out of his wound. Things don't look too good for him.

"I don't think he is," I respond.

"Then we have to go while they're distracted," he says. I nod my head. We both slyly get up in unison and lightly sprint to the back door. With all the noise and chaos happening, the two don't even notice us slip away to the exit

Isaac carefully opens the door, it smoothly glides open without a sound. He holds it for me and then with steady hands, like he's conducting surgery, he closes it.

The moment it's shut, we start to run. We don't really know where, we just know to get as far away as possible. The night light creates shadows of our rapidly moving bodies. They flicker on the ground like sunlight leaking through a windy field. Our scampering echoes through the barren streets, creating a cadence of hectic footsteps. Gusts of winds blow on our faces, it intensifies the adrenaline fueled rush of our escape.

For a few minutes, I feel invincible. We have fled from certain death, from a group of highly trained individuals. Nothing can catch us, we'll run forever. But then reality starts to set in: we're getting tired. My legs move slower, my breaths get heavier and heavier, and then Isaac and I have to stop.

We are under Primm's lights, tired and bent over. I realize that standing in plain sight will get us killed, but I'm too exhausted to care.

"We can't run forever," I say exasperatedly.

"Don't worry," he says. "No one is on our…"

Right on cue, we hear metal clang from behind us and run to a corner. I slowly peer out from behind and far, far away, I see the back entrance of the casino that we had departed from. Something is nudging its head out, sliding the door open with its body. The dog is on our trail.

"Isaac," I say worriedly, "the canine is after us."

"Shoot," Isaac says in a panic, "He's probably on our scent, he'll find us in no time."

"What do we do?"

Isaac looks around and tries to think of something on the spur of the moment. He looks downward and something catches his eye.

"I have an idea, sis," he says. "Follow me."

He walks to a metal grating on the ground and grasps it. He struggles as he pulls hard. Eventually, he's able to lift and slide it to the side. A putrid smell radiates from the opening. I look in and see a ladder leading to the darkness below.

"Are you sure about this?" I ask him. I'm ready to jump in, but the odor is a bit deterring.

"Got any better ideas? The dog will have a hard time finding us down there. If anything, the smell will help mask our scent," he says.

"Okay," I say reluctantly. I climb down the ladder first and Isaac follows. He slides the metal grating back over the hole to cover our tracks. After descending a few feet, I feel the ground and stand. It's hard to see anything, but my eyes gradually adjust to the dim lighting.

Isaac plops his feet on the ground and we look around to figure out where to go next. The tunnels seem to stretch on forever, so we just start walking in the dried, caked-out grime of the underground.

I can't believe we've been reduced to walking in the sewers. Things have changed so much in the past days. We went from hiding in refuge to having our family break apart to watching the execution of our brother and sister. And now we're running scared in the dreariest of places, a literal dog and cat chase.

I wonder how long we'll be doing this, what our next move will be. Isaac wonders the same thing.

"We can't be on the lam forever," he says. "Even if we lose the dog, this is not where I want to live the rest of my life. And with the United Species Alliance on our tails, we could be running a long, long time."

"We need a place to hide," I tell Isaac.

"So far, hiding hasn't worked out," Isaac says. "And if we do find a place, they'll catch up to us."

"There's nowhere for us to go," I say. "But you're right, there's nowhere on Earth that will keep us safe from the Alliance."

"Maybe there isn't a place on Earth that we'll be safe, but there is somewhere else. Do you know what I mean?" He asks the question, and I know his answer.

"Tiago," I say. "You want us to go with Tiago's plan."

"He's the only family we have left."

"But what about my visions? The slaughter, the gunfire, the death?"

"I don't know if they're always right. Why didn't your visions show what happened to Oscar? Or Maddie? Or us?"

I pause, not really knowing how to answer him. "You know that's not how it works, Isaac."

"Then how does it?"

"I don't know, it just does."

When we were young, things kind of came to me. I was able to see, on more than one occasion, what the weather would be on certain days, when arguments with family members would arise, where my brothers and sisters were when the others couldn't find them. I saw visions of future events.

I couldn't and still can't see everything, though. I didn't know mother was going to die or that we'd be on the run from the government. I didn't see that Lombardi or Leonard would be killed either, and I certainly didn't see that Oscar's plan would turn out the way it did. Things come at me randomly, but when they do, I'm never wrong.

I never could fully explain my powers to my brothers and sisters. Even I'm unsure what I'm capable of since it happens so infrequently. For the most part the others recognize that there's something special about me, especially Tiago and my twin.

I didn't see a lot when we were hiding, but once Tiago mentioned his plan to go to the Moon it came to me. His plan would end in disaster and those who went along would die. I personally had no qualms with his idea. On paper, I think it's a good plan and if anyone has the gall to try to attempt it, it's Tiago. But what I saw in my vision gave me chills.

Smoke rising, things exploding, a hail of gunfire, a bright light, and lots of dead relatives. No one made it to the moon, just to their graves.

After that, I was desperate to find a way out and when Oscar volunteered to leave, it was my opening. If I were to live, I needed to be as far away from Tiago as possible. I convinced Isaac it was the only way to survive, so he went with me. But now that Oscar is dead, he's questioning my abilities. He never really wanted to leave in the first place, it took a lot to persuade him.

"I still have that bad feeling about Tiago and his grand scheme," I say to Isaac worriedly.

"I know," he says, "but this isn't the weather or finding out where one of our brothers snuck off to, this isn't some trivial thing. This is life or death, this is for our survival, and I'm sorry to say, sister, but things are getting hot and heavy. I don't know if I want to risk our fate on your unpredictable guesses."

He breaks my heart. Isaac never questioned his faith in me before. He believes in the abilities I've been gifted. But then again, he's right. Maddie and Oscar died, we're getting chased, and I didn't infer anything suspicious.

Maybe I could detect the little things, but it seems that my knack for clairvoyance may be a liability in heavier situations.

"What about what that guy said, their leader?" I ask Isaac. "He mentioned something about a note, meeting and talking, and Oscar looked confused by his words. What do you suppose he meant?"

"I'm not sure. They were speaking quietly," he says. "I couldn't make out what they were talking about."

"Do you think Tiago had something to do with them showing up?"

Isaac scoffs at my suggestion. "Don't be ridiculous, sis. Why in the world would you say that?"

"I don't know, I mean, it's a possibility."

"Is this one of your senses?"

"No."

"Then don't even think about it. Sure Tiago and Oscar never got along, but he wouldn't tip off the law. I know Tiago's rough sometimes, but that's extreme."

"But he didn't like Maddie, either."

"But it's not just Oscar and Maddie, we were there too," Isaac says defensively. "You know Tiago has always had a soft spot for us, especially for you."

"That's true," I say. Tiago sees something in me. Whenever we talk, he says I understand things better than most. I'm unsure what he means because his words are always so cryptic, but, according to him, I'm special.

"At this point, Tiago and the others are the only ones we have left, everyone else is dead," Isaac says. "We have to go to him."

I'm still skeptical. "Are you sure he'll take us back? We did leave him, after all, and he didn't seem too happy about it."

"Once he knows that Oscar is dead, that we have nowhere else to go, I'm sure he will. He can't dump us out on the street."

"I...I suppose you're right," I say reluctantly. "You supported me when I wanted to leave, I'll support you now."

"Thanks, sister," he says smiling. "Okay, now that we have a plan let's get out of these tunnels and..."

The sound of dragging metal echoes throughout the sewers. Someone has opened the grating from which we entered.

"The dog is still on our case," I say with a hint of fear.

"Damn, he's good. Can't believe he followed us here," Isaac says. "With his skill, even the stench won't deter him from our trail. I have to think of something..."

He sees some metal pipes on the floor and races toward them. He picks two up, hands me one, and keeps the other for himself.

"Even if we try to out run him, his nose will know where we are," Isaac explains. "The only way we can stop him is if we take him out."

I look at Isaac hesitantly. "I've never fought anyone before."

"Don't worry, we'll sneak up on him. I'll create a fake trail that circles around and we'll obscure ourselves. Then, while he's figuring out our location, we'll jump him from behind."

"Then we make a run for it?" I ask him.

"Then we make a run for it. Follow me. We have to stay quiet."

We walk forward ten or twenty steps, then backwards. Isaac points to a small opening in the wall and motions me to go and hide there. He then finds another groove and places himself in it. And we wait.

I hear the dog's footsteps getting closer. He walks lightly, but even his delicate stride echoes throughout the tunnel. The sounds of his sniffs get more and more rapid as he traverses the ground.

He's only a few feet away. He's so close that I hear his uniform crunching and rubbing on itself as he moves toward us. And then, only a few paces to the right of me, he appears.

The dog is practically standing next to me, but away from Isaac. I look over to my brother and he motions me to strike my blow. I stare at the pipe in my hands, cold and heavy, and wonder if I have what it takes.

Isaac starts to motion more furiously than before. He wants me to make my move. The dog is already out of my striking distance and will soon reach the end of our trail and circle back. I have to hit him before he turns around and sees us.

I stalk him in the dark, staying graceful on my feet. I see him halt and I raise my weapon in the air.

But then he says something, and it catches me off guard. I stop in my movements, and the dog blurts out. "That's odd. Why is it going the other…"

I don't think, I just react, and bat a mighty swing at the back of his head. His neck flails up and he lets out a sharp yelp before falling to the ground like a ton of bricks.

Isaac emerges from the shadows as I look at the dog. He's not dead. In fact, he's not even knocked out. His eyes are still open, though it seems they are fighting hard to stay that way. They rapidly blink and look left and right, towards me and Isaac.

"What should we do now, Isaac?" I ask him.

His face narrows and starts to intensify. It glowers a frown.

"We should kill him for they've done," Isaac says, his voice shaking. He raises his pipe as if he's about to thrust it into the dog's battered head.

I'm surprised by my brother. I had not known him to be an angry person. Then again, we had just seen our brother and sister murdered before our very eyes. The thought of it fills me with rage.

But then I look at the dog. He's lying down, eyes hollowed out, and holding on to whatever consciousness he has left. He's so helpless.

"But he's defenseless right now," I say.

"So was Oscar," Isaac shoots back.

I remember when Maddie and Oscar were killed, the dog was the voice of reason. He was like the human, he didn't want us to die. It was the pig who fired the first shot, the pig that started this mess. After that, things got crazy, that's all. I'm sure he didn't want things to turn out this way, either.

"No Isaac," I say. "It's not right. It wasn't his fault, it was the pig's."

"Sister, if we don't kill him now, he and his team will kill us later."

Isaac might be right, but the human commander was adamant that we stay alive and so was this dog. Even if they find us eventually, I don't think he would do us in. If anything, sparing one of them might actually help us in the long run. They would see that we're not the monsters they think we are.

I just don't want anyone else to die. What's the point of all this killing? Four of us are dead, one of them is dead. Haven't enough lives been taken? Will killing this one help our cause? We can escape, we can run, but I don't want blood on my hands. It's not right.

"Isaac," I say as my eyes get watery, "please don't do it, please."

He looks at me on the verge of tears and starts to relent. He never could bear to see me cry.

Isaac drops the metal pipe and slumps his body down in disappointment. "Fine, sister, we'll do it your way."

We turn the other direction and start to walk, leaving the dog behind.

"We need to make it to Tiago as soon as we can," Isaac says, "but I'm not sure where to go. He's probably at the teleporter now, but it could be either of them."

Suddenly, an odd feeling hits my brain. It's sharp, but not painful, just unexpected. I stop in my footsteps and pause. My eyes widen open. One of my visions comes to me.

"They're at the Li station," I say.

Isaac had noticed my odd behavior. "Another one of your visions or whatever?"

I nod.

"Okay," he says. "I guess that's where we're going."

"So, now you trust my ability?"

"Little things, remember?"

As we walk away, I turn around to see the dog still on the ground. His eyes are closed, but he is still breathing. He must have passed out from my blow, but I am glad that Isaac didn't kill him.

"Thank you for listening to me, brother," I said.

"It wasn't an easy thing to do," he says. "I still think he shouldn't have lived."

"You sound like Tiago."

"And you sound like Oscar."

Things stay silent between us for a few moments.

"One day, sister," he says in a serious tone, "you'll realize that the world isn't always such a nice place, that you have to do what you have to do to survive."

"If I ever come to that realization, I don't think I'd like the person that I've become," I say.

Isaac looks at me unusually then looks back ahead. We don't say another word for the rest of our trek.

Chapter 22 – Fenrir Snow

Conflicted

November 17, 3040 2:34 AM

Almost an hour and half has passed and we still haven't gotten the call from Commander Trevor. I'm tired of waiting, I want to make our move now, I want to storm this teleportation station and end this mission.

We've already done plenty of recon. I've run circles around this building and didn't find anything suspicious. Erawan and Colbo remain at their posts on the opposite sides and have reported nothing. If there was someone here, they weren't outside, and they certainly didn't get past us. The only thing we have left to investigate is the station itself.

But no, the Commander has made it very clear that we are not to engage until he's done checking out the casino. I think this strategy is wasting my time. What information could he find in his meeting that would help us? He says he can get us numbers after he's done, scout who we're dealing with if he talks to them face to face, that we will be more prepared for what's coming if we take our time. That's fine if our targets were taking theirs, but they're not. Time is something they cannot afford and every moment we wait gives them more and more minutes on the clock.

I remember when we killed that bird halfkind, Lombardi. I could smell the desperation in the air and I didn't need my powers of scent to sense that.

Colbo treated the kill as if it was a trophy, another achievement on his list of accomplishments. He probably didn't sense what I was feeling. It wasn't pride, I don't feel that when I finish these missions. I never felt one ounce of happiness through all the things I've done for the Brotherhood of Wolves. I do it because they ask me to. It's what I owe my kind.

Yet, all those times, I didn't feel any remorse either. Every mission I've done, every task I've been assigned, I was okay with. Even when I killed creatures I didn't know, even when I saw the fear in their eyes, I never felt the burning sensation of guilt. I think.

And I've done a lot in the name of my brothers. I've tracked human supremacist groups who wish to take back the world that was never theirs in the first place. I've hunted lions who captured wolves and used them as slaves. I've ransacked shanty towns of dogs and cats who cooked up drugs. I've killed these beings without hesitation, without moral conscience. They deserved to die.

But this time, things are different. These halfkinds are on the run, scared and alone. They pose no real threat to society, they're a small group of misfits trying to live, yet we hunt them down like they're criminals. It's not right.

And why? Because we don't want another Ark Project to happen? We don't want another Event to occur? Because the humans can't create more of their precious toys? We want to make sure no more genetic mistakes are made. Yet my superiors fail to realize these mistakes turned us wolves into what we are now. The irony isn't lost on me.

When we killed Lombardi Lawton, Colbo approached me to get a gauge on how I was feeling. I didn't say anything or bat an eye his way. Instead, I walked away from the kill and said I was fine. But inside, I wasn't.

When I blasted that shot through his head and saw his charred body lay limp, a part of me mourned for my victim. It seemed wrong killing him. I'm not under orders from the Brotherhood of Wolves, I'm under orders from the United Species Alliance. To me, this is a human directive. I agreed to this mission because the Brotherhood asked me to, but they're being played like puppets. I vowed I would never take an order from a human unless it was completely necessary. This mission isn't necessary, yet here I am, a grunt under their command.

Why did I even take this task? I wondered that as I watched Lombardi Lawton's dead body, the end result of my success. Is my sense of loyalty so high that I'll do anything?

But I can't think this way. Now is not the time to crack. One second of weakness could get me killed. The bird man threw a bomb at us and if I didn't have my instincts, I could have been killed. As much as I sympathize with their plight, I'd rather be the one who comes out alive.

The more I think about that kill, the more I'm surprised they want to meet us at all. It seems like poor strategy to invite your enemies into your lair to negotiate when you don't have anything to bargain with. My peers didn't seem to think twice about it, though. They're foolish because they completely underestimate what these halfkinds are capable of. Am I the only one to see the obvious? That it could be a trap? Am I the only one who gives the halfkinds any sort of credit?

We haven't heard from our leader since he embarked on his operation. I wonder how things went. I wouldn't be surprised if Commander Trevor and his crew of heroes got captured and it was up to me to save his sorry ass. Though, to be honest, I would find satisfaction in that.

Then, as if fate is listening to me, I hear a beep on my communicator. The others react to the beep as well. I receive the signal and a graphical holo display appears before me. I see boxes with Colbo, Erawan, and Commander Trevor on my screen. We're all linked up.

"Where's Apollo?" I ask Commander Trevor.

"He's recovering from an injury," he says.

"What happened?" Colbo asks.

Trevor pauses a bit, hesitant to tell us the answer. I see his eyes looking away from the screen nervously. "Borton's dead."

"What?" Colbo says, shocked by the news. "What happened?"

"When we got to the casino, we ambushed a small camp of halfkinds there. It was Maddie, Oscar, Iris, and Isaac Lawton. We were able to subdue them, but Borton fired without permission and killed Oscar. This led to an argument between the three of us and, while we were distracted, Maddie impaled Borton with a piece of debris."

"Good job," I say sarcastically.

"Shut up!" Trever yells.

"I thought you were there to negotiate," Colbo says to ease the tension. "Why did it all of a sudden become a stand down?"

"Because they didn't know we were there to negotiate," he says. "Someone had set them up. They had no idea we were coming. Then Borton, against my orders, went in firing a barrage of shots and things got messy."

"Why would someone set them up?" Colbo asks. "And who?"

"We think it's one of their own, but we can't confirm," Trevor responds. "We just know they weren't expecting us like we thought they were."

"When did all this happen?" I ask Commander Trevor.

"About thirty minutes ago," he says.

"Why didn't you tell us sooner?" I demand.

"Because I was looking for Apollo."

"And where was he?"

Once again Trevor pauses. "He was chasing after two halfkinds that got away, Iris and Isaac Lawton. He followed them all the way down to the sewer and they attacked him, knocked him out cold. When he didn't return, I went looking for him and found the open manhole cover he entered from. It didn't take me long to discover where he was. He was unconscious and I had to attend to his wound. He's okay now, though, but he lost their scent and doesn't know where they went."

"And now those two are gone?" Colbo says. Trevor nods his head. "Well, isn't that fantastic."

"Why did Borton disobey your orders?" I ask Trevor.

"Because he was only thinking about himself," he says. "I gave the call to capture them, but he refused to obey. Borton took it upon himself to do it. He was more concerned about what the Alliance wanted than what I directly told him to do."

Colbo has a confused expression on his face. "Excuse me for my rudeness, Commander, but wasn't Borton right? Shouldn't we be concerned with Alliance orders? I mean, the goal of the mission is to eliminate the halfkinds and it seemed you were in the position to do so."

Trevor narrows his brow.

"I know what we're sent here for, what our goal is," he says in a raised voice. "But we do things my way. Unless these things are threatening your life, I don't want any merciless killings, you understand? When we encountered Oscar's group, they came peacefully for the most part. I already had this discussion with Borton, I'm not going to have it again with you."

"Borton is dead and Apollo is injured," Colbo says. "Seems they didn't come as peacefully as you thought."

The Commander looks even angrier than before. "This is the end of this discussion. I'm not going to talk about it anymore."

Colbo has a skeptical look on his face. "As you wish, Commander."

"So, now what's the plan?" I ask the group.

"I assume you all have been staking out the Gonzalez station?" he asks us.

"That is correct," I respond.

"See anything suspicious?" he asks.

"No," I say. "We arrived at 1 AM and set up a perimeter as you commanded. Nothing has gone in or out. The lights are off inside, there doesn't seem to be any activity there, but I can only guess since we haven't been able to investigate inside."

"Okay, that's good that you stayed your ground," he says. "I want you to finish up your search, head inside, and inspect from there."

"But it doesn't seem that there's anyone inside," Colbo says. "Shouldn't our focus be on the other station?"

"We'll get to that one soon enough. Just do a quick sweep and nothing more. If you have reason to think there's something suspicious then continue, but if you don't we'll meet at the Li Station. Shouldn't take more than ten minutes. Apollo needs some time to recover from his wound, so I'm going to give him a breather while you guys fulfill your order."

"Fair enough," Colbo says.

"Keep your communicators on, at least in sound mode," Trevor says. "I want to hear what's going on, understood?"

"Understood," Colbo says. "And what about the twins?"

"We'll have to worry about them later. Right now the priority is the teleporters. This is Trevor signing off."

His display shuts off, but the others are still signed on.

"Meet me at my location so we can go over our tactics," I tell the others. I see them leaving their posts and they come walking my way. I then turn my communicator off and they do as well.

"So, how should we do this?" Colbo asks.

"We've already swept the boundary," I say. "And there doesn't seem to be any activity inside. There are three entrances on the north, west, and east side. Let's split up and enter from the three sides and then start our search there. Agreed?"

They all nod their heads. Colbo starts to walk to the station, but stops and turns around. "Man, that Borton had some guts to defy the Commander's orders."

I scoff at his comment. "Yeah, and now he's dead because of it."

Erawan doesn't say anything, but Colbo looks a bit unpleased by my comment.

"Hey, he was one of us, have some respect," Colbo says.

"I don't respect hot-headed soldiers who defy orders and kill innocent, unarmed individuals."

Colbo looks shocked by my statement. "When did you have a change of heart? Is this world going crazy? Am I the only one who realizes that this is what we were sent to do? If the Commander wants to puss out, that's fine and dandy, but I'm not going to balk at fulfilling my duty, especially when it's an Alliance order."

"So, you would murder harmless bystanders if your boss told you to?"

"Um, excuse me, last time I checked, they attacked and killed Borton," Colbo says like he's offended.

"And last time I checked, Borton provoked them. I doubt he would've died if he had listened to the Commander."

"It's his fault for not being careful," Colbo says. He lifts his gun from the ground into his arms. "Don't expect me to be the same way."

"Confident as ever," I say sarcastically.

"What's wrong with you?" he asks in an irritated manner. "Before this evening started, you seemed to be willing to do what it takes to get the job done. Now all of a sudden, you're going soft. What gives?"

I look at the ground and then I look back up to the others. "After our skirmish at the supply depot, I started to think about things. We've been sent to kill these things, yet they haven't done anything to us. They only thing they want is to live. And how do we, our leaders, as a society, react to their discovery? We come in with guns in the air. They weren't even given a chance, we sent them out for execution the minute we knew of them."

"Well," Colbo says, "you know why we're doing this. I mean, we've talked about it so many times now."

"Just because I know why doesn't make it any more right."

"That's too bad for you then, but when it comes down to it, if our lives are on the line, I want to know that I, the rest of the team, can count on you. You're not going to get cold feet because you've got a case of guilt all of a sudden?"

I look at Colbo. His face is humorless, his lower lip protrudes, and his brow tightens. He's dead serious.

"Don't worry about it," I say callously.

"Good." He turns his back to me and starts to stride away. I look at Erawan who hasn't said a word the whole time.

"You don't talk much do you?" I ask him.

He lowers his head so that we are eye level and looks directly at me.

"No, I don't," he says sternly. He then turns around and marches in Colbo's direction.

At least one of us understands what the hell is going on.

Chapter 23 – Curtis Lawton

Lair

November 17, 3040 2:34 AM

I got to the Gonzalez station at about midnight. Candy's programs worked like a charm. The window she set to disable security was from 12 AM to 12:30 AM and, like clockwork, I walked through the doors without a hint of struggle. Once inside, I turned the security systems off and started to lay the foundations of my final resting place.

I walked around a bit to see what I was working with. The teleport station wasn't too big, but it was roomy enough for me to conceal myself from the view outside. The walls were high and the floor was checkered black and white. Multiple screens hung from floor to ceiling, but they were off when I arrived. Everything was off, the station was in full charge mode.

There was a lot of furniture on the floor: benches, some food stands, ticket counters, and other things. There was also a large metal box with safety signs on it. That must have been the generator that Candy mentioned. Lastly, there were ten or so teleport pods lined up against the wall. I wouldn't be using them, though, maybe just for cover.

After I was done surveying the area, I looked inside my pack to see its contents. A small handheld device was at the bottom, I took it out to observe. It was a transmitter, a wrist mounted one. It wasn't a fancy holo display model, but it was what I needed. Tiago wanted to make sure I sent him a sign when I executed my plan. That way he would know when the deed is done.

I attached it on to my wrist and it fit snuggly. The transmitter had a button in the middle. All I had to do was press it and Tiago would receive a little beep. That was the signal I had to give. After observing it for a few seconds, I continued rummaging through my backpack.

I felt something hard yet light touch my hands. They were the two energy pistols that Ace had swiped from his earlier supply run. I took one out to inspect. It was fully charged and felt light in my hand. I gripped it and got comfortable with my aim. My finger caressed the trigger. I looked at a trash dispenser nearby, pointed my gun at it, and took a shot. A quick light dispersed from the barrel and grazed the side of the unit. I'm not that skilled of a shooter, but my goal isn't to kill, it was to lure them in.

I set the gun aside and dug through the bag again. This time I pulled out a flat disc like object. They were garden mines, compact and precise. It was extremely light and I probably could have tossed it clear across the station if I wanted to. There were a lot of them, at least fifty in my bag.

Tiago's instructions about these were simple. I press the small button to arm them. After they're armed, they'd beep a few times and then stop. There wouldn't be a way to figure out where I placed them after that, no lights, no sounds. I'd have to remember where I put them exactly. If I didn't, I could very well blow myself up. My plan was to lay them around the perimeter and stay clear from it afterwards. I'd be waiting in the center, anyway.

I'm surprised these things were at the supply depot, so I guessed they're not very strong, probably made to scare away small animals in the woods for someone who might need that sort of thing. I highly doubted they would do enough damage to injure a trained operative, but, again, it was just to lure them in.

Those items weren't for me, it was for any possible intruders I might run into. The last thing in the pack was for my use.

I pulled it out, a long metal cylinder custom made by Candy. It was an explosive, the same kind that she had made for Lombardi, only much more powerful. According to Tiago, it could take down this whole station if need be. It worked the same way, clutch the handle, the bomb arms, let go of the handle, the bomb detonates within a few moments.

These were the tools I would use to do my work. Like an artist and his brush, I respected the equipment I was given. I made sure that no resource would go unused, everything was important.

With all the items in hand, I went to work setting the trap. I took the garden mines and walked around the perimeter, arming and tossing mines around like I was sowing seeds in a garden. I concentrated all of them towards the entrance doors that hug three different walls. They were the only way anyone could get in, so when our enemies entered, they'd have a nasty surprise for them.

I then grabbed whatever I could and constructed a fort smack in the middle of the station. Benches, trash dispensers, pieces of wood and metal, anything I could get my hands on became a part of my reinforcement. This was where I planned to hunker down when the enemies came. While they blast their shots, I'd be hiding, waiting for them, drawing them in.

That's what the guns were for. I didn't plan to kill anything. My shot proved I wasn't that great. I wanted to bait them in, like flies. As long as my fort held up, I could stay there until they come close enough for me to make my last move, my master stroke, the reason I was in the Gonzalez station in the first place and not some corpse in a grass field.

The creatures that were after us, they know we were headed to a teleporter. There were only two in Primm, the Li station and the Gonzalez station. The Li station was farther from the depot where they found Lombardi, farther from our hideout. Tiago said, tactically, our pursuers would investigate the Gonzalez station first. Little did they know I'd be waiting for them.

My mission was simple - when they come, I'd draw them in. I'd fire some shots and the mines I placed would go off if they got near them. They'd be stunned and filled with adrenaline, then rush to their target without even thinking twice about what was in store for them. The second I felt like they were within range, I would set off Candy's bomb and it'd be goodbye to our enemies.

Tiago would have the time he needed to make his escape. I'd have my rest and, in doing so, I'd help my family. I've wanted both for a long time. I thought about it, talked about it, and now I could finally do something about it.

Tiago mentioned that I could turn back whenever I wanted to. He shouldn't have wasted his breath. I was only going forward, not backward. Though I had my doubts here and there, though I didn't fully trust Tiago, I was and still am ready to end this. I don't want to live anymore. My encounter with that drunk lion proved beyond a shadow of a doubt that this world would fear me, that I was a monster. Monsters get burned at the stake, I'd rather end my life on my own terms.

Some think suicide is selfish. I think those people don't know what it's like to hate yourself so much that you question your existence. Only then would they know what it's like to want to take your own life.

What I'm doing isn't selfish, what I'm doing is for the family. If anything, it's selfless.

After I had completed the setup of my lair, I heard some noise outside and carefully crept to a window to see who it was. I saw the wolf and gorilla that Ace mentioned, the ones that killed Lombardi. They also were accompanied by an elephant. Tiago was right, they did come. These were the creatures that I would have my revenge on, the ones that I could put an end to so that my brothers, both Oscar and Tiago, won't have to worry about them anymore.

I was ready to take them on, but for some reason they stayed outside. They set up camp and resided there, didn't even bother to come near the doors. I was ready for them, ready to pull the trigger to bring them in, to squeeze the handle of my bomb so it could blast them to pieces, but I had to wait.

I considered drawing them in anyway, but if they weren't coming, I would leave them alone. They couldn't go after the others if they were in my sight. I wanted to buy Tiago as much time as possible and if I acted hastily, the clock would be much shorter. I only saw three of them and I was sure there were more. There was no need to set off the alarms, it might have sped up their actions.

So I waited, and waited, and wait. It's now two and a half hours past midnight, and they're still outside. I wonder if they're ever going to storm the gates. From an obscure position, I'm able to see where they are. Before, they were scattered around on each side, watching the perimeter like guardians. I'm surprised they didn't notice me. It must be hard to see what's inside since they've been hovering away from the building. But now, they're congregating in the distance. I can faintly see them with their headsets on, talking on a holoscreen to someone. That must be their leader. I wonder where he is right now. Maybe he's observing from a command station, maybe he's looking for the others. I hope they're okay.

I worry about Oscar. This mission is supposed to be for Tiago, but I still think it's to help them all. If Oscar is in danger, then all of this will be in vain. I'm not here to serve the interests of one family member, I'm here to serve the interests of everyone. We've always had a strained relationship, Oscar and I, but I like to think there's a mutual respect through all the cautiousness. Though I hung with Tiago, I hope he never got the wrong impression.

Suddenly, the team breaks apart. Their communicators are off and they start walking towards the station. This is it, their commander must have given them the go. I scamper back to my wall of benches and parts. I have my guns ready, the bomb is by my side. It's time to stop thinking, it's time for action.

If I succeed, I'll be happy because I know I'm going where I belong. And I'll be happy because I know the ones I love will be safe. It's time for this broken soul to find some peace.

Chapter 24 – Fenrir Snow

Killzone

November 17, 3040 2:45 AM

Our communicators are on, we're in our positions. The building is rectangular, one story high, aged, and plain. I'm not even sure what the walls are made of, probably carbonidium, an old alloy that hasn't been used for decades. A few windows adorn the side looking dusty and unclean. This place, like everything else in this city, is shabby and run down. I can't believe people make cross country trips using this station.

At almost 3 AM, the November air is cool, but I barely notice thanks to my fur. The city lights create an orange tint that paints the walls of the building and I stare at it while the others enter. We haven't seen or heard anything suspicious, not even a peep. It's a simple sweep job, but we can't be too careful. So far, these halfkinds have proven themselves to be rather resourceful.

Our communicators have been switched to sound mode. I'm not sure if Trevor is listening, but per his orders, it's on. I'm at the east entrance, Colbo is at the north, and Erawan is at the west. Our weapons are drawn, we're fully equipped and alert. All three of us have the access keys provided us by Primm officials. It's mounted on top of my helmet, all I have to do is put it in front of the scanner and I'm ready to go in.

"I'm in position. Confirm that you are all ready," I say.

"Confirmed," Colbo says on the communicator.

"Confirmed," Erawan responds.

"All right, on the count of three, use the keys and open the doors. Enter slowly and cautiously, got it?" I ask.

"We got it," Colbo says.

"On my count," I say. "One, two, three."

I present my key and the scanner automatically engages. I hear a beep and the doors slide open. I take my first steps in.

I can't see the others. I've only had a glance at my surroundings. I know Erawan stands on the opposite side, but there's too much blocking my view. Benches, teleport pods, item stands, and structural pillars are some of the things that are in my way. Even then, it's too dark to see clearly. The only light are the moon beams and street lights that shine through the cloudy windows.

"Can any of you see?" I ask the others.

"No," Colbo says. "It's damn dark in here. Even a hawk would have a hard time seeing this mess."

"I have a light on my helmet, give me a second," I say to the others.

"It'd be appreciated," Colbo says.

I'm about to equip my flashlight, when I sense something odd. Colbo and Erawan continue to move forward as I hold my position and try to figure out what is off. I don't see or hear anything funny. It's quiet, too quiet, but that's not always a bad sign. It's something else, something I can't put my paw on. It smells funny in here like a hint of sulfur. And then, I realize what it is. Oh, shit!

"Colbo don't move!" I yell. It's too late. The quaking hits my feet and a piercing noise vibrates through my ears.

"Goddamnit!" Colbo yells. I hear him on my communicator. His bellow echoes through the walls.

"My foot, it feels like someone clamped it with spikes. It hurts! Fuck!"

"Erawan, are you okay?" I say through my communicator.

I don't get a response. I can't really see through the rising dust, but I think I see the shape of an elephant. Sure enough, Erawan responds.

"I'm okay," he says.

Colbo continues to curse in pain. Meanwhile, I take another sniff into the air. The scent is familiar to me now.

"What happened over there?" a voice asks me. It's Trevor. I guess he is listening in after all.

"The place is booby trapped with garden mines," I say through the communicator. "They're small and non-lethal, but they can cause damage if tripped."

"No shit, asshole!" Colbo says.

"You'll live. Stop being a pussy," I say to him.

"They totally fried my foot, so screw you," he says, grimacing through the pain. "It doesn't seem to be too bad, just hurts like hell. I think I might be walking funny for the rest of the night."

"That's okay," Trevor chimes in. "Fenrir, you'll need to find a way to disable the mines."

Disable the mines? I can barely see, let alone know where they are. But suddenly an idea pops into my head.

"I'm going to use the marble shooters," I say. "If I put them on low charges, they'll hit the mines and set them off. I can clear out the ones in front of me and then go to Erawan's and Colbo's locations to set theirs off. All of you need to stand back."

"Do it," Trevor says. "Everyone fall back!"

I nudge my nose on the black box located above my front paw. A red light discharges from it and I stick my wrist out, aiming in front of me. Small, bright neon blue flames pour out of it like a cereal box and hit the ground running. It only takes seconds for them to make contact with the mines and I see puffs of smoke and flying metal shoot into the air. The mines are being detonated one by one, each little flame doing its job, each little flame clearing my path.

In less than a minute, all the traps in front of me are gone and I can see a well-defined road of dead mines in my way. I head towards the other's positions when, suddenly, another peculiar smell hits my nose. It's pungent, dirty, like the back of an alley or swamp. It's the scent of a living thing.

"We're not alone!" I yell to the others. Once again, I'm too late. Swift whizzing noises fill the air and bright, meteor like streams fly from the center of the building. Before I even realize what's going on, I promptly run behind a nearby item stand for cover. It's the dash of my life, but with my nimbleness, I'm able to make it.

I take a few seconds to recover, then moderately peer from the side and see that the projectiles keep coming. We're being fired at. Some are aimed at me, others are aimed at Colbo and Erawan, and they're all originating from the middle.

The ammo fires at us fast and reckless. I'm not even sure what our enemy is trying to hit. It seems he's bombarding us with random shots. I realize that whomever is shooting isn't an expert. A true marksman wouldn't be draining the power on his gun, he'd conserve what he has.

"Whoever is doing this is a horrible shot," I say to my comrades over the communicator.

"Agreed, he isn't hitting jack," Colbo says.

"I think with his unfocused nature, I can charge at him," I say. "I'm the smallest of us and you still have mines in front of you. I have a straight clearing to this guy, I'll try to rush and overwhelm him. Whatever he has coming for me, I can dodge it."

"Being the hero, eh, wolf?" Coblo says sarcastically.

"No, just taking the best option."

I stay behind the item stand and continue to hear him waste away his ammunition. I gently peer out and try to get a fix on his location. At this point, the smoke has cleared and my eyes have adjusted to the dark. I can see his outline, hiding behind an assembled fort of benches. It's an unobstructed line from me to his little barricade. Time to make my move.

I don't think, I simply churn my legs. My top speed is 65 miles per hour and, at this moment, I'm certain I'm hitting it. The creature is only 40 or 50 feet away, I'm near the fort in less than a few seconds. With all my might, I lunge forward, colliding through the benches and nail him head on. Chairs and scraps fly everywhere, a thunderous crash echoes through the walls. I've hammered him with all that I got and he goes sprawling across the floor, taking his blockade with him.

For a moment, I'm out cold. I overestimated my distance and applied too much force on my victim, which causes me to get slightly knocked out in the process. But when I come to, I see the broken and deformed pile of seats in front of me. My victim is trapped under it.

I pounce on the stash and bury my head underneath, but, to my surprise, I feel nothing, see nothing, and smell nothing but broken benches. I am utterly perplexed, but I don't have time to think about it. The muffled screams of my comrades enter my ears. I can't hear them with my head encapsulated by this mountain of mass, so I pick it up to see what the commotion is.

"Behind you!" I hear Colbo yell.

"What?" I respond.

For the third time, I'm too late. I feel a massive fist hit my back and I drop to the ground in milliseconds. The blow takes a few moments of my consciousness, but when things come back to me, I feel something cold, rough, and slimy wrap around my neck. It's firm and stiff, like a boa constrictor. Before I even realize what's going on, it's completely squeezed around my head.

If I was able to see myself, I'd see an enormous half man, half crocodile creature choking the life out of me with its colossal tail. Unfortunately, I'm not watching as an outsider, I'm experiencing it. I struggle mightily, trying to position my head so my jaws can clamp down on him. It's no use, though, there's no way I can twist my head in position. My paws flail around uselessly, the energy starts to fade. I feel myself letting go. My awareness is fleeting, slipping away from my reach.

He uses his appendage to turn my body around so that I'm facing him. I stare into the face of this thing as my vision blurs and my air passages tighten. I see beady yellow eyes and a protruding snout snorting directly at my nose. His skin looks like it's tough as nails, harder than any kind of synthetic leather I've seen before. And his teeth are terrifying. They are sharp like blades and stick out of his mouth in random, chaotic directions.

The last thing I think before I'm about to pass out is that I'm going to be this guy's early breakfast. But something amazing happens. His tail loosens and I fall straight to the ground with a thud. I'm once again out for a few seconds and, once again, when I regain my consciousness, he's gone.

But not for long. I hear the pounding of his footsteps from behind his makeshift fort. He jumps beyond it and lands in front of me. His mammoth feet are the first thing I see. I then raise my head bit by bit to see the rest of him. He's wearing a tattered shirt with cut off sleeves and loose jeans. The muscles on his arms are well defined and the scales on his body make the ones on his face a pale comparison in roughness. His hands are webbed. On the tips of his fingers are thick, jagged claws. His body is hunched over and he's breathing heavily. He stands in front of me, a massive tower of flesh and bone, and raises right arm high in the air. He outstretches his fingers and prepares the claws. It's time for him to strike a fatal blow.

I'm still recovering from nearly being choked to death and I am too weak to fight back. I try to react, but it is in vain. Things flash in front of my eyes, from the beginning of the mission to this moment. I trace through my thoughts on the objective, my disagreements in its purpose, my understandings of the enemies, and the moral ambiguity of it all. So many of my questions will remain unanswered. I didn't want things to end, not until I've become satisfied, not until I understand things clearly.

But I guess this is it. I helplessly watch him thrust his arm in my direction and close my eyes.

A second has passed and I feel nothing. His swipe should've been struck by now. I open my eyes to see him staggering backwards, landing on his back on top of the piles of benches. He clutches his chest, breathing deeply, and I see a blackish red liquid leak from behind it. It trickles down to his leg, where another wound oozes from his thigh. I didn't realize it earlier when I scanned him, but the first wound was there before the second one. He has been shot twice.

I look behind him and see Colbo with his cannon of a gun. It's smoking. I then look at Erawan. His firing baton is also smoking. Two shots had been fired indeed, the first from Erawan, who stopped this halfkind from choking me to death, the second from Colbo, who saved me from getting disemboweled.

The halfkind is now completely incapacitated, lying on his belongings, life fading away. I gain a second wind and recover from my encounter. I arm my weapon. A shot in the head should do it.

I look at him. He's helpless and his eyes tell the story. I don't have to kill him, he's already dead inside. The toll of running and losing family members must be quite heavy. Poor guy.

"Trevor," I say. "We've subdued one of the halfkinds. He was firing shots and I engaged him physically. Colbo and Erawan then fired a few of their own and he seems to be mortally wounded."

"He's not going to live?" Trevor asks me.

"No, he's not."

"Was he the only one there? No others to be found?"

"That's correct. He was alone," I say. The halfkind coughs out some blood and continues his struggle to hold on. "Should I end his misery now?"

"Not yet. See if you can get any information from him, like the location of the others."

I look at him, his condition getting worse. Even if he was healthy, he wouldn't talk, but an order is an order.

"Do you know where the others are?" I ask. He says nothing. "He's not going to talk."

"Very well, then," Trevor says. "End it."

The barrel from my helmet juts out. It's armed and ready to go. I take one last glance and say, "Sorry, guess you'll be joining your brothers and sister."

Suddenly, his eyes widen and he shakes his head.

"Brothers and sister?" he coughs out. "Who are you talking about?"

I look at him cautiously. The expression on his face is of utter confusion.

"The bear and the cow, Oscar and Maddie," I say. "They're dead."

Even though he's approaching his last breath, he has enough energy to display the shock he is feeling. I'm no mind reader, but he looks like he has no idea they're dead.

"You killed... them?" he agonizingly musters to say. "But, how... did you know where to find them? They were... hiding."

"We found a clue to their whereabouts, a letter on our vehicle," I tell him bluntly. "It said your brothers and sisters wanted to meet us, but when my colleagues got there, they only found, Oscar, Maddie, Isaac, and Iris. Then a standoff occurred and those two died in the process."

"Letter...? Clue...?"

Astonishment still carries on his face and it starts to shake. I see him moving his mouth, but no words come out. It's like he's talking to himself, figuring out some kind of brain teaser while I watch him, dumbfounded by his actions. After he's done, he lets out a small laugh.

"That.. bastard," he says to himself. "He sent you your clue... everything... the bomb... the betrayal... even my death... was part of his plan... we were all pawns... family duty indeed..."

I stand there confused by his words. "Excuse me? Pawns? What are you talking about?"

He looks me dead in the eye. "My brother, Tiago, they're... at the Li station. They're planning to... use the teleporter to get out of this... city...first to San Francisco, then... to the...Moon. If... you... want to...stop him... you and... your team...will find him there."

He picks up a wrist transmitter that is next to him. He must have been wearing it, but it probably flew off in the heat of battle. He clutches it and uses his finger to press a button. It makes a beep and he tosses it away.

"I've given him the signal," he says. "He'll think everything... is... going according to ...plan. He won't know what's... coming his... way."

"Signal for what?" I ask him.

He then lifts his other arm, which he had hidden behind the rubble during our whole conversation. He's gripping a bulky metal cylinder. It looks familiar only because I've seen it before. Lombardi Lawton had tossed one at us when we were fighting him. It's a bomb. Crap.

The trigger is squeezed tightly, and I pray that he has the strength to hold on.

"Sorry... I armed ... it before... you told me... about Oscar...and Maddie...This one... is supposed to be...pretty... big," he says, blood spewing from his mouth. "Better... run... fast...neither... of us... has ...much time."

Those are his last words. His eyes close and his head tilts back, the bomb he clutched so firmly releases from his hands and hits the floor with a clang. Seconds seem like an eternity. I turn around and sprint as far away as possible. The ground jolts behind me and a tidal wave of force flings me forward.

After that, I don't hear or see anything. I lose my breathing in a typhoon of fire and a swirl of objects. Gravity seems to be going up and down, left and right. My mind gets lost in a sea of nothingness.

Chapter 25 – Tiago Lawton

Abandoned

November 17, 3040 3:01 AM

"How are things going, Candy?" I ask her. She's on her infocube looking at some monitoring programs. She, Ace, Alex, and I got here about two hours ago and went to work right away. The teleporter wasn't going to start itself.

When we arrived, she disabled the security systems. It was easy enough, at least for her. When we were hiding, she had hacked into the central security mainframe the teleportation stations use. Since it's all maintained remotely on a cloud, she got access into their servers, changed some of their code, and set an open window of time to disable the locks. She put a thirty minute window of down time between 1:00 AM and 1:30 AM. We arrived at 1:10 AM, and disabled the security programs for the rest of the evening.

Candy also covered any traces of her code that could be detected by the guys upstairs. She said big companies, like the transportation ones, usually had programmers constantly on duty to make sure there are no security irregularities occurring. There are no cameras or visual recorders inside, everything is done through the cloud and programs. If you have a smart enough hacker, and I mean really smart, like Candy, masking your moves, you won't have anything to worry about. Those guys in their comfy chairs won't even know what's going on.

We did the same for the Gonzalez station, so Curtis could get in and out with ease. Candy disabled it an hour ahead of ours, since he arrived earlier to his location.

With all the work she's been doing, I'm surprised she's not stressed. Even under these circumstances, she's easygoing. Candy has this way about her that's nice. Everyone gets along with her and she's straight forward in her opinions. Her motives for supporting me are different from Ace and Alex. Those two joined me out of pure allegiance. Candy is a true believer. She knows that my plan to the Moon sounds crazy, but it's also the best shot we have at staying alive.

"They're going on schedule," she says, answering my previous inquiry. "The power modulator is charging up as we speak. It will probably start up in thirty minutes. All I had to do was move the scheduled start time from 3 AM to midnight. These things normally charge for three hours before the station opens. That charge supplies enough energy for these transporters to run on until closing time, which is ten at night. Then they cool down and the whole process starts over again."

"Why do the stations need separate power sources to do all this?" I ask her curiously. "Why can't they get power from the energy companies?"

"I think it's a political thing," Candy says ambivalently. "It takes a lot of power to run these stations and the energy companies are worried about putting too many resources into the operation of these teleporters. There are so many now and this could prove costly. There are two of them in Primm and we're just a small town. Imagine how many are out there in the world. The only way these things could operate without the globe running out of power is if the transportation companies offered to sustain it themselves. That's why these things aren't open 24 hours, at least in Primm, they need the time to cool off and charge."

"But we're kind of jump starting things, so they won't have enough time to cool. Won't that damage the source?"

"Probably, but I guess it doesn't really matter to us. We'll be long gone by then, right?" She asks this with a hopeful smile on her face.

"We sure will," I respond.

"I wonder how the others are doing?" she asks me earnestly. "I hope they're okay in their hideout."

I want to avoid her question, because it reminds me of the things I've done to get us four to this point. We started as a family of eleven, now only a few of us remain. The faces of Leonard and Lombardi flash through my mind. For so long, I had deemed them useless members of my family. But was that enough justification to use them in my schemes? Yes, it was. If they had continued on with us, they surely would have slowed us down.

Then I think about Curtis, a brother on the brink of suicide. I saw him about to take his life and I didn't save him. I pushed him over the edge. I could've helped him, I could've veered him away from ending it all. Instead, I sent him on a suicide mission, knowing that he wouldn't return. I loved, love my brother. I've tried to help him for a long time. I know him better than any of my siblings and I knew persuading him to live would be a pointless cause. Eventually, he would break and we would mourn. At least now he can die a hero. My brothers and sisters will remember him for his bravery, not his cowardice. I gave him the chance he wanted. I even made sure he could bail out anytime. But I know for him, there's no looking back.

And then there's Oscar and his followers. My younger brother has been a great ally, but also a great enemy. He couldn't accept the choices that must be made if you want to survive. In a time where we have to make tough decisions, this difference is what drove our family apart. He lives in a fantasy world that doesn't exist. If only he could see the reality in front of him, then perhaps we'd be leaving this godforsaken city together.

It's too bad he took the twins with him. They, especially Iris, are special, and when they decided to leave us, it burned a hole in my soul. I will forever be hurt by their decision.

I ratted out Oscar, but that's the decision I had to make to buy us time and get the agents off our tails. I don't know if my ruse worked, but Oscar and the rest are dead if it did. A part of me feels the guilt, but another part of me knows he made his choice when he decided to leave. When we make it out alive, the regrets I have will sting, but eventually they'll subside.

Curtis, Lombardi, Leonard, Oscar, I did all these things for the sake of survival, for the family I love, for the family that can make it to the end. This is for Candy, Ace, and Alex, this is for those who are loyal to me, who share my vision. In the long run, whatever has happened, whatever sacrifices I made, it'll be worth it.

I realize I haven't responded to Candy's comments.

"I'm sure they're fine," I tell her. Sometimes, the truth is best when it's hidden from the world. "I'm going to go check on Ace. Good work so far, sister."

"Thanks, Tiago."

I make my way towards the exit of the station and press a button on the wall to open the outside door. I see no one, so I raise the transmitter on my wrist and press a button. It sends out a signal to a receiving one and I hear footsteps hurrying my way. Within seconds, Ace appears in front of me.

"You called, Tiago?" he says.

"Yeah, just want to see how things are going out here," I respond.

"Nothing unusual. I haven't encountered anything, not even a raccoon."

"That's good."

I have Ace patrolling the perimeter. If anything suspicious is going on, he has a transmitter to warn me. I don't expect any visitors, though, especially after all the plotting I have done.

"You think your plans worked?" Ace asks me. He's well aware of what I did to Curtis and Oscar's group, but he doesn't care. Loyalty will make you look past the worst atrocities.

"I don't know," I say. "I haven't gotten the signal from Curtis and I don't even know what's going on with Oscar."

"I can go to their hideout if you want me to scout."

It's a good idea, but not worth the risk. Ace is far too valuable at this stage of the game.

"No, that's not necessary," I say.

"Okay," he responds.

"You're doing a good job Ace, keep it up. I'm going back inside."

"Thanks."

I can tell he's elated by my approval. That's always been the case, I'm the big brother whom he idolizes. I'm not sure if it's a feline thing or not. Or maybe it's an inferiority thing, because he isn't exactly the brightest bulb. When I trust him with responsibility, he probably feels smarter than he really is. Whatever the case, he gravitates towards me.

And, in all fairness, I treat him pretty well. I'd do anything for him because I know he has my back.

I open the door and walk back inside the station. The last person I approach is Alex, who is tinkering with some of the weaponry that Ace smuggled from the supply depot. There's a pile of pistols and a large stash covered by a musty old blanket.

"How are the preparations going?" I say to Alex. My tone is much more serious than when I talked to Ace. It's always been like that when talking to him. He's much bigger than me and I could be overpowered in seconds. Yet, I'm the boss. It's small things, like the way that I talk to him, that allow me to grasp power and reinforces my leadership.

"Good. I've tested the pistols, they're the real deal. Let's hope Curtis was able to use them."

These are the same pistols I put in Curtis's pack. Alex raises one in the air and inspects it. He points it forward, shooting at an imaginary target.

Alex is my other right hand man. I tell him what I tell Ace. I need Ace for his speed and grace. I need Alex for his intimidation and brute strength. He is the last line of defense I have if it ever comes down to that.

"And have you prepped Candy's bombs?" I ask him.

"Sure have, they're under here. You sure had a lot of work in store for Candy this week."

He lifts up the blanket and reveals a cache of ten metal cylinders.

"Well," I say, "it's good to be prepared."

These bombs are slightly different from the ones that she made for Lombardi and Curtis. It's not a squeeze and explode type grenade. There are strings attached to the trigger device. If you pull the string hard enough, it arms and explodes.

I sometimes wonder how Candy was able to assemble all this. She said it was easy given that our hideout used to be an industrial chemical plant. As she explained, there was enough stuff to play with that she could've made an array of homemade explosives, if she had more time.

Once we're almost ready to leave, I will call Ace back in and instruct Alex to set these around the perimeter. The teleportation stage of my plan is fragile and can't be interrupted, so if someone does crash the party they'll walk right into my trap. A simple trip on the strings and they'll be blown to kingdom come.

"What about this one?" Colbo says. He presents me another cylinder shaped canister, but it is much bigger than the others. It's similar to the one Curtis has and it's just as powerful.

"Give it to me," I say. "I'll be the last one through the teleporter. Before I go through, I'll toss this one into the station to make sure this place is destroyed. It'll be much harder to figure out where we go if they don't have anything left to inspect. I'll make sure this place is burned to the ground in order to secure our safety."

Suddenly, my transmitter lets out an earsplitting beep.

"Ace?" Alex asks me.

"No, this is for the other thing," I say.

I'm referring to Curtis. That was the signal to let me know his deed is done. Alex looks at the ground and shakes his head. "Poor guy."

Words cannot express the mixed feelings I have at the moment. My brother is dead. Yet, it was what he wanted, it would've happened with or without my interference. I can't turn back time now.

"Yeah, poor guy," I say solemnly.

"Do… do you think he got all of those bastards? Those people who are coming for us?" Alex asks.

"He did send the signal, so that means he got the job done. I trust him on that."

We stand there in awkward silence. I don't know if it's appropriate to continue talk of our plans. Luckily, I don't have to. Ace bursts into the station, astonishing the three of us inside.

"Tiago, you won't believe it!" he yells.

I'm prepared for the worst. I'm expecting Ace to tell us that a full cadre of soldiers are outside our hideout. But to my surprise, it's not that, it's two people I thought I'd never see again.

"Iris, Isaac," I say stunned.

"Hello, Tiago," Isaac replies.

"What are you doing here?" My voice is shaking. I'm not sure what happened with Oscar and I'm worried that Isaac discovered my deceit.

"We, we, were attacked," Isaac's voice trembles. "Oscar and Maddie, they're dead."

All of us look shocked, but only Candy's is genuine. We're not stunned that Oscar and Maddie are dead, we're more stunned that the twins are still alive.

"What happened?" I ask him.

"We were ambushed by a human, a pig, and a dog, agents of the United Species Alliance. They killed Oscar, Maddie killed the pig, and they killed Maddie. We were able to escape in the chaos and came here."

"And the human and dog, they didn't follow you?" Alex asks.

"No," Iris says. "The human tended to the pig, but the dog chased after us. We were able to… incapacitate him."

"Impressive," Alex says.

"So, what brings you here?" Ace asks.

Isaac clears his throat. "After what happened to Oscar and Maddie, we don't have anywhere to go. We only have you guys left. We want to rejoin you on your mission to the Moon. I'm sorry we left earlier, but now, we know. Iris and I, we trust you. You're a good brother and I know you'll help us out."

The last thing Isaac says pierces me like a dagger. He trusts me. I then look at Iris, whose demeanor is a bit more cautious than Isaac's. I'm afraid of her in some sense. She's been different her whole life. She knows things and from what I see, it appears she knows something right now.

I wonder if I should let them rejoin my crew. They'll no doubt be helpful to my cause. Yet, I cannot. When I look at the twins, all I can think about is that they turned their backs on me. They went with that deserter, Oscar. They know how much I revere them, how I think they are extraordinary individuals, but when I needed their support, they let me down. How do I know that it won't happen again? My emotions get the better of me.

"I'm sorry, Isaac and Iris," I say, trying to show as gruff of an exterior as I can, "but you cannot join us. You've made your choice when you left and so did I. We will be making this trip without you."

"Tiago, no!" Candy yells.

"I'm sorry, Candy, but that's my decision."

Candy looks hesitantly at me and then at Iris and Isaac. She walks forward and gives Iris a big hug, tears rolling down her eyes. Iris receives her embrace. She looks heartbroken, while Isaac looks enraged.

"Why are you doing this, brother?" he yells with tones of confusion and frustration. "You would abandon your own kin out of a petty sense of pride? Don't you care about us?"

I do, but I can't trust their loyalty.

"I used to," I say. "But not anymore."

"Where will we go?" Iris asks desperately.

"I don't know and it's not my problem," I say unemotionally. "Walk east, walk west, walk north, walk south. Just make sure it's away from here."

Isaac walks up to me, his fury flushed across his face. We stand eye to eye to each other. He extends his head forward, past my ear, and whispers, "I hope you die for this."

He then does an about face and walks the other direction, towards the exit. "C'mon, Iris, let's go. There's nothing for us here."

Iris starts to follow him and looks behind one more time at the family she'll leave. I expected her to be remorseful, but she isn't. Instead, she looks relieved. I don't fully understand it and part of it scares me. What does she know?

"Where will you go?" Candy asks as they leave.

"Back home," Isaac responds. "Back to where this all started."

The door opens and they leave. I probably will never see them again.

Ace sneaks up next to me and asks me quietly, "Do you want me to follow them? You know, keep tabs, in case we need them?"

Iris's goodbye still haunts my mind. I stand there perplexed, trying to figure out what she was saying with her face. I could get Ace to follow them, to force an answer out of her. But that's too much, even for me. Some think I am ruthless, but I have my limits.

"No, leave them alone," I say. I think about the past night. "I've done enough already."

Chapter 26 – Apollo Bradley

Hindsight

<u>November 17, 3040 3:25 AM</u>
The last twenty minutes have been hell for
Commander Trevor and I. We last heard from Fenrir and
his company a little under half an hour ago. He had
Curtis Lawton cornered, but after a short conversation
and a bang it's been nothing but silence from their end.

My head had been hurting like hell up to that point.
The halfkinds whacked me pretty hard. It felt like an
anvil landed on me. I must've been out cold for ten or
fifteen minutes before Simon found me in the sewers. He
was able to wake me up, but I still felt really groggy. My
head was throbbing and my body was sore. I wanted to
vomit all the time, but I could only dry heave.

Simon eventually led me back to the Spades and
Diamond Casino where the bodies of Borton, Maddie,
and Oscar Lawton lied, covered with blankets. From his
arms to his feet, the Commander's uniform was stained
with blood. When Borton got speared, it was a mess.
Blood squirted everywhere. Since I wasn't there, I
wonder how long it took for him to finally bleed out, or
maybe the Commander performed a mercy killing. He
didn't say one word about what went down, but that
might have been the case.

Losing teammates is something that always brings the
Commander down. Even though Borton was a scumbag,
he was a colleague, a pig that Simon was responsible for.
It's never easy to have a squad member die on you. I
think Simon sees Borton's death as a reflection of his

failure. He didn't just let Borton down, he let himself down.

I took some time to rest while Simon debriefed Fenrir about what happened. They discussed their upcoming task at the Gonzalez station. My head was still throbbing. I had taken some meds that eased the pain. It was stuff that Simon gave me, high grade human pharmaceuticals. Still, it wasn't strong enough to keep me on my feet for more than a few minutes. I needed at least an hour or so until I was ready for action.

That's the real reason why we didn't join up with Fenrir. Commander Trevor wanted to assist. He was aching for an opportunity to redeem himself. But then he saw my condition and realized I was not combat ready. It was a tough decision for him, but it's situations like these where his integrity shines.

That didn't mean he was taking it easy here. Once Fenrir, Colbo, and Erawan started, he was glued to his communicator. He trusted them with their duties, but he also wanted to make sure they were safe.

After the mines were disabled and Fenrir went to pursue Curtis Lawton on his own, Commander Trevor's concern grew greater. We had seen pictures of Curtis. We knew how big he was and during their skirmish he had the upper hand. When Fenrir was getting strangled, Simon frantically demanded to know what was going on. Fenrir was probably too choked up to respond or even hear Commander Trevor, but Colbo gave the play by play. With Fenrir's life on the line, Simon barked for someone to take action. Fire a shot, throw a bomb, whatever, just intervene. Fortunately, Erawan was there to make the save.

I had never seen Simon so intense. Not during our first mission, not during our many meet-ups and outings.

He's usually a professional guy with a cool exterior. But perhaps the pressure was getting to him, especially after Borton's death. He didn't want anyone else to die on his watch.

Once Curtis had been subdued and Fenrir had him at gunpoint, that's when things went into chaos. We heard Fenrir have a conversation with Curtis, but it was hard to make out what they were saying exactly. There was too much interference, probably from some kind of transmitting device. Then, without warning, a large boom echoed through my communicator. It blared into our ears like a fireball. Commander Trevor and I looked at each other confused, but we were thinking the same thing - a bomb must've gone off.

After that, it was static and the sound of silence. Commander Trevor immediately looked at me and said, "Apollo, how are you feeling now?"

"I'm better," I responded.

"Good, because we're going to the Gonzalez station on the double."

Both of us quickly assembled our gear and high tailed it out of there. There was no time to do anything about the bodies, we had to leave them. Our transport wasn't parked nearby, since we entered on foot, so we rushed over as fast as we could. I've never seen a human run so fast, even I could barely keep up with him.

When we got to his vehicle, Commander Trevor powered up his hovercar and in seconds we were in the air, charging to the Gonzalez station.

I'm now sitting in his transport in silence. I look at the Commander and I see him doubting himself. It's something I never expected to see.

His eyes are slanted and his mouth is quaking. He wraps his hands tightly, too tightly, on his controls, and under his breath I can hear him mumbling out curses.

Ever since I met him as a young, naïve operative of the Dog Alliance, I've admired him. He was my role model, what I wanted be like in all facets of life. His career, his honor, his ability to make his team members feel welcome, inspired me. But to see your idol on the brink is disheartening. You realize he's not perfect, not indestructible.

His shoulders were carrying an amount of guilt I had never experienced and I could tell his head was filled with questions. What if I had done this? What if I hadn't? So many choices were being evaluated in a matter of seconds.

"Damnit!" Simon yells in frustration.

"Commander?" I ask him in a concerned tone.

"What the hell was I thinking? Why didn't I see it earlier. Fenrir pointed out the obvious and I still ignored the signs."

"Commander, what are you talking about?"

"It was a trap, Apollo. From the beginning, Fenrir said it was a trap and I didn't listen to him. Now he might be dead because I made the wrong call."

"No, don't think that. Your judgment was right. It was the smartest move to make at the time. I mean, they couldn't hide forever, they had to act. The transportation station was the only way out and we all knew that."

Commander Trevor appears a little calmer, but the frustration on his face still shows.

"But I should've been more careful," he says, his head leaned to the side, his elbow pressed against the window. "I shouldn't have split us up. If Colbo, Erawan, and Fenrir had more reinforcements…"

"Then we all might have been dead," I say. "Splitting up the team was right. We had no other option, especially since we were on our own mission to the casino."

"And that turned out to be a red herring, one I should've seen a mile away! But I didn't!"

He punches the side door in frustration and it startles me a bit.

"What the fuck was I thinking?!" he yells. "There's so much I did wrong! I bit on the wild goose chase, I lead my other team into an ambush. Years of experience and I walked into it like a dope."

"Commander…"

I don't know how to respond. He glances over and sees me blanked with a half confused, half scared expression.

"I'm sorry, Apollo," he says. "I shouldn't lose my composure like that, especially as a leader."

"It's okay, Simon," I respond.

"It's just, I don't know. We've known each other for a long time, right, Apollo?"

"Yes, of course."

"Can I ask you something then and get your honest opinion?"

"Sure."

"After what's happened tonight, do you still have confidence in me?"

I've never seen the Commander as vulnerable as this. The mere notion that he's coming to me with uncertainties in himself is crazy. And the fact that he's asking me for advice is nuts.

Any of these actions would be preposterous on any other night. But then again, it's not any night, it's a night where the mission has gone awry and over half the team could be dead. Even the greatest of men are only human.

"Of course, I do," I respond instinctively.

"Apollo, this isn't some kind of test, you can be honest with me."

I hesitate to say what's on my mind because I don't want to distress him any more in this fragile state, but I know he wants a real opinion.

"There's one thing I think Fenrir was right about, ever since we started this mission," I say.

"And what's that?" he asks. His voice is accepting, so I know there won't be any hard feelings if I speak my mind.

"We've underestimated these halfkinds greatly," I say bluntly.

"I see."

"We came into this situation headstrong, with little time to prepare. The strategy you made was fine, but our attitude towards it, Coblo's, Borton's, hell even you and me were arrogant. After we first killed Lombardi Lawton, we were handfed all these leads in a matter of hours. Sure we were cautious, sure we considered that it might be a ruse, but we overlooked it. Why? Because we didn't think our enemy to be capable of such ingenuity. You thought it, I thought it, the only creature who didn't was Fenrir. We saw how easy it was to kill the birdman and thought it'd be the same for the rest. But these halfkinds have proven to be much more dangerous than we thought. Their planning has been meticulous and they've been able to figure out our moves. Us, a highly trained group of soldiers, and we've been played so easily. It's because we let them play us."

He doesn't look angry or sad. He simply processes what I've told him.

"After our encounter with them at the casino," I say, "I've learned not to underestimate them. I mean, when we came in, we had them captured, the mission should've been over."

"But it was Borton's fault, he charged in and caused the chaos," he says. "He disobeyed me."

"True, but even after all that, you chose to take on Oscar one on one, without a firearm. It was reckless. If you saw him as a bigger threat, I'm pretty sure you wouldn't have tried to be a hero."

"So you're saying I should've killed him, like a murderer? Like Borton did, in cold blood?"

"No. What you should've done was treated him like any other hostile and not like some scared civilian."

"I see your point."

He doesn't seem disappointed by my words, but rather regretful of his actions.

"I'm guilty of this, too," I say. "I chased after those twins like a rabid dog chasing frightened kittens. But I could've very well been killed."

"But they did spare you."

"True, which shows you the power they possess. They made the decision not to kill me, like a god over a mortal. And it shouldn't have happened in the first place, but my carelessness allowed it to happen. All I'm saying is we have to start realizing that these halfkinds are a lot more cunning than we anticipated. We can't let our guard down anymore."

He is about to say something, but pauses first. He then speaks. "Looking back on things now, would you have done everything the way I did?"

"I probably wouldn't have and I'm not just saying that to be kind. As I said, I had the same cocky attitude as the rest of us and we really didn't know what we were getting ourselves into. But looking at it now in hindsight, we made the wrong moves. The important thing is we learn from them and move on."

Commander Trevor turns his face to mine. "Apollo, I appreciate your honesty. As always, you're someone I can rely on. And I'm not saying that to be cordial, it's from the heart. I'm glad you're on this mission with me."

In the beginning, I was fearful that my words would have strained our partnership, but it looks like they strengthened it.

"Unbelievable," Commander Trevor says while looking at the view ahead.

In the distance we see a partially destroyed building, smoldering, smoke leaking from its wreckage and rising to the sky. Debris is scattered about everywhere. It's a sea of metal, wood, electronics, and death. We've arrived at the Gonzalez teleportation station.

Commander Trevor lands his car immediately and I jump out to survey the damage. Whatever explosive they used was powerful enough to take down the whole station. There are so many things crackling in flames that it makes it hard to identify a source. There's a glow coming from the edge of the wreckage, the remnants of the power generator. It smells like sweltering metal and the wind blows ashes into our faces.

The Commander puts on some goggles and assesses the damage while I continue to survey the area.

"Apollo, use your skills to see if you can locate the others," he says.

I equip my scent booster and get to work. There's so much wreckage, it'll be hard to sort through everything. Luckily for me, I'm able to catch a scent right from the get go. It's Colbo.

I press my nose on the ground and sniff furiously. I breathe in deeply and walk up and down until I home in on a trail. From there on, I tread steadily, examining every inch and crevice until I can locate Colbo.

Sure enough, I find him and he's dead. His body is smoking, the hair on his back charred to a crisp. I see dried blood and slightly torn pieces of flesh. Half of his face is scared, small chunks seem to have disappeared from it. His mouth still flashes his trademark frown, but some of his lip has been ripped apart, making his teeth very visible. There's a small cavity in his chest, but it's blackened and burnt. Most of him remains intact, nothing seems to be dismembered, but he didn't go peacefully. When the blast happened, he must have been engulfed in the flames, as his weight was too large for force to fling him.

"Commander!" I yell. "Colbo is over here and he's gone."

Simon sprints to my location and sees his remains. He doesn't say a word, he just kicks a nearby piece of debris across the carnage.

"We'll find something to cover him with," he says sternly. "For now, see if you can locate Fenrir or Erawan."

I once again sniff the ground to see if I can catch a trail. I walk toward the perimeter, past a bent and scorched teleporter until I'm able to pick up Erawan's familiar odor.

I don't have to do much digging for him because I already see part of his body sticking out from the ground. His head seems to be buried beneath the piles of rubble. The rest of his him is turned over on one side and is under some scattered metal and wood. I swipe the ruins away with my paws.

His body isn't charred like Colbo's. It's actually relatively clean and as I scan it with my eyes, I find it hard to figure out what happened to him.

"I found Erawan!" I yell to Simon. He runs over and sees what happened.

"He doesn't look as bad as Colbo," Simon says to me.

"Yeah, but something doesn't look right."

Commander Trevor looks closely at him, eyeing every inch available.

"You're right, Apollo," Commander Trevor says, "something looks off. Help me lift his body out from the wreckage."

He goes over to lift one leg and suddenly jumps back. I don't understand why he does it until I sniff under the corpse. It smells like embers. His body isn't turned over on one side, it's the only side. The other half of his body is completely black. And his head isn't covered beneath the piles of rubble, it simply isn't there. Erawan's body had been disfigured beyond recognition. He didn't deserve this.

Commander's reaction to Erawan's death is different from his reaction to Colbo's. He looks utterly disgusted by the sight in front of him. It is the kind of mutilation you wouldn't wish up on your worst enemies, the kind that stays with you forever. He was a member of the highest guard in his society and there he lies before us, a barely recognizable corpse of his former self. You never think such warriors can go out this way, but he did. Simon gets on one knee and lowers his head in respect. I lower mine as well.

"I'm sorry that things ended this way, my friend," Simon says, "but don't worry, your death will not be in vain."

We stay there in silence for a few minutes. Commander Trevor then gets back to his feet and looks around.

"Were you able to pick up the scent of the halfkind responsible for this? Curtis Lawton?" he asks me.

"No," I reply. "He probably was vaporized since the bomb was in his possession when it went off."

"Good," he says.

Commander Trevor drops his gun and puts his hands on top of his head.

"I can't believe this happened," he says to himself. "All this destruction, it's my fault."

I want to console him, but I feel that silence is the only appropriate response.

After a few moments, he turns to me and asks, "Did you find Fenrir?"

I shake my head no. "There hasn't been a single trace of him. If he died, I would've found his scent or something."

"Lucky for you, he didn't," a familiar voice says. It's Fenrir and he looks like he's been through hell.

Chapter 27 – Fenrir Snow

Recovery

<u>November 17, 3040 3:46 AM</u>

I feel like shit. My fur smells like ashes, while specs of blood spot it red. My legs hurt, my back hurts, my head is pounding, and I can't even move my tail without feeling pain. I look around and see only the scattered remains of the teleportation station. That Curtis Lawton sure did a number on us.

The instant he let go of the trigger, I thought I was done for. All I could do was run as fast as possible. By the time the bomb exploded, I was already near the exit where I had cleared out the mines. I was fast, but not fast enough. I felt the ground shake and a ripple of wind jettison past my legs. Before I could get farther, I was in the air, head facing down, ass facing up. I remember flying straight forward until I felt a violent thud hit my back. After that, it was lights out.

When I woke up, I was greeted by murkiness. My vision was obscured by debris. Once I lifted my head, the rubble fell off, and I saw the carnage that had unfolded. The whole station was demolished. The smell of soot hit my nose so abruptly that I sneezed it out. Fires raged on and smoke filled the air.

I looked at myself to survey any injuries I might have obtained. I felt funny on the inside, so I pulled out the bioscanner and gave myself a quick read. A few minutes later, the results came, some broken ribs, a hairline fracture on my hind leg, and cuts on my back, nothing big. But I do have a large trail of blood running from my face. I must've been cut pretty deep, I'm lucky that one of my eyes wasn't taken out.

I was healthy, for the most part, so I started to look for the others. If I was able to survive with no major injuries, I was hopeful that they did, too. But it didn't take me long to discover their bodies. I found Erawan first. The discovery I made was grim. He didn't talk much, but I respected him. I knew of his reputation and I knew the warrior's heart he had. And now he lies before me, his body defiled like vermin.

Then I found Colbo dead under some other junk. I didn't like his smart ass attitude, but I did owe him my life. I will remember that. Two team members' lives ended so suddenly, it left me wondering how I was still alive.

I also wondered what Curtis Lawton was trying to say with his final words. He mentioned something about being a pawn, about being betrayed. From what Trevor told me, the halfkinds he encountered didn't know about any proposed meeting, that they were set up. Then this halfkind tells me in his dying breath that he was a fool who was played and rats out the location of his brother.

Tiago - that was the name he mentioned. According to his files, he was the oldest and most likely the leader. He must've orchestrated all the events that happened today, from Lombardi's raid to Oscar's standoff to Curtis's kamikaze mission. Judging from Curtis's change of heart, he wasn't playing nicely. He probably used and abused his siblings in some kind of master scheme.

With my thoughts and realizations coming to fruition, I decided that it was time to run back and warn Commander Trevor. He had to know what Curtis told me. Only problem was I didn't have my communicator on me, it must've been destroyed during the explosion.

The only way I could inform him was if I left on foot. I was injured, but I could still run like the wind. I darted in the direction of the Spades and Diamond Casino.

I didn't have far to go. After a minute or two of running, I saw a familiar hovercar in the air approaching the wrecked teleportation station. It was Commander Trevor and Apollo.

They landed and were inspecting what was left of the station. I hear them talking and I barge into the conversation.

"Lucky for you, he didn't," I say. I'm exhausted and aching, and it's the only line I can think of at the moment.

Both of them stand there astounded by my appearance. I don't think they were expecting me to be alive.

"You found Erawan's and Colbo's remains, I take it," I say.

"Unfortunately we did," Trevor responds.

"So, how did you come out of this alive?" Apollo asks me. "From the looks of things, I thought no one survived."

"Luck, I guess," I respond. "One second I was running for my life, the next second I woke up conscious and surprised. When the bomb went off, there was a moment when I thought death was certain. It looks like someone, something, up there likes me."

"I'm glad fate is on your side," Trevor says. "It's been a tough night, half of our team is dead. First Borton, now Erawan and Colbo, not sure if Apollo and I could've taken all of them alone."

"How many of them are left?" I ask.

"By my count, six. There's Candy, Ace, Alex, and Tiago Lawton, and the twins who got away. But we're plumb out of leads. The completion of this mission is in jeopardy, we don't know where they are at this point."

"You didn't hear my conversation with Curtis Lawton?" I ask Trevor. "I thought you were listening in."

"No, you started breaking up before he let off the bomb. Why?" Trevor asks curiously.

"Because, he gave them up. He said Tiago Lawton and the others are hiding at the Li station. They're planning to use it to get to San Francisco. From there, the ultimate destination is the Moon."

"I see," Trevor says. "If they get to the Moon, they could hunker down at one of the uncharted, unsettled plots of land there. They could live there for the rest of their lives, hell, even build a society. The Moon is still an undeveloped free space, they'd be near untraceable if they wanted to."

"Why did Curtis reveal his brother's location?" Apollo asks.

"I was thinking about that," I respond. "When he died, he said something about being a pawn, that he was just a part of Tiago Lawton's schemes. I suspect he had something to do with Curtis's death and your meeting with Oscar Lawton."

"So you think Tiago is the master planner behind all of tonight's events?" Trevor asks.

"It seems so," I say. "I would say Tiago Lawton is extremely dangerous."

"You know what that means," Apollo says.

"Yes, we have to stop them at all costs," Trevor responds, clutching his pistol. "Fulfilling our mission will be the number one priority. We must eliminate them."

Their response intrigues me. "You seem to be acting different. I thought all you wanted to do was capture them and let the Alliance deal with them. I thought you had the whole we 'come in peace' mentality."

Trevor looks at me. "After our last encounter, I've changed my mind. Apollo and I have discussed things. We've been underestimating them. They are dangerous. They're against the wall and all they can do is fight back. We either kill them, or be killed by them. We can't take them lightly anymore."

"Seems like a drastic change in strategy after one incident. Those twins must have really rattled you two, huh? You know, you kind of sound like Borton."

"We're different," Apollo says, "And we won't be killed like Borton. He wanted to massacre them. His overconfidence got him murdered. We respect our enemy and that is why we have to take every precaution necessary."

I smirk off his comments. "Sure, whatever you say, dog. Tomato, tomotto. It sounds the same to me."

I can tell he's slightly annoyed.

"And what about you?" he says. "All of sudden it looks like you're getting soft on us. Still think this is a walk in the park, even after Curtis almost blew you to smithereens?"

"I never thought things were going to be a walk in the park!" I snap back. "Wasn't I the one who told you fools not to underestimate them? Wasn't I the one who warned you of their traps? Well, guess who was right."

He wants to go at it with me, but Trevor looks different. He kneels with one knee and wipes the grime from his face.

"You're right, Fenrir, you did warn us," he says. "And I'm sorry that I didn't listen to you. I didn't expect much from our enemy. If I had given them the credit you gave them, then perhaps three of our team members would still be alive. I bear this responsibility and I'm not going to fail at it again."

He takes a quick glance at Colbo's body and continues.

"Listen, I wanted to come in peace, I truly did," he says. "I wanted to extend my hand and let these halfkinds know that we won't be their executioners. The last thing I wanted was for anyone to get hurt. But things haven't turned out the way I expected, and because of this desire, this weakness, Erawan and Colbo are dead. Perhaps what we're doing isn't ethical. I think the same thing, but the halfkind that's left, Tiago, we've seen what he's capable of. He's turned on his family members, he's sent some to their graves. If he's willing to do all this, what other lengths could he possibly go to in order to achieve his goals? If we don't stop him now, we may be letting a monster loose on the world. It's true that we may not know our enemy that well, maybe his motives are virtuous, but I'm not going to take that risk."

Commander Trevor makes some valid points. Whoever we're dealing with, this Tiago Lawton, he's done things so ruthless and cruel it makes me wonder what else he'll do next. He could go away forever, or he could come back with a vengeance. Against us, against the High Dog Council, against my Brotherhood. Perhaps coming at him armed and prepared is the only way to go if we want to prevent any of this.

"What we do going forward, what we do at the Li teleportation station, it won't be easy," Trevor says, "but based on what we've seen today, it will be necessary. Decisions like these are hard to make, but I finally feel like it's the right one. I'm done making the wrong choices. My order is to take on Tiago Lawton with full force and I need all the team members I can get. We three are the only ones left and I intend to finish things that way. Are you in?"

When I started this quest, I wanted to do what the Brotherhood of Wolves asked me. As the night became darker and the task became grimmer, I started to question my objective. Even now, even after they have nearly killed me, I wonder if hunting these halfkinds is the right thing to do.

But then I think about Tiago Lawton, the architect of all this deceit and madness, and I feel compelled to join Commander Trevor and his dog.

"Okay," I say, "I'm in."

"Thank you, Fenrir," he says.

"So, what is the plan?" Apollo asks.

"They're at the Li station, right?" Trevor asks me.

"Yes," I respond.

"Apollo, find directions and an ETA, stat," he says.

The dog pulls out the graphical interface hooked up his helmet and does a quick search. "It's about 11.7 miles away from here. ETA by hovercar should take ten minutes, tops."

"Good," he says. "Fenrir, what kind of defenses do you think they'll have? You've seen them in action tonight."

"Most likely they'll have mines of some sort, possibly like the garden mines that we encountered."

"I'm not sure about that," Apollo says. "Such puny arms might be good for some decoy operation, but if this is their ticket out, I think it'll be heavily fortified."

"I agree," Commander Trevor says, "when we arrive, I want both of you equipped with scent boosters to scout the area. I want to know what's in there before we make our attack. I know wolves don't like relying on that tech, but I don't want to take any chances. Equip your scent booster, got it, Fenrir?"

"Fine," I say begrudgingly.

"Once we're in, keep your communicators on at all times," Trevor says. "I'll give you commands from there."

"I lost mine," I say.

Commander Trevor takes a communicator out from his belt and hands it to me. I'm surprised because it's a wolf model.

"Always be prepared," he says.

"Thanks," I say. I think this is the first time I've thanked him for anything all night. Who was I turning into?

"Stay focused and be prepared to eliminate anything onsite," Trevor says. "I don't want a moment of hesitation. As we've learned tonight, that hesitation could get you killed and no one else is dying under my command."

"Understood," Apollo says. Like a stereotype, he's loyal as ever to the human, it kind of makes me sick.

"Fenrir," Trevor says to me, "are you ready?"

I think about the moral questions swirling in my head, about what's right and what's wrong. I think about Curtis Lawton's last words. And then I think about our opponent, Tiago Lawton. He's not above sacrificing his own brothers and sisters. The most dangerous types of people are the ones who are willing to do whatever it takes. In the end, they think their actions are justified.

But we're doing the same thing.

"Yes, I'm in. Let's go," I say reluctantly.

Chapter 28 – Iris Lawton

Memories

<u>November 17, 3040 4:04 AM</u>
We've made it back home, back to 1523 Chakming
Drive, back to where it all started. Dawn is approaching,
rays of sunlight stretch into the landscape. The journey
from the Li station to home was far, so we had to scurry
as fast as we could if we wanted to stay under the shade
of nightfall. I didn't think the walk would take so long
and I was afraid that we would get lost since we were
journeying through unfamiliar territory. Fortunately,
things looked familiar enough from all the moving we
had done this past week.

When we arrive, it's like I barely recognize the place.
Nothing has changed. The walls are still dented, the front
is unkempt. Pieces of garbage float by from the gusty
Nevada winds. The windows are barred. It's always
been a little grimy, a little dingy, a little bit rough. I can't
say it's ever been the most welcome looking place, but it
just doesn't feel like home. It was where I grew up in,
but that's now a memory.

When I step on the front porch this time, it feels
different. When we lived under this roof, it was a place
that I found comfort and joy. I must've sat on this front
porch several times. Mother let us hang out in the front
and backyard since our house was so isolated. Each time,
I felt like I belonged here. Now, I feel unwanted, that I'm
a stranger in a strange land. I can already sense how
deserted my home is, how empty the rooms are inside,
without setting foot in it. I look at my house from the

outside and I see a body without a soul. I don't feel happy coming here, I feel wrong. I never thought that a homecoming could be so unwelcoming.

I step inside and things hit closer to home. Ace said the United Species Alliance Science Division was here earlier. They must have inspected and cleared out our things, because the house is empty. Every precious memory, every item we couldn't take with us, they confiscated. I knew that the USASD was thorough, but I didn't think they would be that detailed. Only a week after leaving, the vacancy of my home is quite astonishing.

No one is here when we arrive. I doubt they need workers showing up at 4:00 in the morning for inspection. Since they already swiped every piece of evidence they could get, I'm not sure when, or if, they will make a return visit. I don't see any surveillance equipment or patrol drones. Actually, I don't see anything at all. For the time being, it seems that we are safe.

I look at Isaac and wonder how he feels about coming back to an empty home, but something else is on his mind. He stands here in rage, still angry over how we were cast aside so easily by Tiago.

"That bastard, I hope you're right," he mutters under his breath.

"About what?" I ask.

"Your premonition, about how you said they'd all perish. I hope Tiago doesn't set one foot on the Moon, I hope he dies trying."

I'm a bit flabbergasted by the callousness of his words. I can see they are genuine.

"Isaac," I say softly, "don't say such things. You may be upset now, but still, he's family. You know he cares."

Isaac sneers at my comment. "He has a funny way of showing it."

He lets out a sigh. He knows his words are reactive, not thoughtful.

"I'm sorry, sis," he says to me, "you're right. He is family. But what do we do now? We have nowhere to go."

"We could stay here," I say optimistically.

Isaac makes an uncertain face. "I'd like to do that, Iris, I really would. But the house is only empty now. I can't guarantee it'll stay that way. You know someone is going to come back. This visit is temporary. It's not safe here. This place isn't our home anymore."

Before we arrived, I was hopeful there'd be something for us here, but my eyes cannot lie, my home is a ghost of what it used to be.

I walk through the rooms and reminisce of the times when things were simpler. I refuse to see the void that my house has become. I visualize the memories that will haunt my mind for days to come.

Our living room is right beside me. It's dark right now, a little dusty, and some foliage has crept its way onto the floors. It already had been wearing and tearing away, long before mother died, but the condition emphasizes how abandoned our house is.

I close my eyes and see the same room in a much different light. I go back thirteen years. The floors and walls are new, shiny, and clean. It's evening, but the room is glowing from lamps that mother had recently purchased. There are couches, chairs, rugs, and decorations on the wall. The room greets me, the comfort I feel warms me.

I am not seventeen, I am four years old. All my brothers and sisters are with me. Mother has a fairytale tablet and it's story time. We all sit on the ground while mother towers above us with her tale ready to read. We aren't bickering, alliances aren't drawn. We don't know about the world outside, how much they hate us, how much they want us dead. Instead, the eleven of us sit there in marvel, hanging on every word she says. The only world we have is her.

She's telling us the fable of the wolf and the dog. A fatigued wolf meets a healthy dog and is impressed over its fit appearance. The dog tells the wolf his life of ease, having free food and shelter, while the wolf has endured a life of hardship. The wolf decides that the dog has the perfect life and wants to join him, and the dog happily accepts his company. However, as they travel to the dog's home, the wolf notices the fur around the dog's neck is worn away. He inquires about this and the dog replies casually that his collar leaves a mark around his neck. Collar? The wolf knows no such thing and soon realizes that the dog is not free, so he leaves him. A full belly is a poor price to pay for liberty.

"Why does the dog have a collar around his neck?" I ask mother.

"Because he has an owner," mother responds.

"But why is that a bad thing?" I respond. "Why doesn't the wolf want to be owned? He's hungry, shouldn't he eat?"

"Because, he isn't free," Tiago interjects. "It's better to have the choice of feeding yourself than have someone feed you."

I am a kid so I make nothing of the story, but Tiago is old enough to understand its lesson. He realizes he is not the wolf in the story, he is the dog, and mother is the owner. She provides us with food and sustenance, but carries our collars high above our heads. It isn't only her who is our master, but the rest of society as well. They force us to live underground and they dictate our actions. This fable is a tale that resonates with him for a long time. That is what drives his yearning for freedom.

I move on to the kitchen. The piles of dishes and cooking utensils are gone. The many spices and canned goods mother had are no longer there, only empty shelves remain. On the counter where the outside window is, there used to be a vase of handpicked flowers that she would fill every month. There would be roses, tulips, daffodils, but even that has been taken away.

I notice a red stain on the floor, and can only picture Leonard face down in a puddle of blood. It sets the grim, new tone of this house.

The only thing left is our round, wooden dining table that we ate so many home cooked meals on. I see myself at age five, eating a bowl of chicken soup mother had prepared while she is busy tending to a boiling pot on the stove. I entertain myself, doodling away pictures of me and my brothers on my tablet as I happily slurp my soup.

"Mom," I call to her.

"Yes, dear," she responds.

"When you were young, what did you want to be when you grew up?"

My question startles her and she drops the metal stirring spoon into her pot. She looks out of the window and stares off to space. I am young and unaware of the effect my question has on my mother.

"Mommmm," I say, nagging at her. "Did you hear me?"

She snaps out of her trance and focuses on the question. "Yes, dear, I heard you. Sorry, mommy was thinking of something else. What was your question again?"

"What did you want to be when you were young?" I repeat my question.

She turns off the stove and takes a seat next to me. She observes my sketches and gazes at me.

"Oh," she begins saying. "I wanted to be a lot of things growing up. I wanted to be a dancer, a singer, a model. I wanted to travel the world and meet the man of my dreams. What do you want to be, my little princess?"

"Oh, I don't know," I say casually. "Maybe an artist, or maybe a space explorer! Oh, maybe I can be a dancer or singer too! Maybe I can be famous! Do you think I can do that, mom?"

She is weary to answer my question. She doesn't have the heart to tell me I could never be those things.

"Maybe one day," she says indecisively.

"So did you get to do those things? Did you get to be a dancer?" I say as I continue to scribble on my tablet.

"Sort of."

She looks away from me and stares at the ground. I continue to color without a care in the world, but she silently reflects on her past. All she can think about are the sins she's committed.

"Did you fall in love with the man of your dreams?" I ask her. I set my tablet aside and look straight at her.

"Well, kind of," she says hesitantly.

"Is that who our dad is?"

She looks at me and doesn't know what to say. I'm a curious child and I want to know the answers to everything, no matter how uncomfortable they may be. I don't know the gravity of the question.

Suddenly, she hears Oscar screaming in the background, followed by Tiago's childish laughing.

"Looks like the boys are at it again," she says, changing the subject. "You finish your soup, sweetie, I'm going to tend to them."

I finish my meal. I never do get my answer.

The memory fades in front of me and I'm transported back to the empty kitchen. My siblings and I had so many entertaining times eating and cooking away in this room, but there won't be any more meals to cook here. I'll only be able to look back on those times and remember how long ago those days were.

The kitchen window has a wonderful view of our backyard. It's unfenced and there's nothing but tall grass fields that outstretch for a mile. Our house is at the edge of town and there is a lot of undeveloped land surrounding us. The backyard was a haven of sorts. Mother let us go out, she wasn't worried about someone spotting us there.

There used to be a tree that stood in the middle of the field. It was old and the roots were weak. It had a makeshift swing hanging from its branch. I look outside and I imagine a time when the tree was there.

I see it not tall and proud, but on the verge of collapsing. It's a clear spring day and I'm nine. Mother has planned a picnic so we could enjoy the wonderful, sunny weather. By that age, we are already plugged into all of our electronics and she wants us to take a break. An outdoor outing is the idea she comes up with.

She had everything ready, sandwiches, drinks, and some stories she could read to us, just like she did when we were young. Some of us aren't interested in that kid's stuff anymore, like my older brothers, so they are begrudgingly forced to join us. Everyone is about to settle in, but mother has forgotten to get a serving spoon for her salad, so she asks me to run in the house and get it.

I gleefully accept my task. I walk toward the house, but I start feeling queasy. A throbbing pain hits my head and I kneel down over, clutching it. I can hear Isaac yelling to see if I'm okay, but I ignore him because the pain is too strong.

It feels like something is pounding at my skull from the inside and I hear a barrage of high pitched sounds. It lasts for seconds, but it feels like minutes. And then I see something. My family is happily munching on their sandwiches when a cracking and crunching sounds speeds through the air. The tree is falling. They desperately try to run away but they're not fast enough. It falls over and crushes everything underneath. I am helpless to stop them.

I start to cry and open my eyes only to realize that what I saw didn't happen. They're still sitting there, talking, starting to eat. It's only Isaac who has gotten up and he stands in front of me.

"Are you okay, Iris?" he asks.

"Um, yeah, I think so," I say confusedly. "The tree is still there."

"Of course it is. Why wouldn't it be?"

Suddenly, a panic overcomes me. I don't know why, but I have an impulse to get everyone away from the tree. I dash over to the picnic area without responding to Isaac's question.

"Iris, what's wrong?" he yells at me.

But I'm already near the others. I wrap up the blankets in haste, engulfing the nicely set plates and food in them. Some of my siblings look confused, others look angry.

"What the hell are you doing?" Alex yells at me.

"We have to move, away from the tree," I say hysterically as I continue to gather everything.

"Why?" mother asks. "What's wrong?"

I've collected all the items and ignore her question. Tiago grabs my arm.

"Iris, what's wrong with you?" he says angrily.

"Let go!" I yell.

This causes him to tighten his grip, so I drag him and the others away from the tree into a safe zone.

"Let go!" I yell again.

"Not until you tell me what's going on!" he says. I don't have time to explain. The tree starts to make the same cracking noise I heard and its base crumbles. Pieces of wood fly everywhere. Within seconds, a thunderous thump hits the ground, right where they were sitting, and clouds of dirt fill the air. Tiago lets go of my arm.

"How did you know?" he says in a stupefied tone.

"I… I don't know, I just saw it."

That was the first vision I ever saw, though I would have plenty more later. That spot always reminds me of it.

Isaac is still in the living room inspecting and I slink away from the kitchen towards a door in the wall. It leads to the basement, to the underground sprawl where all our rooms are. I wonder if they took all our belongings from there. I walk down, guided by the streams of light leaking through the small windows that are barely above the ground.

Sure enough, when I get down to the bottom level, I am not surprised. The rooms have been cleared out. Every single corridor is bare.

I walk to the end which leads to a big room that was our study. Mother homeschooled us there and taught us about the world outside. I remember the first time she told us about the world's history, about the Event, about the Ark Project, about everything.

"What about us?" Candy asks her. I see her and my other brothers and sisters seated in our desks. I'm ten years old.

"What do you mean, Candy?" mother replies.

"You said that the Ark Project led to intelligent species, but none of them you named look like us. What are we?"

Mother doesn't know how to respond to the question. "You? Um, you are special."

"No, we're not," Tiago says bitterly. "If we're so special, why do we live underground? Why do you keep us hidden from the world?"

He is now a teenager and rebellion courses through his veins. He is older than us and he's been here longer than anyone else. He yearns for freedom, but mother denies it from him.

"Because, they won't understand who you are," she says.

"They? Who, humans? Wolves? Dogs? Lions? How do you know that?"

"I just do, trust me, Tiago."

He is still young, so parts of him obey our mother. He sits his down and rests his head in his arms despondently.

"Children," my mother says, "I know some of you are curious about the outside world. I would be, too. But I can tell you that your curiosity will be unsatisfied. There is nothing for you out there, only pain and misery. People, animals, they will all want to hurt you. You're only safe here with me."

Some of my brothers and sisters look terrified, others look skeptical. This is when our family started to divide, when factions started to rise, factions that would shape the events of this evening. They weren't pleasant memories and I walk away from the room.

I traverse back through the corridors. Each one belonged to a different sibling. One was Isaac's, one was Maddie's, one was Lombardi's. All of us had our own special little place and I make my arrival to the one I claimed. It's empty.

My mind travels to a few days ago, right after mother had died. I am frantic, messily packing my things into a bag, carrying whatever I can. I know there's a chance I'll never come back home. My room has so many memories and I don't know what I should take.

The essential survival items come first. Food, bottles of water, and several changes of clothes fill my bag, leaving only a little room for other things. I see a picture that's framed, one that has all of our family members. It was taken only months ago, one of the few times that all of us were in a photo together. We took it on the porch and I remembered how happy it made mother knowing that after all these years, we were still a family. She was so ecstatic that she made copies for everyone and made sure we cherished it as much as she did.

Tears hit the frame as I look at it. She was dead and that picture reminds me that I will never see her happy again. But it's also one of the few reminders that, for a time, we helped her find some joy in life. Our mother had a tough life, but in her eyes, we were the reward for going through those challenging years. I will be forever grateful. I wipe the tears from the glass and put the picture in my bag.

Everything is packed and I'm about to leave when one more thing catches my eye. It's the story tablet mother had, the one she read fables from. When we grew old and had no interest in those stories, she threw it in the trash. She hadn't read to us in years, so I guess she had no use for it. But I did and I plucked it from the receptacle without ever telling her. I needed something to remind me when times were simpler, when I had no worries.

I remember standing there with my bag. There was no more room to fit any items. I take one last look at the story tablet, the last piece of my childhood and walk away.

The room starts to darken and I snap out of my trance. It's no longer filled with mementoes. I'm back to reality.

I walk up the stairs and return to my brother.

"So, what do we do now Isaac?" I say.

"I've been thinking about that, Iris," he says. "We should wait until sunrise and then we'll have to find another place to hide. It won't be safe here for long."

"I know, I never thought our home wouldn't be."

"Huh?" Isaac asks.

He's unaware of the things I've been thinking, unaware of the emotional journey I've taken through the past.

"Are you okay, Iris?" he asks.

Tears start to flow down my eyes and I let out a light sniffle.

"Yeah, I'm fine," I say, struggling through the words. "If it's okay with you, I'm going to sit on the porch for a while."

"Sure, sure," he says softly.

I plop myself on the front porch and let the tears come out. So much flashes through my mind and every image makes it harder for me to regain my composure.

There was a time when I could sit on this porch and find moments of peace. Tiago could be fighting with mother, or I'd be distraught about my future. It didn't matter, though, because on that porch, I could look up at the sky and let all my troubles drift through the wind.

"Sister?" Isaac says from behind me.

I wipe away my tears and sweep aside my misery.

"I'm fine, I'm fine," I say.

"What were you doing earlier?" he asks.

"Nothing, just thinking about things."

"Like what?"

"The past. You know, when we were young."

"Oh," he says. He treads cautiously. "Those… were good days, right?"

"Yes," I say, wiping another tear away. "They were."

Those days were some of the best I ever had, but now they are tainted. I can't look back on the past and find happiness anymore. If I do, it'll remind me of what I used to have and what I never will again.

Chapter 29 – Simon Trevor

Storm

<u>November 17, 3040 4:10 AM</u>

I landed my hovercar in the distance, like I did when we approached the Spades and Diamond Casino. I want to have the element of surprise on my side because I don't think they're expecting us.

I've sent Apollo on scout duty to see what we're up against. He's been running circles around the building and hasn't raised any alarms, but he'll have a hard time determining who is in the building without a clear view. The Li station has very few windows to peer in and even if we could see what was going on inside, there are no lights on. It appears they're working in the dark.

It might be another ruse set up by Tiago. Perhaps Curtis was lying to Fenrir before the bomb went off, to throw us off the trial and lure us into another trap. But in order for that to happen, Curtis would have had to know that someone would survive and who could've predicted that? I certainly doubt that any of these halfkinds can tell the future.

"So, looks like this is the final charge, eh?" Fenrir says to me. "We're storming the gates before the sunrise."

"I suppose so," I say.

"Commander, I hope you're right."

"Right about what?"

"About what we're doing," he responds. "Shoot first, ask later. Don't let your guard down, hit a preemptive strike. Do you really think they're that dangerous?"

"We didn't think so before. Look how it's turned out."

"I suppose you're right," he says reluctantly. "But, as I asked before, do you think what we're doing is right or not?"

I dodge around the question because the answer isn't simple. "It doesn't matter if it's right or not, what matters is what will happen if we don't do anything."

"And what do you think will happen?"

"I don't know. But judging from tonight, it doesn't seem to be any good."

"That's the human way, I suppose," he says gruffly. "Either destroy, destroy, destroy, or create, create, create. Why can't your kind leave things alone?"

"I can't answer for all my kind," I say defensively. "But I suppose doing something is better than doing nothing."

"So you think," he responds vaguely. It's odd, when we started this mission, Fenrir was the one who seemed most likely to hold nothing back, while I was the one who wanted to use restraint. Now the roles are reversed.

Apollo returns from his scouting mission and interrupts our conversation. He can sense the tension.

"I hate to break up the party because I know you and Fenrir must be having an enlightening conversation, but I think Curtis was telling the truth," he says. "There's one of them out on patrol right now."

"Which one?" I ask.

"The cheetah halfkind, Ace Lawton," he responds.

"And he didn't see you?" Fenrir asks.

"I doubt it or he would've reacted sooner," Apollo says.

"Good job, Apollo. Did you get a look inside?"

He shakes his head. "Sorry, Commander, it's closed shut."

"It's okay."

"What's the plan, Trevor?" Fenrir asks.

"No more sneak attacks," I say. "We do a frontal assault. It'll be at most six halfkinds and we brought in some extra fire power, so we're prepared for whatever they have."

"Ahh, you're referring to the Spitfire?" Apollo says.

I pick up the heavy gun from the ground and secure its strap around my torso.

"Yes, I am," I say. "And this."

I pull out some mini grenades from my pockets. They're called mini grenades because of their size, not because of their damage capabilities. Their blast radius is quite remarkable.

"What do you guys have?" I ask. "Don't tell me you only have those single barrel energy pistols equipped in your helmets."

Apollo swishes his tail in an odd motion. The sensors in the back of his helmet pick it up and four more barrels protrude from hidden compartments. Fenrir does the same.

"Try five barrels," Apollo says. "We can switch it to higher caliber, too, if you want."

"Um, that's not necessary," I say. "Fenrir, do you have any more marbles left in your shooter?"

"Only a few, I didn't have time to restock or recharge," he says.

"That's okay. Everyone's armor equipped?" I ask. They both nod. "Okay. We'll take out Ace first and then carefully make our way in. Equip your scent boosters. Got it?"

Both of their helmets switch gears and out come the scent boosters.

"Good," I say. "Let's go."

We march prudently towards the station. It's about 200 meters away. We walk through some shrubbery that hugs a hovercar parking lot. It leads to the entrance and it's our only cover, as the area around the station is quite open. I crouch down and make sure my head doesn't stick out. The canines tread lightly on their paws.

We're now about 100 meters away and I can see someone moving along the side wall. He's strolling about casually and appears to be holding an energy pistol. He grips it loosely with his hands. I give the signal for the others to stop and their steps come to an immediate halt.

"You see him?" I ask the other two.

"Yes," Apollo says. "That's Ace."

"You think either of you can get a clear shot from here?" I ask.

"It's a tad far," Apollo says.

"Yes, 100 meters is a bit much," Fenrir says. "Even with my homing sensors on, I'm not sure how accurate I can be."

"I don't know how much closer we can get without attracting attention," I say. "If neither of you think you can do it, I'll take it."

"Be my guest," Fenrir says. "You're the Commander."

Apollo also nods.

"Okay," I say. Both my hands clamp down on the handle of my pistol, my right index finger grazes the trigger. I hold it up in front of my eye, keep my arms steady, and zoom in on my target. A deep breath goes in and then exhales out. My mind is clear, my focus is strong. I take one last look at my target and pull the trigger.

The flare streaks out of my gun, arcing in the air until it homes in my target. It travels fraction of a millisecond by fraction of a milliseconds. I'm wide right. I miss by a few inches.

Ace reacts to the impact of my shot. A small hole is on the station wall. He sees the dent and is confused by what has happened. He doesn't make the connection that it was a pistol that fired at him, but knows something very peculiar is going on. He peers closer at my miss and inspects it.

"Let's move!" I yell. "Full strike!"

The three of us emerge from the bushes and charge towards him. He turns around and it looks like he's about to vomit. He doesn't have time to think and bolts for the door, his pistol still in hand.

We're about 20 meters away and we're closing in on him. He's in front of the entrance and knocks a few times on the closed door. We fire a few shots his way, but aiming on a full sprint isn't easy and they miss him left and right. He sure is taking his sweet time entering the building. As we approach, I notice he's not trying to get in, but phoning in some kind of code.

Sure enough, I'm right. Out bursts a behemoth of a creature, a pistol in each hand, firing like a maniac.

"Try and take me down, assholes!" he yells.

The glare of the street lights shine off his massive frame and they hug his colossal and well-defined muscles. He has a horn stuck in the middle of his head. It's Alex Lawton.

The three of us split up and take cover. I hide behind a trash bin, Fenrir dashes behind small metal wall, and Apollo jumps under some raised plant holders. I delicately pop my head up, but I'm hit with a barrage of gunfire.

"Apollo, Fenrir, do your helmets have something that can help us see past our cover?" I ask them on my communicator.

"Yes, there's a camera installed on the top," Apollo says. "I can use it to peer above this plant holder."

I wait a few seconds and he chimes back in.

"It's out. Those two definitely know where we are, they're firing recklessly at our locations," Apollo says.

"We don't need your fancy device to figure that out, the barrage of energy shots tell us the story!" Fenrir shoots back. "Give us something we don't know."

"Their location is about 20 meters ahead of you, to the left. Can you sneak in a marble and distract them? We can use it as cover fire."

"Got it," Fenrir says. I see him press a button on his leg mounted box with his paw. A blue, bouncy ball of energy fires from it. I stick my head out and see Ace and Alex looking at it, entranced by its gentle glow. But then Alex realizes what it is, pushes Ace out of the way, and jumps to the side. The sphere goes off, emitting a concentrated explosion that sends pieces of the ground flying into the air.

Now is our time. I jump out from behind the trash bin and start firing at Ace. Apollo and Fenrir also start charging. They team up and throw a volley of fire in Alex's direction.

Ace and Alex both roll around until they find something they can hide behind. They take a few seconds to rest and then continue their stand, firing shots left and right. It's too much to dodge, so I'm forced to find something to hide behind. I see another trash bin and use it as a temporary fort.

Apollo and Fenrir have a different strategy. They're aggressive and continue going forward, side by side. I see Alex pop up from behind his cover and fire a shot straight at them. Fenrir is able to dodge it, but Apollo gets hit square in the abdomen. I hear him yell out a sharp cry.

"Apollo!" I yell. "Fenrir, get him out of there!"

Fenrir stops dead in his tracks and turns around toward our fallen ally. Alex continues to fire, but his other shots miss wildly. His first shot must have been a fluke. Fenrir clamps his jaws on Apollo's uniform and drags him away behind an abandoned hovercar parked in front of the station.

"What's his status?" I yell frantically over the communicator as Ace continues his bombardment of shots.

"I'm fine," Apollo says. I'm surprised to hear his voice. "His shot hit my armor, I just have the wind knocked out of me. Thanks for getting me out of there, Fenrir."

"It's my job," Fenrir says taciturnly.

"We're getting in closer," I say. "Continue the assault. Our priority is to get inside the station and take the others out."

"Understood," both of them say.

I stick my gun out and fire a few shots blindly at Ace. He responds to my gunfire with more gunfire. Back and forth we go, our standoff switches from one side to the other like a seesaw. I look at Apollo and Fenrir, and the same thing happens to them. This is going nowhere. We need to change up our approach.

"I have a plan," I tell the others via the communicator. "I'm going to draw them out and when I do, find cover. I'll take care of the rest."

"How are you going to do that?" Apollo asks.

"With the big guns."

I dig in my pocket and pull out a mini grenade. I unstrap my Spitfire and set it to my side. I press a button to arm it and lob it overhead to Ace's direction.

"What's this?" I hear him yell. "Shit!"

A giant blast shakes the ground and I can see smoke fly into the air. The second this happens I stand and hold the Spitfire up. Alex is too distracted to see me rise and Ace has made it to the door, back turned to me. Damn this guy is fast, I thought my grenade would've damaged him in some way, but he was able to react and dodge it with his speed.

It's irrelevant. The Spitfire is already armed and aimed at him and with one pull of the trigger, I fire.

A wall of blood sprays the door and his body violently pushes forward. His back is painted red and his shirt has been torn to pieces. He falls forward, arms out stretched on top of him, and slides against the door as his wound wipes against it and creates a streak of red.

Alex, not wasting a moment, takes this opportunity to dash inside. I see him and fire another shot, but I miss. I usually don't miss at such a close range, I suppose he's blessed. He makes it through and forgets to shut it in the chaos. It's wide open.

I look at Apollo and Fenrir. Both of them have risen from their concealments and we approach the open door.

I take a look inside and see Alex's back as he continues to stumble into the hideout. There's a chimp halfkind who was working three compcubes at one time, but now her focus is on the three of us. As we stand on the front doorstep, Ace's body is right below our feet.

And then I see Tiago. I stand tall and for a moment put my firearm to the side of my body. He returns the gesture and straightens his back. We look eye to eye at each other, leaders locked in a dead stare.

"Something smells off," Apollo says. "I can't quite put my paw on it."

Suddenly, I hear a scratching sound, like sandpaper. It's Ace. He's still alive and is crawling slowly in agonizing pain back into the building.

We look at him in astonishment, dumbfounded that he isn't dead yet. There's a few holes of missing flesh on his back. His skin and fur has been singed from the extreme heat of my weapon, yet here he is, doing whatever it takes to try to get back in.

I look back at Tiago, still standing confidently, arms folded up on his chest. There's something different about his expression. He's smiling.

"Wait, I know this smell," Apollo says.

I look to where Ace is crawling and I move my head closer. I see a glimmer of light glint in front of him. My eyes sharpen in on it, it beams faintly.

I realize what it is, a wire. My eyes madly follow the string. There are metal canisters strung along the wall, near our position. Ace is now in front of the string and raises an arm above it. With one final burst of energy he lets it fall, right on the wire.

"Bomb!" I tell the others. We turn around and do a mad dash away from the door. I feel a ripple shake the ground and the front view lights up from the explosion behind me. It can't end like this, it won't. I see the trash bins I was hiding behind earlier. It's our only chance, so the three of us jump behind them. I sure hope they're made out of something sturdy.

The blast is smaller than anticipated, the only thing that reaches us is dust. We're fortunate. I stand up and see the doors are charred. The inside of the station is slightly damaged, but capable of working.

The bombs were only meant to blast away intruders, not level the building. In his last moments of life, Ace Lawton tried his best to kill us. He failed.

The lights turn on and I can see the others hiding behind a makeshift fort of furniture. Fenrir said Curtis Lawton did the same thing. They're concealed, but we'll smoke them out. The final assault has just begun.

Chapter 30 – Tiago Lawton

Meltdown

November 17, 3040 4:32 AM

I'm hiding behind a flipped over metal table and I see the human and his canine companions entering through the front door, guns drawn cautiously. I immediately fire at them with my pistol. They split to the sides, the human and dog go right, the wolf goes left. I try to hit them as they scurry away, but they're too fast and within seconds they find something to hide behind.

I empty my gun at both targets, as does Alex. Candy hides behind a table, per my instructions. I tell her whatever happens to stay there, I can't afford to lose our family prodigy. They return fire promptly and we both duck and wait for them to recharge. They have heavier weapons, like the human's hand cannon, but our fort is remarkably sturdy. Back and forth it goes for five, no, ten minutes. Our fortifications are strong, but our weapons are too weak. Their weapons are too strong, but there's too much clutter to do any damage.

We're at a standstill.

It's not dark like it was a few minutes ago. The bulbs now glow, making everything visible. Candy's many compcubes, food, clothes, and our other belongings can be clearly seen. Before they barged in, the station was almost fully charged and power started to flow throughout it. As a result, the lights turned on. My eyes had to adjust, as we'd been working in the dark the whole time. Yet it's nice to see things lucidly when it was so difficult earlier.

"We have to do something," Alex says as the shots continue to rain in.

I take a look at my surroundings to formulate a plan. About fifteen feet to the right is the teleporter, our ticket out of here. It's a twelve feet high pod that has a sliding door made of teleranium, a special metal used to handle teleporting. A faint glow leaks from the outlining of the door, signaling that it is powered and ready to go. To teleport, all one has to do is set the destination at the control panel, and when it is ready the door will slide open. Once you step in, the door closes, and in a dash you're in a new city, country, or even the Moon. You see a flash and you're done.

But there's one complication that prevents us from busting out of Primm: the control panel is on the other side of the station, right in firing range of our enemies. Candy was working on getting the teleporter fired up before they arrived, but once the battle started and a bloody Ace fell through the door, she had to abort her mission.

Ace, my loyal brother, didn't deserve such a gruesome death. When I saw him crawling in agonizing pain towards the trip wire, I knew what he was going to do. I wanted to go out there to tend to his wounds, but he looked up at me and shook his head. He let me know it was okay, he had a plan. I gave him a sneer. If things worked out, Ace would trigger the blast and we'd be rid of these hunters forever. Candy, Alex, and I would be free. My smirking face was the last thing I wanted that human to see, a final "fuck you, we made it."

I watched him crawl, and all I could do was think about the times when we were young. He tried to win my admiration. Whether it was by taking my side in fights or doing anything at the whim of my command, I could only think of one word to describe him: devoted. There hasn't been a moment when he wasn't looking for my approval, when he wasn't trying to make me proud. Well, brother, you did.

"We have to get the teleporter running and make a break for it or Ace's sacrifice will be in vain," I say to Alex.

"Obviously, but there's no way we can get it started in all this chaos," he says. "We'll be killed on the spot. And Candy is the only one who knows how to operate the thing."

"Wait a minute, something is off."

I hear something that I haven't heard since the assault started - silence.

I stand up to see that there has been a cease fire. The human, dog, and wolf are still hiding behind their cover, but nothing is happening. That is until the human pops up from his position and uses his right arm to volley something in the air. It's small and hard to see, but he launches it far enough for it to come flying in our direction. I reach up in the sky and catch it, plucking it like a low hanging fruit. I open my hands and in my paw I see what it is. Oh, shit!

I throw it back in their direction and, like rats, they flee from it. It explodes right when it lands. Broken bits of concrete, metal, and wood erupt into the atmosphere.

The three are still alive, though. They've moved forward and hunkered down behind some more fortifications, away from the blast, but closer to the control panel. They start to fire again.

"They're moving in closer," Alex says. "It'll only be minutes until they come close enough to kill us. We're out-powered and out-matched. We have to make our escape now."

"And how do you suppose we do that?" I ask Alex. "Whoever is going to start the teleporter is embarking on a suicide mission!"

"I know," Candy says. Her hallmark smile and her uplifting demeanor are nowhere to be found. It's been replaced by a no nonsense attitude and grave stare. She's serious about it.

"No, Candy, you don't have the same stake in this as Alex and I. You're too valuable and intelligent to sacrifice," I say. My tone is stern. I really don't want her to go.

"It's not a sacrifice," she says. "It's a choice. None of you know how to operate the controls, only I do. If I don't do it, then we're all dead. It's better that two of us make it than none."

"No, Candy," I say harshly. I'm hoping I can scare her out of it, but she doesn't budge.

"She's right," Alex says. "She's the only one who can get us out of here."

"Shut up, Alex!" I yell. Wave after wave of ammunition continues to hit us. I start to see holes and cracks forming in our stronghold. We won't last very long if we wait around. But this is a choice I do not want to make. Candy has done so much with so little. Her future holds so much greatness. I could never live with myself if it was thrown away.

"I'm sorry, Candy, but the answer still is no. We'll figure something out instead," I say.

She looks disappointed by my decision, but abruptly lifts her head up and says, "Tiago, there's nothing left to figure out."

Candy gets up from where she was sitting. Her legs start to churn as she begins her race to the teleporter controls. In a last, desperate act, I grab her foot, but she promptly kicks it away and continues towards her goal.

Energy shots fly past her. She jumps and ducks to avoid getting hit. But it's no use, I see her take one to the arm. She falls over and clutches it in pain. Lucky for her, she tumbled right behind a column and it blocks her from the team's aim.

"Candy!" I yell. "Stop! Come back!"

She peers out from behind. "No, I'm too close to quit now."

Candy gets back up and makes a mad dash to the panel. I see her run, savagely with all her might and, amazingly, she makes it. She only has seconds to fiddle with the panel and she works on the controls in incredible time. I look over to the pod and the door opens. She did it. San Francisco, here we come.

But it will only be two of us. The human and dog circle in on their target and direct all their firepower on her. She's hit with a shower of fiery light, her body jerks around like a puppet on a string. It only last a few seconds but seems like an eternity. Every small flail of her limbs, every agonizing expression she makes on her face, I can see so vividly.

Her violent dance stops and there's nothing left but my sister, torn up from head to toe, leaned against the wall, any life extinguished from her.

As I see her lifeless body slumped against the wall, visions flash in my mind. I see her as a scientist finding cures for diseases that have just been discovered. I see her as an engineer, developing new tech that could revolutionize the industry. I see her as biologist, unlocking the secrets of not only our origins, but of every creature on this planet. She is the future, a mind unmatched in this world.

But, I realize even if she lived, the brightest gem can't shine when people can't see past the rough edges. She'd never do those things and it makes me mad.

This world is ignorant, this world is blind, this world is a horrible place. All they see is what is on the outside without realizing the gifts that lie inside. What a stupid place indeed. The anger I feel fuels my fire to make it, to avenge not only her, but all of us who were never given a chance.

"The teleporter is live," I tell Alex. "It's time to leave. Get the final present ready."

He grabs Candy's last bomb.

"I hope when we get out of here, there won't be a trace left of these guys to weep over," he says.

I grab two energy pistols and lead the way to teleporter pod. Its door is still open, all Alex and I have to do is walk in and we'll be gone. I empty sphere after sphere of bright lights at the enemy, creating enough cover fire for us to make a straight dash to it. They duck under their barricades for safety as I lead the way. Alex is right behind me and adds to the pandemonium with fire of his own.

They don't return anything back and I can taste the freedom. We are feet away from the pod and I make a final leap towards it. I'm inside, but nothing happens. I'm confused. I wonder if I'm already in San Francisco, but I look forward and still see the damaged Li station in front of me. The teleportation pod has been powered down, the mesmerizing glow that emits from it has now disappeared. What could've happened?

I scan my surroundings and see the cause, the control panel has been destroyed. The human had his gun aimed at it, but he draws it down and back to me. The fraction of a second before I made my final dive into the pod, he blew it to pieces with his hand cannon. Without the control panel, the teleporter is useless. It automatically shut down. My attempt failed.

I look around to see where Alex has gone to, but he's not in my view. I am alone, left to confront my killers, the ones fighting in the so called name of justice. The game is over. My chance to be at liberty has slipped away from my fingers and now I stare down the barrel of a gun. I close my eyes and think about what I've done. I should've known my greedy ambitions weren't worth it. I'm sorry, I'm so, so sorry.

I feel my torso imploding and then exploding. It feels like an anchor has jammed into my stomach and ripped it inside out. Then it burns like I'm being branded, everywhere. The pain is excruciating and I feel the blood trickle from my stomach down to my leg. I smell the smoke emitting from my burning flesh.

I open my eyes and look down to see a large wound encompass the front of me and I stumble backwards in a state of shock. I land ass first into the teleportation pod. It's a fitting way to die. I wanted to reach this stage so badly, risked life and limb, made sacrifices I never thought I could make, and it looked like I was going to spend my last moments here. Karma indeed.

But I am not dead, yet. Despite the agony I feel mentally and physically, I'm still breathing, I'm still aware of my surroundings. I see the human, dog, and wolf approaching me, guns still pointed straight in my direction.

"Don't move," the human says.

"Don't worry," I say, moving my lips slowly. "I don't have anywhere to go."

"Apollo, Fenrir, go look for the other one, Alex. We lost him in the firestorm with Tiago, he's probably hiding…"

A bright light hits my eye and it appears to go through the human. His head swings back and I see a cloud of blood puff from his front cranium. He falls to his knees and his back bends on his legs awkwardly. His arms collapse to his sides and the gun in his hands plunges to the ground. Finally, the back of his head slams on the floor. His eyes are still open, glazed over, but I'm sure he was already dead before he hit the ground.

The wolf and dog look stunned and even I'm bewildered by his sudden death. It happens so fast, I don't even have time to think about what happened.

"Commander!" The dog runs over to his body to see if he is okay, but it's useless. He's dead as a doorknob. I see his snout shaking and lips snarling, but his grief is interrupted by someone's presence. He looks up and I look to the right where the dog is staring.

Things now make so much sense. There I see Alex, smoking pistol in one hand, bomb in the other. Suddenly, I can't help but jeer a little. At least one of us might make it out alive.

Chapter 31 – Apollo Bradley

Fable

November 17, 3040 4:47 AM

I've felt anger a few times in my life, but never rage. Rage is different from anger. When you're angry, you become mad for brief moments. Perhaps you do something you regret, but there's still something holding you back from going over the edge.

With rage, there's nothing holding you back. No morals, no conscience, just raw emotion. It blinds you. The moment that Commander Trevor died, that's what I felt. It was pure, it was unbridled, it was personal.

Commander Trevor, a mentor, a colleague, an idol, lies motionless on the floor. Blood trickles down from the hole in his cranium, his body bent in an uneasy position. Just a minute ago, he was barking orders while we were in the fight of our lives. He was our main support, I looked to him for guidance not only in this shootout, but in so many other facets of my life. He was the person I wanted to model myself after. I wanted to climb the ranks of the Dog Alliance and eventually become what he was, a respected leader and model soldier.

He was also a good guy. Sometimes you have friends that aren't truly your friends. Dogs, humans, whomever, that you call late in the night for advice and would be annoyed that you rang. Friends who tell you they'll see you later, but you never hear from them again. Commander Trevor was far from this. He was a great friend, honorable, dependable, and caring. When times got rough, or when I'd worry about an upcoming mission, he was the guy I could call to make sure that things were going to be okay. It wouldn't matter when I bothered him because it wasn't a bother at all. They have that saying about how dogs can be loyal to humans. After meeting Simon, I know that it can work vice versa.

He was a leader through and through. Sure, he had moments of weakness, what human doesn't, but there isn't anyone else I would have heading this mission. He commanded the charge against the enemy and he paid the ultimate price for it. He didn't die heroically, he died from the shot of a coward, who killed him at the least suspecting moment.

I look at the culprit, a whopping, enormous mass of creature and I see nothing but the enemy. This waste of life we call a halfkind is responsible for killing my best friend. I will make him pay dearly. I will give him agonizing wound after wound, and it's not until I have him, and all his kind, begging for mercy that I will fire my final shot.

We gave them a chance to come peacefully. We tried that with Oscar, yet he wanted to rip Commander Trevor's head off. We held back against Curtis and he blew our teammates out of the sky. We let our guard down against this freak. No more holding back, it's time to recognize the enemy and take him down.

"You better stand back," Alex Lawton says to us as he holds a metal canister. "This thing is like the one Curtis had. I activate it and all of us are gone, so stand the fuck back!"

He looks agitated and scared. His arm shakes, eyes blink furiously, and his snout twitches. He took a coward's shot at Simon. I see nothing but weakness in him, so I step closer.

"I said, get back!" he yells frantically.

The gears in my helmet move a little and a barrel sticks out.

"Fire," I say softly.

A shot rings out of my head and hits him directly on his shoulder. His mouth opens wide and he roars out a bellow that echoes through the station. His canister drops harmlessly onto the floor and I see his wound smoking, smoldering as pieces of red and black float into the air.

"Ow, goddamnit!" he says.

"Fire," I say again.

The shot hits him in his other shoulder and his body twists in reaction. He wobbles back a few feet, as if he is going to fall, but his legs catch him before his knees buckle. The gun he has drops from his hand and falls to the floor. It bounces for half a second until it succumbs to its weight.

"Ugh," he says. He doesn't react as strongly to the second one. The pain overloads his mind.

"Fire," I say once more.

The shot careens forward and hits him square on the knee. His leg falls limply to the ground and causes him to kneel over. His arms are dull, unresponsive, and collapse to his side. He grits his teeth and clenches whatever he can as he tries to comprehend the agony that shoots through his body.

"Fire," I say again.

Another knee cap has been demolished and blood bursts from it like a broken water balloon. His legs give in and he lands square on his ass. He adjusts his body a bit. The only thing he can control is his back and he tries hard to keep it straight. But it's pointless.

"Fire," I say one last time.

This shot goes directly into his chest, above his heart. He instantly falls over backward, head on the ground, looking straight up. He's still alive, but I've completely disabled him using my pistol. Like a surgeon, I've dissected my target using nothing but focus and precision. I don't want to grant him a quick death. I want him to feel every shot piercing him, I want him to know that his demise will be painful.

Fenrir looks at me stunned, but also inquisitively.

"He's not going anywhere," I say to him. "Keep your gun pointed at him, make sure he doesn't do anything funny."

I walk over to where Tiago is laying. He's still alive, but his wound and heavy breathing suggest he might not last that long. I don't have much time to get my answers.

I stare him down and he does the same. His lips are tight, his eyes narrow and unfriendly.

"Where are the other two?" I ask him.

He's taken back by my question and looks at me peculiarly.

"I don't know… what you're talking… about," he says.

"Don't play dumb with me," I say. "I know about the twins, I met them personally. We had briefings on your whole family before our mission. They're the only two left. Where are they?"

He reacts with a hint of surprise, but goes back to his stonewalled demeanor.

"I don't know," he says. "They left with… Oscar and I haven't seen them… since."

"Is that so?" I say. "That's too bad. I was going to offer you some medical help in exchange for the information. Your wounds are bad, but treatable. With the right staff working on you, you'll survive. Tell me where they are and I can guarantee that they'll be here in ten minutes."

"You think... I can still... be saved? You do see what I see... right?"

"It wouldn't hurt to try. Cooperate and I might even throw in an order to release you."

He looks at me hesitantly and thinks carefully about my offer. "You're bluffing. The second... I tell you... you'll kill me."

"I'm a dog of my word. It won't happen," I say.

"Why do you want them... anyway?"

I pause and think about Simon. "Because my commander died before he could complete his mission. I intend to finish it for him. Besides, during my run in with the twins, they beat me. Let's just say I think they're dangerous, especially since they have an older brother like you."

He shakes his head cautiously. "No, you're wrong... they aren't dangerous. And I don't care what you offer. You can throw me a tablet... with an order from the United Species Alliance that would guarantee my freedom... that I'll never be persecuted again... and I would throw it back at you if it meant ratting out... the twins. I've done a lot these past few days... done some horrible things... but this is where I draw the line."

"You betrayed the others. What's one more?"

"They're different. The ones I gave up were useless... incompetent. The twins are special. I'd tear up a million... of your petty contracts."

"Really?" I ask. "Freedom is a valuable thing you know. Us dogs, wolves, animals as a whole, we've spent hundreds of years trying to grasp it from the clutches of humans, and through much sacrifice, struggle, and opportunity we got it. I'm offering it to you for a much lower price. Don't you want that?"

Tiago lets out a light chuckle.

"I do. But I don't... trust you."

"That's too bad."

I arm the barrel in my helmet straight at his head.

"No, wait!" someone yells. Alex Lawton's head is lifts up, grimaces, and looks straight at me. "I'll take that deal."

Tiago looks over and, at first, doesn't seem appalled by the betrayal. It's almost as if he thinks it's a joke, that Alex would never do anything so out of line. From his face, I can tell Tiago doesn't believe the words.

"I want to live, I want to be left alone in peace," Alex adds on, his face showing nothing but truth.

I don't sense that he is bluffing. And as Tiago figures out the situation more and more, he doesn't either. A few seconds ago, he looked confident and skeptical in his brother, but now he looks upset and flabbergasted.

"No, Alex... don't," he warns him. "You can't... trust them."

Alex shakes his head. "My wounds hurt, but they can heal with the right treatment. If I don't get it, I'm dead. Also, I can be free if I take the offer. I have nothing to lose."

"And the twins?" he says desperately.

"I don't think they're as special as you do. You've revered them for years and I never understood why. It's your weakness and you've taught me that weaknesses should be disposed of. I'm sorry, brother, I'm done taking orders from you."

"But they're your... brother and sister," Tiago says sadly.

"I care as much about them as I do for the others that have died," Alex muses. "To me, they're another sacrifice so I can live."

A heartbroken Tiago shakes his head in disbelief. "Where did you learn... such treachery?"

Alex looks squarely at his brother. "From the best."

Tiago doesn't respond, just looks up at the ceiling despondently and remains quiet.

"So," I say, "where are they?"

Alex closes his eyes and musters the strength to say it. "They're back where this all started, back on the corner house on Chakming Drive."

"Thank you," I say. I think of Commander Trevor. "Fire."

The blast speeds through my helmet and through Alex's skull. His head blows backward fiercely and the shot vibrates the rest of his body, swaying it up and down on the ground for a second until it finally stops and he lies motionless.

I then turn my attention back to Tiago. He doesn't look startled at the events that just transpired, only disappointed. He sees the barrel on my helmet adjust and knows what's coming for him.

He looks at me and he looks at Fenrir. He closes his eyes and says, "I am no dog... I am no wolf... I am only myself. I am... free."

"Fire."

I take a final shot and it screams out of my helmet into Tiago's heart. He grimaces a tad bit, but with his last ounce of energy, he tilts his head backward in peace and smiles.

I walk away from him and past Fenrir, who has kept the same dismayed expression throughout both killings. He doesn't say a word, just looks at me with careful eyes.

"C'mon," I say. "We have work to do."

Chapter 32 – Fenrir Snow

Sunrise

<u>November 17, 3040 5:32 AM</u>
We've made it to 1523 Chakming Drive. It took about twenty minutes, of traversing through the dawn-lit Primm streets, but we are here.

Apollo's gears have switched, he's in full rampage mode. The only thing that guides him is his blind fury. Tiago and Alex Lawton felt his wrath for killing the Commander, his teacher, his comrade. Now it seems that the dog is here to complete the job and finish his circle of revenge.

He's made things personal. Any halfkinds left alive are no longer individuals to him, just enemies that need to be eliminated. He wants to get even. It's no longer about the mission, or the honor of duty for the United Species Alliance, it's about himself. Completing our mission will be his final parting gift to Trevor's corpse.

I find myself in a mixed frame of mind concerning the events that have transpired. These halfkinds may have killed more than half my team and our fearless leader, but I can sympathize with their cause more than our own. If we had left them alone, if the order had never been made by the United Species Alliance, perhaps things could've ended peacefully. We didn't have to kill them, we could've co-existed. Instead, the order is the order and it's caused a lot of unnecessary bloodshed.

We backed them into a corner and the only thing they can do is fight back. It's for their survival. Unlike the dog, for them it's been anything but personal. We are their faceless enemy. We are not victims, they are. We are the murderers, it's just that we murder in the name of our leaders.

Things made themselves so clear during our raid on the Li station. With wrath coursing through his veins, Apollo brought out their vulnerabilities and exploited them in order to finish them off. He tricked Alex and rubbed Tiago's demise in his face. Trevor's death has completely transformed him into a dog on a mission, a relentless killing machine that now won't stop until his friend is avenged. There is no honor in that.

I already had doubts about my role as an assassin for the Brotherhood of Wolves. Now I'm at the brink of quitting. I don't want to fail my colleagues, but as we get closer and closer to the end, things feel so wrong. These halfkinds aren't criminals or dangerous crime bosses, they're civilians.

I think about Tiago's last words, dog and wolf and himself. What could he have possibly meant? The question leaves me confused and I thought about those last lines on our way here. I still haven't come up with an answer.

We're at the porch and the front door is cracked open. The house is dilapidated, the paint, chipped and worn off. The inside looks vacant. Apollo has his scent booster on and gives the ground and air a sniff. He looks around and breathes the smells in deeply.

"They're here," he whispers. "Their odor is everywhere around the premises and it's fresh. Alex was telling the truth. Let's proceed."

"Let me go in first," I tell Apollo.

"Be my guest."

I nudge the door open with my nose and stick my head out. I look to the right and see nothing. I look to the left and see a cat halfkind with a giant stick that crashes down, right over my back. Crap.

It hits me hard and I fall flat on my stomach. Luckily, my armor absorbs most of the impact, but it still hurts like hell. I roll around so my head faces the ceiling and I see the cat halfkind raise the stick again, preparing for another strike. He swings wildly downward, but I evade it and roll out of the way just in the nick of time. I recover and get back up to my feet.

We stand face to face. He's lean, but toned. His face is an odd but appealing mixture of whiskers, hair, and a pink nose. His alluring yellow eyes narrow and look at me harshly. The stare down thickens the air with tension. Neither of us are willing to make a move, we stand there and gaze at each other cautiously.

However, a move is made, but not by either of us. Apollo storms in and shoots at Isaac. A blast hits him in the arm and he falls to his side. He keels over, but Apollo continues his assault. He shoots another ball of energy and it hits him again in the arm. Now the cat halfkind is on the ground, doubled over.

The adrenaline takes over his body and the cat halfkind gets up. But Apollo's attack is relentless. He shoots him again, now on his forearm, and he kneels on one knee, the other hand clutching his wounds. This time he stays down.

"No!" Another voice creeps up behind me and I see his twin running towards him. She lunges and embraces her brother as he struggles to maintain his posture. Her body covers his completely.

"Move over!" Apollo yells.

She doesn't budge an inch.

"Do it, Iris," her brother says. "He'll kill you if you don't."

She reluctantly complies and stands to the side.

"Now on your knees, hands behind your head," Apollo barks out.

She's frightened and trembling. Tears are rolling down her eyes. She's about to cry hysterically at any moment. Iris Lawton slowly puts both knees on the ground and raises her hands behind her head.

Apollo looks at Isaac Lawton. "You too."

Isaac lowers his other knee and raises one arm behind his head.

"I said both arms," Apollo demands.

"I can't," he retorts, scowling over his injury. "You kind of shredded one."

"Very well," Apollo says.

I take a look at Isaac Lawton. He can barely open one eye from the pain shooting through his body. His teeth grind so hard they might crack. He inhales in air intensely with intermittent pants coming out here and there. Blood flows down his arm like a steady river flow. It empties in drips and stains the floor with dark, thick crimson circles.

"So, you're going to kill us?" Isaac asks bluntly.

Apollo isn't expecting the question and dwells before he answers. "Yes."

"Why?"

Apollo lowers his head, not knowing the answer. He struggles to understand the reasoning and all he can say is "Because we were told to."

"So you always do what you're told? Even if you think what you're doing is wrong?" Isaac shoots back.

Apollo doesn't hesitate this time. "I wasn't sure if I was doing the right thing before taking on this task. I sympathized with your cause, I saw that we were the big bad hunters picking on the little guy. But, you know what I realized?"

"What?" Isaac says dejectedly.

"You aren't the little guy. You are the future. You represent a change and from what we've seen, change is dangerous. Much like yourselves."

"Change? What are you talking about?" Isaac says in a perplexed tone.

"I assume you know what the Event is?" Apollo says.

Isaac thinks about Apollo's question in his head. After a few seconds it seems he's come to a conclusion.

"That's what this is all about, you think we're going to blow up the world?" he yells. "Our little family? You think we're capable of that? You're delusional."

"The humans who were against the Ark Project were also viewed as delusional, and they ended up being the ones who were right," Apollo says.

"Yeah, and now you're free because of it."

"The irony is not lost on me."

"So, then we come along and you think we'll form some kind of secret society, one that will blow you up? That's the wave of destruction you speak of? Why? Because we're not like you, because we're abominations? Savages?"

"I suppose," Apollo says quietly.

"How do you respond to that? With more destruction. It doesn't matter if you're a dog, wolf, human, whatever. You all walk around and think you're civilized, that your new intelligence makes you better. But, inside, you're as savage as you were before the humans gave you the smarts. You just don't want to admit it."

"Say what you say," Apollo responds apathetically.

Isaac's voice quickly turns angry. "Don't kid yourself, you don't believe in any of the junk you're spewing. When you captured us, you and your human friend didn't want us killed. And now all of a sudden you're going to execute us like criminals? What happened? Your friend die or something?"

"Don't say anything about Commander Trevor!" Apollo says furiously. He speaks with anguish and raw emotion. "That human was killed because of your kind. He was my friend, my brother in arms. Is it personal? Perhaps, but don't even pretend that I don't know what you halfkinds are capable of. His death opened my eyes - I now see the damage your kind can do. I saw it in Tiago, that's why I killed him. All of you are so thirsty for freedom, you'll do anything for it. Our ancestors had that same thirst and we all know how that turned out."

Isaac, a little astonished asks, "Is Tiago really dead?"

"Yes," Apollo says.

He shakes his head in disbelief and says, "Well, I'm sorry your friend died."

"I don't believe anything you halfkinds say anymore."

I look at Isaac and his face sours. He realizes that no matter what he says, nothing will help.

"I should've killed you back in the sewer," Isaac says sorely.

"Yeah, you should've," Apollo responds. "Fire."

Just like the others, a comet of energy zips from his helmet and through Isaac's brain. He probably doesn't even have time to realize what has happened before he blacks out of consciousness and his head hits the floor.

Immediately, Iris Lawton bursts into hysterics. She lunges at her brother, and picks up his body to place it on her knees. She grabs him tightly, holding on for dear life, and buries her head into his chest as tears pour out of her eyes.

Iris then let's go of her grip slightly and rubs his face with the back of her hand, wiping the blood off his fur. She gazes into his soulless eyes and cries even harder as she places his limp head over her shoulder, clutching her dead brother's body like a mother and a newborn.

I watch and I can't help but feel her pain. Her tears are the culmination of a lifelong struggle to be accepted, to have that one word that has been tossed around so much - freedom. And now she sits there, dead brother in her arms, the last of her kind, looking up at the barrel of a smoking gun.

Apollo has it aimed directly at her head, but she doesn't feel fear, she doesn't feel anxiety, she only feels the grief of her loss.

His helmet is armed, his shot ready to fire.

"I'm sorry it had to end this way," Apollo says.

"Fire."

Iris Lawton sits there, still clutching her brother's body, in shock. Apollo turns around and looks at me, bewildered at what has happened. Blood trickles down his snout and he sniffs it. His legs start to shake and he strains his body to stay up. It's no use, though, because his legs give in to the weight and he collapses. He falls lifeless in a pool of his own blood.

I snort the air and breathe in the smoke from the barrel on my helmet. He's the only kill I plan to make.

Iris is still stunned and slowly sets her brother's corpse to the ground. She approaches me softly, curious yet reluctant.

"Are you going to hurt me?" she asks me.

"No."

"Why... why did you do it?"

I look at Apollo, blood still spilling from his head. I think about how in the blink of an eye he changed from easygoing suck up to a maniacal, cold blooded murderer. It was done all in the name of a human, his master. It is at this moment I realize what Tiago was trying to say.

Dog and wolf, that's how it ended.

"I did it because I call no one my master," I say.

Iris is unsure of my words, but her reaction tells me she understands the subtle message in it.

"Are Tiago and the others really dead?" she asks.

"Yes," I say.

"Then, I guess I was right all along."

I don't know what she means, but it doesn't matter. She gets up and stands over her brother. Iris is the sole survivor in a family of eleven, possibly the only halfkind on Earth. She takes a few moments to soak up this information.

I still see water coming from her eyes and she walks around the room, pacing slowly, peering at walls as if there's something to look at. I imagine that she's looking at faded memories in her mind, places and events that will only haunt her for the rest of her life. And as these thoughts consume her, she falls to the ground and weeps softly and tenderly.

I approach her warily, unsure of how to react. But as I see the raw emotion pouring from her soul, I lose my inhibitions and nudge my head against hers as a sign of comfort.

At first she scoots back, surprised by the gesture, but she looks at my eyes and sees that my intentions are genuine. She lets go of any fear and moves forward to give me a heartfelt hug. Her eyes bury into my body and I can feel her tears as she lets her emotions go.

As she sits there, gripping my fur tightly, I look outside. Through the door, the sun stretches out over the horizon. The streaks of warmth hit my paws and warms my coat.

I close my eyes to imprint this moment in my memories. I want to remember it as long as I can.

338

Chapter 33 – Iris Lawton

Countdown

<u>December 31, 3040 11:57 PM</u>

I walk outside of my quaint little cabin and breathe in the crisp winter air. I have a large coat on and I sip on freshly brewed hot chocolate. My legs tread through the snow as I lose myself in the millions of stars that fill the sky. The moon is glowing, radiating its bright blue and green shade across the landscape. It's quiet, the only thing I hear is the rustling of pine trees in the wind.

The Northern Lights flicker across the sky so beautifully. Its illumination is vibrant and haunting. The colors dance wildly, the stars are their partners. It's a sight that I thought I would never see.

It's been over a month since my ordeal in Primm. After my brother died, along with his murderer, Fenrir Snow helped me escape from that hellhole. He confirmed that I was dead to his superiors and we waited until nightfall to make our move. The Li station had been damaged, but Fenrir made the quick fix and it became usable, so I said goodbye to my home and left Primm forever.

We secretly arrived in the Wolf's Den, the northern part of Canada. We journeyed far away from the cities, deep into seclusion. Using his contacts, he found me this abandoned cabin in the woods. It was rundown and empty, but in a month, I was able to shape it into my home. Thanks to the insta-item he provided me, I'm able to get what I need to survive out in the cold. It's now furnished and I have enough food to last me for months.

It's just a start and eventually I'll have to figure out a way to make credits to sustain myself. Perhaps I can sell things via the infospace, while continuing to live anonymously. I can't rely on Fenrir forever, but, for now, I am happy with what little I have.

I wouldn't be alive if it wasn't for him. When he shot his partner and I saw the dog fall limply to the ground, I was stunned. I thought I was going to die right there and then, but when I looked up, I only saw the affliction on Fenrir's face. He looked tired and weary. Perhaps he was broken from all the death that evening. I felt the same way and when he came to comfort me, I could sense his grief, his conflicted feelings. I hugged him because he needed one.

He still stops by once in a while, to make sure I'm safe, and in this short month, we've gained a mutual respect for each other. Hell, it's not even that, I'd say we've become foundations for each other.

I consider this wolf that had a heart of stone as my family, not as a replacement for what I've lost, but an addition to what I will remember. And, although he doesn't say it, I have a feeling I've become the one thing in this world that has helped him come into terms with himself, his purpose in this world.

That is a bond that cannot break.

I look in the darkness of the forest and it reminds me of the way I would view the world when I was young. I would look from my front porch in that house in Primm and see such a mysterious and hardened place. I was afraid of what it would bring to me, I was afraid of all the things my mother told me. There was so much uncertainty that it scared me. The only experience I had with living was in the confines of that house. Knowing that one day, I would face what lied beyond, it terrified me. I looked at my future and I saw the same darkness I see in the trees now.

When mother died, and then Leonard, and then all the others, I felt my fears were justified. We had faced so much adversity and all we wanted to do was to be left alone. That was really it. Oscar wanted to live in peace alone in Primm and even Tiago, though hard headed and angry, just wanted to be left alone on the Moon. But the powers that be couldn't let us go and the ones I loved paid the price.

Yet here I am, the last one, the last halfkind, and I suppose I've done what my brothers wanted, I'm living in solitude. If only they could see me now, they would be so proud.

I take a sip from my hot chocolate and realize that it's getting cold, so I walk back into the cabin. A fire is burning in the fireplace and I cozy up in front of it. I turn on my video feed so I can catch the countdown to the new year. The screen captures the atmosphere. Crowds are cheering, some drunk, but all look so happy. I see humans partying with dogs, pigs sharing the moment with tigers, rhinos and crocodiles downing a New Year's toast together.

The moment looks so joyous and I think that could've been us. We could've been mingling with all these animals, we could've had the good times with them. If only things had been different.

Exactly five hundred years ago, the animals started their fight for freedom. It seems I'm starting mine as well.

I sit in the cabin and observe the scene, my first New Year's Eve alone. I'm a bit envious. They don't know what they have. I didn't know, until I lost it all. But I won't let it get me down. For the first time in my life, I feel hopeful about my future. I don't know what it will bring, but I promise myself, I won't be afraid anymore.

It's 11:59, and the countdown starts.

Five…four…three…two…one.

Happy New Year.

Chapter 34 – The Superior

Postscript

January 1, 3041 9:05 AM

"Working on a holiday?" Bastion says to me as he walks into my office.

"Of course," I say. "You know there are always things to be done."

"I sure do," he replies.

"I take it you're here to give me your status. I understand you've finished your report."

"I have."

"And?" I ask curiously.

"As you detailed in your findings, Maya Lawton died of synconium poisoning. It seems it was caused by our implants."

"That's a shame," I say disappointedly. "I hate it when our work goes to waste. And what of her children?"

"The United Species Alliance acted fast. They sent in a team to hunt and kill them."

"Did they notice you?" I say sternly.

"Negative, sir, I was able to follow their movements unseen."

"Good. So what of her children?"

"The Alliance was able to kill ten of them," he tells me. "But, fortunately, the one you're interested in still lives."

"Excellent!" I exclaim. "So, where is she?"

"That's the thing sir, she disappeared," he says. I'm mildly annoyed by the news, but he carries on. "The

United Species Alliance thinks she's dead, but she was aided by the wolf agent, Fenrir Snow. They vanished through a teleporter. I should've stopped them."

"No, that's quite all right, Bastion. Remember, we are to remain in the dark at all costs."

"Understood. Since they left Primm, we've failed to find any clues on Iris Lawton's location."

"Well our priority is to find her. She's different from the others," I say to a concerned Bastion. "She's special."

About The Author

Andrew Vu is a novelist who was born in San Jose, CA. He graduated from UC Berkeley in 2007 and currently resides in Oakland, CA. During his spare time, he enjoys movies, video games, and watching sports. He roots for his California Golden Bears, the Kansas City Chiefs, the Golden State Warriors, and the Oakland A's.